The Adventures of Sir Goblin, the Feline Knight

The Adventures of Sir Goblin the Feline Knight

Barbara E. Moss

Illustrated by Emily du Houx

Polar Bear & Company
Solon, Maine

Polar Bear & Company
Solon Center for Research and Publishing
P.O. Box 311, Solon, Maine 04979, U.S.A.
polarbearandco.org, soloncenter.org
info@soloncenter.org
Copyright © 2008 by Barbara E. Moss
Cover art, design and illustrations, Emily Cornell du Houx.
galleryfukurou.com
Gallery Fukurou is at 20 Main Street, Rockland, ME 04841.
First paperback edition March 2009 ISBN: 978-1-882190-03-4
Second paperback edition June 2022, ISBN: 978-1-882190-98-0
Available via local retailers and online worldwide, wholesale via Ingram.
Library of Congress Control Number: 2008021589
Manufactured on durable, acid-free paper in more than one country.

To Sanford

Contents

Acknowledgments
-ix-

Goblin Meets Snow Beauty
-1-

Goblin Knighted
-29-

Sir Goblin's Christmas
-43-

Sir Goblin's Spring
-105-

Sir Goblin's Quest
-137-

Sir Goblin and the Unicorn Hunt
-165-

The Knight's Assailant
-207-

Glossary
-315-

The Author
-323-

THE ILLUSTRATOR
-325-

Acknowledgments

Many people helped me bring these stories to fictional life and I am most grateful to all of them. I especially wish to thank Richard White for reading early versions of the Sir Goblin stories and providing helpful criticism and encouragement. I am in debt to the late Cynthia Stowe for her encouragement and editorial suggestions. Shirley Rousseau Murphy generously offered suggestions. Many thanks are due to Siegfried Engelbrecht-Vandre for offering his expertise and advice on European wildlife and to Susan Sellers Mueller for generously answering my many questions about the behavior of horses. Most of all I wish to thank my husband and children without whose love and tolerance this book could not have been written.

Goblin Meets Snow Beauty

One.

GOBLIN WAS HUNGRY. His shrunken stomach screamed for food. Three days ago, the cat had raced into the forest to escape an angry pack of slavering hounds that he feared would tear him apart. The forest floor offered little food but grubs and insects, nothing that would fill a big tomcat's stomach.

At last, he came to cleared land and a rude shed made of rough-cut boards and repaired with sticks jabbed into cracks to keep out wind and rain. Within were a sow and her piglets and two old ewes, sheep doomed to meet the butcher's knife soon. Goblin ran inside and in no time cornered a mouse. He hooked it with a claw, and his fangs sliced deftly through the spinal cord in its neck. The fresh meat warmed Goblin's stomach, making him feel relaxed and drowsy. He had just closed his eyes when suddenly he heard a shout.

"Get that mouser, Roman! Kill that witch's imp!" an old tom-human's voice squeaked in rage.

Too late, the cat recognized the hurried, four-footed gait of a dog that had seen him run into the shed. Encouraged by its human master, the hound would kill him. With his terrified eyes dilated wide into black shining discs, the starving cat leapt to the top bar of the sow's pen, still holding a part of the mouse pinned between his teeth. He scrambled along the rail. Roused, the sow also got to her feet and wobbled her disc-shaped snout up and down as she smelled, rather than saw, the possibility of cat for dinner.

With the speed of Mercury, Goblin dashed across the tops of the stall railings and leapt toward the patch of light that was the doorway. The lanky old hound dashed though the hut's entrance, made a twisting jump, and snapped at the small intruder; Goblin flew over the dog's head, and the hound's fangs raked at his haunch. The cat shrieked once and, bleeding, fled to freedom.

Fueled by fear, the cat ran and ran. He left the village and the small shed far behind. He was deep in the woods and two or three miles from the village when the searing pain in his leg forced him to stop. He could no longer hear the human's cries and accusations of witchcraft. He had easily outrun the thumping trot of the hound.

Goblin curled up in some soft green herbage bearing bumpy red fruit. He licked his haunch. His immediate need for food somewhat satisfied, he tended to the wound. It must stay clean. He knew that. It was just good cat sense. And so he licked and licked, but the pain did not ease. He tried purring; his mother's purrs had always helped. But the dog had ripped his flesh deeply, and the pain was unrelenting. The smallest movement felt like flames all over his body. He purred a cat prayer.

Would he be able to walk in the morning? The sun was already setting, and night would fall early in this deep wood.

The morning will have to take care of itself, thought Goblin, and he washed himself until he could lick no more.

Now relatively clean and scentless, he hoped no nighttime marauder, no boar, wolf or fox, would find him. He did not fear the dog or the human; he knew they did not go into the woods much, and never at night.

Madelyn rolled onto her side as the first blush of dawn came through her window. She listened to the birds singing for some time and then slowly propped herself up on her elbow. She sat up and pushed her feet into the wooden clogs she had put at her bedside the night before. She always woke up early now; her arthritic joints would not let her sleep late. How things change! When she was a girl she had never wanted to get up early, and many times her softhearted mother began the milking, Madelyn's task, for her. Now there was only one goat, and her pains eased only when her old legs started moving.

Madelyn stood up stiffly. She pulled her dress on over her shift and wrapped the wooly shawl that hung on her bedpost around her shoulders. In the feeble dawn light she entered her main room and stepped deftly through the darkness to her left, unlatched the south-facing door, and pulled it open. Light streamed in and bathed the central hearth. Madelyn stirred the coals. Soon she had her morning porridge and raspberry tea sitting before her on the large plank table. A little goat's milk made the porridge tasty. Madelyn breakfasted alone, but she ate well.

She sat for a while at the table, looking about her, satisfied with her life. It was still a good house, a grand house. This main room was where she cooked, spun, and prepared her salves and other treatments for her visitors. A workbench, spinning wheel, and, in her back room, a loom, made it known that an industrious housewife lived here. The fleece and carding combs stuffed in a basket by the spinning wheel and the spools of spun thread stacked on a stool were evidence of the normality of her life. Completing the furnishings were several stools like the one she sat on now, drawn up to the large table. Another was next to the spinning wheel. A long oak bench stood against the wall by the door. Across the room, opposite her bedroom, stood a low cot. A crisp, fresh sheet was spread tightly over the thin mattress, and a blanket lay folded at the foot as if waiting for someone to lie down and draw it up. A doorway in the wall opposite the front door led to a small back room, where the loom took up much of the floor space and where kegs and casks of stored food, spools of spun flax for weaving into cloth, and a bolt or two of fabric cluttered most of the remaining space.

Every housewife had similar possessions. But extraordinary were the huge clusters of dried plants and flower heads that hung from the ceiling and were jammed into baskets and tubs about the main room. Mortars and pestles of various sizes, knives, scissors, other odd implements and several dozen stoppered vials—some large, some very small—stood on the worktable. Like her mother and grandmother before her, Madelyn was a wise woman, gifted in the arts of healing and advising.

Her house stood almost two miles beyond the village, but not many days passed without a visit from a maiden in need of advice about young love or a matron wishing to mend the ailing heart of her much older love. They paid her when they could, with gifts of food or the occasional small coin.

Having finished her porridge, Madelyn tied her long homespun cloak under her chin. She pulled up the hood to keep the early damp off her hair. Carrying a large basket, the old woman stepped out into the sunshine. She turned west and began the quarter-mile walk to the ruins of an old mill. The mill stood at the first ridge of hills where the millrace could catch the falling stream's tumbling water and direct it over a mighty wheel whose revolutions had once turned the grindstones within.

Madelyn's grandfather had been the last miller, and Madelyn's whole family had lived happily and prosperously in that house. Little Madelyn had loved the excitement of people coming from all the nearby villages with their grain and returning with flour and meal for their bread. She used to climb atop a great boulder that stood at a bend in the road. From her high vantage point the little girl would call out to her brothers and father as soon as she saw a cart lumbering toward the mill.

But that was before the Great Sickness. Madelyn's grandfather fell sick first with great black sores in his armpits and groin; for all their skill, Madelyn's mother and grandmother could not cure him. They had not seen anything like it before. No one had. Within days, her grandfather was dead. The following summer the plague returned with greater fury.

Madelyn still shuddered when she recalled that horrible time. It began when her Aunt Helen and her young cousin arrived one morning just as Madelyn came into the house with the morning's milking. Footsore, bone-weary, and soaking wet from walking all night through the damp woods, Aunt Helen spoke in a rapid tumble of words and tears. While her aunt sipped some restorative tea, Madelyn's mother packed a bag of healing herbs. The girl heard her aunt explain to her grandmother how Madelyn's woodcutter uncle had broken his leg.

"I must go to him immediately. I'll take Madelyn. She can help carry the things, and it will be good training for her," said her mother. It was this journey to the woodcutter that saved Madelyn's life.

Weeks later when they returned, they found no one at the mill. Its great wheel was silent. Where were the menfolk? Nobody was at the house.

"Where's Grandma?" cried Madelyn.

Only a thin goat and some chickens moved about. The sheep lay dead, stinking in the grass. Fear turned to horror as they discovered the filth and disarray that was inside their house. When Madelyn's mother saw only empty crocks instead of her salves and balms she knew a great sickness had passed through. A pile of filthy, blood-soaked linen was heaped just outside the door.

"Where could Papa and my brothers have gone, Mamma? Where is Grandma?" Madelyn asked over and over.

Madelyn's mother only replied, "Tomorrow we will sell some pullets in the village, and we will hear news." She kept sweeping and picking things up. She handed Madelyn a bucket. "Draw some water; then see if you can get some milk out of that goat. Keep busy."

Yes, the plague had indeed reappeared in the village. In the weeks when Madelyn and her mother were tending to the woodcutter, a third of the village had died. The survivors dug a pit and threw in the corpses as they arrived off the carter's wagon. The priest had not the courage or faith to stand over them long enough to say even a few sacred words.

Madelyn's grandmother had been the last of the family to die. She, they were told, must have dragged the men from the house. A villager came later to the millhouse seeking a midwife because his child demanded to be born at his chosen time, plague or no plague. As he drew near to the house, he startled the scavenging birds. They flapped their great black wings and settled clumsily in nearby tree branches. Madelyn's grandmother lay dead in the doorway, and the men were scattered in the yard.

Two.

T HAT WAS MANY, many years ago. Today Madelyn rested a minute against the great boulder. She glanced at the mill, now a ruin of stone and vine-covered timbers, and sighed at the memories. For a moment she heard, or she thought she heard, footsteps and voices at the mill. *My imagination*, she thought. She shook her head to return her thoughts to the present. *In spite of it all, I have had a good life*, the old woman told herself. She picked up her basket and crossed the road to where the berry bushes grew.

"What's this? Why, it's a little gray-striped mouser!"

Goblin woke up. His eyes stretched wide open in terrified amazement. A human was standing right in front of him! He wanted to run, but his wounded leg had stiffened during the night. He had to stretch before fleeing, but then fresh blood bubbled from his wound, and he fell down. Madelyn easily scooped him up and laid him in her basket.

She tucked her apron around him and shut the lid, cooing, "Poor little soft creature. Do not be afraid. Flesh is flesh. Madelyn can heal human flesh; she can heal cat flesh, too."

The old woman's purring tones, repeated like a magic incantation, calmed Goblin. Quickly, Madelyn picked several handfuls of bumpy raspberries, tossed them in on top of her apron and walked home as swiftly as she could. As she hurried down the path, she hummed and chanted a repetitive soothing rhyme to keep the cat calm.

Two black-robed figures emerged from the woods near the mill. One had stopped to shake a stone from his sandal. While he stood tying it back on, his companion had seen Madelyn scoop a cat into her basket. "Look at that," he whispered to the other, "Did you see that?"

They were two itinerant friars who earned their living begging alms

Madelyn can heal human flesh; she can heal cat flesh, too.

and preaching repentance to whomever would listen. The younger one, the man with the painful pebble in his sandal, had not seen the old woman put the cat in her basket, but he saw her and heard her song. So he dutifully replied, "Yes, yes, suspicious, very suspicious."

They followed Madelyn at a quiet but attentive distance, and, noting the house she entered, they continued their journey to town.

A saucer of warm goat's milk comforted Goblin's stomach as nothing had in a long, long time. Madelyn had stirred in a tiny half spoonful of her restful, calming potion that she normally prescribed for farmers during drought. The farmers would then doze off more easily at night and got at least a decent night's sleep in spite of their anxiety about the possibility of crop loss and future famine.

The cat went to sleep on the hearth mat. Madelyn cleaned and salved the wound. A drop of her strongest pain potion allowed her to draw a thread through the deepest part of the tear and close the wound sufficiently for nature to do its healing work. Little by little and day by day, Goblin spent less time licking his wound, and the tear healed cleanly. Then, one day, a few weeks before Michaelmas, Madelyn saw Goblin biting furiously at his haunch.

"Ah!" said the old woman, "The threads have begun to itch! Time for them to come out."

That afternoon as Goblin lay stretched out as long as he could make himself, in the manner of happy cats, Madelyn stroked him tenderly, humming her little magical chant. Goblin purred and closed his eyes. Arthritic fingers parted his fur where the wound had been. Goblin lifted his head and chirped once. Then he settled down and closed his eyes. With surprising quickness and dexterity Madelyn slid her slender embroidery scissors under the threads, snipped them open and pulled them free.

That same afternoon Goblin presented Madelyn with a beautiful, fat, gray mouse in grateful payment for his treatment. He marveled that she did not eat it but instead praised, petted and exulted at length his usefulness as a mouser. So *he* ate it.

"Why you gobbled that right up, you little gobbler! You are a regular goblin, you are!" The old woman said, her eyes crinkling, and her bosom bouncing as she laughed at her own little pun. The name stuck. He was Goblin.

As summer days cooled into fall, Madelyn was busy collecting the last cuttings of the herbs she would use in her medicines. Often when she went into the woods after leaves and seedpods, Goblin followed, and she chattered to him constantly.

"This is useful for tea for a lady's cramps," she'd explain. "And this weed, when properly applied as a poultice, eases a man's sore muscles."

Goblin chirped as if he understood.

Laughing, she said out loud, "You know, cat, I sell it mostly to women. In fact, if a man comes to get it for himself, I not infrequently later have his good woman coming complaining of marriage problems. And I counsel more tender care on her part. Rub his back, I say."

"Mew, meow," said Goblin, not understanding fully but always polite.

When Madelyn walked along the road, however, she was always very quiet. Once, when Goblin followed behind her, meowing, she stamped her foot and shooed him as a richly dressed man passed on horseback. Then when they got home she patted and petted him and covered him with kisses.

"But you mustn't follow me close, kitty pet. It's not safe."

Goblin did not understand, but he was forgiving, and the food was good.

Madelyn's patients paid her in either coin or food, often little meat pies or eggs. Goblin shared in a very good diet, although he still preferred to catch his main course. He grew sleek, his fur lustrous and marvelously contrastive in its pattern of gray and black stripes.

Madelyn understood Goblin's need to be free, to visit with the lady cats as he saw fit and to go on extended hunting trips. Goblin was freer than most men were, she thought, as he was neither tied to the land like the serfs nor obligated to a feudal lord by vassalage. He usually returned from social calls tired and scruffy, but happy, and from hunting excursions with a gift of mouse or bird for Madelyn. The woman's heart loved Goblin's company, and he found regular warmth and food irresistible. And, truth be told, he was becoming rather fond of the old woman.

Born in the woods, Goblin had never wanted or needed to associate with humans. He had heard many, many stories of their cruelty to cats from his lady cats and the other toms he met while courting the ladies. But Madelyn was different. He noticed that his dish was placed outside when there were frequent strangers seeking advice, as there were during certain festivals and market days. He had to stay outdoors then. *Ah, it's for my protection from cruel human visitors*, thought the big cat. He heard Madelyn explain clearly to guests that the dish was for "the goblins that lived in the woods" that were thought to bring either good or bad luck according to people's treatment of them. All humans, he knew, had certain superstitions, and Madelyn's patients found the idea of goblins in the woods perfectly reasonable. Although Goblin had never met any such creatures, the humans knew for certain there were fairies, unicorns, griffins and dragons in the woods. Why not goblins? Indeed, Goblin on occasion met with other cats who were the lucky beneficiaries of a "goblin" dish and who rewarded their householders with fresh-killed mice. Madelyn's reasonable idea was catching on. Yes, he was becoming rather fond of the old woman.

Fall turned to winter, and Goblin spent many hours snuggled by Madelyn's fire. Never had he had such a luxurious winter. If he could not find a mouse or vole or other suitable beast for a feast, the old woman usually had a bit of meat or cheese or egg for him. Or at least little sips of broth. Life was good, so good.

One day Goblin woke up from a nap behind the woodpile and discovered his back was covered in a blanket of sparkling white flakes.

Oh! remembered Goblin. *It's that season again.*

He could remember two snowy seasons, his first when he still followed at his momcat's side with his sister. Good huntress that she was, she could not provide for three. Out of necessity that winter Goblin honed his hunting skills to a keen perfection. He learned to use his claws to dig through hard ground and unearth grubs and sleeping insects. He found the winter hiding places of mice and their little relatives. If he or momcat brought down a bird, they declared a feast day. In the spring they emerged lean and ragged-furred, but alive.

His sister and his momcat were expecting kittens in the early summer. Goblin and the rest of his family all agreed it was time for him to leave the family group to seek his own fortune in the world. So Goblin struck off on his own. The beauty of this, his first spring, enchanted him; butterflies fluttered by and tickled his nose; the air was sweet with flowers, and the mice seemed particularly careless. He ate well. Little by little his yearnings for his momcat came less frequently and were not so painful anymore. Summer was downright fun for the playful, young Goblin.

By the time the white, sparkling flakes arrived again, Goblin had learned many lessons—one being that farms and other isolated human endeavors often provided a plentitude of the fresh meat that all cats craved. He grew big and strong.

This, his third snowy season, would be different. Goblin stood up, stretching and arching his back and letting the snow tumble off. His heart swelled with happiness as he thought of a winter by Madelyn's warm fire. What incredible good fortune was his!

Time flew swiftly with just enough "dish days" to add spice to life. Soon it was red berry season again. One morning, while the wise woman was grinding herbs into powder at her worktable, Goblin heard tom-human voices. Madelyn, despite arthritic joints, suddenly jumped off her stool and tossed Goblin out the back window. He could smell her fear. From his hiding place he saw two men, dressed in blackish robes and carrying sacks, pass by. They hesitated outside Madelyn's house and pointed at her little window. Goblin could hear the zing of her wheel spinning. They went on by. Her wheel stopped. She went out to her well and called the cat in.

"They come by every few months, begging alms and bringing medicines to the townspeople. They mean well. But they are suspicious and very rigid minded. Stay away from such men, pet." The wise woman murmured to her cat, stroking his back and scratching under his chin.

One morning, a few days later, as Goblin lay purring and flexing his claws on the sunny doorstep, a slender girl stepped up to the doorway blocking out his sunshine. As she carefully stepped over him, her skirts swept his ears. Her hems shivered. He sensed deep tension and possibly sickness and fear. The girl was Rosemarie, the village blacksmith's young daughter. Goblin slipped quickly around the corner of the house.

"Did I see a cat?" asked the young woman—for at thirteen years of age she was indeed a young woman, and a woman whose heart was rejoicing in the glory of first love.

"Oh, just a goblin," Madelyn waved a hand dismissively. Like the hound Roman's master, Madelyn was well aware of the Church's attitude toward people who kept company with cats—they might be committing the heresy of witchcraft.

"I thought I had seen one here before."

"What brings you here today, my dear?" the old woman asked, changing the subject. "Has Will not smiled upon you yet?"

But Madelyn had already spotted a rash on the girl's cheeks and forehead and guessed it was not for more advice on romance that the maiden needed her.

She had come to Madelyn not many weeks ago for one of her famous love potions, in reality a concoction of strawberry juice and herbs that added a red color to the lips while new hope put a sparkle in the eyes. It worked. Or so the maidens claimed.

On that visit to Madelyn's house, Rosemarie had told her how her father had thrown back his head and laughed uproariously when he noticed her making calf eyes at his apprentice, William. His laughter quickly turned to anger, and he snarled, "Not that plodding, dull boy. You can do better than that, girl." He then tried to keep her out of the smithy.

"Yes, Will, we——," today the girl blushed and dropped her eyes.

Madelyn's potion had acquired another very good recommendation.

"He is so sweet," the girl continued. "Today he . . ." Rosemarie's chin trembled.

"You have the red fever, my dear. I can see the rash already. Come sit here."

The girl sat down. She pulled a bundle from under her cloak. It wriggled.

"Today Will helped me make this," Rosemarie burst into tears. The bag slid to the floor. "Fa . . . Father . . . Father told me to . . ." She could not say more.

Her shoulders shook, and she covered her face with her small hands and cried as if her world had ended. Madelyn opened the bundle and pulled out a cat, a delicate creature with pure white fur and eyes the color of summer grass. Madelyn understood. Rosemarie's father had told her to dispose of her pet, probably to drown it, and her father's apprentice, the young man she loved, had helped her sneak the cat away.

"Ah, my dear, you have many cares. But the fever first. You must take this tea."

The wise woman sprinkled a spoonful of ground herbs into a pottery cup and poured boiling water from her hearth cauldron over the leaves. "Here. It will calm you. Rest on my cot. I will go to the village and tell your family you have the red fever and should stay with me a few days. I will say nothing about your kitty."

"Oh, thank you." Rosemarie's delicate face had flaming red cheeks, scarlet bumps across the forehead and, now, red-rimmed eyes.

She looked up shyly at the old woman and almost inaudibly whispered, "I call her Snow Beauty."

The old woman shouldered the bag of salves and herbs that she always carried with her to the village and left her house. She expected to be gone but a few hours, back with plenty of time to give Rosemarie her next dose of medicinal tea. Madelyn never for a minute thought that she would never see her house again.

Three.

GOBLIN ZIPPED BACK through the door as Madelyn went out. Already his cat sense had informed him of many things about *his* visitor. He was dazzled. Never had he seen a creature so exquisite! He sat down and licked himself, shoulders, paws, and face, until he was satisfied that he was the spiffiest tomcat on the continent. Then he swaggered up to Snow Beauty with steady steps, tail held high and stiff. His heart hammered against his ribs with love, hope and fear—fear that he might be spurned. Snow Beauty had observed his antics sharply. Her green eyes shimmered with yearning. She crouched and kneaded the floor with her front paws.

Rosemarie sipped the last of the tea. Her hands trembled, and the cup clattered against her teeth. Her fever rose, and, shivering, the girl lay down on Madelyn's cot and pulled the blanket over her. She drew her trembling knees to her stomach for more warmth. She drowsed, woke, turned over and turned back again. She tried to make herself warm by tucking the blanket more tightly around her. She saw Snow Beauty crouched by the hearth. Somehow just seeing her cat was calming. The animal's white loveliness was the last thing Rosemarie was certain of as her fever climbed. She heard a fierce screaming meow. Then several more yowls. She tried to see what was going on, but the girl understood nothing. It was not her room, but some strange nightmarish place instead. Pots and plants stood about. A large gray animal jumped onto her belly, hissed and disappeared.

Madelyn started down the road to town. Her gait grew steadier as her blood stirred and eased her ancient hips and knees. A half-mile down the path, she was walking with a steady gait that she could have kept up half a day.

As she walked she wondered. *What was it that girl was actually coming to*

Goblin meets
Snow Beauty.

see me about? The fever? Was it her cat? Did she want me to keep her cat? Maybe that was it. A few steps further. *But did she know I had or liked cats? She obviously did. Maybe she thought I could make hers invisible or some such magic. I hope not. I hope no one thinks my medicine extends to such tricks.*

She plodded on, and, except for the comforting rhythm of her leather salve bag creaking against her shoulder, the world was completely silent. No birds were singing. Madelyn looked up and saw what she expected to see, a great goshawk, circling, searching for feathered prey.

It took about an hour for Madelyn to arrive at the town. There seemed to be some hubbub about, but she went straight to the blacksmith's home. As she padded by his shed, a stripling of no more than sixteen stared at her; his jaw dropped, and his eyes popped wide open. Madelyn had given him only a brief glance noting the gold-blond fringe poking out from the front of his leather blacksmith's cap. Supposing him to be the wonderful Will, she moved on in search of his master. But the surprised boy dropped his hammer on the anvil, and its sudden clang made her jump.

"Ma'am, Ma'am," the boy cried, rushing to her.

At that moment the blacksmith appeared in his doorway, and Madelyn turned to speak to the older man. "My good man, your daughter Rosemarie lies sick abed in my house. She has the red fever and must not be moved for a day or two. I have tended to her well. Fear not."

"I do fear. But why did she go to you?" The smith asked, seeming much distracted.

Then he seemed to think of something, some possibility—a mystery to the old woman—he moaned. "Holy God! Oh, no! She didn't take that—Madelyn, we have much trouble in this town. Get back to your place now! Don't let anyone see you. Don't speak of Rosy."

But even as he spoke, a ragged man ran up and pulled at Madelyn's sleeve. "Oh, mistress midwife, my Mary is in such dreadful travail. All day. She has little strength left."

"I must go to her."

"No," yelled the smith, blasting out the word as if from great bellows.

"I must."

The old woman walked across the square with the poor man. She saw friars in the square with a group of townsfolk around them.

"They have been here preaching for several days now," remarked the poor man as they hurried by. "They have been getting the folk all worked up about purifying their souls and such things. But in the end those kind always want money, and I have no money so I stay away."

Madelyn heard Mary's pants and groans long before she entered the dark hovel. The woman, no longer young, lay on a cot raised but a few inches from the floor. Beneath her hips and bent legs were wrinkled sheets and blankets already wet and spattered. Her gown was thrown back over her huge belly; her chemise tented over her knees. Her sweaty hair was tousled about, long ago out of its cap. Dull eyes stared at the ceiling from gray lids. Tear tracks had painted her face in stripes of agony. Two little girls, dressed only in patched chemises, crouched on either side of her, helplessly patting her arms.

"The baby lady is here, Mama," whispered the older one.

Mary arched her neck forward to look, then dropped her head back down and arched her back involuntarily as another contraction began.

Madelyn rubbed the woman's belly and cooed soothingly, "Fear not, Madam. You will live."

Madelyn's initial assessment of the mother's condition, however, left her with many doubts. She pulled up a stool near the woman's feet, and, searching in her salve bag, she procured a small lamp. Lighting it, she placed it on the stool and pulled up a second, lower stool for herself. The lamp's feeble light revealed a scarlet tear at the bottom of the birth opening and the shiny pink surface of a new life presenting itself.

"Are there no women to attend?" asked the midwife of the husband.

"No."

He did not add that they had fled when he went for Madelyn for fear of the friars who were preaching about dangerous women who kept cats, who cast so-called healing spells, and who might be witches.

"Then you must hold her legs apart. Is there nothing clean in this house?"

"Some swaddling cloth for the baby," replied the husband.

"Bring it," ordered Madelyn, "and, if you can, warm some water for her washing up."

The words "washing up" with their implied end to her labors and possible survival heartened Mary. Her spirits rose.

The head of the baby struggling to come into the world did not look right to Madelyn. She had helped many babes make their grand entrance to life: big, bawling boys; pink, little girls; the baldheaded and curly topped. But this one? Something was very wrong.

With linen draped over her hands, Madelyn pressed her fingers into the birth canal on either side of the peculiar presentation. She wondered if she should try to turn the babe but dismissed the idea when she felt the easy pliability of its head. The midwife worked her draped fingers into the birth canal, stretching it a bit wider. Then came a ferocious contraction;

Mary screamed, blood spurted from the tear, and the infant slid out. The cord and the afterbirth came, and Madelyn directed the father and the girls as she tended to the whimpering creature in her arms.

She carried the baby to the light at the doorway.

The father came up, but, before he could say anything, she whispered, "It's a girl but badly formed. She will not live long. I will take her to the church for the priest to baptize. Look to your wife."

Wrapping the baby more securely, she hurried across the green to the church. She did not hear one of the friars say to his audience, "That's the woman. Her with her cats and magic cures."

With her free arm and all her ancient strength, she yanked at the church door. It opened a few inches. She stuck her foot in and twisted to shove the door open with her back. At the far end of the nave she saw some holy men. Dipping her fingers into holy water, she crossed and blessed herself. She scurried toward the holy men, crying out as she went.

"Oh, please, holy father," she cried, clutching the wet, unwashed newborn against her chest and attempting a curtsey, "this child is weak and must be baptized now!"

The priest mumbled something, shuffled his feet and seemed both embarrassed and horrified at the sight of the infant's malformed head. The other men were part of the visiting friar group. Even in its swaddling cloth, the men could see that the child was monstrously deformed. It had no forehead. Madelyn glanced down at the babe; its face was turning blue. She looked into the priest's face, her old eyes pleading. He turned away to get the ewer of baptismal water.

Misunderstanding him and on a sudden inspiration, she ran to the holy water stoup; she splashed a handful of water over the child's face and said, "I baptize thee—uh—Mary Elizabeth, in the name of the Father, the Son, the Holy Ghost. Amen."

As she uttered the word "amen," two friars grabbed her from behind and spun her around. They pulled the baby from her arms and shoved the infant at a crone who was on her knees praying and lighting a candle.

"How dare you perform this holy sacrament yourself! You witch!" shouted the friars.

The priest tried to pull the friars and Madelyn apart, saying it was an effectual baptism, but they ignored him. They shouted accusation after accusation to her face.

In the morning Rosemarie's mother carried her risen bread dough to the baker's oven. As she walked through the center of the town, she saw the men-at-arms making preparations in the square. They seemed to be propping up a tall post, but few people were up and about—certainly no mob—and it seemed a lovely morning. The woman's thoughts were of her daughter and her strange visit to Madelyn's house. *What was that girl up to?* She had noted Rosemarie's dewy glances at Will and heard her sighs, so she suspected the young man was at the bottom of this odd affair. *What trouble these young people are!* She planned to get her bread baked, go quietly to Madelyn's house, perhaps give the old woman a loaf of freshly baked bread, and bring Rosemarie home. The girl would be somewhat better by now and could recuperate at home.

As soon as she reached the baker's brick mound of an oven, she knew things were not right. Something horrendous had happened. One woman turned and looked hard at the smith's wife; the women stopped talking and stared at her.

"She came to your house," one said accusingly.

The smith's wife cringed. The babble of many wagging tongues came harshly to her ears, fingers pointed, and she was shocked to learn that the old midwife, so harmless and so kind to all, had been accused, tested and convicted. Remembering Rosemarie's white cat, she dropped her breadbasket on the ground and ran.

When she reached the doorway to her home, she called out to her husband, "Husband! Madelyn did not go home last night. That woman's child was a monster. She's been accused, made to confess and will be burned as a witch. My poor sick girl!"

The man was not in their house. The mother turned on her heel and burst into the smithy. "Who knows that Rosemarie is at Madelyn's house? My child is in danger! We must get Rosemarie!"

"Stop your screaming, woman," demanded the smith.

He took her by the shoulders to shake sense into her.

"Do you want the world to know she is at a witch's house?"

"They are saying that even now."

Four.

SHOUTS CAME FROM the town common. The smith's family heard cries of "Shame! Shame! Shame!" resounding from the square; whether it was directed at Madelyn, the men-at-arms, or the friars, they could not tell; but, from their dooryard, they could see the men-at-arms dragging out an old hag. Her hair was shaved off but for a few white wisps. Madelyn had been stripped to her chemise. As she was turned to be tied to the post, it appeared doubtful she was alive. She slumped to the ground. Men pulled her upright by chains, and the townspeople could see that her chin, neck and the whole front of her chemise were dark with blood. People who stood nearer to the spectacle than Rosemarie's parents could see the executioner slip the hanging cord and something else around Madelyn's neck. Another armed man nailed a small oval of shiny pink flesh—her tongue—to the post above her head, as was the local custom. She would speak no more heresy. Perhaps her eyes met those of the executioner for a moment, for he patted her cheek as he tucked a little bag into the neck of her blood-soaked garment and tightened the hanging cord. He stepped back and commanded the kindling be lit and the faggots added. A few wisps of smoke rose in the morning air.

"I will go for Rosemarie," announced William.

He turned sharply on his heel, and was away to the stable behind the smithy before the father or mother could say a word. The smith and his wife could not look as the first flickers of flame licked at the post and at the crumpled figure tied to it. They hurried into their house. They did not see the four louts carrying torches and running down the road toward the millhouse. Nor were they looking out their window when William led out a big, raw-boned farm horse, just recently shod and waiting for its owner to return to town to reclaim it on this, the market day. The horse, fully saddled and carrying bulging saddlebags, laid its ears back and snorted at its unaccustomed attire. It was more used to pulling a plow or a cart than to being ridden. After leaving a bag of coins in the stall for the horse's owner, William climbed up and urged the animal into the road.

Suddenly, a blasting roar, louder and more cracking than any thunder, shook the ground and rattled houses. The gawking crowd, expecting to see a grisly, fiery entertainment, fled to their doorsteps and now stood quaking, unbelieving. In the blast's wake, the silence was utter. The executioner had filled the little bag tucked under Madelyn's neck with gunpowder, and the first tall flames gave her a quick, merciful death. Madelyn had delivered his wife's children and cured her of childbed fever. *A swift death will at least deny the wicked friars their hot, red amusement,* he thought.

The room in Madelyn's house darkened and grew light again as Rosemarie lay tossing on the cot. Day dawned with a light breeze hushing through the trees and a bird singing softly. Rosemarie opened her eyes and recognized the room.

"Madelyn," she moaned.

No one came. Awake now, the girl felt a gentle scraping over her forehead and heard a low, rumbling sound. She reached her hand to her forehead. Snow Beauty let out a cheerful little chirp and went on licking Rosemarie's fever sores cool. Against her leg, a large gray cat lay purring and kneading. The girl was attended by two nurses, two feline nurses, who had met, courted, and consummated their marriage during her feverish nightmares.

Rosemarie pulled Snow Beauty to her chest and stroked the cat's cheeks, murmuring, "Snow Beauty, my kitty, my dearest kitty."

Goblin stood up, stretched his back into an arch, walked straight up Rosemarie's leg, and plopped himself down on her stomach, purring loudly.

"So you want to be petted, too." She scratched his chin. "You are the Goblin."

She laughed a little as she recalled how Madelyn tried to pass him off as a little demon.

"But where is Madelyn?"

Rosemarie pushed the cats gently aside and sat up. She made her way unsteadily into the old woman's sleeping room. There was no sign of her. Nor was she outside. Back inside the house, Rosemarie realized she was very, very hungry. She tore at a heel of dry brown bread and nibbled some cheese. Sitting at the plank table, she happened to glance at the hearth. The fire was not banked and not fed. The hearth was stone cold. She jumped up and kicked at the ashes. The fire was never allowed to go out at home. Madelyn must have been gone for a long time. What had happened? Without the fire, Rosemarie had no hot food, no drink, no light.

She felt lost. Was she well now, or would she give the fever to her family if she went home? Or to Will? She could not part with Snow Beauty—no matter what her father said. *Oh, Will, dear Will! We had so many plans!* Rosemarie paced about the house, trying to make sense of her situation. Often she glanced outside, down the road, looking for Madelyn. She sat down at the table and, resting her woozy head on the table's surface, dozed a minute or two, picturing the apprentice as she had last seen him, hammering a shoe onto the hoof of an old dappled carthorse. She would go home now, she decided. She had to talk to Will.

Sitting up, she looked around for her bundle. Unnoticed, Goblin slipped quickly out the door. Rosemarie found her bag under the plank table, next to a box that was sided with wooden rails. It was made for carrying chickens to market and had a strap. *This is a little heavy but will be more comfortable for Snow Beauty*, she thought. She dragged it out and set it on the table. Snow Beauty sprang onto the table and sniffed all around the coop. She rubbed her chin against its side.

The front door squeaked open, and Goblin strode in. A fat, gray mouse dangled from his jaws. He leapt onto the table and presented the rodent to the white cat. The cats shared a hearty breakfast. Unable to watch a mouse being eaten, Rosemarie turned her back and ate the last of Madelyn's cheese.

The morning breeze sifted through the cottage, gently rustling the herbs hanging from the ceiling. On the breeze, Rosemarie smelled smoke. Curious, she went outside. She stood on the tips of her toes, craning her neck back to see over the treetops. Looking in the direction of the village, she spotted a thin column of smoke that got thicker and blacker as she watched. Now and then she heard strange shouts and noises. Rosemarie ran toward the mill and climbed the great boulder for a better view. Great billows of black smoke and sparks rose into the air. She climbed back down. Just as her feet touched the ground a thunderous explosion shook the whole earth. Never had the girl heard a sound so deafening. She ran back to Madelyn's cottage in terror, screaming, crying, tripping over stones, and once tangling her foot in her own skirts. When Rosemarie reached the cottage door, her stomach rolled, and she felt chilled to the bone from fright.

The thunderous clap had left behind an eerie silence. Not a bird sang. Not a breath of air stirred. Rosemarie's heart pounded in her ears, and her hands trembled. When Snow Beauty slunk out from under the cot, the girl snatched up her prized pet with shaky hands and pressed her face into the animal's soft, warm fur. She patted the cat's shoulders, and the little animal purred. *Snow Beauty, you are such a comfort*, thought the girl. Then, taking the white cat by the scruff of the neck, Rosemarie plopped her into the coop. No Goblin was about. As the lid fell into place, Rosemarie stood up, determined to go to Will. It was then that she heard voices outside—men's rough, crude voices shouting and chanting the same words over and over. They were coming closer.

Rosemarie shouldered the coop and went to the door. She saw two or three men pushing their way through the brush, holding torches aloft.

She could hear their singsong raving clearly now.

"Burn the witch's house! Burn it to the ground!"

Jamming the door shut, Rosemarie fled to the back room. She pushed the coop through a window and then tried to get out herself, but the sill was up too high, and she couldn't hoist herself up. She had to go back to the main room for a stool.

She was straddling the windowsill when the first man flung his torch into the main room. Its flames licked greedily at the dry herbs and flowers. Rosemarie raced into the woods, not looking back, not following any path, pushing branches from her face as they slapped and scratched at her cheeks. The coop slammed against her thigh and back. Snow Beauty slid forward and back. Twigs and leaves jabbed at her in her small prison. The cat trembled and screamed meows in terrified confusion.

As a second man threw his arm back to fling his torch, long iron forge tongs slammed into his cheekbone, smashing his face and dropping him to the ground. William's iron weapon next came down hard on the first man who had pitched his torch, who was frantically grabbing at William's horse's reins. He was stunned and also fell. Young William's plow horse shied, terrified of the fire, tossed its head, and showed the whites of its eyes. In panic, the beast pranced over the fallen men. A third man risked the flailing hooves, trying to reach the youth and set his hair afire. Will knocked him and his torch aside and let his horse gallop down the road. The two soul-purifiers who were still on their feet had had enough. Throwing their torches more or less at the house, they ran back the way they had come, leaving their fallen comrades on the ground.

William's plow horse shied, terrified.

When he got his horse under control, Will rode back towards Madelyn's burning house. He tied the horse in the woods just off the road and went to look around behind the house. He felt sure Rosemarie was not in the house, but he thought that maybe she had hid in a shed or the cesshouse or even the well. He reasoned that, if she had run down the road when she saw those ruffians coming, they would have caught her. When he could not find Rosemarie, he remounted and urged the horse into the woods in search of her.

Rosemarie ran until she came to three tall rocks standing sentinel-like among the trees. She slipped behind them and set the coop at her feet. There she hid, with her hand on her breast, gulping for air, her back pressed against one of the sun-baked pillars.

She could still smell smoke and hear shouting and arguing, but the sounds were not coming closer. Once she heard the distinct whinny of a horse. Then silence. Rosemarie remained behind the rock, too scared to move or think. After what seemed like a very long time, she heard a strange cry. *Was it human or some strange bird calling?* she wondered. A sick fear rose in the girl's throat, and she pressed a hand tightly over her mouth. The call was getting closer.

"Oooh-ah-eeee! Oh-ma-eee!"

Closer still. Branches snapped and cracked. Someone or something big was coming through the woods.

"Rose-ma-rie!"

"Will!" shrieked the girl, as a horse and rider broke through the brush.

The boy jumped down from his horse. He and the girl found each other's arms. They clung together and kissed until breathless. Rosemarie pressed her cheek against Will's strong shoulder and breathed in the smoky but delightful smell of the boy who made his living at the forge. Tears of joy dampened her branch-scraped face. He kissed her forehead and each pink cheek until the scratches stung.

"I love you," William whispered over and over into her ear.

More kisses, and then he pulled away from her a little, "But I really must flee, Rosy. I think I may have killed, or at least badly hurt, one of those men back there and maybe another. If only I could have come yesterday as we had planned! I had everything ready. But when Madelyn came and said you were ill . . ."

Rosemarie interrupted him. "You came to protect me. No one will—," but seeing the fear in his face, she simply finished with, "Oh, Will, I will go with you to the ends of the Earth!"

That said, she abruptly asked, "Tell me, surely you heard the thunder?"

"The Devil's been at work in our town."

Will put his arm around her waist, reached for the horse's reins, and began to lead them to the road.

"Snow Beauty," cried the girl, twisting free.

She ran back to the tall standing stones and pulled out the chicken crate. The little cat's eyes were dilated and as black as obsidian; she was trembling all over. Rosemarie reached her fingers through the bars of the little animal's prison and stroked her paws.

Softly she crooned to the cat. "It will be all right, Snow. We will go for a ride and then things will be all right."

The cat settled into a crouch and stopped shaking. Together William and Rosemarie rigged the box with its furry, white resident across the horse's rump. As William turned the horse, Rosemarie asked again about the thunder.

"The thunder? It was gunpowder. The executioner tried to be merciful, I suspect. Madelyn had brought all his children into the world."

"Executioner!"

"Let's get away from here, Rosemarie. We haven't much time. They'll be back shortly. There will be a hue and cry. I'll tell you everything as we walk," he said.

Rosemarie saw his face had gone very pale.

"Let's be going." She pulled at the bridle.

Together they led the horse through the woods. When they came again to the road, Will lifted Rosemarie onto the horse and swung himself up behind her. He urged the horse toward the abandoned mill. Bit by bit, he told Rosemarie what had happened while she lay in Madelyn's house. "A man asked her to help his wife, who was in labor. The babe had no proper skull, they said. It was a monster. She hurried it to the church to be baptized before it died, and the visiting friars there accused her of witchcraft."

"What? Madelyn was the kindest person in the world. She was certainly no witch!"

"Were it not for the monster child, no one would have listened to them. But, apparently, she confessed when they, you know, did what things they do."

"No! My God, no! Confessed to what?" Rosemarie asked, still incredulous.

"To conversing with a gray, striped cat that was her familiar." Will could not tell the tale gently.

"That smoke! Oh Madelyn, Madelyn!" The girl sobbed, "She was like a grandmother to me."

"She was everyone's grandmother," said Will, kicking the horse to a bumpy trot.

At the great boulder, a demanding yowl rent the forest calm. A gray face appeared over the edge of the rock. Paws shuffled, judged the distance, and jumped. Goblin crashed down onto Snow Beauty's box. He tottered, meowing and clawing at the wood. The girl made a gesture, and, without a word, Will slid the cat into the coop with the beloved Snow Beauty.

"A cat's risky," warned Will.

"It's all I can do for her. He was hers."

William saw the two cats touch noses and heard them begin to purr.

"They are together. We are together," the youth added, as he hugged Rosemarie's waist and kissed the back of her neck.

At the millstream, Will walked the horse upstream through the water for a hundred yards.

"To lose the hoof marks," he explained. "So no one can follow us."

He steered the horse through the woods, and, after an hour, they returned to the road. Rosemarie sank against Will's chest. His arms felt strong around her. She whispered, "I just want to be with you. Anywhere. With the Lord's help, we will find a home."

Goblin Knighted

One.

ROSEMARIE WOKE UP. She rolled over onto her side, crunching the leafy branches that made up her bed. No wind rustled the trees. It did not matter whether she opened her eyes or held them closed, as there was only blackness and silence throughout the forest.

Will, her young husband, had spread his leather blacksmith's apron over the branches to make their bed smooth and less damp. He also had coiled her cloak into a roll so it could rest beneath their heads like a pillow. It was warm when they had lain down to rest that night, but now the air had a chill. Rosemarie turned to snuggle against Will's warmth. As she turned, she winced in pain.

Her toe was throbbing. Yesterday, her shoe had worn through, leaving her toe exposed to blister and bleed. In the black silence, the throbbing seized Rosemarie's groggy imagination, and all the girl could think of was the frightening picture of her toe, and then her whole foot, becoming black with disease. Over and over again, she imagined a festering infection seething and streaming through her blood, rotting off her toe and, in the end, leaving her young body a corpse in the woods, a pile of bones. She prayed for a miracle healing, making promises to the Blessed Virgin. Still, the blistered toe throbbed, and sleep would not return.

A night bird screamed. *What was that?* she wondered. Her heart raced. They were lying in the midst of a deep wood. Would bears or wolves come for them? Could their horse be trusted to whinny an alarm if any beast came near? Horses must sleep, too. She rolled over. *Oh that toe!* She turned back toward Will. She squeezed her eyes closed and, after some minutes, slept a fitful, dreaming sleep. When the sky bloomed pink and morning birds began twittering, a raven's raspy cry woke man and beast.

Goblin mewed from his chicken coop house, and his beloved Snow

Tall trees blocked out the sun.

Beauty slanted her green eyes toward him. Rosemarie, sighing, rubbed her eyes and then reached over and undid the latch on the coop. A little pink nose pushed open the lid, and the big gray cat slipped out, followed by his mate, Snow Beauty. Off they both bounced in search of breakfast.

Will jumped up and began stretching. The girl propped herself up on her elbow and watched her husband's antics with a resigned amusement that made her forget most of her nighttime terror. Every morning he greeted the day by bending deep at the knees, standing again, and flapping his arms like some great mythical bird learning to fly. After the third repetition of this routine, Rosemarie giggled.

"Gets the blood awake. My grandfather always said this is what the Teutonic Knights did."

"Your grandfather—it's always your grandfather," the girl laughed.

"No," grinned Will, "but he always said that."

After a minute or two more of this flapping exercise, Rosemarie decided her husband's blood was awake enough, and, whimpering dramatically, she pulled back her skirt and held up her wounded foot. Her lower lip jutted out, and her eyes pleaded silently.

Will, reading her need for pampering, kissed her foot and washed her toe in a little ale before wrapping it in a bit of linen. "That's all I can do for it now."

Seeing his grimly pursed lips and the slight squint of his eyes, Rosemarie understood that he was more worried about the possible festering of her wound than he admitted. The girl said nothing, but she was worried too and knew their journey must not—could not—last much longer. *He smiles*, thought the girl, *and says good fortune is around the next bend in the road, but even I can see how thin the horse is. And by the saints! We aren't even traveling down a road that could have a bend in it!*

For the most part they had been pushing east through the deep Swabian forests, where tall trees blocked out the sunlight and the consequent lack of undergrowth made walking easy for both man and beast. But the crunchy, brown leaves and evergreen needles that paved the forest floor provided little food for the horse. Rosemarie kept her fears to herself.

The girl heard a rustle among the leaves. Snow Beauty appeared carrying a large grasshopper, alive and dangling by its big back leg. The delicate white cat sat down in front of the coop and began to munch on the insect. A moment or two later Goblin appeared; no one had heard him return to camp for he was a savvy and stealthy hunter. He dropped a husky, furry creature at the feet of his mate, and the two cats shared a substantial breakfast. The two humans had no breakfast.

After the cats finished eating, William and Rosemarie packed up their things, loaded them onto the horse, and set forth again on their journey, walking always to the east, the girl limping badly as she tried to walk by placing just the heel of her injured foot to the ground. The two cats traveled in the barred cage, made originally to carry hens to market, across the ample rump of the carthorse.

Their travels had begun months earlier, when William inadvertently killed a man in defense of Rosemarie, and the two lovers were forced to flee their home village. William, with the confidence of youth, had assured Rosemarie that, as a journeyman farrier who was very good at general blacksmithing, he would have no trouble earning a living.

During the bright days of summer, fortune had initially smiled on them. They found enough work in a series of small villages to stay well fed and hopeful. A good life surely awaited them. They had only to find it. Welcomed everywhere, William shod horses and oxen and mended farm implements. Rosemarie picked up more than a few pennies spinning. But, as yet, they had not found a village large enough to support them permanently.

They had spent the harvest month at a small village, earning wages by helping to bring in the crops. That village had had many more people living in it a year ago. But a crop failure and winter disease caused many people to go hungry, get sick, and die. Then, their manor lord wanted to take over his neighbor's lush fief, and he found an excuse for a private war. He filled out the ranks of his army with village men, as was his right. Their lord won his battle, his plate armor being far superior to his neighbor's mail, but the humble folk, the foot soldiers, had to fight with only farm implements, pitchforks, billhooks, and the like, and without armor. Thick-padded vests, pulled over their tunics, had to suffice for protection. Many died.

So few people remained that William and Rosemarie were able to live for nothing in one of the empty houses, there being no family left to collect any rent. Every evening they returned from the fields with sore muscles and their young backs aching but with coins in their purses. Rosemarie would boil porridge over the fire pit in the center of the little hovel. After eating, they would sit on the ground by the fire, playing with the cats, and watching the smoke twist and turn dreamily as it rose to find its way through the opening in the roof. The young couple snuggled together, spinning their own dreams of their future life together. The two cats sat across from them, purring late into the evening and kneading their claws into a straw floor mat, thinking thoughts of their own. Snow Beauty was fat and round. They worked hard, but it was a pleasant time.

The village blacksmith was among those who had not returned from the war. And now, his wife, supposing herself a widow but still young and strong, tried to continue the business. William taught her to repair the iron tips on wooden spades and to mend sickles and scythes, which were the repairs most needed in the village, especially at harvest time. But, in helping her learn to make a living, William in effect put himself out of a job. The widow would have enough work to keep food in her belly if William did not compete with her. If he remained, there would not be enough work in the tiny settlement for two blacksmiths. William, ever optimistic, decided to move on. He paid the woman blacksmith a portion of his wages for a small anvil, completing his set of equipment needed for his trade. Heavy as the anvil was, it still weighed much less than a person, so when they left the village, with his horse well fed and healthy, Will had no concerns about strapping the chunk of iron onto the back of the creature. In his younger days, the big, old horse had enthusiastically pulled many a heavy cart over rutted roads filled deep with spring mud. His previous owner had called him, rather heroically, Noble Puller. Will just called him Nob.

When William and Rosemarie had packed their few things onto Nob's back and were ready to leave, the village folk generously supplied them with lentils, beans, and greens fresh from the harvest. The travelers bought some bread and dried meat to eat and weak beer to drink on their journey. And, with many smiles and hugs and pats on the back, the people of the hamlet directed the young couple to travel east and told them they would soon come upon a large village where they would certainly have sufficient work.

That was weeks ago, and no village whatsoever had come into sight since then. Nob was downright bony, and, except for Snow Beauty's odd round belly, the cats looked lean and stringy as well.

Two.

ON THIS, A sparkling morning, after William bandaged Rosemarie's toe and loaded their heavy gear onto Nob, he whistled a merry tune as he walked, to keep Rosemarie from suspecting just how worried he really was. William was beginning to think the villagers had tricked him. *I have been fooled,* he thought. *Rather than feed two more mouths in the winter, they sent us into the woods to die.* Now, in his mind, the villagers' kind smiles and nods seemed to him sly and cunning.

They had walked for only an hour or so. The sun was still low in the sky and the day pleasant, but Rosemarie hobbled along, trying not to moan. When the heel of her injured foot slipped off a stone and her toe hit the ground hard, she screamed. "Oh, I am sorry, husband. I did not mean to make such a noise," she said quickly.

"I think we should rest for a little while," William said, taking her arm, and helping her to sit down on a boulder. "A throne fit for a queen."

Rosemarie sat down and unwound her dirty bandage. The young man smiled bravely at his wife. "I have an idea," he said, and turned modestly away from her. Bending over and lifting the edge of his tunic, he began to untie the laces that held his hose. Rosemarie giggled.

"What?"

"It's not you. The cat licked my toe."

He inched his hose down his legs, kicking off his boots when the cloth bared his knees. The leaves and evergreen needles that covered the ground tickled his bare feet. But no stone bruised his foot, and no thorn pricked his toes as his tender feet gingerly tested the ground. William rolled up his hose and stuffed them in with their baggage on Nob's back.

"Here, you will wear these boots. Take off those flimsy shoes. The ground will toughen my feet."

She giggled again. "Oh, you have such a rough little tongue!"

Goblin was licking her toe clean.

"Stop that!" protested the husband, swatting Goblin away.

"Mrrt! Meow!" cried the cat, meaning, *Don't you know I am giving her foot good cat medicine?*

Switching his tail in annoyance, Goblin turned away and pounced on a wood bug. William cut a strip of cloth from the hem of Rosemarie's under-tunic and used it to make a new bandage. He reported that the sore toe looked no worse and possibly even better. The couple walked on.

Near noon they saw bright, yellow-green leaves on the trees ahead of them, where sunlight penetrated more readily, dappling the foliage with a sparkling, bright light. Pushing forward faster now, their spirits lifted by the sunlight, William and Rosemarie hastened to the spot where the forest seemed cheerier. The woods were more open; squares of blue sky peeked through the leaves, and even some grass and wild flowers pushed up through the leafy litter on the forest floor. Nob stretched his neck down hungrily to nibble the tender blades. William could not argue with the poor, thin horse. They decided to rest. It was a very good spot for their noontime meal.

As the big animal munched greedily, Rosemarie prepared lunch. She unfolded a now much spilled-upon linen cloth and laid out a meal; a pot of lentils—served cold but cooked up the night before with a little carrot, onion, and parsley for flavor—formed the bulk of their repast. They shared a sliced pear and apple and drank a small cup of beer. Their bread was long gone.

William and Rosemarie had discovered that, while traveling, it was more sensible to break with custom and have their main meal at night rather than at midday. Every evening, when they halted for the night, Will started a small fire, not for heat or light, since the days were still rather long and warm enough, but to cook some food. They then had plenty of time to sit by the fire, talk, relax, and play with the cats while they boiled up something from their supply of dried legumes and root vegetables. They would usually quench their thirst by drinking the boiled water in which they had cooked their vegetables, wasting nothing. Occasionally, Rosemarie found some late berries or mint leaves to add variety to their meals. Although they had, by now, eaten all the bread and dried meat that they had with them when they left the woman blacksmith's village, the couple were not yet concerned about the sparseness of their diet. They had both survived many winters on nothing but pottage.

After they had eaten their food, Rosemarie put away the lentil pot, wiped off their spoons, and folded the linen cloth. William, wiping his mouth with the back and then the heel of his hand, leaned against a tree and closed his eyes for a quick nap. But the cats were romping with a squirrel and clambered over Will's bare ankles.

"Ouch! Watch those claws!"

The young husband jumped up and brushed himself clean of leaves and dirt. He was about to ask his wife how her toe was feeling when he saw that Rosemarie was smiling and gazing skyward.

"Look, Will. A branch has been sawed off that tree. And that one too."

When they looked about, the couple saw sawn trees all about them.

"Why, this is a coppice!" exclaimed William. "A village must be near."

Excited by the discovery of a place where people came to cut firewood, and at the prospect of an end to their journey, the two tried to gather up the cats. They had to play chase-the-cat first, though, because Goblin and Snow Beauty were still playing chase-the-squirrel and wanted to stay longer. Snow Beauty actually hissed when Rosemarie picked her up and put her hands around the cat's round belly.

"What's wrong with you?" asked the girl. "Lately you always seem angry at me." In a bit of a pique with her pet, she slammed the coop lid shut with the cat inside.

William tugged at Nob, and the big horse very reluctantly left his grassy paradise.

"Praise the Lord!" both William and Rosemarie exclaimed as, a quarter mile onwards, they emerged from the woods and beheld a hedge-bound field of late summer hay, half mown. Tiled rooftops broke the horizon beyond with their jagged squares and angles.

Buildings! People! Hope they need a blacksmith! William's mind was racing.

Three.

WILLIAM STARTED TO push through the hedge.

"William!" snapped his wife. She pointed to his knobby knees, "Your hose!"

It would not do to meet strangers half dressed. William pulled on his hose and reclaimed his boots. Rosemarie tied on her flimsy shoes.

Then, breaking through the hedge together, they beheld one man out alone in the field. He was on his knees, looking heavenward, his hands clasped as in prayer. The cowl thrown back onto his shoulders and the rim of hair around a shaven spot on his head revealed his status as a monk. Will could hear the rhythms of Latin speech. Groaning, the monk threw his face to the ground. William and Rosemarie walked their horse slowly up to him.

"Ahem. Excuse me. Er, good day to you, sir monk; I am William the farrier, a blacksmith." Will introduced himself to prepare for asking directions to what he thought must be a large town just ahead.

The monk leapt to his feet. Babbling, sometimes in Latin, bowing deeply from his waist, he eventually made it understood that William was the answer to his prayers. His scythe was broken—the last decent one the monastery had. The lay brothers were taking in the apple crop and attending other fields. How would the hay for the mules be cut? The young monk burbled on.

His name was Innocent. Innocent's glance now took in Rosemarie. A woman. Young. Beautiful. He blushed. Now the monk's short life's story tumbled out. It seemed that, at the age of four, when his father remarried, he had been left at the monastery as a gift from his father to God. His mother had died giving birth to a stillborn girl.

Rosemarie was the first woman he had stood close to since he last saw his mother. His face flushed scarlet; his ears turned the color of blood. He was embarrassed, and he quickly pulled his cowl low over his face and turned to look at William.

Used to speaking little, and then often in only Latin, Innocent struggled to convey by gesture and words of local speech, dredged from his memory, that the monastery was obliged by their Rule to provide food and shelter for weary travelers. And, with rather little tact, he suggested that William could more than return their kindness if he mended what broken implements he could. The farrier answered that he was more than happy to assist them. Secretly, William hoped there would be enough repair work for Nob to get several days' worth of good food.

As they approached the abbey gate, Rosemarie swathed herself in her cloak to shield her feminine form as much as possible, not with an intention to deceive, but to prevent any more monkish blushing. Even so, she received a wide-eyed scrutiny from the porter.

"Ah, I must inform the Abbot," he whispered and scuttled off, leaving them all standing outside the door.

Its stone walls made the monastery look like a fortress, but without slits for archers. No preparations for any defense were visible. The residents had shut out the world, its sins and its temptations, and trusted the grace of God for protection. The porter returned and let the travelers in through a narrow gate. A few monks, who were crossing the courtyard, glanced with gawking curiosity at the visitors. Spotting a woman, they quickly directed their gaze to the ground and pulled low their cowls over their faces. Even so, upon glancing over her shoulder, Rosemarie caught a few of the holy men sneaking a quick extra peek at her.

The young couple was to be housed in the guest quarters. The porter brought them to Brother Ambrose, who was responsible for the accommodation of guests. Brother Ambrose was an amiable old man of some forty years with a soft, pink face, a twinkle in his eye, and the stubble of a gray beard wreathing his cheeks. The monks stood together and spoke in Latin. Brother Innocent told his story with great animation, whipping his hands about in excitement. Brother Ambrose listened, smiled, and nodded. He quieted the young monk with a pat on the shoulder. This was not the first relation of a miraculous answer to prayers that the old man had heard.

At Ambrose's signal, a lay brother led the starving horse to the stable. In no time the faithful Nob was dining on a meal finer than anything he could dream of—oats, hay, and even a carrot or two.

The porter returned to his post, and two monks helped to move Will and Rosemarie's personal things to the guest quarters. The two lovers carried in the mysteriously covered chicken coop themselves. Fortunately the residents of the chicken coop did not meow, and no questions were asked about cats. The blacksmith tools were brought to an outbuilding where an old forge stood. The monks helped Will get a good fire roaring, and the youth set about mending whatever he could, mostly scythes and sickles.

Rosemarie now found herself alone in a long room. She looked about. Stone walls and tall, glazed windows reached toward a high ceiling. The floor was wood, smooth and scrubbed clean. Along one wall, four bedsteads jutted into the room. All had straw-filled mattresses and wool blankets, and linens were neatly folded at the foot of each bed. Curtains between the beds could be pulled to close off a cubicle. At the far end of the room, poles, for visitors to hang their spare clothes over, stretched from wall to wall. Two tall braziers stood at opposite ends and lent a modicum of warmth to the great room. A prie-dieu stood against the window wall, as did a trestle table and benches. Some tallow candles, affixed to tall, iron candlesticks, stood on the table.

The young woman whirled around in amazement. She, who had been sleeping in the woods for weeks, had never lived in a house made of anything but wattle and daub with earthen floors. Here, she had even been shown the location of an indoor privy, off the passageway between the men's and women's quarters. What astounding luxury—almost decadent!

"What should 'Lady' Rosemarie do next?" giggled the girl.

She hung her woods-damp cloak over a pole, pulling some leaves and pine needles off as she smoothed it out. The coop emitted little grunts and mews.

"Oh my darlings, how wicked of me to forget you."

She heaved the coop to the table and pulled off its disguising cover. She saw Goblin reach out a soft paw to Snow Beauty who was lying on her side. The white cat lashed with bared claws and growled and spat. Goblin leapt back, switched his tail, and licked his paw. His body language clearly spelled, *Humph, women!* As Rosemarie opened the cage, the big tabby flew across the room and took refuge under a bed. Murmuring soothing words, the girl reached in to pet her snow-white darling.

Slash! Growl! Spit!

"Oh! Bad girl!" Rosemarie slammed shut the door and pulled the cover over the coop.

After a few moments, her calm returned, and she made up the bed,

under which Goblin crouched. As she sat down on the bed, she realized
her toe was not hurting so much. She was about to pull off her shoe and
re-bandage the toe when she heard footsteps outside her door. She heard
a grunt as something was set on the floor, followed by a sharp rap on the
door and then hastily retreating steps.

With some trepidation, she opened the door and peered out. "Oh,
thank you," she called to the fading footsteps.

A bucket of hot water stood at her feet, covered by a washbasin
and two linen towels. Rosemarie hauled this offer of hospitality into the
room. The girl tipped some water into the basin and set it on the table.
She dipped one towel into the water and sighed with pleasure as the
wonderful comfort of the warm water caressed her hands.

After washing her face, neck, and ears, the girl barred the door. She
kicked off her shoes and slipped off her tunic and shift. For the first
time in many weeks the girl mopped off and dried her entire body. The
hot water felt so good. After a few minutes her arms, legs, and shoulders
relaxed into a warm, melting softness, forgetting their hard trudge
through the forest.

She opened her bundle of things and shook out her spare shift. It was
soiled, but not as caked with grime and sweat as the one she had been
wearing. For a moment she considered wearing the new houppelande
she had had made for winter, but it was heavy and really should be kept
for a special occasion. She dressed in the spare chemise and pulled over
it her same tunic, after she had shaken it out, of course, and brushed it
off as best she could. Rosemarie liked to look nice for William. Quickly
she combed out her long chestnut braids, re-braided her hair, and pinned
it up under her cap.

Goblin pulled himself out from under the bed. He began kneading
and purring loudly into one of the neatly folded linen sheets.

"Yes, Goblin, that's exactly what I should do. It's wicked but
needful."

Rosemarie searched her bundle and retrieved a small knife. It was
no little matter to cut herself a bandage from the sheet. When she had
a strip of cloth cut free, she wiped her sore foot with the same linen
towel, now somewhat damp, that she had used to dry herself. She re-
wrapped her wounded toe. It really was much better, no longer red and
raw. Her prayers of the night before answered, the young girl, forgetting
to offer a prayer of thanks, happily told Goblin how her toe was almost
entirely well. The cat purred loudly, kneaded the blanket with his claws,
and slowly blinked his big eyes at Rosemarie. He knew the toe would get

better; after all, he had given it good cat-licking medicine. Rosemarie, now feeling elegant with her new cleanliness and good health, dipped the cat a deep curtsey.

Finally, she plunged her grimy shift into the bucket and began washing it. Except for the sound of her scrubbing and wringing, the room was silent. But, from time to time, she heard small noises emanating from the coop. When she could wring no more water from her shift, she spread it over the poles to dry.

Sitting on the bed she had selected for herself, Rosemarie gently scratched Goblin's cheeks and stroked his ears. He had begun to purr again when another soft sound made the girl look toward the cat coop. She crossed the room.

She flipped back the cage's cover and cried out, "Holy Mother of God!"

Snow Beauty lay on her side. Three wriggly little creatures snuggled against her stomach. Goblin knew Snow Beauty's time to kitten was at hand. He now stood up as if to take a bow. He stretched his front legs out before him then extended his back legs, and finally, curving his back into a full arch, he resettled on the bed.

"You needn't look so smug," Rosemarie said to him.

Just then, loud voices and the tramp of feet echoed from the stairwell. She threw the cover over the coop and ran to the door to listen. Mixed with the tread of booted feet, she heard the rattle of metal. *Is it weapons? Armor?* Doors opened and shut. Amongst the jovial, backslapping banter, the young woman picked out William's laughter. Hearing the men's cheerful voices, Rosemarie suddenly felt very lonely. Her heart cried out for her husband's company. She whirled around and propped her hands on her hips. She stamped her foot. Her young brow wrinkled.

Jutting out her lip, she then demanded of Goblin, "By what right has he all these jolly companions, while I'm alone—like a prisoner in an empty cell?"

Her grand accommodations of a few minutes ago now appeared to be the stone-cold walls of a prison.

Four.

KNUCKLES RAPPED LIGHTLY on her door.

"Rosemarie, are you ready for guests?" Will called from the passageway.

She threw open the door. Excitement and curiosity bubbled up within her, dispelling her annoyance. Will stood in the hall with a tall, curly haired, blond man; a cluster of men's faces loomed behind them.

"Your room has the only large table, and, since there are no other women staying here now, we might as well dine together," Will explained, as they all tramped in, a total of eight men and one slight, pimply faced youth.

As unobtrusively as they could, Rosemarie and Will moved the cat coop to the far end of the room. A lay brother hustled away with Rosemarie's wash water. Brother Ambrose and yet another helper brought in a ewer and pottery bowls for them to rinse off their hands before the meal. After each had dipped his hands into a water bowl and patted them dry on a towel offered by Brother Ambrose, the old monk inquired whether there was anything else anybody needed; satisfied there was nothing further he could do for them, he wished everyone a good evening and toddled out. The lay brothers followed him but returned almost immediately with a supper of bread, soup, cheese, wine, and ale.

Before the dining group had settled around the table, William made the introductions, finishing with, "Sir Rudolph, my wife, Rosemarie," and, turning to her, "Sir Rudolph is a knight in the service of Baron Robert von Schwartzfeld. He is on a noble quest."

"At your service, Sir Knight." The young woman dropped a deep curtsy.

The plain food was filling, the drink plentiful, and the talk soon turned merry. Differences in rank and social status were all but forgotten for the evening. So many tales, plots, and plans were exchanged over pots of ale and wine that Rosemarie forgot for the moment her own excitement and her desire to tell William about the kittens. A real, radiant, golden-haired, blue-eyed knight was sitting at their table. Never mind the thin scar that crossed his forehead and divided his left eyebrow or the sparseness of the yellow locks at the very top of his head; this was a man whose adventures were the stuff of minstrels' songs.

The only other fighting man whose name Rosemarie would remember from that night was Gerhard, Sir Rudolph's equally fair-haired, but somberly quiet, second-in-command.

Sir Rudolph was undertaking a difficult and possibly dangerous task, but, upon hearing of the young couple's plight, the ever generous and chivalrous knight offered his assistance and protection as far as his probable destination, the market town called Johannesmarkt. There, he was to negotiate with the lord who held the manor.

Hearing that a town large enough to support them might be within one or two days' journey, her heart jumped with joy. Will, even more enchanted, saw the adventure of a lifetime before him. Surely this knight would need his services to shoe his horses and bang out the dents in his armor. By evening's end, Will and Rosemarie felt they had known the knight forever and were fully committed to his mission.

"It's a dangerous mission," Sir Rudolph said.

The knight glanced at Rosemarie, but the firm set of her mouth told him not even to suggest leaving her behind in the sanctuary of the blushing holy men.

"My liege, Baron Robert, served the duke honorably," he continued. "He was captured and is held by a petty lord whose ransom demands are exorbitant. He is not eager to negotiate and wants to get all the money he can from the baroness, Lady Alfreda von Schwartzfeld. She has gathered together a huge amount of money, gold, silver, and jewels to buy her husband's freedom. It is this great treasure that I bring with me to offer to the brute in exchange for my lord, the baron. The man has no right to refuse such a ransom."

"Who is this greedy lord?" Rosemarie wanted to know.

"A great, gray-haired brute named Johann de Forrest who sided with the Duke's enemies. Baron Robert was neither among the dead nor the prisoners exchanged, and this Johann slipped away before the peace talks were completed. Some six months later, men claiming to be sent by this Johann came to Lady von Schwartzfeld seeking ransom money.

"Their proof was a small gold reliquary containing a lock of Saint Agnes' hair; her ladyship knew at once that it was her husband's. Apparently the reliquary was clamped by gold hooks and rings to a plain iron cross of no obvious worth but for the small stone at its base. It's an amazing little gem said to flash red, or blue, or sometimes even clear, depending on the light it is held to. A greedy man could easily pull off the reliquary, according to Lady Alfreda, and never notice the cross or stone. The baron wore it always around his neck."

It was near midnight when the men rose from the table and clomped out to their quarters. Goblin scurried out from under Rosemarie's bed and began to devour the gravy-soaked crumbs on the floor. Then he leaped onto the table, where his rough tongue scoured any remains from the bowls. Rosemarie wiped up some tidbits and threw them to Snow Beauty.

William spent the next day at the forge. Rosemarie took advantage of the quiet hall to rest and play with Goblin. She didn't dare interfere with Snow Beauty who was much occupied with her kittens and exceedingly snarly. The girl attended a morning service at the monastery church with the young squire, who had few duties that morning and was bored.

Sir Rudolph dined at midday with the abbot. It was an elegant meal—roast quail and fine wine, served on silver platters and in silver vessels—in a warm, wood-paneled dining room. Still, the knight returned to the guest quarters in a somber mood and immediately sat down to talk with his men. The abbot had told him that Johann was dead, and the manor was managed now by his son Hubert who if anything was more brutal than his father. No one knew much about the supposed prisoner, whether he was alive or dead. After hearing all this, Sir Rudolph decided to entrust the treasure intended for the ransom to the abbot of the monastery, additionally protected by two of his own men. He and his five remaining warriors, his young squire, the carter, and the farrier and his wife would push on to Johannesmarkt at daybreak.

Because they understood that Johannesmarkt was only a day or two's journey from the monastery, William and Rosemarie decided to leave Nob with the monks to eat and regain his strength. They would come back for him once they were settled. After watching Sir Rudolph's men haul chest after chest of treasure from the heavy wagon—to be stored under lock and key in the abbot's private library—Rosemarie climbed into the wagon with the soldiers' remaining gear, Will's anvil and tools, and their few other possessions. For her own comfort and that of her pets, she arranged folded blankets on the floor of the wagon so she could sit next to the cat coop.

The wagon would jolt along over the rutted road, affording a rough ride, jarring and sliding its passengers. Will would be much more comfortable on a horse. He would ride the lively steed previously ridden by one of the men who stayed behind. Sir Rudolph had said nothing to the young couple of his conversation with the abbot, and their hearts were merry as they set forth on what they thought was the last leg of their flight.

Five.

SIR RUDOLPH, MOUNTED on a dapple, gray palfrey, rode between two of his men at the head of the little procession. Next came the squire, leading the knight's warhorse. The clumsy wagon followed. Will was not far behind, and the remaining three fighters brought up the rear. Midday of the following day brought the traveling party to Johannesmarkt. Alongside their path a brook rushed its watery energy down the hillside to a gaily creaking millwheel. Its energy spent at the mill, the stream meandered peacefully into the town, skirting the edge of a green common where a milk cow grazed. Bridges arched over the brook. People, horses, and dogs bustled about their tasks. The church bell's low, throaty tones rang the noon hour. The travelers dismounted and stood with their heads bowed for the noon prayer.

As they raised their heads after the prayer, Will and Rosemarie thought the little town looked like a most inviting place. But when the travelers looked up at the barren hill just beyond the village and at the forbidding stone dwelling atop it, they stood aghast at the bleakness of the lord's manor house. Hacked tree stumps were all that graced the grounds. A tall palisade surrounded the house. Some of the posts were whole tree trunks set into the ground; it was so high they could not see the ground floor of Lord Hubert's home. Armed guards stood at either side of the gate.

Then, as the knight and his companions watched, a great ox-drawn farm wagon, piled high with hay, lumbered toward the gate. As the wagon inched through the portal, a man ran out, squeezing between the wagon and the palisade. He was not quick enough, and two guards seized him by his arms. Their cudgels pounded his back, and he crumpled to the ground. Grabbing his wrists, the guardsmen dragged him on his stomach back inside the palisade. The unfortunate man kicked and pushed with his feet, sending up clouds of dust in his struggle to get up. The cudgels slammed his shoulders once again. The farm wagon kept rolling in as if nothing had happened.

Rosemarie moaned, clapped both hands over her mouth, and ran back to the cart, where she huddled on the blankets next to her cats. She could hear her heart pounding in her ears. *What kind of place have we come to?* wondered the girl.

The knight's men stood a minute as if stunned, each wondering what the violent little scene might mean for them.

Finally Sir Rudolph spoke. "Behold the abode of Hubert de Forrest."

He urged his horse forward into the town. Townsfolk whispered and stared as the clanking armed figures passed them.

Again Sir Rudolph pulled up his mount, this time before a substantial slate-roofed building. The wooden sign over the door rocked gently in the breeze. A tankard overflowing with froth, painted on the swaying board, advertised the refreshment offered inside.

"We'll have something for fortitude," said the knight.

He led them all in, where they were readily seated at a trestle table and soon were munching dutifully, if not happily, on bread; sipping a thin, soupy stew; and downing very good ale.

Despite the hearty food and good drink, the somber appearance of the manor and the tense mood of the knight's men had a chilling effect on the young couple's spirits. The fighting men ate silently while Sir Rudolph got up from the table once or twice to have a word with the innkeeper. Rosemarie sipped her soup carefully and from time to time surreptitiously spat pieces of meat back into her spoon. She dropped these onto the bare wooden table. Then, pushing the meaty pieces behind her bowl, she pressed any juice out from the meat with her spoon and slipped the little nibbles into a leather purse that hung from her belt. Only when she had acquired a small handful of cat snacks did she eat her fill.

When they had eaten enough and could find no more reason to linger at the tavern, they returned to their horses and wagon and headed up the manor road. In spite of their trepidations, once at the manor, Lord Hubert's guardsmen received the travelers courteously. Their wagon was drawn around to the back of the manor house where a two-story wooden wing had been added for guest rooms, making a sort of second-floor dormitory. Their horses were stabled. The knight's men hauled all their gear and the young couple's possessions, with the exception of the anvil which they left in the wagon, into the second-floor guest hall in the dusty wooden addition.

Sir Rudolph's men knew all about Goblin and Snow Beauty. They were not all convinced that traveling with cats was safe or lucky, but they did not think that Rosemarie could possibly be a witch. They kept their mouths shut. As a matter of practicality they accommodated their furry fellow travelers with a shallow, earth-filled box that served as a portable commode. This they also hauled into the guest hall.

They hustled Rosemarie in when Lord Hubert's men led the carthorse off to the stable. Sir Rudolph thought the presence of a woman in the party might be awkward to explain. He had gleaned information at the tavern that caused him to think he must protect the couple carefully until his dealings with Lord Hubert were completed.

They now found themselves accommodated all together in a long room where the sole amenity for guests was comprised of some bare, straw-filled mattresses stacked against a wall. They were informed that they would meet their host, Lord Hubert, at the evening meal. The lord of the manor, having no idea which day, or even week, Sir Rudolph would arrive, had ridden out to his tenant farms to collect taxes and fees he claimed were due to him. William noticed that Sir Rudolph pursed his lips when the steward rubbed his hands together and smirked as he spoke of collecting taxes.

"Beat out of them every coin he can, is more like it," the knight muttered under his breath after the steward left.

The group arranged the mattresses and shifted their luggage, so they could get at what they would most likely need. Rosemarie was disturbed that the knight emphasized easy access to their weapons. Having made themselves as comfortable as they could, they were quenching their thirst with a round of sour-tasting beer, home brewed and provided by their host, when Lord Hubert's falconer appeared at the door.

A spry, wiry little man, he was virtually jumping up and down with enthusiasm. He said he had the most beautiful and best-trained birds in the duchy. He offered to take Lord Hubert's guests hunting, saying that they simply must not miss this opportunity to see the falcons perform. There being several hours to fill before the evening meal, all the fighting men joined the hunt.

Six.

AFTER THE FIGHTING men left, Rosemarie opened her purse and fished out the small bits of meat that she had strained from her midday soup; she dropped them into the cats' cage. Snow Beauty bestirred herself, jostling her kittens, to snap up the largest bit of meat. Goblin quickly smacked down the rest. Rosemarie gazed in wonder at the three tiny bundles of white fur with gray-striped tails—three new lives. Snow Beauty growled a warning, and the girl shut the lid, leaving them to their business.

Since she was not required to stay in the "women's quarters," as at the monastery, she and Will decided to stroll around the grounds. Rosemarie covered the cats' coop, and they went outdoors. It was a sunny, crisp autumn afternoon. The young couple strolled hand in hand, as there were few people around to see them show such youthful affection. There were no trees and no birds singing within the palisade. Weeds and patches of trampled grass held down the dust. They passed several outbuildings— stables, a barn, sheds—and came around to a walled-in kitchen garden at the back of the manor house. Next to it, a stone building with three huge chimneys proclaimed its function as the kitchen. A covered walkway connected it to the main house.

Beyond them, a baker bent before a brick mound of an oven, pulling out loaves of bread. A bone-thin girl, bare legged, her hair tumbling from its cap and whipping in the breeze, used her fingernails to pick off the loaves from his peel and drop them into a basket.

As they walked around to the kitchen door, Rosemarie blurted out, "Oh, let's see the kitchen! Perhaps I can help."

"Silly thing! I will not have my wife a scullery maid," cried Will, pulling her back from the door.

Just then, the door flung open, and a vile-looking man skulked out. He carried a foul-smelling bucket that swung as he walked, splashing and spilling some sort of black slop. His boots were covered with mud and possibly dung. He hurried to the manor house. As he stepped off the doorsill, a woman of giant proportions appeared in the doorway. One of her muscular arms held the door flat against the wall, and, in her other hand, she waved a wine jug.

"Don't let me catch you at my wine cellar again! Stick to your own affairs!" She turned her red-faced glare toward Rosemarie and Will. "Well, what have we here, my little brown mousies?"

"I, I wanted to see the kitchen," Rosemarie said, summoning up all her courage.

The big woman tucked a strand of her graying, yellow hair into her cap and smoothed her gravy-stained apron over her belly with her immense paws. "Why? Who sent you?"

"No one," said the girl.

The big woman stepped toward the girl, glaring. For an instant, Rosemarie could see inside.

Three maids were scrubbing kettles and tureens. A young man scraped at a blackened spit. Another piteously thin girl was chopping something white, perhaps turnips, at a table in the center of the room. Fires blazed with various degrees of intensity in three hearths.

"Come, Rosemarie," William whispered and tried to steer her away. "She just thought she might help. We are guests here, that's all."

"Guests?" the big woman bellowed in surprise. "Guests of Lord Hubert! Heh, heh, must be the Second Coming that milord sends his guests to help Joanna! Get thy behinds out of here! You pig's—"

The two did not wait to hear what part of the pig they might be. They both ran off as fast as their legs could take them.

Returning to the guest hall, Rosemarie said only, "I think I'll lie down."

She threw herself down on a straw mattress and pulled a sheet over her head. William tried to do likewise, but he could not stop thinking, running over again and again everything that had happened in the last few days. Goblin mewed. The youth lifted the cat from his cage. Goblin ran straight for his shallow box. He pawed around in the dirt and squatted to relieve himself.

Rosemarie groaned and buried her face in the dusty mattress. "Oh, that awful smell!" she whimpered.

The young farrier scooped up the cat and returned him to the coop.

Next, he scraped up the cat's droppings with his dagger and flung the stinking stuff out the window. William left the window open to air out the room a little.

"This hall stinks so of mouse nests and Lord knows what all that no one will notice much," said William, more to the cats than to his wife.

When Sir Rudolph returned to the guest quarters in the late afternoon, Rosemarie was sleeping.

William, gesturing toward the still form on the mattress, said, "Sir Knight, with your permission—"

"I'll have them send over food," Sir Rudolph replied.

The knight was actually much relieved that the young commoners would not be present at the meal. He did not want to have to explain their presence in his party. Knights, being aristocrats, did not dine with commoners. The warriors went to supper.

After a scullery wench brought food to the guest quarters, Will let loose the cats. Goblin and Snow Beauty ate very well on dove and quail. Will woke his wife. She ate, and the little family spent a pleasant hour playing with the cats, teasing them with straws drawn from a mattress. Snow Beauty soon returned to her kittens, but Goblin enjoyed the game, leaping high in fanciful arcs and amazing the humans with the supple twists of his spine as he jumped and turned. *Good Heavens!* thought William. *If I flipped like that my back would snap in two.*

When they heard men's footsteps on the stairs, they boxed the cats. When the knight stepped into the room, he found the couple gazing out the window at the stars.

"Beautiful night, milord," said William.

"For you, perhaps," answered the knight. He sat down heavily, grunting with weariness, and his squire knelt to pull off his boots.

"Hubert got wind that there is a woman in our party. He was very persistent with his questions. I'm afraid he now thinks your wife is a distant kinswoman of my squire; he thinks her parents had despaired of finding her a husband, for she lacked grace and beauty—forgive me, dear girl—talked of God to a fault, and dressed like a mendicant, like a beggar. You see, the abbot had mentioned there was a convent a little beyond Johannesmarkt. Therefore, I conceived the idea that you," here the knight smiled at his own cleverness, "much to your parent's relief, had had a vision of St. Anne that left you mute. The nunnery was your destination. So I told this villain I carried fine plate for the nun's chapel, along with the ransom money, as your dowry. Your clothes are not those of a lady, obviously, and I can't trust your speech to be that of one either."

"Thank you."

The girl bobbed a curtsey and dropped down on the bed. Far from insulted, she was relieved not to have to attempt conversation with noble society.

On the following day, the main meal would be served as usual at noon. They would dine formally with Lord Hubert and his lady, by which time the knight hoped the negotiations for the ransom would be completed. His distrust of Lord Hubert was so great that he ordered his men to wear armored padding under their shirts; this padding was itself a type of armor, being reinforced with horn and strips of steel. His men were to spend the morning searching every corner they possibly could for the baron while the knight dealt with Hubert. Their plans made, they trooped out.

William and Rosemarie set about cleaning and cutting smooth the girl's fingernails, trying to make her look a little more like a nobleman's daughter. After months in the woods, she might more easily be taken for a highwayman's daughter. She had some balm among her things, intending to use it this winter on chapped, raw hands. They did their best to make her hands look like those of a lady. Then they fussed with her hair, finally settling on pinning it under a linen towel that might possibly pass for a coarse mendicant's veil.

Rosemarie slipped into her gray wool houppelande. She had been so proud of its thick, rich folds; it was an elegant winter garment for a farrier's wife but still not what a noblewoman would wear. She had pictured herself wearing it to Midnight Mass on Christmas Eve at their new home, but, to these high people, even her best dress would seem like the austere garb of a deranged, would-be nun. That thought caused a little surge of resentment that stiffened Rosemarie's spine. She stood tall, determined to play her role well.

"The man's a vile devil. I cannot get a simple yes or no from him about anything," Sir Rudolph complained bitterly to his men later that morning when they gathered again in the guest hall before dinner. Ale splashed from his flagon as he gestured. "I can't get a clear answer as to whether our liege lord is even alive."

"We searched every inch of the grounds, milord," one of the men said. "There are no cellars here but the buttery under the kitchen, and it was as much as my life was worth, milord, to get by that bear of a cook. Still, the buttery is just that—filled with butts of wine, sir."

"He tricked me into conceding that the ransom money was held at the monastery. I didn't like the way he looked when he heard that. So I am posting you, Gerhard, to watch if any of his men ride for the monastery. Oh, give me the clank and clash of a good battle! This negotiating is not for me."

"Sir Rudolph, do you not remember that I am a farrier? I could very legitimately stay in the stable. You may need Gerhard."

"Well said, young William! Take your pliers and hammers and go."

"Yes, sir." Proud to be a part of things, the youth ran out. A little shiver of fear ran down Rosemarie's back. Suddenly, she felt very alone.

The knight had another word with Gerhard.

And so it happened that at noontime the humble blacksmith's wife entered the great hall on the arm of a nobleman. The master of the household sat on an ornately carved, high-backed oak chair at the center of a long trestle table that was covered with a wide linen cloth. The cloth hung down some thirty inches on both sides of the table; it was used to wipe hands and mouths during the meal. Hubert's sixteen-year-old wife, the Lady Frances, sat to his left on an oak chair of her own. All other diners sat on benches. Rush mats covered the floor to absorb crumbs and spills. Behind Hubert, a great fire crackled and roared in the fireplace. Sir Rudolph and Rosemarie sat opposite the lord and lady; Rudolph's squire sat, frowning, next to his "kinswoman." The knight's men sat in a row on either side of them. The lord's steward, clerk, and retainers were arrayed, according to their importance, on the opposite side of the table, on either side of the lord and his lady.

Pageboys brought in ewers of rosewater, first to the lord and his lady and then to the other diners according to rank. When all had washed their hands, the clerk said a blessing. Rosemarie made the sign of the cross three times, attesting to her supposed religious vocation. Then, the lord's pages returned, parading platters of spiced, broiled fish—fresh from the manor pond—and an ornate silver tureen of soup. Each diner had a round loaf of bread, scooped out like a bowl, to serve as a trencher. The feast continued with dove, quail, and meat pie.

Beyond her initial "good afternoon," the young Lady Frances said nothing to Rosemarie, but glared suspiciously at this new dinner companion. Rosemarie had merely curtsied and nodded. Not having to add anything to the conversation, she kept her eyes on her food and determined to make the best of the bounty before her.

Lord Hubert joked and taunted Sir Rudolph about the whereabouts of Baron Robert. Stirring his spoon noisily in the soup tureen, he wondered aloud what peculiar dish lay before him. His spoon flung some of the hot liquid onto his wife's sleeve. She let out a squeak, scowled, and wiped at her sleeve with the tablecloth. Hubert roared with laughter and slyly winked at Rosemarie. "Look sharp; you don't want to swallow a bit of His Excellency's finger, or toe!"

Smirking, Lord Hubert was enjoying Rosemarie's horror. He eyed her as she gasped. Quickly, she tore off a piece of the soup-soaked trencher bread and put it into her mouth.

"By the saints!" exclaimed Lady Frances at Rosemarie's social gaffe. "This woman has the manners of a serf! Do you not know—wherever it is you come from, *lady*—to leave that for the almoner to give to the poor!"

The girl sat rigid, saucer-eyed, almost too scared to breathe.

"Ho!" laughed Lord Hubert. "What have we here?" he asked of the knight. "Your sweet little cabbage?"

Rudolph jumped up, knocking the bench away from himself and Rosemarie. She scrabbled for the table's edge and kept her footing.

The knight slammed his knuckles onto the table and shouted into Hubert's face, "I will not have you insult the honor of this innocent child!"

His last words were not heard. The door to the hall slammed open, banging loudly against the stone wall. Two men ran in and dropped the chicken coop onto the table, directly in front of Lord Hubert. "We found these in their room, milord. Cats, milord, a whole family of them!"

"God's wounds! You're a witch!" screamed Lord Hubert, glaring at Rosemarie.

He ripped open the coop, reached in, and grabbed the first bit of fur that his fingers touched.

"The girl's a witch, a witch I tell you!" raged Hubert.

His coarse fingers squeezed the life out of the tiny creature as he flung the bit of fur over his shoulder into the fire. The flames licked up the newborn kitten with only the slightest sizzle.

"No, no, no! No, no!" Rosemarie rushed at Lord Hubert.

The knight held her back, but there was no end to her screams.

"A loud mute," Lady Frances remarked.

Goblin shot up from the coop like an arrow released from a bow. Ten claws ripped into the evil lord's face. Ten stained claws sliced rivulets of red from forehead to chin, blinding the lord with his own blood. Goblin dropped back into the cage. Immediately, he again leapt out, this time followed by Snow Beauty, each carrying one of the remaining kittens. They were outdoors before the humans—distracted by the bloodletting and Rosemarie's hysteria—noticed they were gone.

It was Lady Frances, rather than her bloodied lord, who took command. "Take the witch to the scullery. Have Joanna keep her," ordered the woman. Her mouth twisted into a satisfied smirk at the mention of the giantess.

Two of Hubert's brutes grabbed Sir Rudolph from behind while Rosemarie was seized and hustled outside. By twisting hard, Rudolph hunched one man off and threw the other over his shoulder across the table. The tossed man's feet knocked Hubert to the floor.

Now it was Lady Frances' turn to scream. "Help him! Help my lord to his feet!"

The only weapons at the dinner were daggers used to eat meat, but the knight's men, all strong men, were well protected by their armor padding, and the general melee broke in their favor.

"Arms!" called the knight.

As a group, his men broke for the stairs and guest hall. In the guest hall, Sir Rudolph tied his padded coif under his chin and pulled a mail coif over his head. It covered his head, neck, and the top of his shoulders. His squire helped to strap on the knight's sword. There was no time for further armor. "Forget the spurs! My gauntlets!"

Having donned what protection they could and gathered up their weapons, Sir Rudolph ordered his men to hold close together and make a fast search of Hubert's living quarters on the upper floor, to try to find the baron. They raced into the upper story of Lord Hubert's house.

Finding no one among the straw mattresses of the guest hall, Hubert's thugs stomped across the corridor and into their master's living quarters. Their shouting, cursing, and the pounding of their boots on the stone floor left Sir Rudolph in no doubt of their whereabouts and the little distance between them and his own men. The knight's troop made their way across the second level, barring each door behind them as they passed into the next room, only to hear Hubert's brutes smash down the oak doors as they followed them. Sir Rudolph's men threw open chests and cabinets, pulled aside draperies, and tore down tapestries and wall cloths in rooms that were mostly bedrooms and storage areas. No baron. Then, they came to Hubert's bedroom, where two frightened maidservants were making ready their master's bed. Like all the servants, they knew the knight was in search of the baron.

"You'll not find a baron here," cried one buxom maid who had a scabbed-over cut on her lip and purple bruises about her eye, her beauty ruined.

"That man! What he did to her!" said the second girl as the first dropped her eyes and brought her hand to her bruised face. "We'd flee had we the chance. Most would."

She tore back the covers she had just spread and kicked under the bed to show no one was hidden there.

"Now's your chance," cried one of the men as they dashed from the room. Sir Rudolph and his men sped down the far stairs and out a side door, into the yard.

As the knight and his men escaped at the side of the manor, they heard Hubert's thugs shouting in the fore courtyard at the front entrance of the house. An arbor of interlocking grapevines between the side door and the front courtyard ensured that Hubert's followers would turn in the opposite direction from the escaping party, if and when Hubert's men realized that the knight would try to get to his horse. The band of brutes would have to go all the way around the manor house and the kitchen, with its connecting passageway to the main house, its attendant bakery ovens, wells, and outbuildings. But, from their side exit, Sir Rudolph and his warriors had a clear path to the stables, giving them a vital few minutes' advantage. At the stable, Gerhard led the knight's warhorse out, armored and saddled. Expecting there might be difficulties, the knight had ordered Gerhard to have all their horses saddled and ready. Will learned of the events of the afternoon as the men mounted. He spoke to Sir Rudolph. "I have been busy, milord." He grinned as he held up the nail nippers that he used to loosen old horseshoes. The knight frowned, but he had no time for talk.

"Please, oh please, don't forget Rosemarie," the youth begged.

"She's safe enough where she is," was the knight's gruff response, but then he reached down and gripped the boy's shoulder and looked him hard in the eye. "Trust me—a little while yet."

They sped off.

William had but a minute to gather up his tools and hide in the loft above before the men loyal to Lord Hubert burst, shouting and cursing, into the stable. They saddled their mounts and raced away after their intended prey. Not one gave a thought to the young farrier.

The knight and his men galloped off, down the manor road, in a cloud of dust. Then, seeing no one was immediately behind them, they paraded at a more dignified trot through the little town, giving the townspeople the impression that they were in control and there was nothing to fear. When they passed the mill on the other side of the village, they clambered up the hill as fast as their horses could take them. At the top, Sir Rudolph found a vantage point to his liking and turned his horse to face the slope. His men fanned out in a semicircle across the road.

It was not long before they heard hoof beats—but they also heard a horse whinny and fall. Another horse mysteriously cried out. Then, Odo, Lord Hubert's second-in-command, came galloping around the bend in the road, racing for the hilltop. Behind him were three more horsemen. The others were but a short distance behind them.

Odo whirled a mace above his head. The man behind him spun an iron-studded flail. Odo led his animal straight at the knight's warhorse. Odo's horse, not trained for warfare, backed and whinnied, showing the whites of his eyes. Sir Rudolph's horse danced in excitement. He trotted so his right side and the knight's sword arm faced the oncoming attack. Odo, getting his mount under control, thrashed at the knight, slamming his shoulder with the mace, but the strong man was shaken for only a second before his sword sliced into Odo's shoulder. Odo fell from his horse, crashing to the ground. The flail accidentally caught the riderless horse on the neck. The animal screamed. Sir Rudolph's squire rode up close his master, thinking to aid him in the confusion of battle. The flail, on its next swing, thumped across the youth's skull, and he slumped in his saddle.

By now, each of the fighters had engaged an enemy. Odo's horse struggled away from the fray and galloped down the hill. Sir Rudolph pierced the flail bearer. Gerhard and Rudolph each had one man more. Most of the thugs had jumped from their horses. Since they were not knights trained to the horse, they were more used to fighting on foot and were now slamming at Sir Rudolph's men and horses with mace, flail, battleaxe, and short sword. One warrior began battering at Sir Rudolph's unprotected left leg.

The knight shouted, "Down!" and his horse, knowing the signal, lowered its head.

Sir Rudolph swirled his sword over the horse's head and plunged his blade deep between the attacker's ribs. The man dropped his weapon and fell to the ground, clutching his bleeding side. He just managed to scramble away from the warhorse's prancing feet before he died. Then, grabbing the fallen man's sword, Odo, mortally wounded, staggered up from the ground.

Roaring like a lion, he put his head down and charged straight at Sir Rudolph, bellowing, "Kill! Kill the—!"

One swipe of Sir Rudolph's sword all but took off his attacker's head. When the blood stopped spurting from his neck and they saw that Odo lay dead in a pool of his own blood, Hubert's men lost heart and began to fall back.

At that moment, one last rider reached the hilltop, mounted on a piteously lame animal. A stone had wedged under a loosened horseshoe. Still not sure of the outcome of the battle, its rider dismounted and bravely approached the melee with a buckler and a war hammer. Only three of Hubert's men remained mounted. Their leader, Odo, was dead; their courage melted, and in a sudden panic, they tore back down the hill, leaving the new arrival standing alone. Sir Rudolph's horse turned its flank toward the new man. Sir Rudolph aimed his bloodied sword at the sole attacker's chest. "Your choice," said the knight.

The man dropped his hammer.

"Bind him."

Sir Rudolph's small force rode back into the village, walking their prisoners behind the knight and his wounded squire. As they reached the bottom of the hill, they saw a horse with bloodied knees standing by the side of the road. Its reins hung to the ground. In the brush lay its master with his neck snapped and twisted at a frightful angle.

All the townspeople had either seen or heard the many riders rushing through the streets, but, fearing Hubert's bloody deeds, only a few brave souls stood on the green, awaiting the outcome of the clattering steel, shouts, and cries of men and horses beyond the mill. As the knight approached the green, his proud warhorse sensed victory and strutted, bobbing his head as if to the beat of a drum, and the daring villagers cheered. Doors then flew open, and women and children flocked to the green to learn the news. They stretched tall to see over Sir Rudolph's horses and to see the prisoners. Perhaps they were hoping some kinsman of theirs had survived, or were saddened that any of Hubert's thugs still lived.

With the sole exception of the unconscious squire, tied onto his saddle and steadied from time to time by the knight himself, Sir Rudolph's horsemen had sustained only minor cuts and some severe bruising. Sir Rudolph's collarbone had received a punishing blow from Odo's mace. Many of Hubert's men were dead, and others lay wounded, writhing in agony on the hilltop. It was with some difficulty that the knight persuaded the jubilant commoners to take a cart up the hill to tend to the wounded. The townsmen wanted to follow Sir Rudolph's men to the manor and finish with Hubert.

Seven.

FTER WAITING FOR several minutes for the clop of horses' hooves to fade into silence, William crept quietly to the stable door, misjudging his own importance, perhaps, in thinking a guard had been posted at the entrance. Looking first to the left, then right, then up to the manor house, he saw no one. He stole little by little across the yard to the kitchen, pausing at times to make sure no one was following him, hiding first behind a cart, then behind a stack of barrels. No one came after him. He heard no sound. William stepped quietly up to the kitchen door. He pulled at it, gently. It was locked. He put his ear against the door. Inside, voices murmured.

He heard a light thump, the mew of a cat as it jumped, and then clearly Rosemarie's sweet voice saying, "Oh, he's going out."

His wife's tender voice brought tears to young Will's eyes. The boy felt the hair of his neck stand up, a chill run down his back, and his fingers turn icy. Reason fled; he had to get to Rosemarie. Grabbing the door with both hands, he pulled, rattling the latch. Heavy footsteps approached from within.

Will heard Joanna's big voice boom, "Who's come to visit?"

The door swung open so fast that Will tripped over the doorsill and into the apron-clad bosom of the giant cook. She relieved him of his dagger, and spun him down onto the bench next to Rosemarie, who sat with her hands bound.

Then the big woman laughed and, putting her hands on her hips, sneered, "Why, it's the little horseshoe fellow!"

Will sat still, wide-eyed. With her paws still on her hips, but pointing William's knife directly at him, she cocked her head to one side and said, "Your little lady, once I got her calmed down, has told me her short life's story, and we even have been visited by your gray-striped friend. He found a rat of monstrous proportions in the buttery." She jerked her head toward the door leading to the dirty steps, "And just left by yon window."

The giantess then busied about the kitchen, still keeping the corner of her eye on the couple. She put platters on shelves and hung up tankards while the lovers murmured together. Her lips worked almost as if she were chewing on something. From time to time she made little humming noises that sounded more as if she were agreeing to something than singing. They were alone. The scullions were not to be seen, although kettles waited for washing. After a minute or two, the cook swung the iron crane away from the fire and ladled out a bowl of broth from the cauldron. "Here," she shoved the bowl under Will's nose, "drink this. It strengthens the spirit. We got to think."

The big woman settled herself on a stool opposite the couple, her feet spread apart and her fingers playing with the blade of William's knife. Rubbing first one hand and then the other on her knees, she took a deep breath and gave William a hard look, as if sizing him up.

She began to speak in short bursts. "My nephew. You saw him this morning. All the family I got in this world. I sent him and the girls up to the house with the fine folks' cold supper. Should they want it. Who knows what they will do. Look you," her voice dropped to a whisper, "that Odo is a hard man, even worse than the master. He does what milord only thinks of doing. I know your girl is not a witch. Truth is, in this town, we liked mousers much until Johann and Hubert—"

Her voice drifted into silence. She sighed, letting out a great burst of air. "You are both such innocents."

Will bristled at that. Only a few months ago he had defended Rosemarie against three men who would have burned her alive, and the couple had survived weeks of wandering. Now he was an "innocent" and, even more humiliating, a prisoner of a woman. Still, he could not see himself pushing a woman around and certainly not such a woman as Joanna.

The cook continued, "Odo will soon make his supper of your fine fleeing knight."

Will thought she might just be right. At that moment, with a whish and a thump, Goblin bounded back through the window. His padded feet came to an abrupt halt as he landed on the rough surface of the chopping table. The cat stood yowling and angrily switching his tail left and right. He glared at William, Rosemarie, and then at Joanna. Goblin's excited, dilated pupils shone like great, round, black diamonds set in rings of gold. They blazed with fury.

"You have little time—but you could run now . . . and maybe have a chance," continued Joanna. "Look, I'll cut these cords. You tie up my hands and then go. I'll say you hit me with this." She set an iron pot on the table.

Goblin spat out a fierce hiss.

Joanna sliced Rosemarie free, but, as she turned to Will, with Rosemarie's cords in her hands, Goblin leapt at them, swatting at them as if playing; he took them in his mouth and ran down into the cellar. In seconds he was back on the table, without the cords, but with a short leather thong between his teeth. A small iron cross dangled from the leather string. Seeing the glint of a bauble at its end, William snatched it up. He grabbed the iron pot and swung it at Joanna's head, hitting her shoulder. She stumbled and dropped the knife. Rosemarie grabbed it. William helped himself to Joanna's cutlery. The woman pulled herself to her feet.

Brandishing a butcher knife at the cook, William said, "We are going to the buttery. You first. Take this lamp."

The cat sped off ahead of them, yowling and looking back over his shoulder to make sure people were following. Goblin pawed the cellar door open and disappeared down the stairs. The threesome started down the mucky steps.

At the bottom of the stairs, Goblin darted into a little hole in the wall opposite the entrance to the wine cellar.

Wondering where the cat had gone, Will worked his fingers over the boards above the hole into which Goblin had slid.

After a minute, Will exclaimed, "This is a door! A secret door!"

"You still have time to run," Joanna suggested one last time but continued to hold the flickering oil lamp aloft.

"Look. There's a latch up here," said Rosemarie, one step above Joanna.

The big woman sighed. "It's your doing, not mine," she said and, with an air of resignation, threw the latch. The door creaked open, revealing five steps curving down into what seemed like a black void.

"Meow."

The lamp threw light only a few feet ahead. The stench of filth, human and otherwise, made the three gag. Hearing Rosemarie retch, Will told her to go back up to the kitchen and get the ax Joanna kept near the kitchen door for chopping kindling. The girl made her way back upstairs.

A small iron cross dangled from the leather string.

She seized the ax and, on sudden inspiration, barred the kitchen door against Odo. Then Rosemarie ran back down to where Will and Joanna stood.

"Meow," commanded Goblin from below.

Taking up the ax, William elbowed Joanna against Rosemarie and smashed the door to splinters.

"You will not lock us in, woman."

They went down the steps into the dark and stink. The ambivalent Joanna went first, carrying the lamp, with William inches behind her, holding the ax to her back. Rosemarie came last, still clutching the butcher knife and William's dagger.

"Me-yow-ow!" Red discs, Goblin's eyes, were like fires in the darkness, reflecting the lamplight.

Then, another sound. Unidentifiable—a moaning? Suddenly, inexplicably, words—thin and papery—words like rustling leaves, like an old man on his deathbed.

"Cat—is it over?"

Will and the cook hurried over to the cat, the wet ground sucking at their feet. Goblin held his position. Now they could see the cat was poised with one foot on the chest of a long, skeletal human being. A man, mostly bones and dirty wet rags, slowly turned his head, and two eyes peered at the three people like great, glassy marbles sunk deep in the orbits of a skull.

"Baron," whispered Will to the man, and knelt.

With the edge of his tunic, William wiped clean the man's parchment-thin lips.

"We need more light," said Rosemarie.

Joanna raised the lamp. A torch was ensconced in the wall. She lit it from her lamp. The red flames revealed the huge stone blocks of the dungeon wall. Leather straps, pulled tightly, tied the baron's wrists and ankles so he could not move. An iron collar was clamped around his skeletal neck.

"He's chained to the wall," whispered Rosemarie.

Three falls of the ax only sank the chain into the soft ground. William tried chopping at the links where they were fastened to a ring in the wall. Again and again he swung the ax. Trickles of sweat ran down the youth's brow as blow after blow rang from the ax. Nearing the end of his strength and puffing for breath, the boy swung the ax over his head and came down with a final fierce whack, and a link cracked. The three worked the chain free.

William ordered Joanna to remove her apron. They tucked the apron, inch by careful inch, under the Baron's fragile frame. Slowly and with great gentleness, they lifted him from the muck. William and Joanna carried him to the kitchen with Rosemarie following and holding up the length of chain that was still fastened to the iron collar around his neck. She carried the knives wedged into her girdle and had the ax tucked under her arm. Goblin ran ahead of them, emitting approving "mrrts." They laid the nobleman down before the fire, and the three set to cutting off his rotting clothing and bathing his body.

Goblin pounced up onto the chopping table, circled, sat, and began licking himself clean: first his paws, then his face, next his chest. When he was satisfied with his appearance, he arched his back, relaxed, and stepped to the edge of the table where he could look down and survey the baron's bath.

Joanna knelt at the baron's neck with a jar of her best wine vinegar. The astringent liquid pleasantly mitigated the smell of the baron's dirty body, but the strong fumes also roused him to a brief consciousness. He groaned. Joanna the cook worked without ceasing, wiping with the patient rhythm of one who had spent many hours kneading bread. Again and again she dabbed a vinegar-soaked towel over the collar's bolts, pressed, and wiped. Little by little the red acid dissolved the rust. At last, William pulled open the cruel necklace, and the baron was free of his chains.

Rosemarie lopped off his long, matted hair and some of his beard. "Can't make him look any worse," she laughed, as she flung the curls into the fire.

Goblin swatted at the flying hair.

It was near dusk before they got the baron washed clean enough to rest on Joanna's bed. All this time the baron said not a word.

"I wonder if he'll live," whispered Joanna, as she pulled the curtain across the ell that served as her bedroom.

Eight.

THE DAY DARKENED, and still they knew nothing of the fighting men. Rosemarie sat on a low stool by one of the hearths, trying to brush the dungeon's muck from the hem of her cherished houppelande. When she had the dress as clean as she could get it, she began wiping off everyone's shoes. William sharpened the ax and, from time to time, looked in on the sleeping baron. Joanna filled the time by taking on the scullions' work, scrubbing out iron cauldrons left from the disrupted noontime dinner. A tap at the kitchen door startled them all.

"Who is it?" bellowed Joanna, assuming her old authority for the moment.

"It's I, Auntie."

"Who's with you?"

"I am alone."

Joanna opened the door for her nephew. He came in smiling, his eyes gleaming with excitement.

"The knight has killed Odo! And put Hubert under guard! They want food."

Joanna hustled about the kitchen, pulling out trays, slicing cold meat, gathering bread, cheese, fruit, and a dozen of her prize sugared dates she found to please the victors' palates. "They'll want drink, too," she murmured.

All the while, Joanna's nephew chattered on with his happy news.

"The one called Gerhard said it was like slicing sausage. The knight said he had never fought wearing so little armor. It seems that Hubert's men soon lost heart—or maybe their heads." The kitchen boy had few actual details of the battle, but he made the best of his report. "Several horses threw shoes. Odd. Some men fled, some were captured.

"The pages told me Hubert was too blinded to do anything to save himself, and no one would defend him but his lady. The Lady Frances became as one possessed, a mad woman. She screamed the most vile curses upon the head of the knight, clawing at the faces of his men and spitting." The youth paused for breath. "More like a witch's cat than a lady, she was," he added.

"I'll help carry these trays across to the house and speak to the knight on your behalf," William assured the cook. "He is a good man."

Joanna looked doubtful. The Huberts and Odos of this world she knew well, but knights? Her jaw worked as she considered whether she had any options. Finding none, she nodded.

Before an hour had passed, Sir Rudolph was kneeling at the baron's bedside. "My liege lord," he whispered over and over, kissing the baron's hands. His broad shoulders shook, and the warrior wept like a child.

William placed the small cross in the knight's hand.

"What? How?"

"The cat found it. Found him," William answered, nodding toward Goblin.

Every time the baron woke, Joanna was there to dribble a rich broth of chicken stock, parsley, and other herbs between his thin lips. After a few days of her diligent nursing, his spirits rose, and he wanted very much to live. When the baron was well enough to be moved, Sir Rudolph saw his lord carried in a litter to the monastery where he spent weeks in the care of the infirmarer.

Despite excellent care by well-intentioned monks—being left to gaze only at bare walls and a large crucifix of his agonizing, nail-pierced Savior—the nobleman found the infirmary almost as bleak as his dungeon. Once life stirred afresh in his limbs, he longed for laughter, green leaves, and blue sky! It took a long time, but he did get well. Once home again, he lived a long, good life.

They brought Hubert to the court of the duke where he was tried and then executed; his wife was shut in a nunnery.

Well before he returned to his own estates, the baron granted the de Forrest manor to his loyal vassal, Sir Rudolph. Gerhard became Rudolph's bailiff. With hard work and careful management, they eventually created a sustaining, if not greatly profitable, demesne of what had been Hubert's fields.

As part of his effort to see justice established in Johannesmarkt, the knight thought it his duty to bring young William before his manorial court, albeit on a day when there were few petitioners present. Sir Rudolph lectured the boy on the wrongfulness of injuring good horseflesh and his sinfulness in overstepping the place in society that, by God's grace, he held as a smith. He was on Earth, said the nobleman, to make and repair tools and to tend to the health of beasts' hooves, never to loosen shoes and do harm. He fined William one heller, a very small sum.

Before William could speak, the knight gaveled him to silence and, smiling, sat back and said, "Now hear you the command of Baron von Schwartzfeld." He shuffled through some documents and picked up one bearing an elaborate seal. Then, after clearing his throat, read, "I command a fair house be built in the town of Johannesmarkt, to consist of two rooms and a loft with a fireplace and stone chimney, for the use of the smith William and his heirs, with land sufficient for living, but not to exceed two acres. I furthermore command that, adjacent to this house, shall be erected a smithy suitable for the shoeing of all beasts needful of shoes and for the conduct of blacksmithing as generally required by the town. And finally I command—," at this point, the knight paused. A hearty snort, a laugh, almost a giggle, exploded from the nobleman's mouth and was quickly stifled as he clapped his hand over his face. He feigned a cough and went on, "Ahem, yes. Let no one say my lord does not remember kindnesses done." Resuming an official tone, he continued to read, "—that the cat named Goblin and his heirs and family, as he so chooses, shall have the right and privilege to live at said shop and house in perpetuity."

Thus ended William's day in court.

The following summer, the baron himself came to visit his vassal, Sir Rudolph. One day, while he was in residence and returning through the town with a hunting party, he stopped at the smithy. Snow Beauty strolled out from behind the forge. Two young, white cats with gray-striped tails followed her. Her bulging sides promised Snow Beauty would soon be a mother again. Goblin sat on the anvil, preening his back toes. A very surprised William hurried out of the smithy and made a deep reverence before the nobleman. "My lord, of what service may I be?"

William's eyes passed swiftly over the horses, wondering if one had thrown a shoe.

Getting down from his horse, the baron commanded, "Will, set that cat down here, will you, please?"

Goblin seemed happy to sit before the baron.

"Cat," said the baron, "I will never know why you did it, but you saved my life."

The great man knelt before the cat and drew a small dagger from

I dub thee Sir Goblin,
Knight of the Smithy.
Whatever you wish, I will grant.

his belt. He tapped Goblin once on each shoulder with the weapon. "I dub thee Sir Goblin, Knight of the Smithy. Whatever you wish, I will grant."

Goblin, now Sir Goblin, stretched out his front legs, as if to bow. Then he walked smartly up to the baron's horse where three hares from the morning's hunt hung over the saddle horn. The knighted feline rose up on his hind legs and sniffed the game.

"Meow."

"Granted."

Sir Goblin's Christmas

One.

THE HARD, COLD ground stung his paw pads as Sir Goblin crept through the woods behind his home at the smithy. The wind shrieked furiously, ruffling the thick coat on his back until the fur blew apart, exposing skin to the icy air. Somewhere in the distance he heard a huge tree blow down and hit the ground with a tremendous, frightening crash. He hurried on, all his senses on full alert. His eyes, ears, and nose tested every crevice and overturned leaf.

The days were short now, and already the sinking sun had brought out the night-feeding animals that Sir Goblin found most delicious. He had killed one mouse and stashed it behind his family's tool shed, so he would not return empty-mouthed, but one mouse did not provide much meat for him and Snow Beauty. Why his humans thought cats could live on their vegetables and thin broth, he'd never know.

Snow Beauty was the sweetest, gentlest of lady cats, and he loved her beyond all measure. A wonderful mother she was, but really a terrible huntress. She had been taken from her mother before she learned the necessary skills and could only manage to bring down bugs and worms. Goblin trained all their kittens.

A flicker of movement caught his eye. He looked up. A dove flitted from branch to branch. Would it fly low enough for him to catch? Already the juices were flowing; he could taste it—nice, soft, warm dove—*mmmm*.

As he thought about how he might most easily catch the dove, a sudden thumping and snapping of the distant underbrush interrupted his thoughts. He crouched low and lay still, as though dead. Coming ever closer and closer, the thunderous stamping pounded the iron-cold ground. Sparks glinted as great toenails slid and scraped over stones.

Foul breath steamed like smoke over Goblin's hunched body. Sir Goblin huddled down into some leaves. He shut his eyes so as not to show his face and to be as inconspicuous as possible.

The monster, whatever it was, passed by him, making the ground shake. Soon after the beast had passed, the cat heard screams—human screams. Grunts, snorts, and the whinny of horses made the hair rise on his back. One long wavering scream ripped far into the cold air. When it faded, the stomping feet tramped off into the far distance.

Goblin crouched there for a long moment, lying still, as if frozen. Once his heart rate returned to normal, his stomach reminded him that he had to find food. His immobility brought him luck. Thinking him nothing more than a gray-striped rock, a dark-furred animal hopped closely past him. In a trice, Goblin was on him. One front paw held down the animal's head, the other its shoulder. With quick precision, Goblin bit through its neck and had his prey. It was a large hare. Goblin's back feet kicked at the soft underbelly, opening it. He hurriedly ate the delicacies inside. He would bring this trophy home to Snow Beauty, and they would have a proper feast.

Knowing humans would not travel through the woods, particularly at dusk, but would instead choose a road, Goblin dragged the hare in the direction from which the human cries had come. The road would be there, and it would be much easier to drag his rabbit home along a smooth path than through underbrush.

Almost immediately, he came upon two tom-humans lying in the road. A pool of blood spilled out all over the ground. Dropping his catch, Goblin sniffed first the taller man. He could smell his faint breath. The second human was there only in part. He had been ripped open by the monster. One arm was missing. All around, Goblin's sensitive nose picked up the scent of the monster. The monster's odor was somewhat familiar, but Goblin was uncertain as to exactly what it was. The cat thought the musk gave off a wild, randy air, and was it perhaps tinged with fear? *Had the monster been afraid?* That thought scared Goblin. He snatched up his prize and hurried home as fast as possible.

Two.

HAPPILY PREGNANT WITH her and William's first child, Rosemarie sang as she stirred the cauldron over the fire in their new home. This would be their first Christmas together in this house. Once homeless wanderers, they had been rewarded with this fine little house. It even had a fireplace, which not many country homes boasted. Most of the common folk still made do with a central hearth and a hole in roof through which smoke occasionally made a reluctant exit.

William, a farrier, had, largely through the efforts of their cat, Goblin, saved the life of Baron Robert von Schwartzfeld. In return, the baron knighted Goblin, henceforth to be called Sir Goblin, and rewarded William and Rosemarie with a smithy in the village and a two-room house next to it. The manor house was awarded to his vassal, the knight Sir Rudolph, who had led the search for the captured baron. Freed from the tyranny of its former harsh master, Johannesmarkt was thriving, and in a little over a year showed signs of becoming not a village, but a small town. After the overthrow of Hubert de Forrest, life for the residents had settled into the quiet hum of most settlements in the mid-fifteenth century.

Rosemarie's cheeks were rosy from the heat of the fire. She had dampened her skirts with water to discourage any stray sparks from burning holes in her hand-sewn clothes. Thin slices of turnips tumbled from her hand, the last items to go into her stew. She had traded two large eggs with her neighbor for two doves, and was very pleased to have so much meat in the pot for Christmas. She stirred and sang. Strewn over the mantel top and tucked above the windows, evergreens declared the advent of the festive season. Every corner of her house was swept and cleaned. Christmas was but two days away.

Sir Goblin and William arrived at the door together. Goblin carried his own Christmas feast, but was bloodied from the carnage he'd discovered on the road. As William bent to pet Goblin and praise his prowess, he noticed a shred of silk cloth caught up with the cat's rabbit. Mystified, William wondered how a piece of cloth, suggesting human involvement, could be tangled about his cat's trophy.

The young man remembered hearing strange, distant squeals between his hammer blows. When working in his blacksmith shop, the clang of the hammer pounding iron kept him from hearing all but the loudest of noises. For this reason, William found his smithy a peaceful, restful place, with no distracting noise, because he usually heard only sounds he chose to make. But now a tingle of fear shivered down his back. *Could Goblin have been involved in something horrible?*

Turning from his door and looking back over the common, he saw other men standing together, talking and gesturing animatedly. He went over to find out what was happening. William had not really known how blood curdling the screams were. But others had heard the screams carried on the wind. It was not long, then, before a group of men carrying what peasant weapons they could gather up—cudgels, sickles, knives, and such—marched down the road in search of whatever accident or crime lay ahead. William went with them.

They were not long in finding the bloody bodies on the ground. Torchlight revealed the smaller one had been but a boy, and the taller, a grown man. He was alive, breathing but not aware. He lay face down, wrapped in a leather cape trimmed with fur around its hem. When they turned him over, they discovered the cape was lined entirely with fur. His head was wrapped round and round with some kind of cloth, fastened at the front with an elaborate clasp. The cut of his clothing was entirely foreign, and he carried no weapon for protection. Supporting the victims in their own capes, the men carried them into the town. They brought the dead boy into the church, later to be washed and wrapped for Christian burial.

Sir Rudolph, the lord of the manor, would have to be told of this bloody breach of the peace—it was the knight's task to ensure the safety of the roads in his fief and to protect the people from danger. But, right now, taking care of the strange injured man was of the first importance. The men decided it was already too dark and late in the afternoon to carry him up the hill to the manor house—he might die on the way or possibly freeze. The church often served as a temporary hospital with the good father as its doctor, but it had no heat. They stomped their freezing feet as they huddled together and spoke from behind gloved hands, their warm breath rising like smoke over their fast-numbing noses. After a few minutes' discussion, the men decided to lay this poor soul before Rosemarie's warm, new hearth.

The young wife hastened to heat stones as the men lingered in a corner, wondering what to do next. By placing the stones against the stranger's back, shoulders, and neck, she hoped to restore warmth and life. When all the warming stones were in place, Rosemarie straightened up. She worked her fingers into the muscles of her lower back, easing its stiffness. Her soft sigh and her protruding stomach that pushed against her dress called attention to the pregnancy. William blushed and looked at his feet, but the oldest man took Rosemarie by the arm and pulled up a stool for her to sit on. "Here, sit down, no more of this for you, girl," he said.

"I'm fine, I'm fine," Rosemarie protested, but sat down eagerly all the same.

Perhaps it was their voices that roused him, for just then, the stranger moved. He groaned. He uttered strange sounds, words something like, "Alla, alla, la, la."

William crouched beside him. The stranger opened his eyes.

"Do not be afraid, sir," said William. "We mean you no harm."

The man rolled his head from side to side; his large black eyes searched the room and rested on the firelight.

"I'm William the farrier, of Johannesmarkt. We will bring you to our lord, Sir Rudolph, when you have recovered a little."

At the mention of Sir Rudolph, the stranger pushed himself up onto one elbow. For one instant, his fingers touched the bloody wound on his forehead; he winced, drawing his hand back. His head bobbed and his shoulders swayed. William expected he would fall back down. But, instead, the foreigner spoke, his words squeezed out between long pauses. He was traveling, he said, to a place called Johannesmarkt to attend to Sir Rudolph's lady. He and his apprentice. All he remembered was that his horse reared. There was smoke and sparks.

After saying something no one could understand, he dropped down again. His eyes closed. William and Rosemarie allowed him lie before the fire all night. It was not a soft bed, certainly, but it was the only truly warm place on this extremely cold night. William did not bank the fire as was customary, but added new logs to keep flames flickering throughout night.

Remarkably, the next morning the stranger sat up and broke his fast at the table with some bread, cheese, and beer. Feeling stronger, he talked at length with William. "I do take my own advice," was his perplexing first comment, after the farrier remarked that he seemed very much better. While not completely proficient in their language, he made William to understand that he was called Caspar the physician. He had practiced and taught medicine in Europe for twenty years. He was on his way to Bologna to teach at the great university in that city, when the duke had asked him for a favor. He was asked to stop at a place called Johannesmarkt to look into the severe state of the health of Sir Rudolph's lady. The common people knew nothing of the noblewoman's daily affairs, of course, so the townspeople had not known that she lay ill.

Upon learning that his traveling companion was dead and their two horses missing, the doctor's great dark eyes brimmed with tears and shone like two black pearls. His speech was halting and his words few. Rosemarie rushed to his side. "Good Doctor, you must rest. Here, lie on our bed. We can go to Sir Rudolph's a little later."

"Omar was . . . a . . . good boy," he whispered. He swayed as he stood up and grasped the table's edge with both hands.

They helped him gently to the bed and almost immediately he fell asleep. Goblin and Snow Beauty jumped up on the bed. Goblin walked up along the length of the sleeping man and, flicking his whiskers back against his snout, sniffed the sleeper's mouth and nose. Snow Beauty sat down near the human's feet, staring at Goblin as if anticipating a report. The big gray cat then climbed up on the sleeping man's thighs, curled up and set to dozing, kneading and purring. Snow Beauty lay down with her chin against the physician's ankles and likewise administered her purr therapy.

Three.

WITH THE DOCTOR asleep, William went out to work at the forge, and Rosemarie set about her morning's work. At one point, she heard someone arrive outside to have his horse shod. Knowing her husband would be busy for a little while in his shop, she went quickly to her clothes chest.

Lifting the lid softly, so as not to disturb the sleeping stranger, she pulled out the shirt she was secretly sewing for William's Christmas present. He would be occupied for some time, and she could work on the fine embroidery that decorated the placket and cuffs without fear of discovery. Tomorrow was Christmas. She hummed a carol. From time to time she glanced up at her cats and, smiling, remembered how they had similarly nursed her when she had the red fever. No one would ever convince her that it hadn't been curative. Caspar slept soundly.

After a long nap and a late lunch of Rosemarie's stew, Caspar felt recharged. It was the middle of the afternoon when the small party started up the hill road to the manor house to report the crime, and for the physician to attend to Lady Alfreda. As she left the house, Rosemarie felt a gentle stirring of her skirts as if a soft wind blew them. Looking down, she saw Goblin and Snow Beauty standing beside her.

They were a group of six—four people and two cats—as they started up the hill. They had asked the old priest to come with them, because he knew a little Latin, and Caspar, while fluent in Latin, was sometimes unsure of the right word in their local language. They thought that, if necessary, the old man could help make Caspar's diagnosis more understandable to the noble couple.

William supported Caspar, on occasion taking his elbow, as they climbed the icy hill, and Rosemarie followed behind. The young wife

had persuaded the men that a woman's presence might be comforting to Sir Rudolph's lady—in spite of the noblewoman having her serving maids—at what had to be a most difficult time for her. Rosemarie had become acquainted with Lady Alfreda when she and William lived for several months in the manor house as guests while their little house and smithy were being built. It had been from the noblewoman that Rosemarie learned some embroidery stitches, and Alfreda had kept the four kittens from Goblin and Snow Beauty's second litter.

"If you go up there with the priest, she'll think she's dying, no matter what the good doctor tells her," Rosemarie had pointed out to the men, convincing them that her feminine company was needed. And so, now, the four of them were on their way to call on the lord and his lady. The two cats trotted right along behind them. Their tails waved high, and an occasional mew reminded Rosemarie that they intended to be a part of this expedition.

There was a surprise waiting for them. As they entered through the gate into the manor's courtyard, they saw one of Sir Rudolph's grooms in the yard talking with a peasant farmer who held the reins of two horses. One animal was a beautiful coppery Arabian gelding and the other a fuzzy pony with baggage heaped on his back. Sir Rudolph himself was just coming down the front steps.

"My horse!" shouted Caspar. He hurried to the animal. He was breathing heavily by the time he reached the beast. A little dizzy from running, the recuperating stranger rested his head against the fine animal's neck for a few moments. The horse nuzzled the back of his master's neck. When he caught his breath, the strange physician whispered endearments to his nickering Arabian and stroked his withers. No one noticed the two cats run off to the barns.

The two horses, obviously lost, had wandered onto the farmer's land, and he brought them to Sir Rudolph, who represented the law in these parts. An honest man, the farmer would not keep what did not belong to him. Now he looked at the ground, shuffling his feet, lingering—perhaps in hope that Sir Rudolph would somehow reward his efforts, or perhaps he simply did not know what to do or say when standing in front of a nobleman.

Caspar wasted no time in rooting through the baggage. "It's all here. My implements, books, powders, everything." Caspar grasped the peasant's rough hand and wrapped the man's thick fingers around a hefty pile of coins. "Thank you, thank you, sir. You have safeguarded my livelihood."

The peasant was speechless. Coins were rare in his experience, and never had he seen so many at once. He stared, open-mouthed, at the strange man wearing a fur-lined leather cape and dark purple headpiece, which seemed to be wrapped around his head like a great towel, fastened with some sort of jewel at the front.

Sir Rudolph stepped in. "Thank you, my good man. You have done well. You may return to your holding."

With that, the peasant bowed to the knight and to Caspar, and hurried down the path. Handing over the horses to the care of the stable lad, Sir Rudolph escorted his guests into his home.

Four.

I NSIDE THE MANOR house, the doctor and the knight spoke together for a few moments. The knight had known that Caspar was coming. Caspar refused the wine that the knight offered his guest but requested a cup of boiled water. It would wash away the bad humors from his injured head, he claimed. After a few more minutes, the physician indicated he was ready to visit his patient, the good Lady Alfreda. The priest waited with Sir Rudolph and William, and the maid showed the physician and, yes, Rosemarie, in to see Lady Alfreda. Because of her severe illness, the couple had invited no Christmas company. Rosemarie, despite her common rank, was known and trusted, and now she and the lady's maid sat by the noblewoman's bed, providing a watchful solace as the visiting doctor prepared to examine her.

Lady Alfreda was much changed since Rosemarie had last seen her. She lay with her head and shoulders propped up by a bolster and a mound of soft pillows. An embroidered coverlet covered her bulging stomach. The bed curtains had been pulled back to let in a shaft of sunlight that played on her yellowed, waxen face. Her red hair was drawn back into a simple braid that draped over one shoulder. She wore no head covering. She had been staring at her book of hours as they entered the room.

She thanked her guests in a thin, whispery voice, pausing every few words for breath. Caspar began his examination by inspecting her hands and thin arms. Next, he looked into her eyes and felt her neck and face, murmuring gentle words to the noblewoman as his fingers pressed lightly against her jaundiced skin. He then pulled up the far end of the coverlet to look at and feel her feet, which were swollen. Lastly, he examined her swollen abdomen. He removed the coverlet and, feeling through her clothing, pressed his hands here and there on her engorged stomach.

"Gracious Lady, you are not with child. It is with a different mass that your belly is full." He stopped speaking. His eyes fell to the bed, and his hand smoothed the coverlet as he thought, *Little time, so very little time.*

For a moment his dark eyes met hers; the small, pale orbs yellowed with disease pleaded; her chin trembled. "I know I will die, and yet I do not feel ready to."

He nodded.

"Turn her," he said to the women, and indicated the direction by pointing to the far wall. Rosemarie and the maid struggled with pillows to lay her on her side. Lady Alfreda moaned, but before she could speak any words, the physician, as if he knew her desire, her fear of losing what little control she still had over things, placed her polished metal mirror in her hand. "You can see who comes in through this . . . er . . . reflector," he said, struggling for the right word.

He left the room, taking Rosemarie with him. As the physician drew near the knight, Sir Rudolph made to speak, but Caspar announced, "My Lord, your lady is not with child." Immediately, the doctor turned to the priest and began speaking in Latin.

William and his wife withdrew to the far side of the room where a servant offered ale. They saw Sir Rudolph drop into his chair, saw him cover his face with his hands, and saw his shoulders start to shake. As their old parish priest spoke to him, he seemed to gather some strength. Rosemarie saw the priest make the sign of the cross and settle a reassuring hand on the knight's shoulder. Together, the knight, priest, and doctor went into Lady Alfreda's room. Almost an hour later, the priest and doctor emerged, and walked up to the waiting group.

"We can go home now," said the old priest.

They walked down the path in silence, no one wanting to be the first to speak. When they reached the village, the priest spoke but once with Caspar, reminding him that the noble couple would send their decision to tonight's Mass. Then, turning to William, he said that the manor steward would handle the case of Omar's attacker.

When she arrived home, Rosemarie boiled eggs for their post-Midnight Mass snack and finished Williams's present. For Caspar, she quickly sewed up a piece of cloth and embroidered it to make a bookmark.

Caspar, meanwhile, bustled around the village, talking to this one and that. As he did so, he cleaned wounds for the injured and prescribed treatments for sick villagers. William worked furiously in the smithy. He too had Christmas presents to finish. Goblin and Snow Beauty came scratching at the door just as the sun began to set.

"Where have you two been?" asked Rosemarie, as if she really expected them to tell her in words. "I haven't seen you since you followed us up the path to the manor." Snow Beauty rubbed around Rosemarie's legs, circling so closely, she wrapped the woman up in her own dress. Goblin, always more direct, went straight to the water jar and began batting at the ladle. Both cats' sides were bulging from good mousing in the lord's stables. If they could have spoke in human speech, they would have solved the mystery of the boy Omar's death, although no one would have believed them. Rosemarie put down the requested drink of water. The cats slurped merrily.

Five.

LOUD AND VIGOROUS peals from the church bell woke anyone who might have fallen asleep before the Christmas Eve Midnight Mass. The townspeople, young and old, all filed into the church. Sir Rudolph remained at home with his wife, but his steward attended. Caspar stood at the back, by the door, where he spoke briefly with the steward. Everyone had assumed the exotic-looking man was a Mohammedan, as many learned physicians were either Arabs or Jews. He was not expected or required to come to the service, but everyone knew he came for word from Sir Rudolph.

The old priest was inspired. In his homily he related the entire Christmas story, from Caesar's decree through the flight into Egypt. When the parishioners came up for the communion bread, the last to come forward was Anna the midwife, who was also the priest's housekeeper, and behind her padded a cat.

She was Magdalene, the priest's cat, and the first daughter of Goblin and Snow Beauty, a pure white animal with a gray-striped tail, as were all of Goblin and Snow Beauty's kittens. She came trotting down the aisle at the end of the service and, emitting a soft mew, lay down in the crèche with the wooden figures of the Holy Family and various cows and sheep, a donkey, doves, a dog, and even a disproportionately small camel. As the people were leaving the church, the priest bent to scratch the cat's ears.

"Magdalene, what is this? You did this last year, too," murmured the old man. "I guess you want to be part of the Christmas story as well, huh? Well, maybe cats *were* there. The story is for all."

Behind them, Caspar laughed diffidently and then pretended to clear his throat. "You know," he said to the priest, "my people came from far east of your Holy Land. We, too, have our ancient traditions."

"Yes?"

"There is a tradition that some of our learned men came to see the infant Jesus, just as you told it tonight. There definitely was something about a star in the ancient writings of my people. But, further, we have this little story. When the Magi, what we call our learned men, were presenting their gifts to the infant, one of their camel tenders, a simple boy or, as you would say, a halfwit, saw a beautiful cat. He ran after it, but the cat ran under some thorn bushes. When the boy grabbed for the animal, it ran away." The physician made a pushing-away gesture with his arm.

"The boy caught up only a handful of branches with thorns on them so that his hand bled painfully. The simple boy then ran into the house where the babe and the wise men were, hoping one of the men would bandage his hand. The baby woke up and instead of looking at the shiny golden gifts, he reached out his little hand and took hold of the thorns, and his—," here Caspar paused a moment, searching for the right word, "—his jiggling little hand pressed against his own forehead. The thorns drew drops of blood from his tiny brow, his fore . . . head." The doctor, again not sure he had the right word, touched his own forehead. "When the Magi next looked at the camel boy's hand, the cuts were gone, healed.

"And, so it was said, the holy babe took the boy's blood, his hurt, to bear himself. This small miracle proved to the Magi that they had indeed found the newborn ruler of Judea. The old story says, further, that the cat went with the holy family to Egypt, where cats are much respected, and his very presence ensured the safety of the little family. But, of course, it is probably just an old wives' tale." Caspar dismissed his own story with a wave of his hand.

"Who knows what the beasts know," said the priest, stroking Magdalene's cheeks.

Six.

ONCE OUTSIDE THE church, Caspar told William and Rosemarie that he would now be staying at the manor house and not with them, and thanked them for all their kindness to him. He was taking some people from the town, whom he had chosen to assist him in the absence of Omar, up to the knight's house this evening. Tomorrow he would attempt to save Lady Alfreda's life. The treatment would be drastic, but he had no other choice.

Just as the doctor finished speaking, the tavern keeper waved to William and called him over. There was to be a meeting at the inn. Sir Rudolph's steward wanted to plan the investigation into Omar's death. He wanted the town's strong young men and Sir Goblin.

William and Rosemarie both went. She wanted to hear about the hunt for the killer, and also wanted to visit with Joanna, now the tavern cook, since it had been rumored that a romance was brewing between the huge woman and the innkeeper.

They entered the warm main room, where sconced torches threw a rosy light to every corner. The fireplaces at either end of the tavern warmed the drinkers more than their own beds would have. An extra table had been set up and stools brought round. Several men already sat at the table, and the young couple joined them. The innkeeper brought large flagons overflowing with ale. Joanna made sure that Rosemarie had a bowl of crackers before her, in deference to her pregnancy.

The steward made an introductory explanation of the evidence gleaned from the condition of Omar's body. "Precious little to go on," he said. "Almost as if a beast had torn him apart."

Silence followed.

The carpenter sucked down the last of his ale. Setting the tankard down on the table with a thud, he wiped his sleeve across his mouth. He began to speak. "That foreign fellow spoke of smoke and fire."

"He said sparks," moderated William.

The carpenter ignored him and went on speaking, warming to his own theory. "Milord steward said 'as if a beast.' Now, there is only one beast I know of that breathes smoke and fire—"

A general moan of derision rose from the men, and the barkeep made sure that another round of ale was quickly put in front of the drinkers, converting moans to slurps.

A moment or two passed, and then a shy farmer ventured, "You know, I did hear tell . . ." all the drinkers leaned forward, " . . . at the fair in Martinsburg last summer, of a green—"

"No, blue," put in another young man.

"Blue, green, what does it matter? Get on with it!" said the carpenter.

"It was named Bry, and it was charmed by the witch Ann. It guarded a treasure in a cave—"

Two farmers spoke at the same time, "—and came out at the full moon!"

"New moon," someone corrected.

"I heard of him! It's true," piped up another voice.

"And I suppose it ate virgins for lunch," sneered big Joanna from behind them. She was standing with her hands on her hips and her tongue firmly planted in her cheek.

"But what treasure could there possibly be in Johannesmarkt?" asked William.

"Oh! Young William!" a chorus of voices rang out. "You were not here when Johann de Forrest lived at the manor. What he did with his riches is anybody's guess."

"Maybe it's his ghost!"

"No, a dragon! I'd rather fight a dragon than a ghost!"

"A dragon! A dragon!" shouted voice after voice. Tankards pounded the table. The innkeeper poured again. Rosemarie and Joanna looked at each other and shrugged.

After some moments of this furor, the steward judged the fighting spirit was at its peak. He stood again to speak. "Tomorrow at midmorning, we will gather in the square and go to the site of the killing, and from there—it depends on what we learn."

With hearty slaps on the backs and shouts of laughter, the would-be dragon slayers spilled from the tavern to return to their homes and a short night's sleep.

Seven.

CHRISTMAS MORNING DAWNED bright but bitter cold. When William woke, Rosemarie was already encouraging the fire to be more generous with its heat.

"Oh, good morning, Will. It's a beautiful Christmas! Bright, new snow everywhere! It's like diamonds all over the ground. Come, see what I have for you." She turned to the chest and pulled out her carefully wrapped present. Suddenly, she clutched it to her breast. "Holy Mother of God!" the girl exclaimed.

William, sitting now on the edge of the bed, had let slip out a word that made her ears sizzle. "I've got to go on that devil's own dragon hunt this morning. Christmas morning!"

"William, I don't believe there are really dragons."

"Well, it can't be proved one way or the other unless we get one. Someone or something killed Omar. Arms don't come off by accident."

Eight men met with the steward in the square. The rest were still sleeping off their extra ale from the night before. As William came out of the smithy with his iron-tipped pike and a sickle, he tripped over Snow Beauty, nearly invisible against the newly fallen snow, as she rubbed and purred round his legs.

"You and your cats!" the men laughed. "Even your big gray mouser will be no good in this fight." As if their laughter were a bugle call, Sir Goblin stepped forward and meowed sourly into their faces, then switched his tail in anger at their derision. He turned and started down the road toward the place where Omar had met his death. Snow Beauty bounced after him, and the two cats walked off in unison with their tails held high.

If he was surprised that the cats started down the very path the men would take, the steward said nothing. In his opinion, a dragon would not bother with such small prey, so he did not try to stop the cats and simply led his small army forth.

The whole world lay hushed under a purifying cover of snow. The path from town was an even white, as if covered by a diamond-spangled blanket. Snow hung on the trees and smothered shrubbery. The men crept ahead with deliberate slowness, looking from side to side for any sign of a dragon. At the sudden shrill yammer of a jay they all jumped and stopped short as one. Rattled by the scolding sound, they peered around and slowly turned to look behind them. Nothing. The cats, meanwhile, continued striding ahead. They seemed to have their minds made up as to what would happen.

When they all reached the approximate spot where Omar met his end, they began searching for some sort of evidence that would suggest what to do next. The new snow had covered any disturbance. On the night of the attack, the ground had been, and still was, frozen to an unyielding hardness, so no prints from boot or hoof were left at the scene of the assault. Sweeping snow aside with their boots, the men did discover some dark patches on the ground that had the look of bloodstains. This proved that they were at the right place. But what should they do now?

Sir Goblin began to yowl. He was sitting across the road, under a broken branch that dangled by only a few strands of green wood. Believing the dragon may have broken the branch as he made his escape, the steward ordered the men to go into the woods at that spot. They headed down a steep bank, snapping and cracking their way through the tangled brush.

The steward turned and hushed them with his finger to his lips. "My good fellows," he whispered, "you make more noise than a herd of oxen. You must step slowly and silently, or this fellow will have warning. Surprise is our best weapon."

"But this bank may be leading down to the dragon's cave, sir," blurted out a townsman, newly made a hunter. The steward scowled at him. The novice dragon hunter looked all around, his eyes wide with fear, at the tangle of undergrowth. Muttering to himself so the steward would not hear, he whimpered, "We'll never get away alive through this snarl of vines and brush."

Despite his disbelief in dragons, a chilling fear tingled down William's spine. Ever so slowly, the men worked their way down the bank, sometimes stepping sideways and grasping at branches to keep from slipping in the newly fallen snow. The two cats always stayed in the lead.

Careful though he was, when the steward's foot stepped onto a smooth white patch of ground, it proved to be a loose rock. His foot slipped, the stone tumbled away, and he fell, hitting the ground hard. "Ow! Oh, God!" he cried, clutching at his knee.

"Hahnk, hahnk!" a beast's voice wailed, rending the frigid air with his loud annoyance and disgust at being disturbed. Leaves rustled below them. Then, from the bottom of the ravine, steam rose. Again the strange honking scream ripped through the air. The underbrush rustled and snapped as if something big were plowing through it.

"Save yourselves! Get back to the road!" shouted the steward, grabbing at branches and pulling himself up. Dragging his hurt leg, he stumbled his way back to the road. Whether it was cowardice or good sense, they all retreated from the ravine. Grunts, snorts, and a variety of horrible squeals followed them and echoed with deafening power off the banks of the little ravine. They felt dragon's breath puff foul hot smoke all over them as it huffed up the bank. The cats, however, sat just inside the edge of the woods, unmindful of the poisonous air being blown over them.

"Goblin, come on!" screamed William.

"Leave the fool cats," demanded the steward. At that very instant, Snow Beauty made her move. With delicate grace, the beautiful cat made a swift leap that landed her on the monster's snout. So wide set were his eyes, and so white was the lady feline, that the monster had no idea an attacker sat within inches of his head. Snow Beauty flicked her white tail across his eyes, blotting out his view of the world and confusing him frightfully. She began nibbling at his delicate round snout, his most necessary and prized instrument. Short puffs of steam blasted from his nostrils; his cries, blaring squeals, pierced the cold air. Then Goblin dropped down from a tree branch and settled near the monster's ear. He meowed, warbling demands into its ear. Understanding the wisdom of the tomcat's advice, the creature submitted, laying his chin to the ground and folding his feet under it.

Snow Beauty dropped from her perch and stepped into the road, where she stood defying the seekers of justice to advance. The men standing huddled together still did not understand what they were seeing. After a spell, William raised his steel-tipped pike.

Snow Beauty hissed and whipped her tail from side to side.

William lowered his weapon. "She does not want us to kill the dragon."

Even the steward, no pet lover, could understand the cat's meaning. Sheathing his sword, he very slowly advanced toward the beast. "Ho!

So this is our dragon! Fierce enough he is, but no monster! A boar, gentlemen, the biggest, meanest-looking wild white boar I have ever seen!"

The great pig, half hidden among the brush, remained in the curiously submissive position, trusting to Sir Goblin's word. The men approached, and a few were soon clambering back down the bank.

"Sir! Sir! See this!" A man had climbed down to the bottom of the ravine and come back. He was holding up a stiff string of bones held together by thin sinews, with a few pieces of flesh hanging from them. The whole thing was thoroughly frozen. "The boy's arm?"

"I think we now know what happened," murmured their leader. The steward scratched his head. *We can't arrest an animal. It is not honorable to kill someone begging mercy, even an animal,* he knew, and puzzled over what to do.

"It's Christmas Day," whispered William gently.

"Very well, Pig. A Christmas blessing upon thee," pronounced the steward. They all sheathed their weapons. Goblin yodeled one more time into the pig's ear, translating the steward's meaning. Then he sprang from the big animal's head and trotted up to William. Only then, when the two cats stood protectively between him and the humans, did the great boar turn and lumber back down into the ravine. The scalding dragon steam now seemed to be nothing more frightening than little puffs of pig breath, huffed from his nostrils, as he struggled through the tangle of brush.

"Still, there must have been some cause for this attack," reasoned the steward, who felt courage course through his veins, now that he knew what sort of dragon he had confronted. "The foreigners were unarmed. They would not have provoked this attack."

"Hunters, poachers on the knight's land, may have been chasing that white boar and frightened or infuriated it," commented one of the farmers, who may have known more about poaching than he would ever admit.

The snow would have covered all traces of poachers. There was nothing more they could do. They returned to their homes.

Eight.

THAT AFTERNOON, WILLIAM and his wife had some quiet time together. Will, since he could not work in the smithy on Christmas Day, was more than happy to help his expectant wife prepare for their Christmas feast. He pulled out the trestles and set up their dining board across the top of them. Rosemarie could well have managed the task—she set up and took down that table for every meal—but she had a few extra frills planned for their holiday meal and was glad for a little help. The young man then pulled up two stools to either side of the table, so they could sit facing each other. Rosemarie set two flagons on the table and asked him to pour out the good, home-brewed beer. Next the girl set an iron vase, made in their own blacksmith shop, in the center of the table, added a little water and filled it with various evergreens to make a holiday bouquet. The trenchers came out next, and were filled with Rosemarie's long-simmered Christmas stew. She laid out their spoons, and the two sat down to the table and gave thanks for their meal.

As the humans lifted their heads from prayer, Goblin and Snow Beauty each pounced up onto the table, settling themselves at opposite ends, as if they were the third and fourth people at the meal. Goblin lifted his nose high and twitched it, sniffing in the lovely fragrance of the stew, which for once had a sufficient amount of meat in it to please a cat. But he remembered his manners and sat still with his tail wrapped politely around his front feet, presenting a tidy, civilized appearance.

Snow Beauty, on the other hand, always the poorer hunter, was quite hungry again. She too sat sniffing the stew's delightful aroma, but her neck stretched high, her eyes half closed in pleasurable anticipation, and she wobbled her head about, to enjoy even more of the aroma. She began to purr with a raucous, almost unladylike rumble, lifting up first one front paw and then the other. A tiny drop of saliva threatened to drool from her lips.

Goblin, fearing she would lose all control and empty Rosemarie's trencher, brought his mate up short with a sharp cry of "Mrrt!" Catching Snow's attention, he jerked his head toward the fireplace and conveyed to her that he had something good for her. The lady cat then crouched down quietly, settled her tail around her toes, and purred softly.

When the young couple finished the stew, Rosemarie cleared the trenchers off the table and came back with her special Christmas surprise—a platter of fruits! In winter! Around the outer edge of the platter was a ring of dried apple circles, nothing particularly special. But as Will looked over the treat, his eyes widened. Next came dried plums and pears, scarcer fruit, but near the center were dates—wherever did she get those? In the very center, most wondrous of all, were slices of oranges! Rosemarie had negotiated long and hard with Joanna the tavern cook, mending aprons and sleeves in return for these treats. William fairly reveled in the fruit. His delight more than repaid the girl for her effort.

All the apples, pears, and so forth, however, bored the cats. Not their style! Goblin made as if to get down.

"No! No! Not yet," cried Rosemarie, "I have something for you." She reached to stroke the cat's head with her fourth and fifth fingers, the only two that were not sticky from the fruit.

When William could eat no more, the young wife licked her fingers clean and wiped them on her apron. Rising from the table, she once again admonished the cats to stay where they were. She went to her chest and rummaged around for a second. Then she drew two little bundles from the bottom.

"This is for you, Sir Mouser." She set a cloth, catnip-stuffed mouse before Sir Goblin. "And this is yours, Lady Snow Beauty. Happy Christmas." The white cat's gift was shaped like a kitten, the creature Rosemarie had seen most frequently in Snow Beauty's mouth. Within seconds the two furry creatures were rolling around in front of the hearth, completely oblivious to anything but catnip.

William stood before the fire, watching their two cats be completely silly and undignified with their Christmas gifts. "What kind of knightly doings are these? I wonder if Sir Rudolph rolls on the floor?" said William.

Rosemarie turned to rummage in the wooden chest again, while her husband was laughing at his own joke.

Suddenly throwing her arms around the man's neck and kissing him on each cheek, she then thrust the beautiful, embroidered shirt into his hands.

"Now it is Christmas," she said, laughing shyly as she waited for his reaction. His eyes sparkled as he ran his fingers over the fine embroidery. *Would those be tears of joy?* Rosemarie wondered, but she did not say anything, not wishing to embarrass him. For a moment, her husband said nothing.

"Not quite Christmas." Grinning from ear to ear, William pulled a small box, made from the fine white wood of the linden tree, from its hiding place behind the evergreens decorating the mantel. He placed it in her hands. Its sides were inscribed with hearts and leaping cats. Two iron hinges attached the lid, into which a rose had been carved. Inside was his gift to her: a belt made of many little links, interspersed with engraved medallions, forged in the smithy.

"Oh! It is so beautiful!" she squealed.

"Now it is Christmas." He took her into his arms.

Nine.

THAT EVENING, ONE of Sir Rudolph's men rapped on their door. William conferred quickly with the man outside who, as he spoke, kept stamping his feet, almost dancing to keep them from freezing in the bitter night air. The messenger's frosty breath swirled like smoke as he uttered a few words and then hurried to deliver his message to the next dragon hunter. Pulling on his boots and wrapping his cape closely around his body, William hurried out. Sir Rudolph had ordered all the dragon hunters to present themselves at the manor house.

Sir Goblin and Snow Beauty modestly did not attend. They knew their story would be told. At home, they dragged out the remains of Goblin's rabbit and augmented it with scraps from William and Rosemarie's trenchers. Eating on the hearth before the fire, where they were not normally allowed to eat, the two cats had a lovely Christmas feast together. For dessert they had more catnip.

All the would-be dragon hunters stood waiting for Sir Rudolph's appearance in the great hall. Long minutes dragged by. Will wanted only to be at his own fireside. Surely Sir Rudolph's steward had given an account of the dragon hunt. When the knight entered the room, Caspar the physician walked a few steps behind him. The men made their obeisances, and as they raised their heads, their eyes beheld a beautiful vision in blue.

Immediately behind Caspar walked a slim, ghostly-white Lady Alfreda, supported by two of her ladies. She wore a blue gown. A white, old-fashioned wimple draped her throat, while a dark blue headpiece covered all her hair, and a gauzy veil of the palest blue floated like a mist about her head and shoulders. She smiled and nodded briefly to all. Her ladies led her to a chaise longue by the fire where she reclined, dropping heavily into a pile of soft, embroidered pillows.

The huntsmen told their strange story of a dragon that turned out to be a wild pig and how it begged Christmas mercy at the suggestion of the knighted cat.

"You see, my lord, that *is* how it happened, incredible as it may seem," interjected the steward.

When they finished, Sir Rudolph sought Caspar's opinion. Did he want to pursue the case further? Perhaps rogues of some sort were hunting the beast. The physician replied that nothing would bring Omar back. Yes, he thought the beast must have been frightened and then, perhaps, the boar thought the rearing horses to be attacking him. Maybe even young Omar had attempted to beat him off. Caspar simply had no memory of these events, having hit his head so hard. He had taken a vow, the physician said, to do no harm; he wished no harm to the animal and wanted nothing but to see the boy buried respectfully and to be able to continue his journey.

Lady Alfreda now sat up, straightened her back, and addressed her company and the doctor who had saved her life. Speaking softly and with effort, she expressed her condolences, her heartfelt sympathy, and her shock; for she had not been told of Omar's existence or death prior to the doctor's treatment of her.

Caspar bowed deeply. "My good lady, gracious lady. I would not have you hear sad tidings now. You must take pleasant rest, hear merry tunes, read of sweet sentiments—all to restore your noble person to its proper balance of humors. Forgive me, I am but a humble physician and a clumsy speaker."

Caspar feared he might have overstepped the bounds of protocol with his medical advice, his words implying that he might be giving the noblewoman orders. He had been much against Lady Alfreda attempting to meet with guests so soon, and had given her his opinion privately. But the woman was so happy to be alive and wanted to make at least this small gesture of Christmas celebration.

The physician bowed again. Then he addressed Sir Rudolph. It was his hope, he said, that when he continued his journey, he would leave with the blessing of his lord and lady. He pleaded that he be allowed to leave them in full happiness, giving the slightest hint that it might take a few days for the good woman's humors to be restored to their correct balance and her energy returned. He said nothing of his own lingering fear for her survival after the brutal operation he had been forced to perform. Much depended on what happened in the next few days. He had to trust the midwife, who seemed sensible and would offer prayers to the Blessed Mother, to perform the cleansings that he had prescribed. God willing, she might live.

When the strange doctor finished speaking, Sir Rudolph ordered a bowl of Christmas cheer be brought in, and a toast made to the physician and to his good lady's health. Caspar honored his hosts with a sip of their heady fruited mead, which he normally did not drink. The dragon slayers raised their cups high and gave a hearty cheer and a toast to Sir Rudolph and Lady Alfreda. Then the hunters drained their drinking vessels dry and looked for more.

At this juncture, Caspar begged to be allowed to retire for the night; he had obviously had a long day. He made his obeisance and withdrew. As the doctor left the room, William noticed a handful of townspeople— Anna the midwife, Joanna the cook, and Theobald the barber among them—standing just beyond the threshold, watching the festivities from the shadows. These were the people Caspar had chosen to assist him.

After a second round of drinks, Sir Rudolph handed purses to the dragon hunters and Caspar's assistants, and wished them all a happy Christmas season. On the knight's orders, the hunters accompanied the physician's helpers back down to the town.

William walked with Anna, taking her arm from time to time, to keep her from slipping as they picked their way down the icy path. The wind howled and whipped his cape open.

"Weather's changing," he said through chattering teeth. He did not know Anna well, but he wanted to be kind and friendly to this woman who would no doubt see to the birth of his child. So, thinking she would want to talk about it—Rosemarie always wanted to talk about everything—he inquired politely as to her part in the day's proceedings.

"Oh, I must say nothing about it," the midwife replied, "but I never heard tell of a man so taken with cleanness." A blast of icy wind blew away her next words, and all Will heard was "vow" and "privacy." The howl of the wind cut short any further talk, and at the bottom of the hill they parted to go to their own homes.

But William heard more than he wanted to know a few days later. In Johannesmarkt, all news was broadcast, cultivated, and bountifully harvested in front of the baker's ovens, while the women waited for their bread to bake. Rosemarie returned babbling on about how Caspar had given the noblewoman something to drink and she fell asleep, how he had actually cut open the skin of her belly, removed ugly, black, bulbous-looking masses from her, and then washed her out and actually sewed her up with thread while she still slept.

"Please, oh, please, woman, say no more!" William pressed his hands tight against his own belly, as if to protect it from a similar assault.

A thaw came in the middle of January. Melting snow dripped from every rooftop and overhanging tree branch, fat drops of water plopping down in a soggy, steady rhythm.

Caspar bade farewell to a rosy-cheeked, happy Lady Alfreda and her noble spouse. He mounted his fine Arabian horse and took hold of the lead to the fuzzy baggage pony. Accompanied by four of Sir Rudolph's men for the next leg of his journey, the physician rode off in a splatter of mud and melting snow.

He accepted no further compensation, reminding them that he had come at the request of the Duke and Sir Robert. But he did accept a gift from Lady Alfreda; snuggled down inside his blousy shirt were two half grown kittens, offspring from Snow Beauty's second litter.

Goblin and Snow Beauty sat on a large tree branch as the doctor passed under them. They caught a glimpse of little white ears and two pink noses nestled among his garments. Snow Beauty mewed a mother's farewell to kittens she'd never see again. Goblin waved a paw and swallowed hard. He consoled himself with thoughts of the great adventures the kittens would have.

It is said that, to this day, many white cats with gray-striped tails live an Italian village not far from Bologna. There, they are known for their adventuresome ways and excellent mousing skills.

Sir Goblin's Spring

One.

SIR GOBLIN TROTTED across the village common toward his house. His fangs clutched a freshly caught rat, and his lips curled into a silly pleased grin. It was a sparkling spring day. The sun was fast drying up the last shining jewels of dew in the grass. Every few feet, the big warrior cat tossed his prey into the air and, when it landed, pounced on it as if he had just captured it. He felt as giddy as a kitten.

Last week, Snow Beauty's green eyes had blazed with the demand to ease her spring yearning, and Goblin found himself joining her in a passionate dance and frolic behind the smithy. All the cats were serenading, caterwauling. Although the dull-eared humans did not much care for their voices and sometimes threw things at them, the cats still sang. And there was much frolicking. It was the time for making kittens! How he loved spring!

As he passed the church with his trophy, he heard alleluias coming from within; they rang out across the town green. The doors of the sanctuary flung open. The people inside were singing the Easter carol that the priest had taught them, *O Filii et Filiae.*

"Oh, sons and daughters, let us sing! of the glorious resurrected King! Alleluia, Alleluia!"

After the service the churchgoers pressed through the arched doorway and down the steps, talking and laughing. Goblin sat down to people watch. He licked his paws thoughtfully.

After everyone left the church, Goblin saw a man slip quickly back into the sanctuary. Something about his furtive movements, the way the man glanced twice over his shoulder, seemed to differ from the mood of the rest of the townsfolk. The warrior cat thought the man slunk about more like a cat than a human.

He felt as giddy as a kitten.

But it is spring, delightful spring! Goblin was having too much fun playing with his captured rat to give the man much further thought.

When they arrived home from church, William and Rosemarie found Goblin drowsily sunning himself on the doorstep. They saw no dead animal. It was safely hidden away for later consumption. The couple was slow in getting home because they stopped often to exchange Easter greetings with friends and acquaintances—they knew just about everyone in the small town. They also took their time because Rosemarie walked at a slow, waddling pace. She was soon, very soon, to bring forth their first child.

"You're quiet, love," said William, as he pushed open the door to their little house, "What are you thinking?"

"When will it be?" she answered, rubbing her hand down and around her huge, taut stomach. "It can't be long."

"Anna says you are doing well, doesn't she?" William responded, searching her eyes and hoping for the millionth time that all was really well and that her women friends and Anna, the town's able midwife, were not keeping anything from him—a mere man.

He felt so useless, so unable to protect and care for his wife.

Rosemarie pulled the iron crane away from the fire and dipped her ladle into the bubbling cauldron. She poured spoonfuls of hot stew into two round bread loaf trenchers. She set these next to the two horn spoons on the trestle table, poured tankards of thin beer, and set a bowl of cheese and dried apples between them. All this time, Rosemarie was again reciting the long list of things she had ready for William just in case, God forbid, anything happened to her during childbirth. With this latest recitation, she added a bowl of beans, soaked and ready to cook.

Her husband groaned, "Girl, I love you so much," and fell silent.

At this point in her pregnancy, he could not possibly tell his wife all the fears he had, or the depth of his love, or with what great wonder—yea, even awe—her bulging form filled him.

They sat down opposite each other and bowed their heads. William said the table blessing. Inwardly, each added a petition to the Blessed Virgin for a swift and safe delivery of their child. The two ate in silence for a few minutes. Goblin and Snow Beauty wove graceful beggar's dances around and between the couple's legs. Then, as if she could contain her silence no longer, Rosemarie burst into a nervous chatter. "I'm so glad Father read the banns today. I was sure Joanna and Paul wanted to be handfast as soon as Lent was over. They are so right for each other."

"Yes, from what I hear, they had better hurry along the wedding, or we'll be witnessing a second Virgin birth."

"Oh, William! But the way people talk, you could be right." Rosemarie blushed a little at their forthright speech and stirred her stew. Then, blushing bright red and giggling, she said, "We'll keep Anna busy."

They were sitting quietly, finishing their beer, when a robin alighted on the edge of the rain barrel just outside their door. As it peered into the water-holder, its song echoed hollowly in the barrel. Its ethereal melody caught William's ear. Later he would recall the bird and its song and understand it as a sign for the baby's name.

As he turned his eyes back to Rosemarie, William saw his wife straighten her spine. Her face tensed and then relaxed. She took a determined swallow of beer.

"You all right?"

"Yes, um," again, she sat up straight. "Uh, yes . . . Oh, William!" Rosemarie wailed. She stood up, shuffled her skirts, and sat back down. "Oh my! Oh my! Get Anna, please! Please get Anna," she pleaded with her husband who sat stunned and motionless. "Anna, now!"

Stumbling over cat legs and tails, William ran out for the midwife. Snow Beauty ducked under the spinning wheel. She was most curious to see a human have kittens. The scene had nothing of interest for Goblin. After all, Snow Beauty had always handled everything perfectly well without his help. He felt disturbed and uncomfortable by all the scent of female activity in the house. He followed William through the town for a while, then turned back and got his rat.

Anna the midwife came. Later other village women came over. There was much moaning, sighing, and then loud groaning. William took refuge in the smithy. He banged loudly on hot iron. Women murmured encouragement. Rosemarie grunted and cried out. It was all too much for the feline knight, so he strolled over to visit his daughter Magdalene who lived at the church.

Seeing a mouse zip into a hole under the church steps, Goblin's predator mind turned to thoughts of hunting. He forgot about visiting Magdalene and waited for the little mouse to stick out its nose. As he waited, one of the church's double doors opened a crack. A man peeked out. He looked to his left and then to his right. He looked back, over his shoulder. Very slowly, the door swung open just enough to let the man slip through. He looked around and then, hunched and hurrying, scuttled around to the side of the holy building. The man ran toward the swale beyond the church. Something in his demeanor, perhaps his hunched-over posture, startled the big cat, and he scampered away across the village green—both mouse and visit to daughter, forgotten.

Later, as the sun dropped to the hillside and the sky turned pink, Goblin met Snow Beauty at the door of their house. Two village women busied themselves with food, and another was washing up linen behind the house, but the fuss had generally settled down. Goblin's quick ear rotated toward a new sound, a softly heard, rhythmic ticka-ticka.

It's the kitten nursing, meowed Snow Beauty.

The? Only one?

Only one. One big one.

Goblin shook his head in such amazement that his ears snapped and crackled.

Two.

J OANNA AND THE INNKEEPER, Paul, were married at the church door on a beautiful, still day. *How different she looks*, thought Rosemarie. A giant of a woman, Joanna looked regal in her russet gown, violets woven into her graying, once-yellow hair. Her violet eyes sparkled, and a big smile stretched across her face as she glanced down at her new husband. Gone were the bloodstained, greasy aprons and the sour smirks that Rosemarie had first encountered when Joanna cooked for the wicked lords Johann and Hubert. The cook's whole being radiated with a happiness she had once never thought possible.

After the ceremony, the townsfolk ran ahead of the bridal couple, toward the inn. They were already dancing on the tavern green to the music of pipers, flutists, and drummers as the happy pair approached. With the help of the barmaids, Joanna's nephew had set up a great trestle table that groaned under the weight of an enormous amount of excellent food. With Joanna as cook, the tavern had become renowned for its delicious fare.

William and Rosemarie, who carried their six-week-old son, Robin, in her arms, took seats at a table inside. Goblin and Snow Beauty paraded in smartly beside the young family; the cats were confident of their place in village society, for the baron himself had truly knighted Goblin for his bravery. They carried their tails high and proud. Once inside, the cats jumped up on the table to be with their human friends. Rosemarie made them sit on the bench like the humans, and William slipped them some meat from the trays of festive food.

One of the last people to take a seat was the old priest. He drew up a stool next to Rosemarie. "And so how is our little Robin?"

"He is thriving, Father, grows heavier every day."

She bounced the infant a little as he lay in her lap, and Robin obligingly produced a gassy smile for the priest.

The old man smiled but asked nothing more about the baby. He watched Goblin and Snow Beauty feasting. Then, after several minutes, he drew a deep breath and sighed. "You know, I have not seen Magdalene since Easter. It's not like that cat of mine to run off. Yesterday, a mouse got into my larder and ate some of the cheese that Anna brought me."

It was a not like the priest to be downcast. William stroked Goblin and scratched the cat's chin.

Still scratching Goblin, William said, "We will keep a sharp eye out for her. Won't we old boy?" He quickly added, "Sir?" in deference to the feline knight.

Goblin arched his back and rubbed his cheek against the blacksmith's hand.

Later in the evening, when the music, dancing, eating and drinking were at a merry peak and the bridal couple were thinking of retiring, a cottager, one of the poorest in the village, who had had more than enough beer, began shouting to one of his comrades. "No, I haven't plowed my strip! And I won't! This year, it must be different."

Two friends came hurrying over to quiet him. They whispered into his ear, and he dropped his voice. His words were nearly inaudible now, as his shoulders were bent over the table, and he spoke with his lumpy nose almost wedged into his tankard. He began a litany of complaints about it being the same thing every year. Barely enough comes from the ground, he complained, to feed his family and pay all the taxes to church and lord.

The priest rose from his stool. The years had made him wise in the ways of his parishioners. He knew when to have a word and when he should sometimes turn a forgiving blind eye or deaf ear and let the Lord deal as he would. The priest was always there for his parishioners at confession.

He made his way across the crowded room and spoke a few words to the poor cottager, and the man grew quiet. His angry eyes grew watery and pleading as he mumbled to the priest. He shook his head as if in refusal, then he seized the priest's hand for an instant before picking up his tankard. The old priest came back to William and Rosemarie's table and sat down heavily.

William said, "You know, Father, Pete's strip of land is the poorest. He does have a hard time getting enough out of it to feed all those children."

"Yes, yes, my son, I know. I will pray for him," said the priest, staring off and rubbing the big, bumpy knuckles of his ancient hands.

His thoughts, it seemed, were somewhere far away. He rose and left the feast.

The cottagers were still huddled around Pete an hour later, but the merriment elsewhere in the room was getting rowdy. William decided it was time to take his little family of three people and two cats home. As they passed the church, Goblin squeaked a little meow and ran up to the front of the building. One of the doors was ajar. He pushed his way into the sanctuary.

"Guess Goblin has to confess to catching a mouse," William laughed.

Rosemarie laughed at the thought of the big cat confessing his sins.

Goblin entered the sanctuary slowly, sniffing the incense-rich air as he walked toward the altar. Candles flickered, giving off a frail, dim glow, but there was plenty of light for a cat to see everything. Goblin was interested only in one thing—one scent that was now faint. He leapt up onto the altar and was wending his way between the large candlesticks and the cross when the priest spoke. "Are you looking for your daughter Magdalene, little Sir Pussycat? She is not here. Ah, I see you have noticed the candlesticks are merely wooden substitutes that I have disguised by binding them with flowers."

Goblin's nose twitched as he sniffed a tall wax taper. Next, he twitched his nose at one of the flowers twined around the candlestick and sneezed, spilling a wet little streak down one petal.

"I have waited since Easter for our own to return. This week, my homily will address loss and the sin of theft. Still, for me, Magdalene's loss is the hardest to bear."

He knelt, crossed himself, and began to pray in Latin. Goblin jumped down with a chirp and brushed hard against the old man, rubbing off a thin line of gray hair onto the priest's cassock. The cat left by the side door.

Little rain had fallen since Easter, so Goblin was able to pick up a faint fear scent that he recognized as Magdalene's. He followed it some distance, slinking low and moving quickly but invisibly through the grass. He lost the scent when he got to a little stream beyond the church.

Back at his fireside, Goblin purred what he had learned to Snow Beauty, who thought Magdalene had simply made a nest to have her kittens safely, some distance away from others. Somewhat reassured, the gray cat lovingly licked Snow Beauty's ears until they shined. As he did so, she purred that tomorrow she would show him the place she had chosen to give birth to her new kittens. Only Goblin would know the location of her nest, just in case there was a threat of some sort.

That Sunday, the homily was a shocker. Not only were Magdalene and the altar candlesticks gone, but, worst of all, the reliquary holding the holy relics of St. John, which had blessed the town for so many years, had disappeared. The townspeople were both angry and frightened. They murmured among themselves, complaining that the aged priest was growing careless. What could the old man be thinking? Would some catastrophe now befall their town? They had so long been blessed. The sacred relics had protected them even from the plague that had devastated nearby hamlets.

The relics were tiny finger bones and black hair believed to be those of the saint. They had, during their long journey through the centuries, been tied and lacquered together in such a way that they now resembled—if a certain amount of imagination was employed—the stubby tail of a kitten.

Some time before any of the townspeople could remember, a goldsmith had made a filigreed container for the holy objects. Apparently, he also noted the resemblance to a kitten tail and worked a cat's face into the design of the reliquary. Whether carved worshipfully or in whimsy, the feline face instilled a certain love, or at least respect, in the townspeople for the little rat catchers. Thus had the reliquary possibly saved the people from the Black Plague by encouraging the keeping of cats despite the strictures of some churchmen. The little hunters kept the number of rats low, depriving disease-carrying fleas of hosts.

The townsfolk clustered outside the church's doors and, after a short discussion, chose four of the town's most important and respected citizens—the priest, the cooper, the miller, and the baker—to approach their manor lord, Sir Rudolph, for redress of their grievance. They went up the hill to the manor that very afternoon.

When they arrived, Sir Rudolph sat at his dinner table, his lady by his side and all his retainers arrayed according to rank, with his bailiff and a visiting knight nearest to him. Retainers of lesser degree sat at trestle tables arrayed to either side of the main board. Table linens hung from each table, almost reaching the floor. Lady Alfreda was spooning up strawberries from a bowl of cream, and, with the good manners becoming a lady, she was daintily dabbing her lips with the tablecloth. When she finished, a young page brought the lord and lady bowls of rosewater and linen towels to wash and dry their hands.

The townsmen waited at the far end of the hall until Sir Rudolph granted them an audience. It was most unusual for townspeople to disrupt his Sunday meal, but, displeased as he was, he still felt an obligation to his honor and chivalric vows to hear their cry for aid. The cooper, whom the people had chosen as their spokesman because of his relative prosperity and importance to the town, stepped forward and bowed deeply.

"My lord, Sir Knight," the cooper began, "there has been a great crime done to our people, and we come seeking justice."

He explained the desecration of their little church, with the old priest interjecting details as the cooper spoke.

"In a day's time I leave for a joust. Really Sirrah! I cannot let a missing pussycat and pair of candlesticks keep me from attending, surely." Then Sir Rudolph demanded of the priest, "This happened at Easter? Why did you not bring this to me immediately?"

The priest responded that he had hoped, by the grace of God, the thief would repent of his deeds and return the stolen objects. "They are good people, my lord," the old man concluded.

The knight sat back in his chair and drained his cup. Then, he slammed down his large wine vessel.

Lady Alfreda, who had busied herself wiping her fingers on her hand towel, looked up. "My Lord, mayhap you need another cup of wine to clear your thinking," suggested the good lady a little testily.

The knight sat up straighter and, somewhat red faced, made another stab at dealing with the matter before him, muttering to himself about the thief or thieves being long gone.

"The theft of the reliquary, however, *is* a matter of some concern," he paused, seeming to think the situation over. "Ah! But we have two honored knights in this town, haven't we? Until I return, let Sir Goblin with his sensitive nose sniff out this affair!"

He dismissed the townspeople.

The bailiff, Gerhard, escorted the men out of the manor hall.

As they neared the door, Gerhard glanced quickly back toward the dining table, and, pulling the priest aside, he said, "It is not like our Sir Rudolph to be so disdainful of this town's concerns, even after much wine. But I think this winter with, you know . . . the . . . ah . . . the near loss of his lady . . . has, ah, greatly affected him. He really is very—"

The bailiff stopped speaking.

Whatever he thought the knight was, he remembered his loyalty to his master and quickly finished, mumbling under his breath, "He really needs to get back to jousting."

All the way back down the hill, the four men wondered how they would ever interest a cat in candlesticks. They went directly to the blacksmith shop to speak to William. Sir Goblin sat atop a hitching post and listened intently. By the time they finished talking, the hands of five men had either chucked Sir Goblin under his chin, scratched his ears, or patted his shoulders. As soon as the four men went away, Goblin disappeared into the house and situated himself on William and Rosemarie's bed for a much-needed washing and grooming.

Three.

ARLY THE NEXT morning, Monday morning, before anyone arrived at the smithy to have a horse shod or any repairs made to their tools, William took Goblin over to the church to have a look around. Everything seemed to be about as usual.

How does one deal with this? thought William, standing in front of the church with his hands on his hips. Goblin circled around his legs, rubbing against his hose, dragging at and twisting the man's stockings. William decided to try to think like a thief. Walking straight ahead would have taken the thief or thieves straight out into the open common. William thought a thief probably would not risk being seen in that open area, nor would he go past the priest's house. So, obviously, he or they went around the other side of the church or out a back door. William brushed the cat hair off his legs and straightened his hose. Then he started to walk around to the side of the church, the way the thief might have gone. Goblin dashed ahead of him with surprising enthusiasm, but the smith stopped suddenly and turned on his heel.

"Let's just make sure there is no other way out from the inside, a window perhaps, Goblin," he whispered to the cat.

Will pulled open one of the great oak doors and stepped inside. The striped knight followed slowly behind him, switching his tail and meowing annoyance. Inside the dark sanctuary, a few candles flickered. William dipped to his knee and crossed himself. He reached around behind him to where Goblin stood. Putting his hand gently on the cat's neck, he pushed down so the animal's head tipped briefly to the floor, satisfying himself that his cat had made a catly reverence.

The priest was at prayer before the altar. William walked slowly along the side of the nave. Brilliantly colored windows each portrayed a scene from the Bible and spilled pink, blue, and yellow light onto the stone floor. William quickly realized that all the windows were too high up to climb out of and were firmly glazed. He tiptoed softly about the holy space, staying well back from the priest. The only other exit was through the room that the priest used and that led out to the yard opposite the priest's house.

"He wouldn't have gone out that way, Goblin," whispered William, "Goblin?"

The cat was not with him. William scanned the empty expanse of the church, looking for his cat. At last his eyes met Goblin's, glowing like two orange lights, just inside the narthex. Goblin sat by the big double doors, waiting to get out. William pulled the doors open, and Goblin whisked out and around to the side of the church, ready to continue their outdoor investigation. William followed, wondering what it was about that cat that always made him seem like he knew something.

Behind the church the grass grew tall and was much trampled in places by men and animals, but no one farmed the soggy strip of land. William walked toward the spot where the stream, freed from its duties at the mill, meandered lazily among rushes and reeds before hurrying to join a larger brother downstream. Perplexed, William stood rubbing the back of his neck for a minute and then turned to the right. The grass was trampled here as well. He knew cottagers crossed this stream regularly to reach their tumbledown hovels. The two or so years that William had been the blacksmith in Johannesmarkt had been busy ones, leaving little time for just exploring. It took him a minute to locate the rocks and rough-adzed planks that formed the primitive bridge. The planks made it possible to get across without getting wet feet, but there were no railings, and the bridge was narrow. A careful horse could get across, but beasts drawing carts would have to ford the brook.

By now many of the town's residents would be awake and starting to go about their business. Several shopkeepers would already have opened their windows. Wives were taking their bread to the baker. Rosemarie would be one of them, and, therefore, no one would be at the blacksmith shop. William thought he should get back to begin his day's work.

The young man turned toward home, but Goblin dashed over the little bridge. Quickly, William crossed the boards to catch his cat. On the far side of the brook, the path led to the right toward the broken-down cottages, but a narrow track led into the woods on the left. William noticed it only because of a small broken branch that swung in the gentle morning air. *Used by the beasts of the woods to come for water*, he thought.

Goblin was intently sniffing the air. His whiskers had flattened back against his face, and his nose pointed to the sky, wiggling, perhaps to take in all the wondrous spring scents. Then, as if he had made a decision, Goblin let out a chirpy meow and raced off toward the narrow track. William had taken one or two steps after his animal when he heard light footsteps pattering along the right branch. A small boy about eight years old flew by, running as fast as he could. William seized the boy's arm as he passed and yanked him to a halt. "What's the matter, young man?"

"Mama wants the baby woman! I must run, she said."

He pulled free and dashed for the bridge.

"Where're your sisters, little Pete?" called William, referring to little Pete's ten-year-old twin sisters who, the blacksmith thought, would have been the natural choice to go for the midwife.

"Father has taken them to some place," called the eight-year-old over his shoulder as he dashed over the little bridge, crossing it in two long leaps.

As William still hesitated at the fork in the path, Goblin began a one-cat chorus of chirrups, "mwats," and outright meows. The cat pushed through the high grass of the barely visible path, stopping every few steps to look over his shoulder and scowl at William. William followed obediently.

Goblin was eager to venture down the little trail, but William doubted the sense of it. True, here and there were some broken twigs indicating someone or more likely something, a deer most probably, had brushed through. But candlestick thieves? It all seemed like a foolish quest. He wanted to catch his cat and get back to his shop.

As he was about to jump and grab Goblin, he stepped on something that bounced out beyond his toe. Some whitish yellow thing lay in the dirt. He picked it up. It was the stub of a candle. Goblin pranced back to where William stood, and the cat sniffed at the taper. The feline knight rolled in the grass. Lying on his back, he paddled his front paws in the air and cocked his head at a silly, teasing angle as if laughing and saying, *See! I told you!*

William raised the wax taper to his nose. It smelt like honey. It was beeswax, pure beeswax, and surely from the church. Most folks in town made do with the cheaper, tallow candles. *So they did come this way*, thought William. He looked around for more evidence. Not seeing anything more of interest and feeling the morning air beginning to stir and warm up, he decided he had best return home to his day's work.

Goblin yowled and meowed for him to continue down the path, but William scooped up the big cat, saying, "Let's go home, boy."

The tabby-striped knight twisted and wiggled. Then, as if buttered, he slipped from his master's arms, leaving William's sleeves coated with gray fur. Goblin scurried down the path and into the woods. William sighed as he watched his cat run off and slapped at his tunic to brush away the cat fur. He really had to get to work. He headed for his shop. Goblin would have to find his own way back. The blacksmith knew the cat could get home with no trouble.

Arriving home, he found Rosemarie behind the house, washing Robin's swaddling cloth.

"Baby makes a lot of washing," she said to William as she arched a long pole from the boiling wash water.

A ball of wet white linen dripped from its end. She let it drip a moment or two. Then she dumped the wad of wet cloth into the adjacent rinse cauldron. Reaching into the cool rinse water, Rosemarie swirled the laundry until she separated out one piece, and, wringing it until she could squeeze out no more water, she stretched up and spread the white cloth over the hedge that separated their vegetable garden from the smithy's yard.

She's beautiful, William mused as he watched his young wife work. If anything, her figure was lovelier now, after the baby had come. With her belly still rounded, the sure sign of fertility, she looked absolutely voluptuous. He walked up to her and was about to give her a hug when his wife turned briskly back to her laundry tub. She jabbed an elbow into his stomach.

"I've got work to do."

It was not the time for hugs. Definitely not.

"William," she called over her shoulder, "If you want something to eat there is porridge over the fire."

Without a word, William went inside and helped himself. He was used to his wife's more cursory attentions since the baby had arrived. He looked down at his pink-cheeked little Robin asleep in the cradle.

"I am a much-blessed man," he thought as he spooned down his porridge.

He had just set down his spoon beside the empty bowl when a villager came with a horse to be shod. William began to work at his trade.

It was not until they sat down together at noontime for their main meal that William had time to tell Rosemarie about his morning adventure. Goblin had not returned. Nor did he return at dusk. Rosemarie had not seen either cat all day. Over supper, the young wife gave her tongue much exercise, prattling on and imagining all sorts of horrible ends for her two cats. Had they, perhaps, been devoured by a wolf, bear, or fox, carried off by Brownies or Gypsies, or cremated by a dragon's fiery breath?

Trying to calm her and get a little peace for himself, William said that Goblin and Snow Beauty were probably hunting as Goblin, at least, often did in the evening. William pointed out that no one had seen a dragon around the town for ages—if ever—and that what they thought was a dragon last winter turned out to be a wild pig.

After the meal, Rosemarie was still upset. Even while she nursed Robin, her husband heard her fussing about the dangerous, big tusks boars had. William remembered he had an order for hinges and retreated to his shop to hammer rosy-pink iron into strap hinges for a barn door until it was too dark to see. Neither of them slept well that night.

Four.

AFTER GOBLIN HAD run off, he slunk low through the bright-green grass. He heard William call to him. He sat up marmot-like with his back straight and his front paws dangling. He meowed to William, but, apparently, the blacksmith could not hear him. The cat watched William's head and shoulders disappear into the tall grass as the man stalked off toward the village.

Fool, thought Goblin. *Was that what he was really after? A candle?*

Convinced that humans were unknowable, the cat continued down the narrow trail. He had two scents to follow, one very strong, one very dear. Goblin walked on at a determined pace. Once, a squirrel chattered at him. Startled by a jay's piercing squawk, he crouched for a moment to the ground. Later, he caught a glimpse of a rabbit fleeing from him. *This adventure is really sort of fun*, meowed the cat to himself. It was a bright, clear day. Sunlight bounced from every twig. *A pleasant day for a journey*, thought Goblin. He had ceased to think of William.

At noon he climbed atop a rock and sunned himself. The warmth on his fur felt wonderful. He dozed. After a minute or two, his head popped up, fully alert to the humming of insects. His ears spun around to the left, then right. Locating the source of a sound, his paw flashed out once, twice. His claws hooked through two white moths. The big cat popped them into his mouth. His lips smacked three or four times, and the food was gone. White moths were among Goblin's favorite snacks. Yum! His tongue wiped both sides of his mouth. He then washed his face hastily, passing his paw just once over each ear. Goblin stood up and stretched and went on his way, feeling much restored.

He was having a lovely time. The sun sank low before he realized how late it was getting. Still he followed the scents. He never needed to leave the trail, which was becoming ever wider. Now, a man on a horse could pass through with ease. When darkness settled in, Goblin located a hollow tree trunk lying along the path. He snuggled in safely and was soon asleep.

In the morning, the relentlessly cheerful din of birdsong woke him up at first light. He stretched, tucking in his chin and arching his back into a tight hump. He wiped the sleep from his eyes with his paws and yawned a big, fangy yawn. Ready to start his day, he heard the rustle of a small animal streaking by him. Whether mouse or vole or something else, he didn't consider but instead pounced and had his breakfast. A full grooming followed. When he had his fur neat and shining, Goblin, feeling presentable enough to meet the king, began the next leg of his journey.

The day was more humid than the day before. The cat sensed it would rain sometime soon. He kept walking, and his journey continued without incident for most of the morning. He had only to follow the scents, to follow his nose, as it were. The path continued to widen.

At a small hill the fear scent of one beast was unexpectedly much stronger. Goblin paused to think. Perhaps there was a rider who laid a whip to the animal's haunch to urge him up the hill. He followed the scent up the rise, and soon Goblin reached a broad roadway where cement lay crumbled between the paving stones. It was the old Roman road. Some powdered cement clung, dust-like, to his paw pads. Goblin sniffed a paw, didn't like the smell and shook his foot clean. There was much that was new to smell on this road, and the cat made a careful study of the air. His nose told him to turn right.

He walked on. Clouds covered the sun. The air turned cooler, and distant thunder rumbled to the south. A few drops of rain began to spot the road. Still the cat walked on. The breeze picked up.

Scents came in strong on the hurrying breeze. Goblin lifted his head and inhaled deeply. His nose twitched, and his whiskers shifted back and down. The gray cat turned aside and crept along a drive that was once also neatly paved with flat stones. It was now little used; Mother Nature had reclaimed her own, and lusty weeds grew high between the paving stones and blocked the cat's view. He heard the voices of humans, of two men. He also saw the roof and upper story of a building. Being very careful, the cat slunk in closer so he could see more.

The two men were strangers to him. One was holding a donkey by a lead. Yes! It was donkey-smell he had been following. It was the strong, ugly smell. But the other scent was also stronger here, and it went straight to his heart.

The men were arguing noisily, one stabbing his finger at the other's

A hissing and crackling came from above.

chest as he spoke. Goblin sat down to watch what he thought were amusing gestures. He placed his front paws evenly together and wrapped his tail neatly around them. Once settled and comfortable, he was ready to size up the scene before him. Thunder rumbled louder and closer. Goblin listened closely to the two men.

"You fool! What do you take me for! You came to me with this?" The taller man held out his hand.

"But I had to provide for my daughters," cried the other, a burly, poorly clad man who held the donkey's lead.

"You said you'd bring me a beast whose fur would be our fortune—"

Lightning flashed and wind whirled up and blew into Goblin's face, blowing away the human's words. Trees swayed, and their black boughs tossed about, swirling first to the ground wildly and then rising up again. But the familiar, dear scent pouring in on the rushing air heartened Goblin so much that he barely heard the man's next words. Or noticed the fierceness of the storm.

"A cat! An ordinary mouser. You must be crazy!"

Goblin listened no more but raced for the building from which the much-loved smell emanated. His eye registered motion as he ran. The tall man flung something onto the ground and drew something narrow and shiny from his belt.

The peasant screamed and screamed. Loud thunder shook the earth. Goblin leapt through the window of the old building and meowed, *Magdalene, Magdalene!*

The thunder now was unceasing. In a flash of lighting Goblin saw Magdalene come toward him. She dropped a kitten softly on the ground at his feet and hurried back the way she had come to fetch the other one of her new babies.

At the same time, lightning flashed brighter than day, a man's scream curdled the air, and thunder crashed as if two Earths were colliding. A hissing and crackling came from above the two cats. Having found each other in the lightning flash, they looked up. Flames flickered, grew, and then voraciously licked at the thatched roof over their heads. The two felines simultaneously ducked their heads, and each picked up one of the mewing, furry bundles from the floor and ran for the window. Timbers fell into the room just as Goblin and Magdalene cleared the windowsill.

The two cats sped across the yard where the terrified donkey reared and brayed, pulling at his lead. A man was lying on the ground, clutching the other end of the lead in his cramped fist. The cats did not stop running until they had reached and crossed the Roman road.

Five.

I T WAS TUESDAY, two days after the Sabbath, when William met at the inn with the village men who had spoken with Sir Rudolph. Storm clouds gathered in heavy, gray, bulging piles above the trees surrounding the village. A few drops of rain sprinkled halfheartedly to the green grass. As William pushed open the tavern door he heard the soft, distant roll of thunder. Inside, the hellos and hearty back slaps made him forget about the weather.

Settled around a trestle table with good beer and bread before them, the men began to consider what options they had in dealing with the robbery. Most doubted there even was a reasonable course of action. The beeswax, the priest assured them, had to have come from the church's candlesticks. It was the length the candles were at the end of the long Easter service. The men had been talking for a while before William thought to mention that Goblin had not returned home. Thunder was rumbling regularly now, and a light, steady rain spattered down.

"Well, William," said the miller, "that cat has strangely hit the target dead center before. He might actually be trying to tell us something."

"But without the knight's men we are not well able to catch thieves."

"Were there strangers about on Easter?" asked one man.

"Who would know!" said the cooper. "We all went from the church to our Easter dinners."

"We had no visitors from away," said the little innkeeper while rubbing grease from a carving knife on his crumpled yellow apron.

"In that case," murmured the priest, "I should like it best if we could settle things quietly, as if among family, rather than bring in Sir Rudolph's men. If we can."

As he stopped speaking, a horrendous crack of heaven's thunderous anger made them all jump. The table was awash with beer spilt from tankards suddenly dropped to its surface.

Rain came roaring down.

The innkeeper hurried to shut the door against the blowing water. Joanna came in with lighted tapers. Setting these on various tables, she rolled the shutters closed across the windows. But for the flickering of two candles, it was black as night inside the tavern. The men sat as statues while nature played out its fierce drama. Hail clattered on the inn's slate roof. Lightening flickered through the cracks in the shutters and under the door. Thunder shook the earthen floor. No one spoke nor would they have been heard if they had. They all sat on stools. Some leaned their elbows on the table; some had wet patches on their elbows where, in the blackness, they had leaned into the spilt beer.

The storm dragged away to its rumbling end. When the rain's tune slowed to a cheerful patter the innkeeper opened the door. Joanna pushed back the shutters. Damp, cold air swirled in and tickled at their necks. The old priest sank down into his robes, shivering. A pink afternoon light pushed the darkness into the corners of the room. Joanna pinched out the little flames and thriftily returned the candles to her larder.

Almost as one, the men stood and stretched. They consulted briefly. The baker pointed out that going through the woods in the direction that William had talked about would eventually bring them to road made by the old "Latin speakers." Goblin had found the candle, and the cat's insistence on going that way suggested that perhaps the candlestick thief had used the trail. It was once a shortcut to a convent leper hospital.

"But the plague had helped the poor souls in the hospital to the next world, along with almost everyone else," the baker continued, laughing bitterly. "We'll take that big old horse of yours, Young Will, push through to the Roman road, and see what we see."

At daylight the next morning, Wednesday, the cooper, the baker, and the miller followed William on his old farm horse, Nob. The smith, having little need to ride a horse since settling in Johannesmarkt, boarded Nob at the inn. He rented or loaned the animal to whomever might need a strong horse.

Nob crossed the little bridge and pushed through the foliage at a steady, slow pace, making the hike easier for the men behind. They came across nothing of any note, no more candles, no cats, and certainly no thieves waiting to be caught.

Late in the morning, the path widened and Nob's hooves clopped on the stone paving of the old Roman road. The men paused to reconnoiter.

So far they had discovered nothing and really had no idea if their quarry had come this way. The paving stones of the old road were barely visible between the grass and weeds that grew knee high.

A gentle stirring of the air caused one of the men to declare, "I smell smoke!"

All together they breathed in deeply, filling their lungs with the sour air.

"No, not smoke," answered the baker, "more like that raw smell of wet ashes."

The men began to walk toward the acrid odor for want of any other clue. Their noses led them to a turn-off.

"Look!" shouted the miller. "Hoof marks! And made after the rain, too. A donkey's."

They followed the hoof prints a few yards back into a driveway. The drive curved so the searchers could not immediately see what was ahead.

The baker spoke quietly as they walked, "This may have been where the leper hospital—oh, my Lord!"

As they walked down the old entrance road, the charred beams of what was once a substantial wooden building came into view. Three corner posts were still standing, but hungry flames had completely consumed the thatched roof. Timbers uneaten by the fire stood twisted and turned at odd angles as if tossed by a whirlwind. Only the heavy rains had saved those beams from reduction to ashes. Little trickles of smoke coming from the midst of the old hospital twirled heavenward from time to time. The three men stood quietly for a minute, attempting to comprehend just what had happened, when, from behind them, they heard the smith shout. "Holy Mother of God!" William was still up on his horse and saw the hospital yard from a higher, sharper angle. His arm shook as he pointed, "Two men!"

He jumped down from Nob. They all ran through the grass to where two men lay dead. One they knew immediately. It was Pete, the father of twin daughters and eight-year-old little Pete. The man would soon have been a new father once again. His face was cut up and bruised. Innumerable donkey hoof prints marked the ground and his body. A small pile of dung lay beside the dead man. Plainly, the animal had been there for some time and had trampled on Pete. But Pete did not die from being trod upon. Blood and flattened intestines smeared the ground. No frightened, pounding hoof could have produced such horror, nor could the animal have made the long, clear-edged slit down Pete's front.

The men soon discovered a shining dagger still lying plunged into Pete's belly. Pete had been stabbed, and the knife had ripped down along his abdomen.

They did not know the other man. He was burned. He was taller and more richly attired than the men of Johannesmarkt commonly were. A full purse and an empty sheath for a knife hung from his girdle.

"He was not robbed," said the baker.

"The sheath, look ye, matches the dagger," said the miller, pointing out that the engraving on the dagger grip imitated the tooling on the leather sheath. "He killed poor Pete, but why?"

"It was lightning that took *him*, I suspect. Both him and the hospital," said the cooper. "God punished him for murdering Pete."

"Surely."

"Indeed. Yes."

"Look around," ordered the baker, who took on a certain authority for being the oldest and for knowing about the existence of the leper hospital. "I'll see what I can do for Pete. See if you can find a candle or candlesticks."

The men shuffled about the ground, ruffling through the grass, searching with their feet. Nob took advantage of his opportunity to graze. He nuzzled some tender shoots then nosed something out of his way with a snort. William, hearing the horse's snuffle, caught the gleam of gold from the corner of his eye.

"Look at this," he cried out. "It's the reliquary!" He held up the little golden vessel. The stolen container for the bones and hair was only about six inches long. He passed it around. Each man crossed himself and kissed it. They were so relieved to have the sacred relics back and their town's protection ensured that it was several minutes before the baker could get them to continue the search. He thought it proper to offer a prayer of thanks for the return of the relics. Still, he had to place them out of sight, in Nob's saddlebags, before his companions could focus on searching for the candlesticks.

Having brought no shovels, rakes, or hoes, searching the wet ashes and charred timbers was not practicable. At any rate, they had to return to town to bury Pete and the murderer. They had to talk with the priest. If only Sir Rudolph were there!

They started on the long walk back to the town. Poor Nob had to carry the two dead men slung over his back, one of whom was more or less tied closed. It was nearing sunset when the four men, bone weary, footsore, and starving from not having eaten all day, trudged into town.

Rosemarie rushed up to Will as soon as she saw him. He was leading Nob from the yard between the church and the priest's house. The others were with the priest, arranging for the washing of the dead men's bodies and for the burials.

"Have you found the cats?"

"Rosemarie, for heaven's sake! By my troth, woman, this has been a horrible day. Leave off about cats."

With that, he buried his face against Nob's neck in weariness, and Rosemarie, perhaps fortunately, could not hear what her tired man mumbled about her pets.

"I must see to the horse." He led Nob to the inn.

He did not see Rosemarie's lower lip jut out or how she punched her knuckles onto her hips. She stamped her foot once. Then, she threw up her hands and marched back to their house. "Snow Beauty, Goblin, what has happened to you?" she wailed.

Robin whimpered in his sleep, and Rosemarie jiggled his cradle to soothe him. Then she poked at the fire and lowered the supper pot closer to the flames. No one saw her cry for her animals.

The identity of the well-dressed murderer, so unknown to the men, was no mystery at all to the women of the town.

As the cloth was thrown back from his burnt face, they exclaimed one after another, "The flax merchant!" "The weaver's agent!" "The wool merchant!" and one even said, "His name was Cuthbert. He came last market day selling beautiful girdles trimmed with the softest fur. I thought it was cat fur and refused to buy."

"That answers that. He came market days to buy the women's spinning and take it to the weavers," said the cooper.

"I wonder if Pete's wife knew him," mused the baker.

"I doubt Marta had either the time or the flax to spin."

"Maybe some wool."

Pete's funeral was on Saturday. They sent the wool merchant's body by two-wheeled cart, pulled by a single mule, to the monastery to be buried in the burial ground for strangers. His full purse more than paid for funeral expenses and a donation to the monks. The villagers expected the Funeral Mass to be a poor affair as befitted a poor man, but the priest sang the mass in a full and glorious voice, a voice not often heard from the old man's lungs. People whispered.

"Is it because the reliquary is back?"

"No, no, he is not a man that cares for things."

"Perhaps it is for Pete, as he could not otherwise help him."

But it was neither reason.

That morning when the priest opened his door to cross the yard and say the Mass in the church, Magdalene stood at his feet, meowing to come in. The little cat was scruffy, much burred, and thinner, but she was definitely Magdalene. Before her front paws a tiny kitten with a gray-striped tail rolled and played. Coming up the path behind her, carrying a similar infant in his teeth, was the great warrior knight, Sir Goblin.

"Ah, I see, I see." The priest understood immediately what had happened. "Come in, my darling, and you, you also, Sir Cat."

He put some cream out for them and the fish that he would have had after mass for his own breakfast. *Some bread will do well enough for an old man*, he thought.

On his knees in the sanctuary, he thanked his Maker with all his simple heart for the safe return of his little companion, Magdalene. He understood that Goblin had somehow rescued her and brought her home safe and with a new family. His heart sang with joy.

The next week, Pete's widow attempted to come to church. After the service, when the women were gathered around her, hugging her and offering what humble aid and support that they could, Sir Rudolph and his retinue tramped onto the green. With a great clattering of weapons, harnesses, and spurs, and with dust swirling around their horses' hooves, they drew up before the little group of townspeople.

From astride his tall mount, the knight leaned down and demanded of the priest, "What news of the theft? Has Sir Knight Pussycat solved the crime?"

The priest sputtered. He was not ready to deal with the haughty, joking knight so soon after the Mass.

But, when the baker started to speak, the priest interrupted him with, "Why, yes, sir, he has. This morning he brought me back my cat, his daughter Magdalene, and her two newborn kittens. Delivered them himself to my door. She, you know, had been taken with the holy things. All that is missing still are the candlesticks, but they are of little value compared to my Magdalene and the reliquary."

That said, he turned abruptly and went into the church, shutting the door behind him. He had answered the knight's question. He would not speak of murder and death in front of Marta.

This was the first the people had heard of Goblin again in his role as knight. They were amazed.

"I guess, for his size and from his viewpoint, he rescued a damsel in distress," they were saying, as William and Rosemarie quietly slipped home.

To their great joy, Goblin sat at their doorstep. He was hungry and scruffy but otherwise fine. Rosemarie presented him with a bowl of stew. He ate greedily for a minute as she hung anxiously over him, her hands clenched. After a few more mouthfuls, Goblin lifted his head. His great, round eyes stared into hers. Then, understanding her silent, anguished plea, Goblin rubbed his flank against her skirts. He trotted to the back door, mewing.

Totally perplexed, Rosemarie let him out but begged the "bad cat," as she called him, not to go away again.

He returned almost immediately, making a great scratching racket at the door. Rosemarie flew to open it. In strode Snow Beauty carrying a kitten. She dropped the white, gray-tailed baby on Rosemarie and William's bed and then demanded to be let back out. Several openings and closings later, Snow Beauty lay spread on the bed like a queen, with five kittens lined up along her tummy, home from her secret nesting place. Proud Goblin sat purring noisily, making a deep, majestic rumble. Picking up first one foot and then the other, he kneaded the bedding.

An Epilogue.

THE TOWN GOSSIPS' tongues were still wagging about poor Pete and about Goblin's adventures, when in September two monks, Brother Gilbert and Brother Innocent, the monastery's herbalist and his assistant, came into the village. They were familiar enough figures. They sometimes dispensed healing herbs to people in need of them in town, but usually the monks passed through, going to the convent to trade honey and beeswax for the nuns' spinning and woven cloth. They never took the narrow path Goblin had discovered but plodded the long way around to the old Roman road with their cranky mules.

This morning the two monks were walking with one of their animals piled with woolen cloth for future habits. Brother Gilbert, much flustered, led a donkey, on the back of which sat two rosy-cheeked, high-spirited girls who could not yet be called women but who were not far from an age at which they could. The nuns no doubt thought the strong but ancient Brother Gilbert a proper enough guardian for the twin girls on their two-day journey, but the young lasses were obviously entertaining themselves merrily at handsome, young Brother Innocent's expense.

As the little party approached the green, everyone heard one girl shout out, "The church! The church! Now you must choose, Brother Innocent, my lord, which one of us will you marry and which one shall be lady-in-waiting."

Their giggles set Brother Innocent to blushing, and he pulled his hood so far over his scarlet face that he could barely see out.

Marta rushed to reclaim her daughters, embracing them and ending Brother Innocent's agony. People flocked around them, eager to hear the news for themselves. Brother Gilbert explained, as he handed the candlesticks to the priest, that the nuns found the twin girls to be the most incorrigible novitiates ever to enter their sacred walls. They wreaked so much havoc on the convent's peace, with their double-trouble pranks, setting fires, whistling during prayer, and what all, that even though they were bright students and learned to write and do figures readily, the good sisters were convinced that the girls had no vocation.

They were herewith returning the candlesticks to Pete, to whom they thought the objects belonged. He had offered them, after all, to secure his daughters' place in the convent. The pious ladies had then instructed the monks to deliver the girls safely to their parents.

In spite of themselves and their pranks, the girls returned home literate, a most rare and valuable skill in Johannesmarkt. The cooper, the busiest man in the town, soon hired one or the other—he was never quite sure which one came in on a given day—to help with his accounts and orders. Pete's family was no longer the poorest in town.

Sir Goblin's Quest

One.

 IR GOBLIN, KNIGHT of the Smithy, sat in the yellow sunshine at the entrance to his home. He crouched with one back leg stretched out beyond his nose. Methodically, his rough tongue combed out the fur between each back toe. Occasionally stopping to bite at a snarl or bit of dirt, he'd then rake out the fur until it lay straight and clean. A claw or two required nibbling down to a keener edge. Thus occupied, the noble tomcat did not notice at first that a young black cat had pranced up to the blacksmith shop. A shift in the breeze brought the animal's scent to Goblin. The knight crouched and glared a defending challenge at the youngster.

Who is this half-grown tomcat? Sir Goblin wondered. The young cat really looked a fright. Fur stood up straight on the top of his head, and his cheeks were bushy. In fact, his grooming was nonexistent. A sorry example of a cat! His eyes, though, spoke of amusement and downright mischievousness. Goblin gave him a low warning hiss, and the youngster bounced away as if blown on the wind. But he returned within minutes, this time crouching submissively before the much-honored, older cat. He sought advice, and the gist of his long tale to Goblin was this.

He and his littermates were taken from their momcat at just about the age when they had begun to scramble about and have fun. A human had tossed them all in a sack and dumped them down the well. They paddled desperately. He and one sister were able to reach the wall of the well and get toeholds on the rough and mossy surface. Inch by slow inch, they clawed their way out of the well to freedom. Then they ran off into the forest. After many twists and turns, eventually his long story brought him to this town where happy cats live. Almost all of them told him they were related to the knighted cat at the smithy, who is very wise, and who could help him find a good home.

Oh, wise, am I? chuckled the great gray-striped cat, with a rumbling purr. *I am not wise enough to know why your fur stands up in shiny peaks.* The younger feline leaped up nervously and showed his other side to Goblin, revealing patches of bare skin where his fur had been cut out.

Oh, Sir Cat, the lady who keeps me now puts this greasy stuff on my fur and sometimes she cuts out my fur. Sometimes she hurts me. She doesn't let me out but for a short time during the day. If I'm not back soon she will put her foot on my tail to hold me down and beat me with her broom. The young cat spoke faster and faster in a stream of pleading meows, then murmured, *I must get back now.*

Goblin, who had said little, was much perplexed by this weird tale, but he gave his word to help, and the young black cat scampered off.

The knight scratched under his chin with his hind foot, stretched, and strolled off to visit his neighbors. At the priest's house, he sat down with his daughter Magdalene. She was a child from Snow Beauty's first litter. He and Snow had had eight litters. By now, many of the cats in Johannesmarkt were white with gray-striped tails, a genetic quirk resulting from the mating of the gray-striped Goblin and the pure white Snow Beauty.

Goblin learned that the funny little cat had approached Magdalene one day for help, and she had recommended Goblin to him. The black kitten was called Tatters by the old priest, because of his ragged, tattered fur coat.

Rosemarie hummed as she stirred the big pot hanging over the fire. Her daughter, who was named Madelyn after the old wise woman in Rosemarie's hometown, was asleep in her cradle. Her son, Robin, was sitting still for once, playing with his new wooden blocks on top of the trestle board that would serve as a table for the noon meal. Goblin settled himself before the hearth. Only he could hear the soft, rhythmical suckling and purring sounds coming from the corner, where Snow Beauty lay behind the spinning wheel, nursing her two newest kittens. Goblin was just about to doze off when—*whop!* Robin, block in hand, gave the big gray cat a thump on the back that the boy probably thought was a pat. Startled, Sir Goblin yowled in annoyance and scurried outdoors. The child cried for "Gobcat," as he called his pet, to come back.

Meanwhile, his mother sighed, and said in her sternest parental voice, "If I've told you once, I've . . ." Goblin was not there to hear the rest.

He slipped into the smithy and settled himself behind the forge, where William was pounding a scythe's great curving blade into shape. The cat folded his front feet neatly before his chest and wrapped his tail around them. Once comfortable, he began to sort out this matter of Tatters.

When the sun reached its highest point in the sky, the noontime church bell rang out, out-ringing William's clanging hammer. It was the signal for everyone to stop for prayer and go home for their main meal of the day. Robin toddled into the smithy and took his father by the hand, and father and son walked the few yards to their house and their dinner. Goblin followed leisurely.

Seated on stools on either side of the table, Robin and William reached for their spoons and began to scoop up the stew Rosemarie had ladled into their trenchers, the scooped-out loaves of day-old bread that served as bowls. She had set the trenchers on pottery platters rather than, as usual, directly on the table. A few wild flowers in a vase gave the humble meal a holiday feeling.

After the first few spoonfuls, William set down his spoon. He ran his finger slowly around the edge of his platter and then looked up into his wife's face. Her blue eyes sparkled. Her cheeks flushed deep pink. She was beautiful.

"Er, It's not your name day, I know. But what is the occasion? Why the platters and flowers?" William ventured to ask. He was sure he had misstepped somehow and should have presented her with a gift, or flowers, at least.

"No occasion, really." Her eyes lowered, and she took an intentionally long sip of broth. When she looked up, she was ready to speak. In a stream of words, prepared that morning, she told William how blessed she felt with a good husband, two lovely children already, and such a comfortable home. She was especially thankful for the fireplace and the great iron crane that William had made. From it, she could hang the stew kettle, a water cauldron, so many things. Her mother, she reminded him, had just a hearth in the middle of their small house, and a hole in the roof whereby the smoke might escape if it were so inclined. Out of breath, she stopped speaking for a moment and then began again.

"With this fireplace I can cook so many ways," the young woman said, "and I have an idea!" Jumping up and going over to her hearthside, she dragged a covered pot from the ashes. Brushing ashes from its cover, she lifted the iron lid and slid two little pies, with their warm red juice still bubbling through the baked crusts, on to a pottery platter. With a great flourish, she presented them to her husband. "Try one."

"Hmmm . . . delicious," he mumbled, as he munched. She edged the second pastry toward him.

"I have talked with Joanna, and she has asked me to sell some in the midsummer fair."

"What? For money?"

"Oh, it's just for a few coins, and only once a year. I want to try things with this fireplace. I can sling Maddie in my cloak, and Joanna will watch Robin along with her boys."

"But, Rosemarie, all sorts of strangers come to the fair!"

"We'll be right across the square the whole time. You'll see us from the smithy." She popped a piece of the second pastry into his mouth and tapped him pertly on the tip of his nose with her finger.

"Guess there's no harm in it. If Joanna recommends them, you really must do it. They are delicious." William got up, wiped his mouth, and kissed his wife gently on her temple. He was patting his stomach and humming as he went back to his work.

Rosemarie remained seated for a while, chin in hands, thinking. It had been easier to get agreement from her lord than she had expected—judging by what some other wives had told her. Now nothing stood in her way but herself. Many wives in the village had little sideline businesses, often beer-making. This, if she succeeded, could be hers. Even if it was a once-a-year thing. The thought of coins she had earned jingling in her purse heartened her. She had to make a tray of pies all baked to perfection. *Will I really be able to do it?* Her stomach gave a little flutter. *What if they burn?* She offered a quick plea to St. Mary and made the sign of the cross.

Robin's singing and the banging of his spoon on his platter broke her reverie.

"Gobcat, Gobcat, get fat, get fat," the boy warbled. He had set his platter on the earthen floor by the hearth and filled it to the brim with stew from the kettle. Goblin and Snow Beauty were gallantly trying to lap up the delicious offering, but were having considerable difficulty. The boy squatted before the dish, slapping his spoon in the broth in time with his singing, spattering the cats' eyes and ears with every beat. Drops of the thick stew hung from Goblin and Snow Beauty's eyebrows and whiskers.

"Robin, what a mess you've made! You're soaked in grease! The floor!" The baby Maddie woke and screamed to be nursed. "Oh! Mother Mary!" Rosemarie exclaimed. "Here. Here!" she cried out and pushed crusts from the trencher bread at her son. "Go feed the chickens out back." She gave her boy a little shove toward the back door.

Shadows were growing long by the time Rosemarie had her hearth scrubbed and the hard-packed earthen floor scraped clean. Robin was "helping" his father for the moment, and the baby was finally sleeping again.

Rosemarie had hoped to finish spinning her flax in time to sell it to the weavers' agent at the fair. She had to finish it by the end of the day, for tomorrow she had to bake her pies. But for little Robin and the cats, the spinning would have been finished an hour ago. Now the sun was getting low, and the room was fast becoming too dark to work in. So much work. Was a woman ever busier?

As the smith's wife stood scowling at her wheel, a gaudily painted four-wheeled wagon rolled by her window and stopped at the smithy. Suddenly getting the flax spun did not seem important. She just had to see this curiosity, this strange wagon.

William appeared at the door almost immediately, and told her that he'd be quite busy fixing an iron tire for these entertainers' wagon and re-shoeing their mule. Would she, he asked, go over to the cooper's and bring back the three nail kegs that the cooper had promised William would be ready today? They were small enough that Robin could carry one. He would keep a ready ear for the baby.

Delighted for the chance to share a sip of herb tea and gossip with Winifred, the cooper's wife, Rosemarie took Robin by the hand and started across the village green. But first, she took a good look at the painted wagon.

The vehicle's sides, though now somewhat faded, still clearly depicted twining snakes, all mottled with green and yellow splotches, and with big, round eyes and fat, red tongues waggling from their mouths. A brown bear danced beside them and, in one corner, a stick-like figure of a man, a juggler, tossed lighted torches that rose and spun above the bear's head. "They don't draw very well," mumbled Rosemarie to herself. After inspecting the wagon, she took a good look at the men. And, yes, the men standing by the wagon—in their parti-colored doublets and hose of red, green, and yellow—were the same group that had come to the festival last year. She remembered their juggling, tumbling, and daring sword-swallowing acts. She recalled especially the thin little boy in a bear costume, who did a dance at the end of a rope. Surely that was he on the back step of the wagon, sitting with his head in his hands. Were his shoulders shaking? Was he crying, or perhaps feverish? She could not be sure.

The three men moved about restlessly, stretching their arms high above their heads, twisting at the waist. One took to doing cartwheels in the dirt before their wagon. They were telling William that they had a splendid surprise finale for their act this year. *They were good last year,* Rosemarie remembered. *This year, Robin will be old enough to enjoy some of their performance.* Rosemarie and Robin left them to their work, and started walking over to the cooper's shop.

They had gone but a short distance when Robin, who had been dragging his feet, pulling at his mother's hand, and staring all goggle-eyed at the colorful strangers, saw Goblin following behind them. "Gobcat's coming, Mama!" The boy planted his feet firmly in the ground, watching the cat over his shoulder.

"Come on," his mother said, laughing, and giving her son a little tug. "He's fine. He's a grown-up cat."

As they approached the cooper's shop, Winifred threw open the door. She stood in her doorway, hands on hips. A mother of five children, she was no longer slim; but being proud of her husband's relative prosperity, she made a point of always being seen well dressed. Today, she greeted Rosemarie wearing a simple wool and linen gown, with long tight-fitting sleeves and a scoop neckline. She had gathered her hair just behind her ears into two large buns held by silvery wire cages. Because it was warm and she was at home, she wore no other head cover. A simple snood covered Rosemarie's hair.

"The kegs are ready, but have a drink of raspberry tea with me first."

Rosemarie was glad to sit, sip, and gossip. Rosemarie leaned back on the prosperous woman's settle and looked around at the meticulously kept room. Not a dish, nor a stool, nor even a floor mat was out of place. The furniture gleamed from polishing.

The women sent Robin to the cooper's shop, where he loved to play among the curly wood shavings. One of the cooper's sons was a year older than Robin, and together they imagined the prows of Viking ships in the curls. The two stormed make-believe castles and raided towns just as they'd heard the Norsemen of old had done. One of the literate twin girls, whom the cooper had hired five years ago to help manage his accounts, was on hand and watched the boys while the cooper went about his work.

Unnoticed, Goblin busied himself sniffing all around Winifred's room. He seemed most particularly interested in the broom that stood against the fireplace wall. His nostrils twitched and his ears flicked back as he carefully inspected each twig.

"I want you to meet my mother-in-law, who has come to live with us. Her name is Wanda." There was a snort—or maybe a snore—and a shuffling of feet from a dark corner of the room, as Winifred said the old woman's name.

Rosemarie turned to look and was surprised to see a grotesquely fat old woman bundled in several layers of garments, with a fuzzy shawl wrapped about her mountain of flesh. She was sitting in a great heavy chair. *She sits like a queen enthroned,* thought Rosemarie.

"She can barely hear or see, and light hurts her eyes," whispered Winifred, "so the dark corner suits her and keeps her out of my way."

Goblin's sniffing investigation brought him around to Wanda. He sniffed at her hemline and laid his ears back. She did not notice him there, nor did she move when he stood up with one paw on her knee and smelt her thick soft hand. He shook his head and sneezed. He stood up again and breathed in deeply over the tips of the old lady's fingers, his jaws gaping with the intensity of his inspection. Once again he sneezed, then let out a guttural "mrrrt" and ran out of the house.

"God love us!" exclaimed Rosemarie, setting down her mug.

Winifred, a polite hostess, finished her thought for her. "He certainly didn't like the smell of her."

The cooper's wife went on to tell her visitor how the old lady doted on her own cat, which she called Devil. It was always getting into something, she said, and the old woman nightly cut burrs from its fur and rubbed it with her greasy pomade, hoping the cat could slip through the brush more easily and not pick up more burrs. Also, the mother-in-law used an herb to entice the cat to her; it made the little black animal jumpy and possessed of a merry spirit. Here Winifred, smoothing her skirts, sighed at the thought of the difficulties the woman made for her.

Then Robin marched in, hugging one of the kegs, with the cooper just behind him. The women stopped their chatter. Their mouths hung open in surprise. What a frightful sight the boy was! Curls of wood shavings sprouted from his blonde head in all directions like weeds. The front of his tunic, his knees, and his shoes were caked in sawdust. Giving her husband one stabbing glare, Winifred, the perfectionist housekeeper, took up her broom, and, snatching Robin by the shoulder, steered the boy right back outdoors.

Rosemarie twittered around her son, pulling the spills from his hair and apologizing over and over while Winifred swept him clean. The little boy stood open-mouthed in surprised silence. Once the child was presentable, Rosemarie paid the cooper and made her swift goodbyes.

She and her Robin walked back home. Rosemarie had a nail keg tucked under each arm. The little boy toddled along with the third keg held tightly against his chest, his chubby arms barely reaching around it. He was so proud to be a "true help to Papa," as he phrased it.

Goblin was working hard at washing the tip of his tail when the two reached their doorstep. "Meorrt," he greeted them, and purred about their legs while they carried the little barrels into the blacksmith shop.

That night, Goblin and Snow Beauty slept stretched full length across the foot of the humans' bed. But Rosemarie and William stayed up late sitting on stools by the window, talking, and hoping to catch any little cooling breeze that might drift into the house. It was too hot to sleep. When they were too tired to sit up any more, they threw their daytime clothes over the clothes rods at the head of their bed and slid between the linen sheets. The mattress's straw filling made little crackling noises as William stretched out his legs. The noise woke the cats. William's big feet bumped into both Goblin and Snow Beauty as he rolled over to give his wife a goodnight kiss.

Not liking being bumped and pushed by big feet, the two cats jumped off the bed.

Humans look utterly silly pressing their squishy lips together, Goblin meowed to his favorite mate.

Snow Beauty offered her opinion. *Humans' lips are soft and floppy because they talk so much.*

She imitated a human speaking. "Meow, mrrt, mrrt, meow, meow!"

"What is that cat meowing about?" whispered Rosemarie, not sure if Will had drifted off to sleep.

"She's saying it is too warm to sleep," responded her husband. He sat up. And since it really was too warm to sleep, the couple talked some more about their day, about the entertainers camped at the town's gates, and about Rosemarie's visit to the cooper's.

"Robin had been a good boy, a big boy, carrying home a keg all by himself," whispered the mother into her husband's ear.

Will said that he was a fine boy, at last yawning as he spoke. Rosemarie began telling him how Mistress Cooper has her hands full with her old mother-in-law and about the old woman's strange attachment to a cat. That part of the news made William snore.

All the cats climbed back onto the bed. Goblin lay with his belly pressed against Snow Beauty's back, his front leg draped lightly over her shoulder. The two kittens kneaded, nursing at her nipples, continuing to do so while their mother slept. The two big cats also discussed their day, mewing and purring sweetly into each other's ears.

Tatters was not kept prisoner in that house, Goblin told his mate, *and he had never been beaten with a broom. There was no cat hair or smell on it whatsoever. That strange little cat is nothing but a mischief-maker.* They went to sleep.

Two.

I N THE MORNING, a red sun rose bright and hot. Rosemarie sat on the side of the bed and thanked the Almighty for preserving her through the night. She reached for her shift and dress. She slipped into her shoes and got up to heat a little water for Will to shave. He would want to be clean shaven for the festival. She got Robin up and into his clothes and saw that he used the chamber pot properly.

By now William was dressed. Rosemarie carried the chamber pot out to the cesspit behind the house. Her husband busied himself setting up the trestle table. They really didn't need the table for their light breakfast—they could easily sit on stools and eat from bowls on their laps—but Rosemarie would need the table for her baking. The young wife changed and fed Maddie and hurried through her remaining tasks.

She snuggled Maddie in a linen sling across her breast and tramped across a fallow field to the bramble patch beyond. Here, she sought the bumpy raspberries for her little pies. She picked rapidly, mindless of the pricking thorns. Her basket was almost filled when the baby wanted nursing. Sitting down on a rock, she opened her bodice to the infant's fierce request. Maddie settled into a comfortable nursing rhythm and Rosemarie relaxed.

Only then did she smell a faint rotten odor. A shadow passed overhead. She looked up above her and saw crows and vultures circling above brambles, not many yards from where she had been picking. The black birds circled and dipped, letting out hoarse squawks, but the buzzards were silent as they floated ominously around and around. *A rabbit or something has died*, she assumed, and then thought no more of it. When Maddie was satisfied, her mother filled up the basket and hurried home.

A long, hot afternoon of baking awaited her. She wanted to introduce her pies on this the first evening of the festival.

Late that afternoon, a raft of purple clouds drifted across the sinking sun, suffusing the little town in a pink light. Rosemarie had succeeded splendidly with her baking. The fragrances of raspberry and baking dough filled the little house. Leaving Maddie in her cradle for the moment—Will would hear her if she cried loud enough—Rosemarie scurried across the green with a large basket of warm pies on each arm.

Joanna had set up two trestle tables outside the tavern and laid white tablecloths over them. Behind the cook stood two large bunged kegs, and a wooden crate lined with wool blankets that the big woman had considerately set up as a cradle for Maddie. She was setting out her own refreshments—mostly her famous meat pies—and flagons for ale as Rosemarie arrived. The cook would be serving the tavern's finest ale for the festival. Rosemarie's baked goods would serve as dessert.

All around the green, vendors had set up tables and decorated booths, each competing with its neighbors for the customer's eye. Colorful awnings and banners fluttered, snapped, and crackled in the air. Musicians wandered about, piping through flutes and recorders, or strumming honey-toned lutes while singing favorite songs. Their tunes—although not usually listened to attentively—added to the festive air as old friends met and greeted each other, and vendors hawked their wares at the top of their voices.

People from the town and outlying hamlets pressed against vendors' carts, searching for gewgaws, or for sewn or crafted articles that they couldn't get most of the year. Eventually, almost everyone made his way to the ale table, and soon the baked meats and Rosemarie's pies were disappearing at a fast rate.

This year's fair had attracted more than a handful of new merchants— sharp dealers, always in search of better markets. One, who called himself Antonio, now engaged Joanna in conversation. He was a tall, rotund man, dressed to the limit allowed by the sumptuary laws. He wore a long, burgundy gown of pleated wool, and a hat of the same color with a flat crown, a narrow brim, and a great black feather curling down to his ear. Rubies dangled from his ears, and his curving, waxed, black moustache and equally dark goatee marked him immediately as being from more southern climes—possibly an Italian city-state. In spite of the generally dry ground, he wore pattens to protect his fine leather shoes from the dog dung and horse urine in the streets. These protective platforms made him tall enough to meet the giant Joanna almost eye to eye.

He was a purveyor of fine delicacies: dried and sugared fruits, nuts, stuffed dates, tangy lemons from Spain, and sweet, succulent oranges. Joanna was eager to give him an ear. He came from Genoa, "that fine city on the sea," he said.

After taking her order—his manservant standing by his side and scribbling down the sales—he slowly introduced another line of conversation. Magdalene, or maybe it was one of her daughters, had zipped out from under the tablecloth, snatched up a tidbit of chopped meat dropped by a careless fairgoer, and dashed back under the table.

"Er, I noticed this town has many cats. Mostly they are of the same white and gray pattern. Only once have I seen similar cats—when I was in Bologna. There, they are held in very high esteem as excellent mousers. Are yours?"

"Hah!" Joanna and Rosemarie both laughed. "They are such good mousers, we now have no mice. We may soon have to cook for them."

"Hmmm," said the merchant, scratching his goatee, as the women explained what a blessing to the town the cats were thought to be, and how an honored doctor had once taken some to that very same Italian city, Bologna. "Hmmm," he said again.

The sun was sinking behind rosy clouds, bathing the town in twilight, when the church bell rang out above the hubbub of the festival. The townsmen supplied themselves with food and drink as everyone turned to watch as a little parade marched into the midst of the festival. The march of the players and the subsequent morality play marked the official opening of the summer festival. The actors were all members of Johannesmarkt's largest association of craftsmen, the Joiners' Guild.

Heading the procession were six men carrying torches, which were set up on posts around the square to ward off the darkness after nightfall. Others followed, playing flutes and trumpets. A drummer walked behind them, keeping time for the marchers. Men, all joiners, in various costumes followed, singing. Two oxen pulled a two-wheeled cart filled with a jumble of props. They all drew up before the church steps, and the beasts were unhitched. Then the cart was propped so its bed was horizontal and could serve as a rude stage.

A trumpeter blew a loud blast, successfully turning everyone's attention to the amateur actors. A stout, red-faced man announced they would now tell the "Story of Jonah." Through song, music, and rhyme, the joiners' brotherhood recounted the adventures of Jonah. Four brawny men heaved the cart's heavy tongue up and down, and the "sailors" in the wagon were duly storm tossed. Sailors jettisoned cargo, played by logs and shocks of hay, to lighten the troubled ship. Then, a terrified Jonah stood up, clinging to the side of the wagon, and sang a mournful tune, begging to be thrown overboard for his sinful disobedience to God.

The rustic's voice was strong, with a sweet resonance that left goosebumps as the townsfolk stood in awed silence and appreciation. The simple song was presented in complete reverence.

The moment of awe passed. The great fish—actually a blanket stretched over a wooden frame and painted with scales, fins, and an eye—lurched from behind the wagon. Jonah jumped over the wagon's side and leaped behind the fish, swallowed. The fish and its dinner scuttled around behind the wagon. The men in the wagon then held up boards and sticks, declaring them to be the towers of Nineveh. The fish reappeared and spat forth Jonah. Jonah preached. The men of Nineveh repented. Amongst alleluias and applause, the actors took their bows. The oxen drew the cart and actors away.

Robin, bored by these grown-up themes of repentance and redemption, pulled his father's hand out to arm's length and, leaning back, did a sidestepping dance, swinging first in front of and then behind the smith. Because the boy's repetitious little dance kept him quiet and occupied, Will let him pull on his arm to his heart's content, while he watched the play alongside his wife and baby Maddie. Next to Rosemarie sat Goblin, watching the performance, his gray stripes making him almost invisible in the dusk. And next to him were two little white spots, the kittens, and beside them sat Snow Beauty looking regal, her white coat gleaming pink in the torchlight.

The performance by the brotherhood always ended the first evening's festivities. William and Rosemarie, carrying Maddie, walked home. Robin, completely exhausted by the excitement, staggered along behind them, whining over and over, "Why did that man jump out, Papa?"

"Because the wagon was shaking," answered the father. Hoping to forestall a stream of "why?" questions, William picked up his son, kissing his curly locks as the boy's weary head fell against his father's shoulder. Robin was asleep before they reached their doorstep. Snow Beauty and the two kittens followed the humans into the house. Goblin came last, as the rear guardian of his family. Only he saw Tatters slip off into the field, toward the berry bushes.

Rosemarie tucked the drowsy boy into his trundle bed and lay down on her bed to nurse her daughter. She fell asleep still in her shift. William quietly laid the baby in its cradle and banked the fire. He crawled into bed and was soon snoring. The cats again curled up at the sleeping couple's feet.

The next morning dawned muggy and hot. Rosemarie peeled off the clinging sweaty shift she had fallen asleep in. She pulled on her frock without its under shift—who would know?—and wrapped her apron tightly around her body. On a normal Saturday, she would have washed their underclothes, so the family could present themselves clean on the Sabbath. But this was Midsummer Festival, and the good Lord, she expected, would understand. Hurriedly, she set out cheese and bread for William and Robin's breakfast. She nursed and changed Maddie. When her husband and son left to help the townsmen prepare for the bonfire, she took up her baskets and went, once again, across the fields to gather berries for the day's pie making.

Rosemarie had not been gathering long when the wind came up and assailed her nose with that same rotten stench. But this time it was much stronger. Crows dived one after another into the brambles. Whatever it was that had died there, it must have been big enough that the birds could not finish it off yesterday. Perhaps it was a fox. She picked as rapidly as she could, afraid that the foul-smelling air might carry contagion.

That evening, when the sun began its long drop to the horizon, Rosemarie stood proudly behind her table of perfectly baked little pies. She kept an eye on the cashbox, and an ear alert for any cries from Maddie in her cradle-box behind her mother. Apparently, the crowd's happy laughter and chatter soothed the infant, and she slept soundly. Joanna looked after Robin and her own twin boys. Her tall twins could wander at will, but they had to keep Robin with them and "present themselves and bow before 'the queen'," their mother, whenever she whistled. Big Joanna could whistle the hair off a dog. Her management system was a game the boys enjoyed thoroughly.

In the center of the town square, men piled bonfire wood as high as a small house. Children scurried everywhere, and the air was charged with anticipation. Grownups lined the square, waiting.

Gloriously resounding peals rang from the church bell. The fair's official festivities were to begin. An acolyte, bearing the cross, descended the church steps, followed by the old priest and two altar boys. After them, the flower-blanketed holy statue of Saint John tottered in stately progress through the town, jiggling first left, then right, with the footsteps of the men who carried it, townsmen selected for the honor both because of their piety and because of their strength. They circled partway around the green, until they reached the point where the millstream flowed into town. Here, the monastery's abbot and a small delegation of his black-robed monks joined the procession. When they arrived at the point where the road from the manor house entered the green, two heralds dressed in burgundy and gold stepped into the road. They raised long trumpets, hung with the burgundy and gold banners depicting the arms of Sir Rudolph. A mighty fanfare sounded forth across the green. The knight and his retinue joined the procession.

For many, this annual pageantry of their manor lord, arrayed in his full armor and mounted on his caparisoned black warhorse, was the highlight of the festival. Directly following Sir Rudolph in the procession, and ahead of his family and retainers, rode the village's other knight. William rode, mounted on a gentle white mare, and dressed for the occasion in a velvet doublet of black and white vertical stripes. On his head was a splendid, black-plumed, gray, fox-fur hat. Charcoal, rubbed into its fur, simulated tabby stripes. Black hose and boots covered his legs and feet. In his arms, William carried Sir Goblin, Knight of the Smithy. For the past five years, townspeople and manor-dwellers alike had thus honored the cat that had saved the life of their overlord, Baron von Schwartzfeld, and been knighted for his bravery.

Three.

THE PROCESSION CIRCLED the green and stopped before the
tavern. Here, Sir Goblin was presented, as he was every year, with
a large pan of Joanna's tasty hare and chicken broth stew. Snow Beauty
and as many white cats with gray-striped tails as could fit around the dish
joined him. When the cats finished their banquet and began washing
their paws and ears, townsmen put a torch to the pile of wood, and the
bonfire crackled into rosy life. Joanna served a round of ale. Rosemarie
sold all the rest of her pies. She had been so very successful. She could
hardly believe the number of coins that jingled in her purse.

Between customers, Joanna whispered gossip to Rosemarie. "Rumor
has it that the Genoese merchant is buying cats to take to his city's
sailors," she whispered, as that same portly man walked away from their
table with a flagon of ale and a raspberry pie.

When the revelry was at its loudest, the jugglers drove their gaudy
wagon in among the dancers, drinkers, and singers. The plaintive eastern
melody of their flute called the merry crowd, as if charmed, over to their
wagon. The entertainers tumbled, cartwheeled, danced, and balanced
along a narrow, raised beam. When they paused for breath at the end of
the act, one juggler passed around his red and green hat. The spectators
tossed in coins. Next, the three showmen juggled balls, jugs, pots, and
big, square, gaudily painted, empty boxes—sometimes bouncing them
off their heads—and never dropped a one. The hat passed again, and
more coins jingled in.

Robin stood squeezed between the skirts of Joanna and Rosemarie.
He was holding Goblin and staring saucer-eyed with enchantment. Now,
one of the tumblers played sensuous tunes on the flute, twisting and
squirming like a snake, while another danced a jig atop a large spinning

leather ball and—at the same time—juggled three flaming torches. He ended his performance by dousing the flames in his mouth. The crowd squealed with delight and mock horror. This was, surely, the grand, new ending to the show, they thought. But Rosemarie wondered what had become of the boy in the bear costume, who had danced to that tune last year while tied to the end of a rope, like an animal.

Then, one of the tumblers moved up against the crowd. He turned his back toward them and stretched out his arms, as if holding them back. He was so near to her, Rosemarie could see the beads of perspiration glistening on his neck and smell his sweat. Another was standing at the back of their wagon, loading in their paraphernalia. The third tumbler began rolling like a wheel in a spectacular circle of apparently unending cartwheels.

Finally, the juggler cartwheeled off to the edge of the green and came running back with a flaming stick. He planted it in the ground in the center of the performance area and backflipped onto the wagon seat, where he took a fast jerk of a bow before the wondering crowd. With a sudden flash, the flaming stick roared and shot into the sky, spilling streaks of red and gold. It banged like thunder. The crowd screamed in panic, running every which way. The guarding tumbler jumped into the back of the wagon. The driver cracked the whip over the mule's head, and the gaudy vehicle rolled out of town.

None of these people had seen fireworks, and only some had heard of the new, explosive black powder. Sir Rudolph sent someone to toll the church bell for order and rode into the center of the crowd.

Still in his armor, he drew his sword and held it aloft, a symbol of law and authority. With his helmet tucked under his left arm, Sir Rudolph waved the great sword so it flashed in the firelight, and shouted for calm. His prancing horse turned in a tight circle amid the panicked people, and a hesitant calm soon settled over the crowd.

Sir Rudolph began to speak to the townspeople. The knight explained about the explosive powder from the Far East, and its possible uses in war. He had heard it could throw iron balls so hard that they could pierce armor and bring down castle walls. He hoped this was not true. But still, its very dangerousness should bring people to their senses. Perhaps, he hoped, people will learn to settle problems peacefully, without warring.

A nervous quiet settled over the festival crowd as they wondered what the knight's words might mean. They began to drift among the vendors, but no one felt like dancing. Some revelers refilled their ale tankards.

It was well past Robin's bedtime and Rosemarie, her pies sold out, wanted to get her son to bed. He was not beside her. He was not near her stall. Joanna joined the search. She could not find him in the tavern, where her boys had run, and she could not see him in the crowd. The big woman whistled but no Robin presented himself. He was not in the church or at home.

Maddie still lay in her cradle box, awake now, wailing at all the confusion. Rosemarie scooped her up and kissed and hugged her close. Chilly terror spilled over her shoulders and ran like ice water down her back. Rosemarie began screaming for Robin, running from house to house with the baby in her arms. Guilt clutched at her mother's heart as she remembered how she had turned away from her child when the fiery stick roared into the air, ducking her head and covering her ears in terror. *I thought of myself and not him*, was her tortured thought. In response to her cries, women ran to search their own houses. Rain barrels were overturned, lofts climbed into, a torch shone over the wells. All to no avail. Men combed the workshops and barns. No one could find Robin.

Frustrated, the searchers began to drift back to where the knight sat on his horse, directing his small band of men in the search. Lady Alfreda had ridden back to the manor house and was even now ordering her maids to search the grounds for the boy. Sir Rudolph had sent some of his people up to search his orchards. What more could the man do? What could anyone do?

Men and women gathered around William and Rosemarie, trying without success to console them. Joanna lifted Maddie from her mother's arms, as Rosemarie had been holding the tiny girl a very long time, and cooed to and patted the frightened infant. As soon as her arms were empty, Rosemarie collapsed against the plump, motherly shoulder of Anna, and gave in to a flood of tears and long, loud, body-wracking wails. After a time, she would weary and her sobbing would quiet into raspy in-suckings of breath, gasping groans that softened into moaning sobs. Again, she would feel the full fury of her pain and begin a new round of terrified wailing and screaming. Anna held her close, as if to smother the pain with her love, but she could not comfort her.

William came over and stood beside his wife, motionless, staring at the ground. Again and again his hands clenched into fists and his nails dug into his palms. His face was contorted into a fearful grimace, his lips pressed together hard; even his cheeks seemed to have sunk in his struggle to control his fear. The muscles above his cheekbones tightened, narrowing his eyes to slits, his eyelids becoming like levees to hold back the tears. The cooper stood beside him, shifting his weight from foot to foot. Two or three times, he tried putting his arm around the young blacksmith's shoulders. He didn't know what else to do. From time to time, the young man was seen to turn his head from side to side and whisper, "No, no, no!"

At just about this time, one of the young joiners, new to the town and not married—and therefore, perhaps not so consumed by the tragedy of the missing boy—began watching a movement in the field beyond. The motion took form as he watched; it was a small cat slinking in from the fields. As the animal came into the torchlight, people could see that it was a black cat and that it was carrying something in its mouth. Some of Goblin's extended family—but not Goblin, who was nowhere in sight—surrounded the little cat and hissed him to a halt. It was Tatters. The joiner, knowing only that William was the same man who had just hours before paraded an honored cat in the great procession, tapped the smith's forearm with his knuckles and pointed silently to the circle of cats.

The man's touch on his arm startled William, and then he too saw the ring of cats. He could never explain it afterward, but in his maddened grief, he plunged his arm into that circle of cats and grabbed up the black cat by the scruff of his dirty neck. Squirming to be free, the cat let something fall from its mouth. The same joiner picked it up, looked at it, cried out, and handed it quickly up to Sir Rudolph. Then, holding one arm tight around his churning stomach, the joiner covered his mouth with his free hand and dashed to the back of the crowd, trying not to throw up his supper.

Sir Rudolph looked at the object placed in his hand. He made a horrible face. Swallowing hard, he called over his bailiff. "Keep this safe, Gerhard."

Although the knight had not said what the object placed in his hand was, not wishing to spread panic, the joiner did tell people. And William had seen it. It was a thumb severed from a young hand. Within minutes, the people standing closest to Sir Rudolph were shouting in horror and rage. Then came cries for revenge.

Rosemarie fell into William's arms. He carried her home. Behind them, a call went up for torches. Angry men started for the fields that Tatters had come from. As he reached their house, William looked back and saw Sir Rudolph and his men draw their swords. The threat of the blades quickly calmed the would-be mob's boiling temper.

"We cannot search at night," Sir Rudolph called out. "The torches would set the woods afire. We will organize search parties at day's break.

Mayhap the boy has fallen asleep somewhere, and will reappear in the morning." By not mentioning aloud the severed thumb, Sir Rudolph had hoped to calm people into thinking they were still dealing only with a missing child and not a murder. "I declare this festival closed."

Buckets of water and shovelfuls of dirt cooled the bonfire down to steaming coals, and the saddened townsfolk returned home. They knew, anxious as they were, that what Sir Rudolph said was sensible. Village children simply knew better than to wander off into the forest where bears, boars, and dragons lived.

Sitting on the edge of their bed, William slipped his arm around his quaking wife and offered ale to her lips. She was shaking too hard to drink more than a sip or two. He then swallowed several gulps himself.

"Rosemarie, Rosemarie, listen to me. That was not Robin's thumb. It was too large and had a long dirty nail. Now let's lie down and get some rest. Tomorrow's sun will reveal all. See, here comes your old comforter." Snow Beauty had crept up onto the bed and laid her chin on Rosemarie's lap.

Man and wife lay down to rest; tears ran silently down their cheeks. The girl's fingers curled into the cat's white fur. Neither slept. At the darkest hour of the night, they heard an owl. Its sad "hoot-hoot, hoot-hoot," seemed to call, "Robin, Robin." The mother and father sat up, put their arms around each other, their head on each other's shoulders, and wept.

Four.

SNORTING HORSES AND men's gruff commands greeted Rosemarie in the morning. Maddie was crying softly. Kissing her and holding her close to her heart, Rosemarie began to nurse one child while the tears streamed down her cheeks for the other. William was already out of the house. Suddenly, she jumped up and went outside, carrying a still-hungry Maddie. She knew she had to talk to William. He was with the search volunteers, who had gathered outside their door. She told them all about the stench in the bramble bushes across the field from which Tatters had come the night before. She reminded William that they had seen the sad little bear-boy the day the wagon first arrived, but strangely, he had not appeared during their performance.

Some of the searchers immediately ran for the bramble patch that lay beyond the fallow field, tripping at times in old furrows overgrown with weeds. Wiser heads notified Sir Rudolph. If murder had been done, he was the one to impose justice.

Within an hour, they were all staring down at a blanket-wrapped bundle, the oddly sweet but rotting smell of which sickened everyone. The knight, sitting high on his horse, ordered the bundle opened. The men who had so quickly run across the field were now hesitant because of the stench. But when Sir Rudolph threatened to jump down from his horse and do it himself, they quickly pulled the folds apart, revealing the dog-chewed, crow- and vulture-ripped body of a boy about ten years old. Flies had settled where his eyes had been, and he was already more identifiable by his rags and shoes than his body. But Rosemarie and William could see that he was the bear-boy. The long, clean slit in his chest that could not have been made by animals proved that he had indeed been murdered.

Catching the murderers, whoever they might be, was now Sir Rudolph's first priority. Still, Robin had to be found; each hour wasted made it more certain that the boy had come to harm. The knight divided the searchers into teams and was about to send William with the group going to the mill and its dangerous millrace, when someone noticed a weary, bedraggled Goblin shuffling down the path from the mill. He was carrying something brown. Fearful now of what *this* cat carried, William ran up to Goblin, and Sir Rudolph walked his horse over to where the cat stood, and dismounted. William plucked the brown, fuzzy lump from his mouth. It was fur.

"Bear fur," said Sir Rudolph, "and well tanned."

Goblin stood meowing and switching his tail from side to side as if in a temper. Having gotten the men's attention, Goblin started back down the path, stopped, and looked back over his shoulder. He walked back to the men, switched his tail some more, and started down the path again.

"'Twould seem he wants us to follow him," said Sir Rudolph, and he mounted his horse. "This is one cat I'm inclined to let lead."

He rode toward Goblin, who then moved further on. But after a few yards, the Knight stopped and dismounted. Staring at some mud in the road where a horse had urinated, he waved his men over.

"What do you think? If I am not mistaken these are wagon tracks." The knight decided to take his bailiff and a pikeman to follow the cat's lead. He ordered William, who would have preferred to search for his son, to follow along on Nob with a basket strapped to the saddle, in which Sir Goblin would ride. They would follow the wagon tracks and then see what the cat had in mind.

As soon as Nob was saddled, Sir Rudolph, Gerhard, and the pikeman—followed by William and Sir Goblin—set off at a brisk trot up the hill path in search of the tumblers. Soon, weeds and grass slowed the horses to a walk. Goblin bounced along in his basket. His front feet hung over the edge. He watched everything with great intensity. His eyes were dilated with excitement. From time to time the cat's throat would rumble with a low growl, as if he thought perhaps the horses were too slow.

They had been riding in this manner for over three miles, still seeing the occasional sign of wagon tracks, when they heard an animal snort and a man curse. The four horsemen halted and listened silently for a minute. Goblin began to yowl and hiss. Not wanting him to give their presence away, William whispered into Sir Goblin's ears, begging him to be quiet. Trying to calm him, the smith scratched the feline knight under his furry chin. For his efforts, the big cat made as to bite William, clamping his mouth around the blacksmith's hand and holding it in a toothy grip, but he did not sink his teeth into Will's flesh.

They all knew exactly what was happening: someone, one of the tumblers perhaps, was trying to back his stubborn mule between the shafts of a wagon.

The foursome urged their horses forward and came into sight of the entertainers, just as they were whipping their mule forward.

"Halt! I am Rudolph of Johannesmarkt!"

The black charger raced forward. Sir Rudolph's sword flashed in the sun.

The driver panicked and lashed his whip hard across the mule's back. The beast screeched, whinnying and braying his anger. It lifted its forelegs, as if to rear, then bolted down the path. The knight's horse kept pace with the racing wagon, galloping beside the mule. They had fled but a few yards, when Sir Rudolph's blade slashed the reins and the nearside trace. The knight reached down from his horse and took hold of the frightened mule's bridle. With soothing words, he brought the mule to a halt.

"You are under arrest. Get down!" shouted Sir Rudolph to the driver.

The man didn't budge.

"Get down, I say."

Still the driver refused to move, waggling his finger before his lips, indicating he was mute.

"Search the wagon." Sir Rudolph's men dismounted.

Goblin leaped from his basket and ran into the woods.

The pikeman broke the latch on the door at the wagon's back. After considerable scuffling, he and Gerhard dragged out the two other tumblers. The pikeman rammed the butt of his weapon into the stomach of one tumbler. As the man doubled over in pain, the pikeman hit him on the head, and he lay still. But the other twisted from Gerhard's grasp.

Laughing at the non-acrobatic bailiff, he sang out as he kept avoiding the men's grasps, "I twist and twine, slither and slime. I rhyme!" He began turning cartwheels down the road.

At a nod from Sir Rudolph, William took hold of the mule, and the knight urged his horse after the spinning tumbler. He caught up with him in a trice. Brandishing his sword, the knight pinned the tumbler against a tree. Leaning down from his horse, the knight's full weight pressed his sword arm against the wiry tumbler's throat. The sword's heavy pommel pressed hard against the great vein in the evil man's neck. The tumbler choked for air; his eyes bulged in panic, but he could not wriggle free. The knight's men bound his hands and feet.

"Would have been easier to run him through," complained Gerhard.

"Yes, but he will have his justice," answered Sir Rudolph.

The pikeman, meanwhile, was searching the wagon. "No bearskin, milord, but I found this." He held up a long bloody dagger. "They are the killers. One of them, at least."

"The others are accomplices. They shall all hang."

At that moment, Goblin jumped out of the forest, carrying a great, black, squawking, flapping starling in his mouth. In a flash, the cat leapt to the top of the front wagon wheel, then to the driver's box, and dumped his catch down the mute driver's shirt.

"Aack! Oohh! Get this thing off of me!" cried the mute. He swatted and batted at his shirt, only to scrape the bird's beak and claws deeper into his chest. In panic, he jumped to the ground. The pike again found work, and the not-so-mute driver, too, was tied up.

Goblin stepped along the driver's box, sniffing and mewing at its edges. Alert to his cat's signals, William climbed up and opened the lid of the driver's box. Inside lay Robin, curled up on his side, and wrapped in the bearskin. The little boy opened his eyes wide when the lid first went up, but then scrunched them shut against the sudden bright sunlight and turned his head toward the floor of the driver's box. His cheeks were stained with tear tracks; his eyes were red-rimmed from constant crying. There was a dirty rag drawn through his teeth and tied behind his head. This gag was soaked through with the boy's saliva. His hands and feet were tied. His knees pressed his stomach, and his bound wrists had been squeezed against his heart. Even at only five years of age, the boy had to be wedged into the box. A piece of the bearskin lay thrown over his torso.

"Robin, Robin. It's Papa. I am here to take you home. It's over." Gently, he reached his hands under Robin's head, and then his shoulders and lifted the child. The boy moaned out aloud as his cramped legs stretched out.

"Are you hurt, Robin?" asked his father. The little boy moaned and started to cry. He could not speak with the gag still in his mouth.

Sir Rudolph stood near the front wheel of the wagon, and William handed down his boy to the knight. Then he jumped to the ground.

With great tenderness, the nobleman laid the boy in the grass and shaded his eyes with one gauntlet laid across the child's forehead. William cut away the gag and thanked God his son had no broken teeth or other injury to his mouth. The knight freed the child's hands and feet and began to massage the boy's ankles. Goblin ran up and licked the tears from Robin's face and purred loudly.

Little Robin turned his face toward the big cat and a trace of a smile

Goblin licked the tears from Robin's face.

graced his lips. "Gobcat." he whispered. Then he looked at William, "Papa!"

After a few minutes, Robin was on his feet and walking around. His legs were a little shaky, but he had no real injuries.

"Papa, I'm hungry."

The rescuers all laughed with relief. Now they knew he'd be fine. The pikeman climbed into the juggler's wagon and took an apple from their larder. He cut a slice for the boy, who sucked thirstily on the tart wedge.

They unhitched the mule and tied the bound men's wrists to the animal's long rein. They could leave the wagon for the time being, but the beast must be fed. They forced their prisoners to start walking back to the town, leading the cranky mule. The mule was not cooperative; he decidedly did not want to go back to the town that had a noisy fair with a bonfire and fireworks. So the pikeman, with no little pleasure, snapped the whip over not the mule, but the wicked men's heads, frightening them into yanking the mule along. They slowly made their way back to the town.

William on Nob, with Robin straddling the saddle in front of his father and Goblin bouncing along in his basket, led the little band back to the town. As soon as they came within sight of the green, a group of women began running toward them. Rosemarie put the infant Maddie into her dear friend Anna's arms, and, hiking up her skirts, she ran toward her husband and son with an abandon not seen since her girlhood. As soon as she could make out the boy's head behind the horse's ears, she began crying out, "Robin, Robin! My boy! My baby!"

Reaching Nob, she pulled at his reins and then stretched her arms to the boy's waist. William lowered the boy into his mother's arms and swung down from the saddle. Rosemarie hugged the boy close, kissing his neck, the back of his head, his ear.

"Mama, Mama," cried the boy. Then she set him on the ground and took his face in her hands. Seeing the red marks and bruises from the gag, she began to weep afresh.

"He's going to be fine, Rosie," William assured her, as he stood behind the lad with one hand holding firmly onto the boy's shoulder, "He's going to be just fine."

William scooped up his son and, putting an arm around his wife's shoulders, led his family home. Joanna led the forgotten Nob and the mule back to the stables behind her tavern.

Goblin took a seat on top of a stack of barrels outside the cooper's shop, to watch as Sir Rudolph hustled the prisoners together into a group before the townspeople. The knight explained that they had presumably murdered their own apprentice for not being well enough to be useful, and that they definitely had kidnapped Robin—and inadvertently Sir Goblin, whom Robin had been holding—during the fireworks panic. Goblin had escaped during the night. The evil men had given little attention to the cat. They did not know he was a knight. Once again, the noble cat led William and Sir Rudolph on a rescue mission, this time saving Robin. He also assisted in the capture of the ruffians. The people cheered the cat, and brought him presents of bits of meat, cake, and fresh cream. One old man offered Goblin a swig of his ale, but the noble cat declined.

"We have just the place for them. Don't we, Sir Goblin?" Sir Rudolph bowed toward the cat who sat tall, licking cream from his chops. Goblin flicked his tail around his front feet and listened. "Next midsummer, Goblin will lead the procession. What other honor can I give him?" proclaimed the knight.

The tumblers were dragged off to the old hole beneath the manor kitchen, where Baron von Schwartzfeld had once been held prisoner, to await their unhappy fate. As they shuffled along, some of the people taunted them, spat on them, and threw rocks, sticks, and clods of earth. Knowing that they would not see these men again once they were shut in the dungeon and later tried at the Baron's castle, Sir Rudolph allowed the people a few minutes to express their rage. It was his rage, too. But he ordered them away before they drew any blood or did them any serious harm. The three entertainers would not see the light of day again until their brief trial and execution.

Early the next morning, Goblin, Snow Beauty, and Magdalene were sunning themselves on a large new barrel outside the cooper's shop. Goblin's ears suddenly whirled around toward a burbling sound. Someone was whistling a happy tune. From behind the tavern came the Genoese merchant. Mounted on a lively horse, the round, fat man presented a glorious sight, with his feathered hat and his burgundy cape fluttering from his shoulders. Two servants traveled with him. One led a packhorse; the other led a donkey pulling a small cart packed with the Genoese's delectable merchandise. From somewhere within the cart, Goblin heard soft, gentle mewing. Just as the merchant caravan passed Goblin, a little black head popped up from among the bundles. A golden eye winked in happy merriment, as if proclaiming, *Adventure, adventure lies ahead!* Goblin waved a paw in farewell to Tatters.

As he walked home, Goblin overheard Winifred saying to Anna, "Humph! I heard he gave good gold coin for a dozen cats, but I had to pay *him* to take that wretch!"

Sir Goblin and the Unicorn Hunt

One.

THE HOT SEASON was coming to an end, and the tasty season just beginning. Yellow leaves fell from the trees in a gentle rain of gold. Sir Goblin loved this time of the year almost as much as when the cold ended and it was kitten-making time. By now all the little mice and other creatures were fat and furry in preparation for the snowy time ahead. They were simply delicious.

The big cat stood up and arched his back. He stretched his forelegs out and then his hind legs, making his body look long and thin. Then, squeezing his eyes shut in pleasure and flopping onto his side, he dozed in a pool of warm sunshine. He was waiting for Snow Beauty to finish licking herself clean as she did every morning on Rosemarie and William's bed.

Suddenly, the clatter of horses' hooves filled the air. The noble cat stretched his neck long and looked over his shoulder toward the tavern across the square. A party of lords and their ladies had rattled up to the tavern door. As Sir Goblin hauled himself to his feet, Snow Beauty emerged from the house, dazzling his eyes with the brilliant purity of her white fur. Together the two curious cats strolled over to the tavern to investigate.

They saw a man dressed in a fine blue doublet, mounted on a prancing chestnut stallion. A short, dark blue cape hung from his left shoulder. On his head he wore a velvet cap, also blue. It sported an elaborately worked gold ornament pinned jauntily at one side. A short, white feather, affixed to the golden pin, fluttered in the breeze. The man sprang from his horse, tossing the horse's reins into his squire's face, and strode up to the tavern door. His spurs jangled as he walked, making noises that, to the cats' sensitive ears, were more like annoying squeals and squeaks than a musical jingle. *Quite the elegant fellow*, Sir Goblin thought.

As the nobleman pulled open the tavern door, Goblin heard him remark to his half-dozen companions and retainers, "We might as well have ourselves a short tankard of their ale while the ladies refresh themselves. 'Twould not be seemly for them to desert Lady Alfreda immediately to repair to the necessary rooms."

Three scurrying, chattering women, clutching at their long skirts and grumbling, "It's about time we stopped," followed the hunters into the tavern.

One was elegantly dressed in a fine, green wool gown with long sleeves embroidered in gold, while the other two were more simply attired and were obviously her maids.

Goblin and Snow Beauty settled their rumps on the ground and wrapped their tails around their front paws, preparing to watch the amusing strangers.

They heard a chirpy "mmrrt" as their oldest offspring, Magdalene, the priest's cat, trotted over to join them. *Who are the strangers?* mewed Magdalene to her father.

'Twould appear to be a hunting party, Sir Goblin answered, nodding toward the mule-drawn cart that stood behind the horses.

Even from where they sat, they could see the cross-barred boar spears projecting from the top of the cart. The crossbars would keep ferocious wild pigs from getting close to the hunters and turning on them.

Humans also know this is the best time for hunting, said Goblin.

As soon as the grownups had entered the building, two children popped their heads above the sides of the cart. The boy swung his leg over the back of the cart and was on the ground in a trice. A girl followed, slowed only by her skirts catching for a second on the top rail of the cart. One of the grooms rushed over and signaled for them to get back in the cart. The boy stuck his tongue out and made bubbly spitting sounds.

By my whiskers, that child can hiss! meowed Snow Beauty.

The girl paused to smooth her skirts and tuck a stray wisp of hair under her cap. When she stretched to get out the stiffness from her long ride and retied the girdle encircling her tiny waist, Sir Goblin observed the delicate curves of a young woman. Her little brother yanked on her arm and called for a game of tag, but she glared at him with womanly dignity. He yanked her cap off. She tried to slap him, but he ran. The girl ran after him. Soon the two were chasing around the cart and around and between the horses. The servants hollered and snatched at them but soon gave up trying for any discipline.

Finally, the girl had her brother by the arm. As the boy and girl grappled, the cats saw something fall from within her clothing. It hit the ground with a soft thud, making little curls of dust rise around it. Before the girl noticed she had lost anything, one of the women emerged from the inn and snarled at the youngsters. They meekly climbed into the cart. The remainder of the adults came out, and they continued the last short leg of their journey up to the manor house.

While the boy and girl were playing their game of chase, another head had poked up above the cart rail. It was light yellow-brown, the color of sand. Tufted ears perched on the top of its head like spear points. The animal pulled himself to the top of the rail and stood with four feet balanced on its edge. It was a cat. The biggest cat Sir Goblin had ever seen. With a great bound, the animal jumped from the cart. He strode over to the watching cats.

Giving the much-honored Sir Goblin nothing more than a perfunctory sniff of his nose, he meowed to Snow Beauty and Magdalene, *Hel-lo-ow, ladies!*

Snow Beauty shrank back at the affront, but Magdalene cocked her head with innocent curiosity.

I am Rodney Ratter, the great beast said proudly.

He puffed out his chest and slowly turned his head from cat to cat to cat. Sir Goblin stretched back on his forelimbs, then arched his back and walked away. Snow Beauty hesitated but a moment. Then, taking a hint from her mate, she turned and followed the knighted cat. But Magdalene's eyes met Rodney's for an intense moment. Then, she shook herself all over, as if stepping in from the rain or, in this case, maybe to break a charmer's spell.

She took one more long look at the sand-colored giant, mewed, *Er, excuse us*, and ran off after her parents.

Rodney strutted slowly back to the cart. His tail poked straight up toward the sky, and his rear swayed as he walked.

He purred under his breath, *I'll be seeing more of that young lady*.

After the strangers with their horses and carts pulled away from the tavern, Sir Goblin spotted the thing that was lying in the dirt where the cart had been. He went over to take a look. It was a brown, box-shaped object, the like of which Sir Goblin had never seen before. It seemed to be made of leather. Sir Goblin sniffed it. He discovered that it carried the scent of two humans. Deciding that the leather smelled good, Goblin tipped the object up with his paw and rubbed his chin along its long edge, thus marking it with his scent. Now all other cats would know that this book—for it was a little leather-bound book—belonged to Sir

Sir Goblin walked away.

Goblin. The feline knight began to chew on the edge of the leather cover, purring and squinting his eyes in pleasure. A shadow fell across his face.

"Eht, eht, eht," warned a human voice.

It was Paul, the little innkeeper. The man reached down and picked up the book. He dusted it off, riffled gently through the pages, and whistled softly.

"Would you look at this! They will certainly be back for this."

Goblin stood up on his hind legs to glimpse inside the book. He saw squiggly lines, sometimes in different colors, and pictures of various animals, often white horses, as Paul paged through the little book.

"I'd better keep this safe."

He slipped the book inside his shirt and returned to the inn.

Later in the afternoon another group of noblemen and ladies, this group with greyhounds, rode up to the manor house. A third party arrived the next morning. Everyone in the village knew the nobles were about to begin their annual fall hunt. Sir Rudolph would hire strong men to drive deer to the hunters. Other commoners would earn a coin or two setting up nets through the woods to keep animals in and poachers out.

All the animals in the woods belonged to Sir Rudolph, and only he and his aristocratic friends were allowed to hunt them. Sir Goblin, being both a knight and a cat, could hunt all he wanted. Who could stop a cat? However, he was interested only in game that was rabbit-sized or smaller. The noblemen sought deer, boar, bear, or possibly a unicorn, if they still existed.

In the afternoon, after Goblin gave Paul the strange book, Sir Goblin, Snow Beauty, and Magdalene went on a short hunting trip of their own. Hunting was not a sport for them as it was for Sir Rudolph and his friends. These cats often had to find their own meat, because their people, being poor, ordinary folks, ate mostly vegetables. The three scampered down the north road and hid in a hollow where they had once met a huge white boar. Soon they heard the rustle of leaves. All three cats pounced. Goblin felled a large rabbit by the shoulders, and Magdalene sunk her claws into its hips. Snow Beauty, never a good hunter, found her mouth full of white, cottony tail. The feline knight made short work of the beast, and the three were soon dining on tasty meat.

The day after Rodney Ratter had sashayed across the town square, and after the last party of nobles had arrived in town, a frisky white pony galloped up to the blacksmith shop. She would have pranced straight inside were it not for a panting, sweating youth who somehow still held onto her lead.

He grabbed hold of the shop's doorjamb and, digging in his heels, shouted, "Whoa! Snowball!"

The youth was maybe fifteen years of age; his chin sprouted manly fuzz, and a soft line of down covered his upper lip. The youngster had lush, curly eyelashes and tumbles of dark golden curls. All the maids in the village would have been in love with him were it not for his gloomy disposition. He was Young Gerhard, the bailiff's oldest son, and stood to inherit his father's very comfortable position at the manor, yet he seemed sour on life. As he calmed the pony, he told William, with something of a sneer, that the animal was to have its hooves trimmed and shoes refitted to be in the finest condition. Tomorrow the little princess would ride her in the hunt.

"Little Princess?" William gave a questioning look.

"You would think. The way her parents both indulge her and guard her." The youthful Gerhard frowned and shook his head. "Actually she is Gisela, the daughter of Lady Clara and Sir Gregory, Lady Alfreda's brother. They are all here for the hunt."

"I thought as much. I'll get right to the little filly."

"I'll be back in a couple of hours. Father has given me a number of errands. And I have a little mission."

At this point, the gloomy youth's lips quivered into what was almost a smile. He strode out of the blacksmith shop, jingling some coins up and down in one hand, and headed for the tavern across the square.

The sun was beginning to drop behind the church tower when young Gerhard, who was usually called Young-Ger or just Younger, returned to William's shop. The farrier turned from his forge.

"She didn't need much work. Heavens! She is a kicky, nippy one. But now she has shoes worthy of a princess, to dance all night."

When he faced Gerhard he was surprised to see that the young man was grinning from ear to ear. He seemed to be bursting to tell someone something.

"Would you look at this!" he all but shouted. He held up the small leather-bound book. Its cover was elaborately tooled and its pages edged in gold. As the bailiff's son fanned open the pages, William saw writing with the capital letters brilliantly illuminated in red, blue, and gold. Throughout the little book were pictures of various animals and unicorns in many different poses. No one needed to tell the two men that a handmade book like this one cost a small fortune.

"Her little ladyship," he meant Gisela, "came running up to me just as Father ordered me to the village. All excited, worried, full of whispers, she was, begging me to tell no one in the house what she wanted me to do. She had lost this book, and it meant the world to her. She gave me all her money and promised me more if I would get it back for her."

"How did you get it?"

"That was easy. She dropped it outside the inn, and Paul had it in safekeeping. He knew it was of value and was eager to have it back where it belonged before anyone made accusations."

"No one would ever accuse Paul of theft."

"I wouldn't be surprised at anything that father of hers does. He is a mean-looking, angry one," young Gerhard replied. "But most interesting is this." He pointed to a passage written just inside the front cover in writing different from that used to make the book. "I can make out that that is a G, and here at the bottom is a J. I can't read enough to make out what is said, but, when young people don't write their names and just use first letters instead, it has to be something kissy-kissy."

"Don't think about it, young man. It is none of our affair." William was embarrassed by this talk. It sounded like women's gossip to him. He wanted none of it.

"Do you have money left to pay for the horseshoes?" the farrier asked, trying to get back to business.

"Oh, yes, Paul would take nothing. I'll give Gisela her money back."

William knew he would. The boy was as honest as the day was long.

William, Rosemarie, and their two children, Maddie and Robin, who were five and eight respectively, were sitting around their table eating their evening meal of lentils with stewed leeks, bread, and cheese, when someone knocked on the door. William got up to receive the visitor. It was young Gerhard.

"I forgot something important," said the young man.

"Well, if you had kept your mind on your work and not romantic imaginings and gossip—"

From the corner of his eye, William saw his wife sit up straight on her stool, all ears, and immediately regretted his words.

"What is it?"

"I was supposed to tell you, and give you, this," he handed the farrier a folded piece of paper, "Lady Alfreda wants you to come up with your cat on the afternoon of the Lord's Day. She says she also wrote it in this note to make it official."

"What's happened?"

William at first thought Sir Goblin was needed because of some infringement of justice.

"Nothing really. Her brother, Sir Gregory, owns a huge cat that he thinks is cleverer than yours. They plan some sort of tournament between cats."

"I don't think Goblin would be . . ."

"It is her command," the youth replied.

William needed no reminder that the village was part of Sir Rudolph's fief. In exchange for his guardianship, they must do as he or his lady wished. Johannesmarkt was fortunate in that Rudolph was a kindly lord, making few demands and keeping taxes low.

"We will be there."

"Rosemarie is invited." Gerhard bade them goodnight and loped off to his father's house.

Will had just barely shut the door when Rosemarie asked, "What romantic imaginings?"

There was no way not to tell her everything Gerhard had said.

"That boy hates farm work. His mother, God rest her soul, always said that. A little gossip or intrigue sharpens his mind."

"He stands to inherit his father's position, and a very comfortable living it is, too. He'll soon have others to do the dull chores."

But William knew his wife was right. The bailiff's son took no joy in his father's work. "It's none of our affair. I have work to do in the shop."

Two.

ROSEMARIE ALWAYS TRIED to make Sunday dinner special. This time, she had added lentils and carrots to the meal and set a vase of red clover and lady's lace on the table, taking pleasure in the way the straggly clover seemed to twist and entwine its pink blossoms among the large white flower heads. William ate quickly, not commenting on his wife's special efforts. His mind was on whatever it was that Lady Alfreda wanted with his cat.

He scooped up Sir Goblin and began the hike up to the manor house.

"I'll be right behind you," called Rosemarie. "I just have to clean things up."

"Don't be too long about it," answered her husband as the door banged shut behind him.

He was always nervous about meeting with the highborn, never sure if his humble blacksmith manners were correct.

As soon as he was gone, Rosemarie untied her apron, and, leaving all the dinner things on the table, she began to fuss with her clothes.

William was trudging up the steepest part of the hill when, suddenly, Goblin stiffened then wriggled and slipped from the smith's arms as if he were greased. The cat crouched in the road, still as stone but for his switching tail. A twittering bird went suddenly silent. A minute passed. Then two. William grew impatient.

"Come on, cat. Let's go."

Goblin slunk, low on his belly, one slow step at a time, toward the bird. William snatched up his cat. The startled bird bobbed its tail and flew off.

"It's just an ordinary sparrow, you silly beast," muttered the farrier, heaving the big cat onto his shoulder.

That was when he saw a beautiful woman coming up the hill. For an instant he did not recognize his own wife. Rosemarie wore her newest gown. A clean, white apron sparkled in the sunlight, setting off her gown's soft russets to an advantage any lady might envy. She had arranged her cap to reveal a little more of her chestnut hair than usual. Behind her scurried Snow Beauty. Together the four continued up the hill to the manor house.

As they approached the great house, William held Goblin snugly against his chest. His wife scooped up her white cat. The smith wanted no mysterious disappearances in search of mice when they were to be presented before the knight and his lady. At the bottom of the stone steps leading to a massive oaken door, William nervously shifted Goblin to his left shoulder and stood looking around. There was no one in sight, no pages, no grooms, no one. Should he just go in, unannounced? He did not know what to do. It was quiet—too quiet. No wind whispered, and no birds sang. William felt the hairs on the back of his neck prickle. Nervous, Rosemarie wanted to go back to their house, and William was about to lead her home when he heard shuffling footsteps. Younger came around the corner of the house, carrying a basket of cabbages.

"Good day, William, Rosemarie, and cats." A ghost of a smile floated over the somber youth's lips. "You have come up anyway, I see." He stared at William and then at Rosemarie as if debating what more to say.

"Do we just go in or what?" William asked.

"Oh, no one's told you anything. Let's see what they want you to do."

Younger set down his basket, took the steps two at a time and tugged open the massive door. William, Rosemarie, and their cats followed. Inside the great hall, all was in disarray. Pages were still clearing the tables of their dishes and cloths left from the noon meal. Serving women were sweeping the floor. In a far corner Younger's father stood talking quietly with the young priest who served as the lord and lady's clerk, accountant, and chaplain. At the other end of the room, behind the center table that was covered with a linen cloth and on which silver *nefs* and serving bowls still sat, Sir Rudolph was hunched over, alone on his throne-like chair. The knight rested his chin in his hand with his elbow propped on the arm of his chair. Slowly, almost imperceptibly, he shook his head from side to side. No one paid any attention to William and Rosemarie or their cats.

"There's been a mishap," said Younger. "I'll ask my father what you are to do."

He took a step or two toward the bailiff and priest.

"No! No. That cannot be!" The bailiff exclaimed.

"I am afraid it is true. I saw it with my own eyes. The women washing him saw it, too. There can be no other explanation." In his effort to convince the bailiff, the cleric had raised his voice loud enough to be heard across the hall.

A boot scraped. With a heavy sigh, the lord of the manor pushed himself from his chair and started down to where his bailiff stood. "Further news? I have questioned everyone about this accident."

"It was no accident," blurted the priest.

Gerhard Senior pushed the undiplomatic priest aside with a rough shove to the shoulder, suggesting strongly to the young man that he had caused enough trouble for the day.

"My lord . . ." the bailiff began.

The chapel door flew open, and a tall woman dressed in black emerged. It was Lady Alfreda. Only a lace snood, not an elaborate headdress, covered her glorious red hair.

She held a girl of about twelve or thirteen close to her side, patting the girl's arm and shoulder as they slowly walked out of the chapel. The girl was crying softly, leaning her head against the older woman's shoulder. Just then, footsteps tapped on the great stairs leading down into the hall from the private quarters above. The smith and his wife stared in amazement at the splendidly dressed couple descending the stairs. She wore a gown of green and gold and he, a doublet of dark blue velvet.

Just as they stepped out on the floor, the woman, seeing her daughter, uttered a screech, "Gisela! What is this? I gave you orders not to go into the chapel! You are not to have anything to do with this . . . this person!"

Gisela's barely controlled tears broke into wails that echoed off the walls of the hall. Rivers of tears streamed down the girl's tender cheeks, already red from crying. "Mother, Mother, but I loved him," she buried her face into her aunt's shoulder.

"Love! Nonsense!" The green-garbed Lady Clara hurried across the hall and snatched her daughter away by the shoulders.

"The poor girl," cried Alfreda.

"You stay out of this."

Lady Clara hustled Gisela up the stairs to the solar, leaving her husband, Sir Rudolph, Lady Alfreda, the bailiff, the priest, the commoners with their cats, pages, and serving girls all standing around, staring at the door swinging shut at the top of the stairs.

"Meow-ow-er!"

A great, sandy colored monster of a cat ran into the hall and up to Goblin and Snow Beauty, who were still being held tightly by their humans. Now Snow Beauty wriggled loose and dropped to the floor. She arched her back and spat in Rodney Ratter's face. Sir Goblin slipped free from William's arms. Rodney stepped up to Snow Beauty and rubbed his cheek against her face as if she had purred a love song to him. Again she hissed and backed away. Sir Goblin pounced on Rodney's back. The two cats tumbled, tussled, and growled. Then, Rodney rolled on top of Sir Goblin, pressing the full weight of his fat body down on the knighted cat and seeming to get the best of him.

Laughing and stabbing his finger at the animals on the floor, Sir Gregory exclaimed so loud that everyone turned around, "Look! Look! Ha, ha! Seems we will have our tournament of cats after all."

But, a moment later, Goblin, a well-muscled hunter, flipped onto his side and tossed Rodney. Then, quicker than lightning, the feline knight jumped on Rodney Ratter. He sat down hard on Sir Gregory's pampered pet. When Goblin pulled a mouthful of fur from his neck, Rodney whimpered, and the fight was done. Sir Goblin stood victorious with his front paws firmly planted on the monstrous cat's shoulders.

"Here, kitty. Let's take you up to your mama."

Pink-faced, Sir Gregory picked up his defeated cat and carried him up the stairs. Rodney the Ratter was destined to endure the sour company of Sir Gregory's angry wife and mourning daughter.

While the two cats were pawing and clawing at each other, Lady Alfreda, Sir Rudolph, and their bailiff whispered together. The bailiff told the nobleman and his lady about the priest's opinion that the young huntsman had not met with an unfortunate accident but had been murdered. The knight looked hard into his wife's eyes. William saw the Lady Alfreda swallow hard, but her back stiffened with resolve. The nobleman raised an eyebrow, and his wife nodded almost imperceptibly. Long married, they understood each other with just a look.

"Bring your cat," said Sir Rudolph, turning on his heel to enter the chapel.

Rosemarie moaned.

"By your leave, my lord. My wife is a most sensitive creature. With your permission . . . ," William begged.

"Oh, certainly," answered the knight when he saw how Rosemarie had gone almost as white as Snow Beauty at the thought of viewing the corpse.

He nodded to his bailiff.

The bailiff turned to Younger and said, "Escort Mistress Smith and her cat home, son."

Younger took Snow Beauty into his arms, murmuring, "Nice kitty, pretty kitty," as he stroked her shoulders and rubbed her ears. Snow pressed her head against his chest and purred.

Rosemarie dipped a curtsey to the men and to Lady Alfreda.

"Good day to you, my lords, my lady."

As they left the hall, William heard his wife say, "She likes you."

"Cats always do. I like them," responded Younger.

The body of a young man lay stretched out on boards supported by trestles. A sheet covered the corpse. Women were still sewing the shroud for his burial. The priest flicked back the sheet from the dead man's head, shutting his eyes and turning his face away as he did so.

"I have not buried many dead," whispered the young priest; he had, in fact, not yet conducted any funerals.

The corpse had soft brown chin-length hair. The women who washed the body had closed his eyes. Only the slightest fringe of downy hair graced his lip. He had been very young. His face had a greenish cast in death, which it never had in life. Sir Rudolph grasped the corpse's shoulder and turned him over enough to see the underside of his head. His back was purplish where gravity had sent his no-longer-flowing blood to finally rest. Clots of blood still clung to the hair on the back of his head. "Yes, I see. You're right. He has been hit on the head. A cracking blow. Unless he fell from a tree, not likely to be an accident."

Sir Rudolph dropped the man's body back down to the table. He stepped back and took a couple of deep breaths. The weather was not warm, but neither was it cold, and there already was a smell. Lifting the corpse had released more odor of rot. Quickly now, the knight stepped up again to the bier and flung the sheet further back to observe the chest wound that his brother-in-law had thought the result of a hunting accident. The priest, however, had said the women cleaned two wounds and that it could not have been an accident.

The knight looked again. He saw a gaping hole about four inches wide just below the breastbone and another, longer vertical slit above the navel. The bailiff was standing behind him and also saw the fatal punctures.

William closed his eyes and begged his stomach, "Oh, please, do not be sick."

Sir Goblin walked around the bier, sniffing. He jumped upon the bier at the corpse's feet, then immediately jumped down and ran to wait at the chapel door. His good cat sense told him to avoid putrefaction—always.

Sir Rudolph flicked the sheet over the body, covering it. Just then, they heard a heavy thud and, turning around, saw Lady Alfreda lying on the floor. She had fainted.

William and Goblin were walking down to the village, Goblin content to amble close at William's side. They had not yet reached the bailiff's house, which stood along the road to the village, when they heard footsteps running after them.

"William!" commanded a gruff voice, "Her Ladyship . . ."

"Is Lady Alfreda not well?"

"She has recovered. It was just the stink of the corpse," said the bailiff.

"She wants you and that Sir Pussycat there," he pointed down at Sir Goblin, who was sitting comfortably on his haunches and licking the tip of his tail, "to look into this matter of a possible murder. You know, she truly believes in the powers of that cat."

William was not at all sure that Sir Goblin would interest himself in a stranger's murder, but he was in no position to argue with Lady Alfreda, so he simply bowed and said, "Yes, my lord."

Gerhard had business in the village, so the two men walked together. By the time William was home, he had heard all about the hunt. He had orders to return to the manor the next afternoon after the funeral.

"I hope the horses keep their shoes on," was Rosemarie's comment when she heard that her husband and his cat would be investigating a murder and that he would not be spending much time at his work.

She poured herself and her husband a stein of beer and settled firmly on her stool with her elbows on the table and her hands tucked under her chin. She was ready to hear all about what had happened in the chapel.

"As you know," began Will, "the bailiff is not much of a talker. But it seems several noble families had gathered for a great hunt. They were after both deer and boar. And possibly a unicorn."

"Yes, I know. About the unicorn."

"You do?"

"Young Ger walked me home, remember. He had a lot to say. I'll tell you after you tell me."

William shrugged. He was not sure he really wanted to hear any of Younger's jibber jabber. Trying to organize his thoughts, he drank a little beer and then wiped his mouth with his sleeve. Rosemarie scowled at him. She thought he was acting like a pig, but he ignored her and began his story. "It was like this. The young man who died was called Josef. He was a penniless orphan whom Sir Gregory took into his service as an act of charity. The boy's father had been Gregory's armorer. He died last winter of some spewing flux."

Rosemarie shuddered at the very thought of someone throwing up and having diarrhea so much that he died.

"Josef was one of the men sent to net off an area to keep poachers out and animals in," William continued. "Then, on the first day of the hunt, he and his best friend Franz were sent to drive deer toward the hunters. The lords succeeded in killing maybe three deer and thought it a satisfactory day.

"It was on the second day of the hunt that odd things happened. The weather was pleasant, and the women planned a midday feast to be held outdoors in the woods some distance from the manor. There was some fuss about seeing a unicorn, and Gisela insisted she and the hunters go after it. It was not until they were all returning to the manor that they missed Josef. And it was not until the next morning that they found him."

"And so Lady Alfreda wants you and Goblin to go up there tomorrow and find the murderer sitting around on a rock just waiting to be caught."

"Yes, something like that. She is most anxious to see justice done. She seems to feel it would be a benefit to her niece."

"What's a benefit, Mama?" a little voice piped up. Maddie was standing next to her mother, her eyes wide with curiosity from all this grownup talk.

"Oh, Maddie! Here," her mother broke the remains of her bread trencher into small pieces, "Go out back and feed the chickens. It will benefit the hens. A benefit is a good thing."

The little girl pulled up the hem of her skirt, making a bag at the front of her dress, and scooped in the crumbs.

She skipped out the back way, calling, "Here chickie, chickie."

"We must be careful what we say in front of the children. Where is Robin, by the way?"

"Sweeping the shop. I hope. Keeping up with those children is a task better suited for a racehorse than a blacksmith," William complained, but he smiled as he thought of his energetic children. "Your turn, Rosie."

"'Twas quite a tale that Young Ger had." Rosemarie brushed trencher crumbs from her apron and settled down on her stool, leaning on the table. "Younger, it seems, was bringing water to the returning hunters' horses at noontime when he sees something he wasn't meant to see." Rosemarie paused to see the effect of her words on Will and took a sip of her beer. "What's-its-name, Snowball, Gisela's white pony, is standing among the horses. Josef—Gisela's father's servant, mind you—is at the pony's head, holding its lead. And right next to him, standing very close, is Gisela. Younger swears she had just kissed Josef, and her hand was still caressing his cheek. So Younger sets his buckets down with a loud clump, so they would think he had just arrived and not seen anything. "Would my lady's pony like a drink?' he asks as innocently as he could.

"Josef turns scarlet and backs away from his master's daughter. He begins rubbing the pony's forehead. 'She does have a little bump here,' he kind of sputters like it was something they were just talking about. But Gisela, acting very much the great lady, looks straight at Younger, 'Thank you, Sirrah. That will be all,' she says.

"Younger had not gone far when he hears, 'Gisela, by all that's holy! What do you think you are doing!' It's her father, Sir Gregory himself, screaming at her. 'Attend to you mother!' Then, 'You insolent puppy! If you ever . . .'

"Younger says here he ducks among the horses legs and doesn't hear the next words because a horse begins slurping up water from his bucket, making a lot of noise. But Sir Gregory's next words, that Younger says he hears, are much gentler in tone, like maybe he has a sudden, different idea. A fly begins to buzz around Younger's head. Between the buzzing and his swatting, he says he could hear only a few of the knight's words. He hears, 'Remember,' and, 'I think it will amuse my daughter.'

"'Oh, yes milord, it will; it surely will, sir!' *Josef sounds surprised,* thinks Younger. *Maybe he is relieved to escape further tongue-lashing or, worse, a beating.*

"'Then be gone with you! And mind you keep your place!' says Sir Gregory.

"'Oh, yes, sir. Yes, sir, I surely shall, my lord.'

"At this point, Josef backs away, bowing and still holding the pony's lead. Younger says he then slipped away to draw more water for the horses without encountering the knight." William was about to speak when Rosemarie added, "Oh, and Younger said Gisela was holding that little leather book when he first saw them."

"She's in love with this—this peasant, then," said William.

"He was an armorer's son, you said. Possibly apprenticed. They make a good living."

"A good match for Maddie, perhaps. But not to be considered by Gisela's class."

"Of course not. I only meant that he was not completely rough."

"Mao. Maaout." Snow Beauty jumped down from the bed and walked to the door.

Rosemarie got up without thinking about it and let her out. Goblin, who had been diligently washing every bit of dirt and the nasty Rodney's smell from his ears and face, followed languorously behind Snow Beauty.

A moment later Rosemarie opened the door again, saying, "What's that horrible yowling? Sounds like cats."

William looked over her shoulder. "I do believe that's that yellow cat, Rodney, over there."

"Your ears may be weak, but there is nothing wrong with your eyes."

The blacksmith's wife could just about make out the yellow cat. It was strolling William and Rosemarie's way. Like bolts fired from a crossbow, their two cats shot across the town square to meet with Rodney. They crouched in the grass in the center of the square. Sir Goblin's tail switched. Rodney meandered over as if bored and sat down opposite them. The cats stared at each other. Time stood still, it seemed, while the two humans watched the three cats size each other up. After some minutes the door at the side of the priest's house opened. Magdalene stepped out and trotted briskly toward the group of felines. Rodney hurried up to her and butted her head with his, most affectionately, and then rubbed his shoulder against her sleek side. He turned back to caress her again.

"What is happening?" whispered Rosemarie, as if speaking louder would disturb the little play unfolding in the middle of the square.

Sir Goblin stood up. His tail pointed to the sky. He arched his back.

"Oh, dear. There's going to be another fight."

The woman burst from the doorway to rescue her cat, but her husband grabbed her arm.

"No. Wait a minute. Let them settle it themselves. Goblin can handle it."

Slowly, slowly, Rodney backed up, looking first over his left shoulder and then his right. Magdalene sat and watched. Goblin took a step forward but then, sticking his nose up haughtily, turned around and walked back home. Snow Beauty followed behind him, looking back just once at Magdalene. Her firstborn daughter tossed her head merrily and trotted toward the priest's house where she lived. Rodney followed hesitantly at a distance.

Goblin and Snow Beauty settled before the fire, busily licking and preening the smell of conflict from their fur.

"A delicate business, raising daughters, isn't it, Goblin," said the blacksmith, addressing his cat as if it were human and scratching Goblin's chin.

He thought of Maddie's growing curiosity and hoped she'd never have problems like Gisela's. He drained the last of his beer and wiped his mouth with the back of his hand.

"Is Maddie still feeding the chickens? I must get back to the shop."

"I'll check on her. It is awfully quiet out there."

The next morning, pink sunbeams were just peeking above the trees when William's snores woke Sir Goblin who was sleeping by the man's feet. The big cat gave the smith a harmless nip on his toe right through the blanket.

That's for snoring, you big oaf, he mewed.

The cat trotted quickly over to the front door where a thin band of pale light seeped under the wooden planks. He sniffed along the line of light. Liking what he smelt, he returned to the bed and crept up to where Snow Beauty slept snuggled against Rosemarie's armpit. He tapped his mate's shoulder, gently at first and then with more vigor. The lady cat sighed and turned her head upside down. He licked her under her chin, where he knew she was ticklish. She woke up with a start and a little mew.

Together they licked up the broth remaining in their bowls from the night before. Then they tried the door. It was barred. They sat down before it and yowled sourly and loudly. Rosemarie stirred and sat up.

She rubbed her eyes and moaned, "But it's still completely dark!"

No, it isn't, meowed the cats.

When the woman's eyes adjusted to the dimness, she picked out her white cat by the door.

"If you really have to go, then by all means go out. I certainly do not want any smells or messes in my house."

She fumbled her way to the door and let the cats out. Then she went back to bed.

Snow Beauty and Goblin scampered off around the corner of the little house, past the chicken house and the shed, through the garden, and into the woods.

I don't know about you, mewed Sir Goblin to his mate, *but I liked the sound of that heavy-footed squirrel I heard this morning. I suddenly have a real taste for a nice, fat squirrel.*

Whatever you like, my Purry, answered Snow as they ran. Purry was her favorite pet name for her mate.

"Where is Goblin?" Will asked his wife after he had eaten his breakfast.

"I don't know. I let Snow out early this morning, just as the sun was coming up. She seemed to have to go very badly. It was so dark that I really couldn't see much. Maybe he went out then, too."

"I hope they're back by this afternoon when I have to go up to the manor."

He brushed some crumbs from his hose; then he kissed Rosemarie on the cheek and went to work. He had just fired up the forge when a workman led a lively young carthorse to the door to receive his first pair of shoes.

The morning passed quickly. William saw nothing of Goblin. At noontime he asked Rosemarie where Goblin was.

"I don't know. I have enough to do without chasing after cats all morning."

Will searched all around the house, yard, and garden, and he even climbed into the loft, thinking the cats might be curled up on Robin's cot for a nap. He saw no cats anywhere. The blacksmith sat down to eat and listlessly spooned in his porridge. He was very worried about what the people at the manor would say if he could not produce Sir Goblin on schedule. Will had even looked in the rain barrel to see if Goblin could possibly have fallen in and drowned.

He was standing in front of his house, scratching his head, when Younger came to take him up to meet with the noble family. The usually talkative bailiff's son was in a sullen mood, remarking only that it had been a very unpleasant funeral and that Gisela took it hard.

"I think you had best come up, cat or no cat."

Three.

GOBLIN AND SNOW Beauty were having a merry morning. The fall air was clean and crisp. Fallen leaves crackled under their feet as they ran with careless joy. When deep in the forest, where they expected to find their prey, the two cats slowed to a stealthy crawl. They chased a rusty red squirrel up a tree. The little animal sped up into some high branches that bent and swayed under its weight. It leapt into the next tree and disappeared into a hole in its trunk. Goblin sat down on the ground and switched his tail in annoyance.

A favorite trick of theirs, he mewed.

The squirrel's escape only whetted his appetite. The woods were noisy with the gabby little red animals busily hunting nuts and hiding them away for the winter. Goblin spotted a squirrel running down the side of tree from a great height. He started to climb the tree from the other side, intending to sneak up on it. At about ten feet from the ground, the squirrel came around the tree trunk, and they met face to face. The rodent had a large nut in its mouth. It swatted at the big cat with its front paw. Goblin hissed and tried to hit back with his own front paw but lost his grip. He fell to the ground, unhurt but feeling foolish. The red squirrel raced up to a high branch and, now holding its little treasure in its forepaws, chattered and cackled in glee at the poor cat.

Enough of this game playing. It's time to get serious. Sir Goblin meowed to his mate.

Snow Beauty, always a poor hunter, was amused to see her mate miss a squirrel or two. He was usually very good. She turned her face away and licked her shoulder so he wouldn't see the laughter in her eyes.

The two cats huddled together to plan their strategy more carefully. Goblin knew he could not climb up a straight tree trunk more than about fifteen feet before his weight caused him to fall to the ground. They prowled through the forest until they came to a tree that suited Goblin's plan. Its trunk was short. Several branches grew out from the trunk at heights the cats could easily manage. Goblin and Snow Beauty crouched on the ground, half buried in leaves and twigs, and sat as still as stones until at last a chubby squirrel came scurrying along. The little nut-eater kicked up a twig which landed on Snow Beauty's nose, making her sneeze. The cat-kerchoo scared the rodent, and it hurried up the bushy tree for safety. Goblin ran up after it and pounced on its back just as it reached the first wobbling branch. The two cats shared a fine lunch.

Now, well fortified and too excited to be the least bit sleepy after eating, the two cats continued their woodland adventure. Once again, Sir Goblin followed a squirrel up a stocky tree and out onto a branch. Snow Beauty ran up the trunk and out onto the branch just behind her mate. The knighted cat seized his victim by the back of its neck. Cat and squirrel both tumbled to the ground. The branch they fell from bounced up and down, up and down. Snow Beauty clung to it with all her claws dug in, tossed about like a feather in the wind. The swaying twigs and fluttering leaves confused and unnerved the pretty lady cat. She fell and landed on a hat.

A huge monster suddenly rose up from the forest floor and snatched the dead squirrel from Goblin's mouth. The frightening creature began chewing at the raw squirrel flesh and sucking at its blood. The monster was a human man who had been asleep on the ground. He snatched hold of the lady cat and would have bitten into her as well, but Snow Beauty, terrified, twisted and turned herself into spinning ball of white fur and flew from the man's grasp. She ran, unseeing, through the woods. Goblin ran with her. When they could run no farther, they hid under a rotting tree trunk.

They could see the strange man crashing through the woods. When their pounding hearts quieted, they heard him moan and cry out.

He babbled insensibly, "Oh, hungry, thirsty, thirsty, dying, lost, hungry, thirsty."

He stumbled over a stone and fell headlong onto the ground. The last sound the cats heard from him was "Ma-ma."

Late that afternoon, Sir Goblin and Snow Beauty sat in the town square, meowing their adventure to Magdalene and any other cat who cared to listen.

He was right below us, and we didn't know it! mewed Snow Beauty. She was amazed that their sense of smell had failed to alert them to danger. *And he would have eaten me!*

Now that I think about it, I did smell something, but I assumed it was the squirrel's fear that I was picking up.

Yes, Papa, chirped an amused Magdalene, looking at her front paw and preening her claws. Toms never like to admit they might have missed something, she thought to herself.

He was covered with leaves and twigs. Grass in his hair. I never saw a human such a mess. Gave us quite a fright, added the feline knight. *He staggered about like a weak, dying sheep. His bark was faint—could hardly hear it,* continued Goblin.

Odd. When you think about it, put in Snow Beauty, *you don't usually see humans alone in the woods. They don't like to get off the roads.*

You don't often see humans alone at all. They live in houses, huddled together by the fire with their few slow-growing kittens, go into the church all together, and work in their fields together. Yes, they are odd creatures when you think about it. Sort of like dogs. Magdalene offered her observations on their human companions.

Suddenly, the three cats spun their heads around. They had heard footsteps. William and Younger were coming down the road from the manor.

The cats overheard William telling the bailiff's son, "As soon as Goblin shows up, I'll be back up the hill."

"Hope your animal shows up soon. Never let us down before."

"He's just a cat, after all! What can he really do?"

Sir Goblin had done many wonderful and unusual things, but William could not imagine that his cat would have any interest in the manor people. He was afraid finding the killer would be up to him. "I have talked to several servants. Everything is one big muddle. This talk about a unicorn confuses me. Perhaps Gisela can be of help when she calms down a little. I am just a blacksmith. Why cannot Sir Rudolph's men find this murderer? Is not that their job?"

"William, they need some kind of evidence before they can clap a man in irons. They have no suspects. And Lady Alfreda has faith in your cat. The killer must be found soon, because Sir Gregory is most eager to return home. It may be that the man is one of his people."

They had reached the blacksmith shop. Younger had errands to run at the cooper's and at the joiner's. Sir Goblin and Snow Beauty found a dejected blacksmith sitting by a cooling forge when they strolled through the doorway.

Four.

THAT EVENING GOBLIN and Snow Beauty were much fussed over and played with. Robin brought in a pan of sand from the creek and set it in the back room. William wanted to make sure the cats knew that the pan was to be their toilet facility for the night. He took each cat and, setting it in the pan, maneuvered its feet back and forth as if digging a hole and then covering up kitty poop.

Sir Goblin muttered little chirps and mews under his breath, saying, *I know what you are trying to tell me, you plodding human. I'm to use the box instead of going outside.*

As if to answer, Will said, "You are not getting out under any circumstances, cat. I need to take you up to the manor tomorrow."

That night Snow Beauty and Goblin each curled into a circle between William and Rosemarie. Snow's last thoughts as she drifted off to sleep were of Magdalene and Rodney. She must remember to talk to her Purry about them in the morning, she thought. Sir Goblin slept with his head upside down and put a paw over his ears so as not to hear his best mate's tiny, whistling snores. His last thoughts of the day were of why he had to go back to the manor. He hoped it was not for another "tournament" with Rodney. But the day's hunting had tired him, and he too was soon whistling snores.

Wide, silvery ribbons of anemic sunlight filtered through thick clouds, making it a gloomy, grey morning. William shut the door of his shop and began the steady trudge up to the manor house. A bulging hempen sack hung from his shoulder. Occasionally, the entire bag wiggled. Sir Goblin was inside. He tried to get comfortable but found himself sitting on his own tail with no knightly dignity at all.

As they approached the bailiff's house, its door swung open, and a grim-looking Younger stepped out to meet the morning. He brightened when he saw William.

"Good day to you, Younger," said the blacksmith.

"We are to take you to where Josef was found," replied the bailiff's son. "But first you are wanted at the house."

As they talked, a big, yellow cat came running up the road from behind them. He mewed insistently. As he walked around William, Goblin wiggled and got his head out of the sack. He growled at Rodney. The sandy-colored cat dropped to the ground and rolled over to expose his soft underside to the knighted cat. It was a feline act of obeisance, a bow, most humble. Before Sir Goblin could meow an answer, William shifted the bag and pushed the warrior cat's head inside.

"None of your tricks," he muttered.

Rodney followed silently behind them.

Inside the manor house, William set the bag down and, pulling at its bottom hem, dumped out his cat. The smith stroked his cat's fur smooth and tried to reassure him that all was well. Goblin commenced licking the nasty smell of the sack from his fur. The two humans stood waiting for the bailiff or one of the nobles to appear. Rodney, however, inched around to face Sir Goblin and mewed. Goblin lifted his nose and sniffed at the yellow cat.

Begging your pardon, Sir Cat. Yes, you are right. You do detect a whiff of Magdalene upon me. She is the most wonderful of lady cats. Truly. Here, he rolled on his back again.

Get up, commanded Goblin, still distrustful of Rodney's intentions toward his daughter.

I wish to remain in this village and to be your daughter's best mate, if you will permit. Oh, yes, it is true I have been something of a lady's tomcat for some years, dashing from one pretty kitty to the next, but never before have I felt this feeling. Rodney's eyes had gone softly wide.

"What are those two cats meowing about?" wondered Younger.

He got down on the floor and began stroking first one and then the other animal. The two cats both shook off his attentions and walked off a few steps where they again sat down and continued their talk.

Magdalene had told Rodney all about her father and his many deeds of knightly valor. Because he loved his mistress Gisela, Rodney now pleaded with Sir Goblin that justice be obtained. The corpse Goblin had seen earlier, now buried, was indeed the victim of a murder, said the yellow cat. He, Rodney, had overheard the lady of the house insist that the knighted pussycat could solve crimes when humans were at a loss.

Rodney begged Goblin for his blessing and for permission to remain in Johannesmarkt near the cat of his heart.

I will no doubt be called upon to find the murderer of this young human, meowed Sir Goblin.

He did not think the investigation would be much fun, but he was, nevertheless, happier to attempt solving a crime than to be forced into another cat tournament. *What can you tell me?*

Rodney mewed his fondness for Gisela. He had lived with her family since his kitten days and had learned to fear people in general and some in particular. Gisela was the only human in that family worth anything, in his opinion. She never hit him or any of the servants, and she, at least, scratched his ears. Every night, when he lay beside her, she told him bedtime stories until she fell asleep. True, he didn't understand the stories she made up about unicorns and a knight named Josef, but they were soothing, and he soon purred them both to sleep.

Josef? interjected Goblin.

Yes, she whispered in my ear at night that she loved him and that I was to tell no one, as if I could, and that it was our secret.

Now that he had met Magdalene, Rodney understood the depth of Gisela's feelings for the young servant.

A little justice is all the poor child can hope for. These humans are so violent, growled Rodney. *We may fight for a fair kitty's paw, but we don't go that far.*

True. Sometimes humans seem to enjoy slaughtering each other, responded Sir Goblin.

He had seen more than enough of what evil-minded humans can do. He pledged to do his best to see that Josef's killer be found and gave Rodney his blessing, resting his paw a moment on the yellow cat's forehead.

The clatter of boots on stone steps turned everyone's attention to the great staircase. Sir Gregory, accompanied by his squire, hurried down the stairs. Lady Alfreda's rich and powerful brother was booted and spurred for riding. He wore his usual blue doublet and cape. His black flat-brimmed hat was set at an angle to keep the sun out of his eyes. He looked very dashing. At that moment the bailiff emerged from the chaplain's office where he, the priest, and Sir Rudolph had been going over accounts.

"I shall take a turn about the orchards while the ladies finish their packing," Sir Gregory said to the bailiff, "I expect we shall be leaving after the noon meal."

"So soon?"

"It is a busy time of year. I have many harvests to see in and a great many taxes to collect," responded Sir Gregory, laughing and pulling on his gloves. Then, he noticed Rodney sitting with Goblin. He turned to his squire, "Here, boy, take this bag of yellow fur upstairs and see that it remains with the women until we leave. I'll see to the horse myself."

With that, he strode out the door.

Sir Rudolph, hearing the voices in the hall, also left the chaplain's office. He was running his fingers through his hair and shrugging his shoulders as if to pull the stiffness from them. He had been looking at the account books since sunrise. Making the small manor pay enough to support a lordly way of life required careful management. Rudolph did not have the heart to starve his serfs in order to put peacock on his table.

"I think we will make it, Gerhard."

"We will, my lord. The crops have been bountiful, and prices are up."

"Ah, the cat is here. Has that Franz fellow shown up yet? No? Please, tell William what he needs to know." With that, he strode out of the hall.

"My lord thinks the young man who is missing is most likely the murderer and that Josef was killed possibly because of a gambling debt or quarrel over a card game," said Gerhard, "Her ladyship's brother continues to believe that it was an accident."

Gerhard had a list of the men who had been hired to assist in the annual hunt. William had talked to some of them the day before. Together, William and the bailiff walked out to the stables. Gerhard sent his son off to work in the barn. Disappointed at not being included in the detective work, Younger slunk away, slouching and shoving his thumbs under his belt.

Standing among the horses, whose busy tails were swishing flies from their rumps, William talked with the huntsmen who had come with Sir Gregory. Sir Goblin busied himself sniffing about the horses' feet, stepping carefully around fresh horse dung. Occasionally, he'd take a swipe at a long tail or a fat fly.

"Tell me what happened on the second day of the hunt," William asked Sir Gregory's men.

Nothing unusual had happened in the morning, it seemed. After the midday meal and a short rest they began again to hunt for deer.

Just then, William, Gerhard, and the men in the stable were joined by Peter, Sir Gregory's squire, whom William had seen in the manor house. He came into the stable to await the return of his master. Upon

Sir Gregory's arrival, he would attend to his master's horse, so the animal would be ready for their departure in the afternoon.

After talking to William for a moment, Peter recalled that, on the day of Josef's death, the hunters had spread out somewhat and headed down into a shallow glen; at that point, Sir Gregory rode off up a hill, looking for deer sign, he said.

"I am called Curly, sir," said a big fellow with ringlets of tight, yellow curls hanging down to the tips of his ears, which were so big that they made his hair stand up like a spaniel's. He nodded a quick bow to William and began to tell the blacksmith his version of the events of the day of the hunt. "It weren't many minutes, sir, 'till I caught a good glimpse of a big buck. Our drivers had panicked him, and he came running right toward us, sir. And I brought him down with my arrow." Here, he held up his stout bow for all to see. "There's few as can string this bow."

Proud as Curly was of the power behind his arrows, he did not kill the deer with one arrow. Gushing blood, the wounded animal ran off into some bushes. Before Curly, who was on foot, could catch up with the wounded deer, Sir Gregory, coming as if from nowhere, galloped up to where it lay. The buck thrashed helplessly on the ground. Sir Gregory jumped from his horse with his sword already drawn and plunged the weapon deep into the animal's chest.

"Then my lord gave three short blasts on his hunting horn and shouts, 'Finest beast I ever brought down!'" said Curly.

"And then?"

"We proceeds to clean it, sir."

"And that's when things got odd," Peter added, "Suddenly someone shouts, 'There's something white running through the trees!'"

"The master," Curly said.

"No, not him, but someone," corrected the young squire with more assurance than his few years would suggest he had.

Curly's shoulders slumped, and, feeling rebuked and shaking his head, he retreated to the back of the stable to pack up his bows and arrows.

"Now we all see a pair of snow-white heels kicking up and disappearing into the forest," continued Peter. "We can still hear it when one of the fellows says, 'Lord a' mercy. Maybe it's one of Gisela's unicorns like she is always talking about.'

"And I say to Sir Gregory, 'She had a book about them, my lord. They are supposed to be in this region.'

"My master laughs real loud and tells me, 'You ride back to the ladies and bring her here. If it's a unicorn, she can tame it. Quick now!'

"We send Curly off to track the unicorn, and I go for Gisela. I come back with Gisela on the saddle behind me, all excited. She jumps down, and her father has her up with him on his horse. We hear Curly shout, and we all charge off."

Peter would have continued talking, but the stable darkened when a man on horseback rode up to the door. "Will someone take my horse! What's all this standing around and babbling! Peter! Impossible to get good help these days! And you mean to be a knight some day! Ha!"

Sir Goblin, who was affectionately rubbing his flanks around the blacksmith's ankles, jumped at the sound of Sir Gregory's barking voice. All the hair on his back stood up. His tail puffed to twice its normal thickness. With one leap the cat was on William's shoulder.

"There, there, my man. Everything is all right."

William stroked Goblin's back and brushed his cheek against the cat's shoulder.

Chastised, Peter rushed to take his master's horse's bridle.

"Let me take you now to where we found Josef," the bailiff said to William. "Good Day, my lord. By your leave, my lord."

They bowed and hurried out, leaving Sir Gregory to rage at his retainers.

Five.

A S GERHARD AND William walked across the stable yard, the bailiff waved to Younger, who was slouching against the barn door. "Come along," he said.

Younger joined the two men, happy to leave his farm duties for the time being.

Gerhard turned to William and chortled. "You know, you talk to that cat as if it were a person."

"He is. I mean, sometimes it seems as if he is. Knows what I'm thinking, at any rate."

As they began to hike through the woods beyond the manor grounds, William put Sir Goblin back into his carry bag. Goblin had had enough of humans and their adventures for a while and happily curled up and closed his eyes. The sun was out now and getting hot. Once they were among the trees, there was little breeze to keep whining insects from spinning around their heads. Soon they were batting and swatting at the bugs.

When at last they paused at the top of a hill, their hair was matted with sweat, and their necks were glistening with perspiration and dotted with bloody bug bites. William let the cat sack slip off his shoulder. "Whew! That gets heavy."

Goblin quietly slunk out of the bag and started walking on ahead of the group. When the men didn't immediately follow, he stopped, glared over his shoulder at them and switched his tail.

"Did the hunters come this way?" William saw no sign of horses having broken through the undisturbed brush. *Odd,* he thought to himself, *noblemen never walk when they can ride. And besides that, they would have brought at least one cart to hold the tables and other things needed for the meal the ladies had prepared.*

"No. There is a road around the other way, but it is longer and mostly all uphill. This is the most direct way to where we found Josef. He was not where they were hunting. It's maybe half a league hence but on mostly level ground," recalled Young Ger.

Sir Goblin ran back to where they stood and pawed at the sack, trying to get in.

"See what I mean about understanding us. He's not going to walk any half a league."

"Amazing. Wonder how he does it."

"No idea," said the blacksmith, holding the sack open; his cat climbed in.

They hiked in silence for about twenty minutes, and then the bailiff said, "Look sharp. Down there is where the netting was strung to keep poachers out. There's a rise and then a sharp drop. It was in the little dip that we found his body."

"Prints all over the place. Horse and human."

"Aye, we brought in a horse to carry the body home once we found him."

"Who found him?"

"Peter and my son. Then I came back with them and the horse."

William squatted and let Sir Goblin out of his carrier. The smith could plainly see bare places on the ground showing where some sort of scuffle had uprooted the grass and some delicate woodland flowers. "These prints are horse, but these are smaller. A pony's?" observed William.

"These appear to be men's footprints here, but they are not clear at all."

Goblin crouched over one print and growled.

"That mark might be a heel print."

"Then 'twould be a boot," noted the bailiff.

Sir Goblin ran down into the little dip in the ground, stopped, and sniffed over a dark reddish spot. When William saw what his cat was doing, he moaned.

"Yes," said the bailiff, "This is where Josef's body was. Down in this little glen. There was much blood. Still is."

Goblin ran from one patch of dried blood to the next, sniffing and mewing softly to himself. Then, he stopped moving and sniffed deeply, hanging his mouth open to take in every subtle scent.

"Merrow," he howled and started scratching at the ground with his front paws.

His claws ripped at something long and dirty white. *A piece of cloth?* thought William. He saw something glitter. Goblin bit at it, growling deeply.

"Here, let me look at that, Goblin."

The cat reluctantly released his find but continued to growl.

"Looks to be a feather attached . . ."

"Let me see that," snapped the bailiff, grabbing it from William's fingers. "Oh, Holy Mother Mary! It can't be! But it is."

Gerhard ran his fingers over the feather, smoothing its vane, and carefully brushed the dirt from the gold piece attached to it.

"What? What is it?" William could see it was some sort of jewelry but wondered at its significance.

"By all that's holy, I'm afraid I know what this means," whispered the bailiff to himself as he tenderly placed Goblin's find in his purse. "This is too dangerous to think about." Then he spoke aloud to William, "Is there anything else here? Search around."

William got down on his knees and carefully ran his hands over the ground. "Come on, Goblin. Help me see if there is anything else here."

But the cat stayed near the bailiff. He meowed and stretched up the man's leg to sniff at his purse.

"There is no doubt, that is what he thinks is important," said William, getting up and rubbing at the ache in the small of his back.

"You know, if you had not seen this, I think I would have left it here and said we found nothing," said the bailiff to the baffled blacksmith.

"Father!" objected Younger, who had been mostly silent during the walk through the woods. "That would be telling a lie!"

The bailiff looked long at his fifteen-year-old son. *He's good. So young and idealistic, but he's right*, the man thought to himself.

To Younger he said, "I said 'I *think* I would have', but I *will* show it to Sir Rudolph. It will be harder that way, but at least we will need confess no lies to the priest."

Gerhard continued, "If we go in this direction, we will come to the spot where the deer was taken, and then it is not far to the road the hunters used. It will be downhill from there. Let's make it easy on ourselves on our way back."

When they reached the road, a light breeze blew away some of the circling insects, and William found it a great relief to walk down a road with no branches or briars obstructing the way. Many thoughts and unpleasant conclusions were whirling through his head. If the gold ornament belonged to the murderer, as he thought it must, because it was certainly not something the orphan Josef would have owned, then the killer was a wealthy man. He must be one of the noblemen in the hunting party. Several families had joined the hunt. He did not know these people. It would be up to others to point out the criminal, he concluded.

The blacksmith believed the bailiff knew a lot more than what he was saying. *That man marches down the road with his lips clamped together so tightly that not even torture would make him speak*, thought William. He tried a couple of times to catch Younger's eye. Maybe the youth would give him some clues as to what was happening. But the bailiff's son looked away as though he found the ground in front of his feet very interesting. They all walked in silence. William was about to yell, "Would somebody please say something!" when somebody did. They all jumped at a moan coming from the weeds just below the shoulder of the road.

"Oh, oh," the voice rustled, more like leaves in a breeze than a person.

They all rushed to the side of the road.

"Someone's lying there! Probably the work of highwaymen," cried Gerhard.

"It's Franz!" Younger recognized the young huntsman in spite of the scratches and bruises on his thin face and the tangle of grass and leaves caught in his hair. Feasting insects had reddened his face and neck. Three of the bites oozed with infection, causing rivulets of pus to run down his face. Gerhard used his dagger to free Franz, hacking away the briars that snagged the youth's clothes. The three men dragged Sir Gregory's servant onto the road. Exposure to the damp woods had left his stockings soggy and torn. Streaks of black mud and grass stains coated his clothes. An elbow poked through one damp sleeve.

"He's alive for certain, but what has happened to him?" wondered Younger.

When they tried to sit him up, his head dropped against his chest and wobbled from side to side. Gerhard knelt beside Franz.

"He is not in good shape." Turning to his son, the bailiff cried, "Run those strong, young legs of yours, Gerhard, to the stable, and come back with a wagon, water—and some wine. Bring help! Go!" He all but slapped his son on his backside as if urging a horse to gallop.

Six.

FRANZ'S APPEARANCE CAUSED a great commotion at the lord's manor. Dinner was delayed. Guests milled about, peering at the poor youth as he was carried upstairs, commenting to each other, "You can certainly see that he has murder in his soul," or, "Such a child could never have done such a deed."

Gerhard immediately took his master by his sleeve, pulling him aside.

"I think, milord, that her ladyship should take charge of his recovery."

Sir Rudolph agreed. It was, in fact, the duty of the woman of the house, in any household from the most humble to the most aristocratic, to nurse the sick. The good lady had much experience with common medicines and the bandaging of wounds suffered by her warrior men. Lady Alfreda needed no persuading. She scurried up the stairs.

As Alfreda disappeared into the solar to seek her medicinals, the bailiff bowed and addressed Sir Rudolph. Whispering, "With your permission, my lord," he pulled the ornament from his purse. "Now that my lady is upstairs, sir. I did not wish to disturb her, my lord. The cat found this at the site. It without doubt belongs to her brother, my lord."

The bailiff's hand shook as he handed over the gold piece with its attached feather.

"My God!" murmured the knight. He turned to William who was standing some distance off with Sir Goblin tangling about his ankles. "Do you confirm this? On your oath, now?"

William, who still did not know that Sir Gregory had worn that ornament on his hat, sensed the great tension of the moment. Crossing himself, he bowed to the knight and gave the only answer he could give.

"I swear by all that's holy, my lord, that this cat," here he pointed down to Goblin, "dug that thing up from under a bloodstained leaf at the place they said this Josef was killed."

"Enough," responded the knight, turning away. "Am I to arrest my lady's brother? How can I? How could anyone? Bailiff, what am I to do?"

Gerhard answered nothing. He dropped his eyes toward the floor. After several long minutes, he took a deep breath, "Perhaps, my lord, when Franz recovers . . ."

"No! We cannot let him take the blame—but to put my wife's brother in that filthy pit of a dungeon!" said the knight.

Ever mindful of his duty to impose justice, he had read a meaning in Gerhard's words that the bailiff had not intended.

"I only thought, my lord, that perhaps there is still some other explanation."

"Oh, yes, Gregory will have 'some other explanation.' He is a quick one. But I am afraid there can be no doubt. He has, after all, something of a motive, albeit it a paltry one."

"Gisela?"

"Yes, Gisela."

Lady Alfreda pulled a blanket up to Franz's chin and called to her maid to put more charcoal on the brazier.

"Be sure to keep it hot," she said as she sat on a chair beside her patient's bed. Wringing warm water from a linen cloth, she leaned over and mopped the boy's face, wiping off the dirt and cleansing the infected sores. Her touch was so gentle that he barely stirred.

A door opened, and Lady Clara strode in. Her skirts bustled assertively as she came up to the bed where Franz drifted in and out of sleep.

"I wanted to see the face of this murderer myself," she announced loudly.

The boy's eyes flew open, and his head tossed from side to side. Loud, unintelligible cries burst from his throat.

"Look how agitated he's become. I think he is feverish. Do take care, Clara, to speak softly and use gentle words."

"Pah! You waste your tender touches on such as he," responded Lady Clara, just as loud as she was before.

"I will stay some minutes with him. Then, sister, I want a word with you before you leave for home." Lady Alfreda stood up. "Let him rest."

Clara understood this was an order; with a swish of her silken skirts, she left the room.

Downstairs, Sir Rudolph's many guests were assembling for the noon meal. The knight slipped Sir Gregory's hat ornament inside his doublet. He did not want anyone, least of all his brother-in-law, to see it until he had decided what he should do. To accommodate all the company that had come for the hunt, extra tables had been set up in the hall. The main table ran across the hall's width so that Sir Rudolph and Lady Alfreda's great chairs stood at its center with their backs to the fireplace. Other important guests had seats on either side of them along the same side of the table. At either end, additional tables were placed so as to make three sides of a rectangle. Guests who sat here were the less important visitors and servants and retainers of various types; they sat on benches on both sides of these tables. William, asked to stay for the meal, sat halfway down the arm of the rectangle to Sir Rudolph's left. Goblin sat on the bench beside the blacksmith, chewing on meat William fed to him. Every time his mouth was empty, the cat stretched his head up to the table's edge and sniffed around at William's trencher. The women across the table giggled, and William quietly pushed Goblin's head down while slipping him a piece of tender squab.

At the head table, Sir Rudolph made a lonely figure in his great chair. Lady Alfreda's chair was empty. She ordered food to be brought to her along with broth for the recuperating huntsman. Sir Gregory had the seat next to his sister's chair, and Clara sat to Rudolph's right. Little Gisela sat somberly beside her mother.

As soon as the blessing was said, Sir Gregory began pulling his bird apart into little pieces. He stuffed several chunks—more than was polite—into his mouth with his fingers. He chewed noisily and smacked his lips, then burped. His eyes darted about the room. He made one bad joke which in his own language was like saying the table, or the "board," was "boring" and said nothing further.

Clara, noting her brother-in-law's somber face, leaned over to ask about his health.

"Forgive me, sister, if I am not being a good conversationalist or a good host."

He touched his throat as if it were sore.

"Certainly Alfreda has a cure for it," Clara snapped. "The number of medicinals and herbs she brought up to that murderer's room! How she can waste so much time on him, I do not understand!" Hearing the word "murderer," Gisela began to cry. Her mother shot her a fierce look, and the girl shrank back. Then, pulling herself up tall, Gisela sat still as if made of stone; only her hand moved, her spoon listlessly stirring circles in the gravy on her plate.

The guests at the distant ends of the table were having a wonderful time; gossip about the supposed murderer stimulated their appetites. Their laughter rang out, resounding off the stone walls. Wine flowed.

Servants cleared the tables and put on clean tablecloths for the dessert course. Suddenly, Lady Alfreda ran down the staircase. Everyone fell silent as she approached the tables, slowing to a dignified walk.

"My lord! He tells such fantastic things!" The lady of the manor stopped before of the rectangle of tables, rubbing her hands in confusion and glancing first at her husband, then Gregory, then Lady Clara, and back at her lord.

Gregory stood up, uttering something about "checking the baggage" or, perhaps, "I'll take care of that baggage." Later, no one was sure what he had said. He began walking around the table. As Alfreda glanced once more at her brother, tears flooded her eyes.

"My lord," she curtsied, "He says . . . that is—"

"Silence, woman," Sir Rudolph mouthed to her. He stood up and hurried around the tables until he stood beside her. Gregory was going up the stairs to the solar and guest rooms.

"I know, I know. I have proof."

"What?" gasped the woman.

"Be quiet a moment. Our guests," Sir Rudolph whispered. He put his arms around her shoulders, holding her close. Then he turned her to face their guests.

"Good friends, as you can see, my dear lady is indisposed. The day has weighed heavily on her heart. I beg your indulgence. Please remain in your seats and enjoy the pies while I escort her upstairs."

There was a general murmur among the people, but the pies arrived, and they turned back politely and enthusiastically to their meal.

"Bailiff! You, and you!" It wasn't much more than a stage whisper, but Sir Rudolph commanded Gerhard, Younger, and William to his side. "Keep him before your eyes."

The three hurried after Gregory. Goblin padded quickly at their heels. The noble couple followed up the stairs.

No hysteric, Lady Alfreda kept herself under control as they mounted the stairs.

Still leaning on her husband's shoulder, she whispered in his ear, "The boy says . . . Oh dear God! He says my brother killed Josef, and he saw it! That was why he did not return. He thinks Gregory saw him there."

"Be brave, Alfreda. I have other proof."

They were standing at the top of the stairs, in the hallway. Franz's room was around a corner and at the far end of the hall; it was a storage room, really, since they still had many guests. Alfreda raised a questioning eyebrow, hoping Sir Rudolph meant proof that another was the killer. Slowly, her husband pulled the hat ornament and feather from inside his shirt.

"Ohhhhh!" the woman wailed, covering her face.

"Perhaps you should go to your chamber, to your prie-dieu, and pray for his soul."

It was, at least, something she could do. With a sigh of relief, the lady slipped from her husband's arms and started for their bedroom. As she reached the door, they both heard a distant shout.

"Go on! I'll see what it is."

He hurried down the hallway. As he came in sight of Franz's room, the door flew open, and William ran out. "Sir Rudolph! Oh, thank God you are here! We can hardly hold him."

In the room, Gerhard and his son were both struggling to hold Gregory by the arms, but the man was a warrior and exceedingly strong. He broke loose again from their grasp. Had not Sir Rudolph been in the doorway, Gregory would have fled from the room.

Sir Rudolph pressed his hand against Gregory's chest and pushed him back. The three pushed him down into a chair. Sir Rudolph looked around. Several boxes stood piled up behind the brazier. "William, see that box over there with the rope tied around it? Cut that rope, and bring it here. Be quick! We'll tie him right where he is."

Sir Rudolph tried to pull out his dagger with his left hand while still holding his right against Sir Gregory's powerful chest.

"That's all right, sir. I have my own," said William.

Once Gregory was bound, they turned to Franz. Goblin was standing at his pillow, licking the huntsman's face clean.

"He breathes yet," said one of the men.

"Look at those marks on his throat," added Younger, "He was trying to choke him, for sure."

"Fool! You cur's whelp! I was just tying to talk some sense into him. Get him to take back his lies!"

"Who're you calling a cur?" Gerhard had Sir Gregory by the chin, pinching and twisting the skin.

"Enough, Gerhard."

Sir Rudolph pulled out the hat ornament and dangled it by its feather before his brother's face. Gregory went white. The two men stared at each other for a long moment.

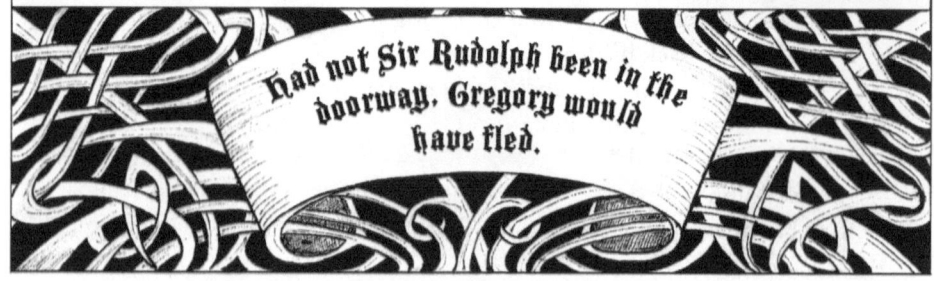

Had not Sir Rudolph been in the doorway, Gregory would have fled.

"But why, Gregory?"

"If you had seen that filthy animal put his lips to *your* daughter's cheek!"

Sir Rudolph made no answer. He would not like to have his own young daughter smitten by someone not worthy of her. But murder, never.

"I will post a guard. Come, smith. You and your cat have done well, but it is time, more than time, you return to your shop."

"Thank you, my lord."

William bowed and lifted Goblin to his shoulder. As he went down the hall, he passed Lady Alfreda and bowed to her. He paused at the head of the stairs, because Rodney suddenly ran down the corridor and stopped at his feet. The yellow cat stood up and braced his front legs against William's leg. Goblin leaned down. They sniffed noses. Then, the two cats meowed a long conversation. William would have stopped them and gone on home, but he was overhearing another conversation—one he knew Rosemarie would want to know about.

"I have decided we will proceed immediately to the baron's court."

"No dungeon?"

"No dungeon, but justice, dearest. He tried to choke Franz. They caught him with his hands on the boy's throat."

"Ooohhh," cried Lady Alfreda and gave way to tears. Then she took a deep breath and straightened to her full height. "My own brother! But he acts like a madman. We have no recourse. But thank you for not throwing him in the dungeon." She looked to the floor, then looked up with resolve in her pale eyes and began speaking again. "I will confer with Clara and recommend they go home at once. They are all packed. And there is much to be done at their estates this time of year."

"Probably best for Gisela."

At the mention of Gisela, Rodney ran over and rubbed against Lady Alfreda's ankles. The woman brightened a little.

"Oh, you big, yellow mountain of love. I'll take you to little Gisela. She needs you now."

With that, the noblewoman scooped up Rodney and carried him down the corridor. William and Goblin quietly descended the stairs, unnoticed.

All the way home, Goblin ran ahead of William. When they came to the village, the cat dashed to the priest's house. He had a long message from Rodney for Magdalene.

It was not two hours later that William stepped from his shop to watch a little party of mounted nobles ride by. The proud Lady Clara, her maids, and several male retainers clattered out of town. The men led three riderless horses and a white pony. Last came a cart. Two children were crouched within, along with the hunting gear. The girl, ghostly pale, with a clenched mouth and circles under her eyes more befitting an old hag, clutched a big yellow cat to her chest. As the cart passed the church, the cat squirmed, and the girl stood up to allow him to look over the side. A little white kitty with a grey-striped tail ran out from the priest's house. She mewed, standing up on her hind legs, the better to see Rodney.

"Mew." *I love you. I know everything. Father told me.*

An answer came from the cart. "Meow." *You will always be my dearest best mate. But this girl needs me.*

"Mew." *Yes, she needs you. I will wait, always wait, for you.*

Rodney pushed a foreleg out of the cart and stretched his head as far out as it would go. But he did not try to get away from Gisela.

"Meow."

"Mew."

Magdalene stretched tall on her back legs and mewed until she could see him no more.

The Knight's Assailant

One.

L ADY ALFREDA PUSHED herself up higher against her bolster and then drew the linen bed sheet up so its edge rested at the hollow of her throat. With the bed curtains drawn, all was blackness. But it was quiet. Too quiet. She listened and realized she could not hear her husband breathing. She reached across to his bolster, searching with her fingers for his thin curls. Not feeling a head there, she swept her arm farther down along the mattress, thinking he had slid lower in the bed. But she already knew. He had left again. She flung the bed curtains back. In the feeble glow of the brazier, the furniture stood as black blocks in the dark room—the huge bedstead, the armoire, their chests, her dressing table.

Lady Alfreda jumped from the bed and ran to the window, grabbing her chemise as she ran. There, she struggled into the garment; pulling it over her head, it caught for a second on one of her thick coils of hair. She leaned across the wide stone sill and threw open the sash. A half-moon threw a silvery light across her face. The whole world below was cast in silver and black shadows. Nothing moved. She saw no one about.

She stepped back from the window. She lit a candle from the brazier. Her soft leather boots stood in front of her armoire. She slipped them on and pulled on her houppelande that her maid had left airing over a clothes pole. She belted the heavy garment high beneath her breasts.

Then taking up the candle, the lady of the manor wended her way along the corridor and down a flight of stairs to the ground floor. The side door—the same side door through which her husband had raced over a decade ago in his pursuit of the wicked Odo—stood ajar. Lady Alfreda stepped out into the night.

A mastiff lifted his head and started to growl. Then he recognized her ladyship and felt embarrassed. His tail beat an apology against the stone porch. She patted his head between his ears. "Which way did he go, Brutus?"

The great dog emitted a gurgling whine and started to get up. His chain rattled.

"Oh, he chained you, did he?"

The woman set the candle down and undid the chain. Whining and eager to join his master, the huge dog bounded down the steps and headed straight for the orchard. *I guessed as much*, thought the woman. The Lady Alfreda hurried after the dog. The big animal ran toward the orchard bench where Alfreda knew her lord often went to sit and think. From there, the knight could see the high hill beyond the town where he had fought his last glorious battle.

As Alfreda drew near the first small apple trees, she slowed to a walk to catch her breath. The dog ran ahead, his hind legs kicking up together and his tail spinning like the sails of a windmill. She saw him stop, turn, bounce back a step or two and start barking.

The noblewoman hurried to where the big dog stood. Her husband was lying on the ground with his face turned into the muddy ruts that his feet had dug when he slid and fell. Licking the knight's face, and washing the soft wet earth from his nostrils, was a large grey-striped cat. At the approach of the dog, all the fur on the cat's back stood up, making him look fierce. Spit flew from its mouth. The feline held his ground and the dog backed up a step or two.

"Quiet, Brutus." Lady Alfreda silenced the dog.

"My lord? Oh, my lord!" The woman pulled at her husband's shoulders, "Rudolph, Rudi, Rudi, oh Ru—"

He moaned. Then cried out "My head! My head!"

"You hit your head?"

"No! Someone hit my head."

Lady Alfreda pulled his arm around her shoulder and tried to get him to his feet. She pulled him to his knees.

He groaned horribly. "Give me a moment." Still kneeling, he wiped at his face with his free hand, wiping off mud and pushing away hair from his cheeks and the corners of his eyes. Then he took a deep breath and tried to stand. Alfreda pulled.

She got him up, but when he tried to put weight on both feet, he screamed, "Oh, my knee! 'Swounds! It hurts!"

Brutus bounced around them, his tongue hanging out, whining and trying to entice them back to the house. *Heh, heh, heh*, the dog panted.

Trying to take a step, the knight fell. His hand landed on the dog's back, and he pushed himself up before he hit the ground again. Little by little they moved to the manor house, one hopping step at a time. By the time they had reached the house the candle had burned itself out into a splatter of wax. The noblewoman got her lord seated on the stone steps and went inside to waken a servant.

It was the first hours of the morning by the time they had washed the man up, bandaged his bloodied head, and sent him back to bed. He complained much of his head hurting and of his stomach rolling. He called once for a basin. But the knight could not—or pride would not let him—vomit in front of his lady or the servants. He waved the proffered basin away again and dropped his head against the bolster. The good Lady Alfreda prayed that their Father in Heaven did not hear—or if he did hear, that he would forgive—the words her husband uttered. She hovered by the bedside, jumping up and smoothing the sheet or wiping at his brow every time he groaned. The man's head rolled from side to side. Again and again he drew his uninjured knee to his abdomen and thrust his leg back out. He clenched his teeth; his bulging eyes searched the dark room, seeking release from his pain. Seeing that he was hurting so much that he would never get to sleep, Alfreda poured a little wine into a cup, and then dissolved a soothing, medicinal herb into the wine. This she trickled down his throat and at last he sank into a heavily drugged slumber.

After the humans had hobbled off to their house with the annoying, whimpering hound bobbing around them, Sir Goblin stood in the orchard, switching his tail angrily. He thought the dog, at least, would have understood that he had helped the knight to breathe again and offered a woof or tail wag of thanks. *Well, I didn't do it for the dog's sake anyway*, thought the big cat after a minute's consideration. *What do dogs know? They are all slurp and no subtlety*. Then feeling a little ashamed of himself for even wanting thanks—after all, he was supposed to be a chivalrous knight—Goblin ran soundlessly back to his house.

Arriving home, he jumped up onto the sill of the house's little front window and patted the pane with a soft paw. A responding white paw patted the opposite side and then worked at the latch. After a minute, the window swung open a few inches and Goblin nosed his way in. He joined the lovely white Snow Beauty, his long time best mate, at the fireside; together they licked Goblin's fur free of mud. Goblin purred into her ear and gently kneaded her side. Soon she knew all about his nighttime adventures. She heard about the nest of rabbits, how he had just pulled out one baby rabbit, but lost it when the strange thing happened to the knight. She listened to him tell how he got the man's face clean to breathe again and how the knight's ungrateful hound could think of nothing better to do but chase him and then maul and kill his rabbit. So he had come home empty-mouthed, but it had certainly been an interesting night. The two cats slept, curled together, Goblin with his front paw over Snow's shoulder.

The next morning when her maid came in to help Lady Alfreda dress, the girl whispered to her lady, "When Hans went to brush the mud from my lord's doublet, there was mud on both the front and back. The back, very like a footprint."

Lady Alfreda jerked her head up, and for a second or two, sat up as straight and still as if she were turned to stone. Then taking a deep breath, without a word, she handed the girl her heart-shaped headpiece, to be pinned into her thick coils of hair. Their eyes met in the noblewoman's metal hand mirror. Alfreda's eyes glinted, then narrowed.

"Say nothing of what you know. And see that my lord's man holds his tongue." And then to ensure her order was followed, she added, "It may otherwise be dangerous."

"Yes, my lady." The girl's eyes widened, as she comprehended, and she began punching the pins through the headpiece and red coils of hair with great, if not helpful, vigor. Again the noblewoman picked up her small mirror. She peered into it and plucked a hair or two from her forehead. She was proud of her long oval face, and would not let the smallest hair suggest her high forehead was not God's own gift.

That morning, after the knight's injury, instead of Sir Rudolph, an exquisitely beautiful and commanding figure met the manor's bailiff and the morning's petitioners in the great hall. Lady Alfreda was dressed in a rich blue damask houppelande, the luxurious heavy folds of which warded off the morning's chill. Above her headpiece floated a diaphanous veil of silk and linen, in a paler shade of the same blue. The wire frame that supported the veil made her taller than even the six-foot tall bailiff. The mist of gauze that floated about her face and shoulders added an air of mysterious femininity to her authority. She stood behind a massive table with a young priest—who served as both her confessor and clerk—to her left, and the bailiff to her right.

"Good day to you, bailiff," she nodded.

He gave a quick bow. "My lady."

She nodded recognition to the others assembled. They all made a quick reverence.

"My Lord is unwell today. I will attend to affairs." With that, she sat and motioned for the bailiff to sit.

Since the annual town fair was about to open, there was much business to be attended to. The petitioners received quick redress of their grievances. The priest, one of the few retainers at the manor who could read and write, collected and recorded fines and taxes. As he wrote down the various transactions for the manor records, he sneezed and sniffed, occasionally blotting the stream from his runny nose with his sleeve. The wet spot on his black robe glistened like a silvery cobweb in the morning light. Alfreda squinted at him and raised an eyebrow in disapproval, but there was too much work to be done for her to send him away. At last, when all the petitioners had been dismissed, the bailiff began his report on the status of the livestock, crops and other business of the manor. Lady Alfreda interrupted him. "Gerhard, I am sure the manor has not fallen into disarray since you reported yesterday. We must discuss this matter of the assault on my lord."

"Assault, my lady?" Gerhard asked with surprise, "I thought he had fallen."

"He says otherwise. You must investigate this matter with all due haste."

The church bell rang out across the town. It was late in the morning but not yet noon, and such a ringing signaled either a death or that a meeting of the town fathers was being called to gather within the old church. Something had happened, but William, who was not rich enough to rank among the town fathers, continued to hammer a shoe for an impatient mule. He had seen the knight's men ride into town and go about speaking to one person after another. Someone had stolen the lord's pigs or some such, he assumed.

Eventually one of Sir Rudolph's men-at-arms came to question William. The questions were innocent enough—had he seen anything unusual or heard anything? But William resented the manner of his questioner. The young man stood with his knuckles resting on his hips and asked his questions with his head cocked to the side and an eyebrow raised. His boot heel impatiently twisted in the dirt. The youth asking the questions was the bailiff Gerhard's son, also named Gerhard, but called Young Ger by everyone in the town or simply Younger. Younger was well known at the tavern. Already his breath was more than a little beery.

Just then Goblin stalked out of the smithy, curious to see what was happening, and sat down beside his companion. His nose twitched, and he raised a paw and pretended to wash his face. His nose covered by a protective paw, the cat shuddered at Younger's smell—beer and sweat, all on top of an excess of the pungent human odor. *When did that man last wash?* he thought. *Cats smell so sweet. Why can't humans lick themselves as cats do? Their tongues are certainly agile enough. They waggle them so much when talking.*

After a few more questions from Younger, William could not resist pointing out that as a blacksmith who had spent years pounding a hammer against iron, his hearing was none too keen. Younger snapped his knuckle against William's chest. "Well, keep a sharp eye then." And he sauntered off.

At their noon meal, William and Rosemarie speculated on Younger's odd questions.

"I wonder what that arrogant knave was after. I hope Young Ger never becomes bailiff. He enjoys lording it too much."

"Well, you know," said Rosemarie, "speaking of odd things happening, I found the front window open this morning. Now that was strange. I know I latched it."

William laughed. "Maybe some thief smelt your raspberry tarts."

Rosemarie was not amused and not convinced of the unimportance of the open window. She looked at their two children.

"Robin, were you up last night? Or you Maddie?" Both children shook their heads. Robin was about eleven years old and Maddie maybe seven, although no one kept exact count of the years.

Rosemarie had begun to clear the table, sweeping crumbs into a cup to feed to her chickens that afternoon, when someone rapped on the door. William got up to answer it. It was the cooper, who was one of the men called to the meeting at the church. "You and the cat are wanted at the meeting."

Before going over to the church, William stood outside his door for a moment looking across the busy town square. He could not help but feel a little thrill of anticipation, for tomorrow the summer fair opened. It was the one time of year that people from all over flocked to Johannesmarkt. Merchants, vendors, entertainers, and all sorts of people, both residents and out–of–towners, were setting up tents and booths. The air rang with the tap of hammers. Rosemarie would again sell her famous tarts, sharing a table with Joanna the tavern cook.

But something serious—not just some petty theft—must have had happened if Sir Rudolph needed to call in the services of the town's other knight, Sir Goblin. Hoping it was nothing to keep him from enjoying the fair, the blacksmith scooped up his cat, waking him from a nice nap, and hurried over to the church.

Stefan the joiner's heart pounded within him. His breast felt too small to contain his excitement. Sometimes he still could not believe that the maid loved him. She was so beautiful, so gentle and kind. She could have any man she wanted, and many had come knocking at her door. But the Prophet had said she would have no other but him, and the Prophet's sayings were true. He was convinced of this now.

Stefan put down his chisel. His fingers swept tenderly over the carvings in the great case's door, as if to impart a little of himself into the very wood. The wardrobe would soon go to its purchaser. He would see it no more. He packed his tools and carefully closed his toolbox. Taking hold of the table beside him, he pulled himself up to his feet.

He took one more look at his work, at the beautiful carvings on its door—the maiden and dancing unicorns on each of the two panels. They each had her face. No one, least of all the purchasers, would know it was her, only he. He, Stefan, was a man in love.

He shouldered his toolbox by its leather strap and limped out the door and locked it behind him. His foot dragged badly tonight, because he had sat still for so long carving. The memory of the sickness that had caused his leg to wither when he was a child flickered once again through his mind. He brushed it away, literally, by brushing his hand across his forehead. In its place, he put the happy thought of his wedding day with Liselotte—Lotte as her friends called her—at his side. How happy they would be once they were handfast.

His path home led him behind the tavern. There, five tomcats were finishing off a large baked carp put out for them by the little innkeeper, Paul. Stefan reached down and scratched the largest cat between the ears. "How are you and your four sons tonight, Sir Goblin?"

Goblin stretched his head up and purred loudly. He raised a front paw and gave Stefan a gentle pat on his wrist.

The other four cats, all of them white with grey-striped tails, while tall, were slimmer and obviously younger than their sire. They stepped back from their feast in deference to their father and waited for their turn to be scratched.

"Tomorrow is your big day, eh, old boy?" the youth said to Goblin, "Tomorrow you ride in the place of honor with that farrier fellow, all dressed in mouser stripes."

Stefan chuckled. He was referring to the procession that began the town's annual midsummer fair. Knighted many years ago, the big tabby cat rode near the start of the procession. He rode in a basket hung from the horn of a saddle cinched around a white palfrey. The gentle little horse was caparisoned in black and white stripes and ridden by Goblin's human companion, William the farrier, also dressed in black and white cat-like stripes.

After petting the cats, Stefan headed for the house that he shared with his mother and sister. A few yards from his door, one of the knight's men stopped him. Had he been out last night after the curfew, some emergency, perhaps? Then, if not, had he heard anything unusual? The same questions—but put more gently by this man—that Younger had asked William that morning.

When the sun started to sink behind the fields, Rosemarie closed the last of the baskets of tarts that she had been baking, with Maddie's help, all day. She set the baskets on the table that had been pushed up against the wall to make room for her next endeavor. She had a cauldron of water warming on the fire. She and William hauled an empty laundry tub into their main room. The woman called her son Robin to her and firmly placed little Maddie's hand in his. "Take her across to the cooper's house, and you two play with their new puppies. See that you watch her closely and don't come back until you see the window is opened. Go straight over and don't wander among the booths and strangers!" She shouted this last sentence to the children as they started across the green. Like all mothers, she did not trust strangers with her children, and there were many strangers in town for the fair.

With the children gone, Rosemarie and William began to pour hot and cold water into the laundry vat; soon they had a pleasantly warm bath. Then William latched their front door and stripped off his tunic, hose, shoes, and underwear. He stepped naked into the tub and grunted with pleasure as Rosemarie rubbed his shoulders with a mild soap, bought for the occasion, and gently bathed hot water over his shoulders. She kissed the bony tip of each collarbone. The little kisses were a ritual initially planted ten years ago when William first participated in the parade and they were both young and silly in love. The important role William played in the procession was the reason for the rare bath. It would not do to have the costume he had worn for ten festivals to be soiled with several weeks of accumulated dirt and grime.

Goblin, Snow Beauty, and their four sons, Mrrt, Meouht, Meuht, and Meohie were all dozing either on the bed or by the fire. Suddenly Snow Beauty leapt to the edge of the laundry tub, where she achieved a tottery balance with all four feet lined up in a row, her two hind feet perched outside her two front paws.

"Oh! Please be careful, cat!" cried William as she wobbled toward the soapy water. But after one quick peek into the tub, she seemed satisfied. Emitting a very delicate, feminine mew, she leapt across the tub and returned to her place beside Goblin.

Rosemarie burst into laughter. "She just wanted a look at you!"

William did not think it funny. He rinsed off quickly. He dried himself while standing on a linen towel that Rosemarie spread on their earthen floor so his feet would not get muddied, and dressed.

After they hauled out the water and returned the tub to its place in back of the house, Rosemarie opened the little window, her signal to the children that their father was presentable again.

Darkness settled over the town and with it came the curfew. All over town both parents and children went to bed and dreamt of the next day's festivities. In the farrier's house, Robin slept in the loft overhead and seven-year-old Maddie dreamed blissfully on a cot at the foot of her parents' bed.

Rosemarie whispered to William as they snuggled under the sheet. "You have been so busy at the smithy and I with my baking, I have not yet heard what that meeting was about."

"They want the impossible again. Apparently Sir Rudolph was hit over the head in his own orchard. Lady Alfreda thinks Goblin can find the thug who did it." William turned onto his side and draped an arm over his wife. He pulled her close, for he knew how upset she would be.

"God preserve us! What a horrible thing! The knight himself attacked in his own orchard! We are none of us safe!"

"Gerhard's men have been questioning people. Let's let them do their job; tomorrow the festival begins. Let's get some sleep so we can enjoy it."

He kissed his wife's cheek and buried his nose in her hair. Wishing to spare his wife additional worry, he had decided not to tell Rosemarie, for the time being, that Lady Alfreda thought she had seen a cat like Goblin at her lord's side when she found him. That was the reason the noblewoman had wanted William and Goblin at the meeting. Now as he lay on his bed, Will suddenly remembered Rosemarie mentioning the open window. He rolled over and began to think, now wide awake. *Had the cat been out? Had Snow somehow opened the latch and let him in?* He would not put anything past those two cats. Perhaps Goblin really had been with Sir Rudolph. It was several hours before the smith fell asleep.

Two.

I N THE MORNING, William breakfasted on cheese, yesterday's bread, a swish of beer and one of Rosemarie's delicious tarts that he snitched from a basket when her back was turned. He set Goblin in his special basket. Today was the procession, and any detective work would have to wait until this solemn obligation was fulfilled. They started for the manor.

William had just stepped out the door when Goblin leaped from the basket and began to scratch in the earth at the corner of the house. He squatted over his little hole. Before William could shout "Bad cat!" he realized what the cat was doing. "Oh, yes," he muttered, "We must not embarrass ourselves during the procession. Horses are allowed to make messes wherever they want, but not knights, Sir Goblin."

As they walked up the hill toward the manor they passed the bailiff's house. All kinds of rattling of crockery, shouts, cries, and laughter poured out from the door. The bailiff had a big noisy family that included Young Ger—who was now eighteen and his son by his first wife—and two boys and two girls by his second wife. Ger would be at the fair grounds, where he was supposed to be keeping things orderly or perhaps disorderly if he had stopped in at the tavern first. The bailiff would be at the stable helping to ready the horses and their attire.

As he climbed up the hill, William thought about how different the procession would be this year without the old priest, who had died a few months ago. Anna, the midwife and the priest's housekeeper, said he had died holding his rosary against his heart and with a smile on his wrinkled, old face. He had seen the angels come to carry him to glory, as befits a man of great faith, Anna claimed. William, not being born in Johannesmarkt, was never even sure what the old priest's name was.

Everyone just called him Father, as if he were their actual father, and it seemed that mostly he spoke of God's love. The new priest, young Father Albert, preached nothing but Doom and watching out that one did not step down the path to mortal sin.

But, it was also true that, with the passage of time, the town had changed in other ways. Sir Rudolph's mild rule had encouraged many people to move to the village. It was now a bustling town. There were many new businesses and manufactories. A number of new potters worked near the swale beyond the church. They made earthen jars, bowls plates. Buyers came from miles around.

But a bustling brickyard also used the swale's clay. There, workers—often runaway serfs—labored long hours, for little pay, baking the bricks needed for the fine homes newly rich merchants demanded. The joiners' guild could barely keep up with the demand for fancy furniture and new buildings. Some of the merchants dressed like lords, thought William smiling, as he shifted Sir Goblin's basket to his other arm.

The festival had changed too. Now it lasted a week. Vendors and entertainers attracted much more of the townspeople's interest than did the holy procession and the guild play.

A sparrow twittered across William's path. Its wings dazzled a brilliant white in the insistent sunshine. William thought no more of Doom or about the changes time had brought, only of the fun his family would have. He loved to watch Robin's face as the boy stared wide-eyed at the tumblers, storytellers, and musicians that flocked to the fair. How pleased Rosemarie was to sell her raspberry tarts! And how pleased people were to eat them!

When he reached the top of the hill, William went directly to the stable behind the manor house. Gerhard already had the gentle white palfrey saddled and caparisoned in black and white stripes. He handed William the black hose and striped tunic. The smith changed his clothes and climbed into soft thigh-high leather boots. He turned down the big floppy cuffs. He placed a large fur hat trimmed with black and white ostrich feathers firmly on his head, and mounted the little horse.

Gerhard fastened the basket to the saddle horn, and set Sir Goblin in it. The cat turned around a time or two and mewed. Then he sat with his front feet over the edge of the basket and his head well above the edge, so as to see and be seen when paraded before the throng. The feline knight knew by now what was expected of him. Gerhard led them out of the stable and tied the horse to a post under the shady branches of an oak.

He next led Sir Rudolph's glorious old warhorse out. It too was caparisoned, but in the knight's colors of burgundy and gold. Armor hinged like rows of scales on a dragon covered the horse's head. The bailiff led the horse around to the back steps of the manor house.

Sir Rudolph owned two complete suits of armor. One suit had a heavy shoulder pauldron that wrapped over his left shoulder like a great shell. This armor was only for jousting, when he needed protection from an oncoming lance. All he had to do, then, was hold on to his own weapon and drive it into the shoulder of his opponent to unseat him. His real fighting armor, which he would wear today, was twenty pounds lighter and a work of art in its flexibility, although by now it had undergone many adjustments. Sir Rudolph was nearly forty years old, and getting fatter each year.

Real warfare was now rare in the duchy, but Sir Rudolph and Lady Alfreda still attended tournaments and jousts. For Lady Alfreda, these events meant a chance to mingle with people of her own class and to arrange a marriage for their daughter and only child, Ruth-Anna. Serious negotiations for a betrothal were underway. And while Sir Rudolph fulminated that the young prince Alfreda had snared for her daughter was chicken–necked and chinless—he had more money than brains, and no brawn at all—Lady Alfreda answered only that he was rich and totally enthralled by Ruth-Anna. No one asked Ruth-Anna her opinion.

On this festival day, while Goblin and William waited under the shade of a tree, Sir Rudolph's squire began to clamp the numerous metal pieces onto the unsteady knight, starting with his feet. This squire was not a youth. He should have become a knight himself a long time ago, but he had been hit hard on the head in the battle for Johannesmarkt. Since that battle, his mind had been like that of a boy of twelve. He played, like a child, with knucklebones, and collected bird feathers and shiny stones. They called him Yodel because of the odd little bubbly song he was forever singing softly to himself. He could not do a man's work. Out of kindness and a sense of obligation, Sir Rudolph kept him on as his squire.

Lady Alfreda steadied her wobbly spouse as this man-sized squire lifted the wounded leg to fit the sabaton to the knight's right foot. Next came the greaves around the calves, which were hinged on the outside of his master's legs and fastened on the inside with straps and buckles. The cuisse, the armor for the thigh, was next. Its attached poleyn protected the knee. Here the squire ran into trouble. The knight winced and uttered un-knightly words as Yodel, singing breathily, tugged the poleyn straps around Rudolph's swollen right knee. Yodel pulled again and squeezed the knee so painfully that the knight's metal-cased foot jerked forward and, perhaps intentionally, rammed the squatting man-boy's chest, sitting him down hard on his backside.

When at last the squire handed Sir Rudolph his helmet, he pushed it aside and asked Lady Alfreda for water. Not wine, not beer, nor ale but cold water. When the tankard came from the kitchen, the knight took a long swallow. Then he pulled off one gauntlet and dipped his hand into the vessel. He splashed cool water over his face, onto his temples and the back of his neck. Then he drank off the remainder of the water.

"These tin clothes are a little warm," he joked. The squire attempted a weak laugh at the feeble jest. But Lady Alfreda frowned, worried. *It is a pleasant day, not hot,* she thought. *Does he have a fever?* With Gerhard at his right and Lady Alfreda at his left, each ready to take one arm should the need arise, the knight limped and clanked down the stone steps toward his waiting horse.

As he swung his injured leg over the horse's back, the world turned black for a moment. The nobleman dropped his head against the horse's mane. Slowly, he sat up straight and took a deep breath. To him, it seemed the manor house and the stable were spinning in circles. When, after a few seconds, his head cleared, Sir Rudolph reached for his helmet and put it on, but kept the visor up. At the manor lord's nod, the little parade of knight, squire, and bailiff, and the ladies and their maids, all riding, and other servants who walked, fell in behind William and Goblin.

Lady Alfreda wore a scoop-necked gown of burgundy brocade; a wide girdle of gold braid circled her waist, its tassels falling almost to her hem. When a whisper of a breeze fluttered her headpiece, a sharp eye could catch an occasional glimpse of her abundant red curls under the gauzy veil that floated around the sides and the back of her head. The ruby color of her gown sparked a flaming contrast with her hair and she was easily the most dazzling figure in the little procession. While all eyes fastened on her mother, Ruth-Anna rode behind her, hardly noticed, dressed in a dull forest green gown with lacing tight at the sides that showed her young figure to advantage. Being young and unmarried, she wore no headpiece over hair that fell to her waist in a splendid display of yellow ringlets gripped here and there in clasps of gold wire. The women rode their gentle mares sidesaddle, and their skirts fluttered against the animals' flanks in a gracious diagonal flow, dropping below their toes. As they rode past, peasant farmers whipped off their hats and bowed. The noble lady on her horse was a vision of loveliness seldom seen by the farm hands. The memory of her beauty would inspire several weeks of increased effort from her poor workers.

The procession began at the church, with an altar boy carrying a golden cross on a staff down the church steps. The priest followed, behind an acolyte swinging a smoking censer. The crowd loved the fragrance of the incense. It wafted an atmosphere of holiness over the procession, making them feel a little closer to God's care and diverting their attention, for the moment, from the savory festival pies and cakes awaiting them. Father Albert loved the incense, too, for it disguised, if ever so briefly, the choking stench of the unwashed peasant mob that closed in around him. The statue of Saint John, borne with tender care on the shoulders of devout townsmen, tottered along at its stately pace behind the priest.

A delegation of Benedictine monks followed. They came every year from the monastery that was two days' journey to the south. While most people in the town attributed feats of bravery to Sir Goblin, the monks came because they believed that the blacksmith William, Goblin's guardian, had been a portent of a miraculous salvation when he appeared at their monastery many years ago.

When these holy men reached the point where the manor road entered the town, two heralds raised their long, straight horns, from which burgundy and gold pennants flapped in the light breeze. They trumpeted a fanfare to announce the noble party's entrance into the procession. Young Robin had been standing at this intersection, waiting for his father; he now took hold of the white palfrey's bridle and gently guided the horse bearing the blacksmith and Goblin into position just behind the statue. Several of the town's leading citizens marched, after the monks and the noble party, as an act of devotion. Lastly came musicians.

By custom this pageant would move in a great circle around the square just outside the booths and tents of all the vendors and merchants. About three quarters of the way around, they arrived at the tavern and honored Goblin in the way a cat would most appreciate—with food.

Next, the program, traditionally, would include a prayer and homily on the life and miracles of St. John, and a favorite hymn. Men carried the statue the short distance back to the church, and then the amusements got underway. Tumblers tumbled, jugglers juggled, storytellers and musicians performed. Ale flowed. People sang, danced and laughed. The world was merry and trouble free.

In recent years, because the town had grown so large, the festival had taken on the semblance of a secular trade fair. Vendors threw open their booths to sell their wares the minute the statue returned to the church. They remained in town almost a week, or until their goods ran out.

This year was Father Albert's first time to lead the procession. On this day the new priest walked with deliberate, measured strides, designed to lend as much dignity to his youthful person as possible. He was tall and broad shouldered. He pressed together his long smooth fingers, as if in prayer, and held them against the jewel-studded pectoral cross on his chest. He was never seen to wear a plain wooden cross as his predecessor always had. It was rumored that he had, in fact, remarked once to Paul the innkeeper that nowhere was it written that he should dress like a mendicant. He bowed his head just enough for reverence's sake, but the sharp-eyed among the spectators could see his little grey eyes flit from side to side as he passed by. Was he observing the reaction of the people to his performance? Was he aware, perhaps, that some of the men made jokes about calling him "Father," when their own sons made better use of a razor than he did? Or was he sneaking a peek at the women?

One young woman would later swear that, as her twin sister held up her new baby girl for the priest's blessing, he winked at her as he made the sign of the cross over her niece's forehead.

Slowly the procession neared the tavern. There Sir Rudolph raised his hand, signaling the riders to halt. The musicians at the rear of the parade fell silent. The monks and the other churchmen moved a little beyond the tavern, stopped, and turned to face the onlookers in the center of the square. Joanna, the tavern's mistress and head cook, had set a long table outside in front of her establishment. It was covered with a glistening white cloth that hung to the ground on either side.

Sir Rudolph's heralds sounded another fanfare on their long trumpets. Joanna emerged from the dark interior of the inn. She stepped up to the white table, and with a great flourish, set a large oval pan directly in its center. She ducked back into the tavern. Young Robin went up to his father's horse and pulled Goblin from the basket. It was all the lad could do to hold on to the squirming big cat, who wiggled and twisted and stretched his neck out toward the pan. He knew the ceremony well. Sir Rudolph removed his helmet preparatory to making his annual speech.

"Sir Goblin, we do thee honor this day," he began. " 'Tis but a small recompense for all . . ."

After a few more words, he stopped speaking, and passed a gauntleted hand across his brow. His wounded head was pounding again, and the world was blackening before his eyes.

"Place the cat," he ordered, and nudged his horse away from the table. He took up a position near the churchmen. Lady Alfreda rode to his side, as did the bailiff.

The musicians hesitated a few seconds, since they, like everyone else, had been expecting a long and florid speech. Then they pattered out a long drum roll. After another trumpet blast, Joanna reappeared the tavern door with a large black iron pot held in both hands. Robin set Sir Goblin on the table. The cat arched his back. He shook himself once all over to straighten his fur after being clutched and mussed by the boy. Then, he stepped up expectantly to the pan. The crowd roared and applauded. Joanna poured her special stew of rabbit and lamb into the waiting dish. Goblin crouched with his tail stretched straight out behind him, and lapped merrily. The musicians ceased their drum roll. For a few seconds, as if time had halted, all was quiet.

Only the delicate sound of the knighted cat's lapping tongue disturbed the silence. Then came a quiet padding of little footsteps. Cats. Dozens of soft feet scurried over the dusty ground. Scores of furry shoulders brushed past the skirts and hose of the spectators to join the feast. Snow Beauty, Mrrt, Meouht, Meuht and Meohie were the first to appear and join their lord at the pan. In a few minutes the entire perimeter of the pan was crowded with cats, mostly white with grey-striped tails, and mostly related to Goblin in some way, joyfully lapping up the tasty feast. A ring of cats sat beyond the diners awaiting a second sitting. The humans chattered and laughed. They counted the cats and made guesses as to which animal belonged to whom, which was the biggest, and which would eat the most. The children laughed and clapped their hands.

A woman looked down as something brushed past her russet skirt. One more cat had arrived. The cat sat down on the ground to catch her breath. Her ribs rippled against her thin skin as she struggled to take in air. Then she stood, and everyone could see how her thin flanks caved in against her spine. Her fur, once shiny white, was matted and a dull, dirty grey. Driven by a stomach-cramping hunger, the emaciated animal gathered her haunches over her hind feet, shuffled a time or two, and leaped for the tabletop. She missed. She tried again, putting all her feeble strength into the attempt. This time her front claws caught the tablecloth and she hung struggling, dangling. Robin stepped up, slipped his hand beneath her, and gave her a little shove onto the table. There she stood panting and desperate for breath, her eyes wide with panic. A couple of the waiting cats turned to look at her, stretching their necks out to sniff her identity. Then one turned back and pushed his nose against

Goblin's shoulder. The feline knight looked up and saw Magdalene, for it was, indeed, Magdalene, his first daughter. The other cats stood aside respectfully keeping his slot at the pan open, awaiting his decision, as he stepped away from the pan. Goblin went to the mangy cat, and gently rubbed his head against her cheeks. Both cats mewed softly to each other. He led the sick cat to his place at the delicious pan of meat. She ate as if she had not eaten in weeks.

The human spectators of this scene of obvious cat love were awestruck. Rarely had they seen a cat so miserable looking. Certainly their cats died when their times came, but usually due to some disease or injury that took them quickly. Johannesmarkt cats were happy cats.

"I think she is the old priest's cat, Magdalene," said a familiar voice from the crowd. It was Anna, the town's most respected midwife, who had spoken. She stood, hands on hips, her feet spread apart to support her bulky body. A formidable person when crossed, she planted her feet solidly against the ground, and let her eyes slowly drift accusingly to where the new priest stood, her lips working as if she were considering her next words.

But before she could speak, a loud groan and then a clank turned all eyes to Sir Rudolph. Once again, he was sliding from his horse and would have hit the ground were it not for Yodel's swift intervention. His helmet had clattered down his armored leg and fallen in the dirt. Even now, Yodel was tying his lord's hands with the reins and fastening them to the saddle horn. Gerhard rode up to his master, righted the fainting man on his horse, and led the entire noble household back to the manor. Gerhard paced the horses as swiftly as he could without them breaking into a bouncy trot—the faster pace would have tossed the insensible knight to the ground.

Three.

A S THE NOBLE party disappeared up the manor road, with a thin cloud of dust eddying around their horses' hooves, a cry of "Murderer! Killer!" rang from one of the vendor's booths. Immediately another voice screamed "Thief! Stop! Thief!"

People ran everywhere at this hue and cry. The priest, calm amid the clamor, ordered his people into the church, and the saint's image disappeared safely behind the heavy doors. Everyone forgot about the cats.

A woman pushed her way through the crowd. It was Liselotte's mother. Seeing William still sitting on his little horse and wearing his striped costume, she headed for the cat table. Goblin stood up, arched his back and stretched his tail toward the sky. Then he settled into a sitting position, tail wrapped around his front legs, ready to pay attention. Magdalene still lapped at the stew but the other cats had all dashed for cover at the outbreak of so much noise and confusion.

Not seeing any of the knight's men or anyone of authority except possibly the farrier, the good woman threw up her hands. "Whom do I go to? Who will help me? I've been robbed!"

William dismounted and handed the little horse's reins to Robin. Putting his arm around her shoulder, he steered the distraught woman back to her booth. "Let's take a look," he said.

Reaching her booth, he saw her daughter Lotte behind the counter and, as usual, a flock of young men gathered in front of it. Just as William stepped up to the booth, Younger reached clumsily across the counter to take Lotte's hand. She snatched it away.

"Aw, come on, Lotte, where's the harm? I'll give you the price of three dolls for just one and a kiss. Jush a leetle kiss."

"No, get away."

Lotte and her mother were seamstresses. The girl's father had died two years before, and the women managed a simple living by sewing. But Lotte also had an artistic streak. She often sewed late into the night by firelight, making dolls. They were delightful creations. The dolls had cloth bodies stuffed with wood shavings, often supplied by Stefan the joiner or donated by the cooper's shop. They had embroidered faces, and sometimes button eyes. Their hair was twisted wool yarn. The dolls' gowns—or, on the boy dolls, doublets and hose—were all made of scraps from the clothes the two seamstresses made for women of the town.

Lotte had sold these dolls at last year's fair. And this year their patrons had rushed to her booth as soon as the awning was up to see if they could buy a doll whose clothes were made of scraps from their own gowns.

But it was not just women flocking to the gaily-decorated booth; fathers and brothers also elbowed their way to the counter to surprise their sisters and daughters. Stefan was there in addition to Young Ger.

The girl's mother pushed Younger away. "Our cash box is gone," she snarled accusingly.

"Oh, ish that the problem," Younger said, slurring a word or two. He had been meditating on Lotte's golden curls and his beery brain was barely aware of the hubbub.

Stefan looked over the counter. He then limped around to the door at the side of the booth. Going into the booth, he dropped to his knees and picked up a wooden box. Grabbing hold of the counter top and pushing hard with his good leg, he stood up. "No, here it is," his thin voice squeaked.

The older woman snatched the box and shook it. No sound. She threw back the hinged lid. It was empty. The mother glared at Lotte.

"I never left the booth," maintained the girl.

"Yes, but do you give your attention to the moneybox, or to the young men?" scolded her mother. She glared again at young Gerhard, who spread his hands in an "I have nothing to hide" gesture.

"Would you mind if I reassured her?" asked William, finding an unaccustomed authority in his voice and not a little secret joy in patting down Gerhard's close fitting doublet after the younger man's insolence of the previous morning. He had no pouch secreted within his shirt. Younger put up with it all with a good grace, even volunteering his own purse for inspection.

"You'll find within, my dear ladies, just enough for—," here he paused and looked again at Lotte, "one doll and a kiss." Coins enough for three dolls jingled from the little leather bag. The bailiff's son smacked kissing sounds at the girl, who turned scarlet, and, scraping up his money again, he headed for the tavern.

"'Twould seem the thief is well gone, Lotte," said William. "But the fair has just begun. There is plenty of time yet to make good money." Then, remembering that he was still dressed in black and white cat stripes, he made his way quickly to Robin and the horse.

Just once he paused to have a word with the cooper, who was complaining of the unruliness of the crowd and that none of the knight's men seemed to be available to enforce order. "We thought we had a murder. There was such a brawl among those brick makers," said the cooper. "The fellow was knocked out cold but seems to have come around. A thick head, he has."

"In more than one sense," said William as he moved on toward the tavern.

"What happened? What kept you?" asked Robin, looking weary and a little put upon for having to hold the horse's reins, when all the excitement of the annual fair was buzzing around him.

"I'll tell you on the way to the manor. But let's see how your mother is doing," said his father, taking the reins and leading the animal over to a busy food table.

Here Rosemarie was doing a brisk business selling her raspberry pies. Maddie sat on a stool behind her. The little girl's smile spread from ear to ear, all raspberry red. William picked up a pie and tossed his wife a coin. He was about to bite into it when his wife scowled and stared at his chest. Remembering his cat stripes were velvet and not washable, he handed the tart to Robin who virtually inhaled it. He bought the boy a second, saying as they left the table, "I must get out of this rigging so I can enjoy myself."

The father and son had made their way across the fairground, leading the horse. Just as they were about to start up the hill to the manor to return the horse and costume, Goblin's head popped up over the edge of his basket and chirped a little meow. Sir Goblin's part in the formal ceremonies was over after he ate his stew; he was now free to wander around the town and just be an ordinary cat. The two humans did not think he was still with them. But during the hubbub over the robbery, the feline knight, like any cat after eating a big meal, needed a short catnap. His basket was just the right size for a curled-up snooze. Now the big cat gripped the side of the bobbing basket with the claws of both front paws. He gazed around him, twitching his nose and gaping his mouth to take in all the wonderful smells flowing and blowing across the crowded fair ground, odors both sharp and subtle, odors that dull humans never imagined existed. He folded his ears back against his head in concentration. His bearings taken, and satisfied that he was on the return trip to the knight's stables, the big cat leaned eagerly ahead with his ears now pitched forward as if in anticipation of some great adventure.

"What could that cat be so excited about?" asked young Robin. It was for him, the farrier's son, that all this was new, not Sir Goblin. He had never been up to the manor, never been near the great stone house with its stables, big kitchens, numerous outbuildings, fields and huge orchard. Robin had heard many times how, long before he was born, his mother and father, along with Goblin and Snow Beauty, had come to this isolated stronghold. They had come in search of a captured Baron. The boy knew by heart how Goblin had found the man, and of how the knight and his father had defeated the evil Lord Hubert and Odo, his murderous henchman. Every winter, the family gathered by the fireplace for the annual retelling of the story, and every winter William's part in the adventure seemed to grow more substantial. So, as they walked up the hill on this warm summer day, Robin suddenly wondered aloud why it was the knight and not his father who was awarded the fiefdom. The smith quickly reprimanded the boy for his sauciness, fearing the boy might say something inappropriate in front of the nobility. Hushing him, William explained he was no swordsman, and that everyone was born to his station in life and could not change it. No one should overstep. It was a lesson learned quickly by an overreaching young farrier many years ago when William was fined in the knight's court. Chastened and embarrassed, the boy walked along head down, kicking a stone.

The sun was reaching the peak of its arc. An eagle soared in lazy circles, black against the brilliant sky, and the knight's bees buzzed by on their way to clover, as William and Robin drew near the stockade's open gate. The guard waved them through and William led the pony around behind the house. Robin gawked at the vast stone walls, so massive and powerful-looking—especially compared to his little wooden three-room house—the wide steps of the front entrance, the sun-spattered glass in the windows of the solar. They passed a serving girl drawing water from a well. Her crisp white apron dazzled in the sun. As they came near the stables, the sweet heavy smell of so many horses made the youth's head spin.

A stable lad came for the pony. Robin had never seen any of these people before. It was another world completely up here.

His father pulled Goblin and the basket from the little horse and the cat scampered off, batting at a dark-blue-tailed butterfly that had had the audacity to flutter over his nose. The cat then disappeared on some adventure of his own. The two townsmen followed the little horse's swaying rump into the stable. Here, out of the sun's midday glare, Robin paused, blinking his eyes to adjust to the relative darkness. Once used to the dimness, he could see two rows of horses' rumps jutting beyond their stable partitions. Sir Rudolph kept enough animals for his family and for a small corps of men-at-arms should he need them. Grooms moved about rubbing down the noble family's recently returned beasts, while others cleaned up saddles and various pieces of tack. Still others pitched hay and poured grain.

Against the wall near the front of the stable stood a rough wooden table, on which some familiar looking clothing was piled. Here, William removed his feathered hat and ran his fingers through the sweaty indentation that the heavy hatband had left in his hair. He tugged a heavy oaken chest, hinged with broad iron bands, from beneath the table, and eased back its cumbersome lid. He was about to place the hat within, when a boy dressed in a fine burgundy linen tunic and the soft shoes of a house servant, not a stable lad's rough boots, ran up to him. He was somewhat out of breath from running up to the stable.

"Here, I'll take that. We'll clean it for next year." William handed over the sweat-soaked hat and bent to untie his hose. The houseboy hovered while Robin helped his father out of the boots. William peeled off the hot clinging hose and pulled off the heavy cat-striped doublet. The servant reached for the warm sweaty clothes. It was a comfort for William to put on his friendly old linen tunic and pull on his own dry hose. He knelt to tie on his shoes at his ankles. Then, standing, the smith brushed straw from his knees and gave his tunic a straightening tug. Robin handed him his girdle with its sheathed knife and purse.

He and Robin walked out of the stable and almost ran into the bailiff, Gerhard senior.

"William! Before you go, do you have the cat with you?" he said, looking around. As if commanded, Sir Goblin's front legs slid out from behind a bucket, pushing a pile of straw ahead of him. A mouse jumped and the cat pounced and snatched the rodent by its back.

"Wait. Come here, Goblin." William picked up the cat-mouse combination and turned to face the bailiff.

"Before you go," the estate's manager began again, "his lordship commands that you and he—," the bailiff nodded toward the cat, "investigate where his lordship fell the other night." With that he turned on his heel and led them to the side of the manor house.

"I hope his lordship is well."

"He is resting," was the intentionally uninformative answer. "He left by this door and went this way," the bailiff continued, pointing. Goblin had snapped the mouse's neck and William removed it from the cat's mouth, receiving an angry growl and hiss for his effort.

"Later, Gob," he whispered and put the limp rodent in his purse.

Following the bailiff, William, Robin, and Goblin tramped in a line down a narrow grassy path to the orchard. They came first to some young, newly planted trees braced with rope against destructive winds. So young were the trees, they gave no shade, and only the smallest sparrow could find a seat on their slender branchlets. Next they came to a rise, the top of the hill. Looking out from this spot, one could see the whole town spread below them with its rooftops slated or tiled or thatched and long blue threads of smoke that streamed tall from the chimneys before dispersing in the rising air. The view of the swirling crowds and bright pennants and awnings snapping and buckling in the breeze fascinated young Robin. Never had he seen his town like this. But the bailiff drew their attention to the hill across from the town, where the rutted road rose up pink in the sunlight past the gristmill, and up to another hilltop almost as high as the one they stood on.

"Sir Rudolph often sat here to look upon the site of his last true battle. You, William, young as you were then, must remember how he was. A great man of action." The bailiff's eyes shone with pride when he thought of the warrior his master had once been.

William nodded. He did remember. He saw again in his mind's eye a younger Sir Rudolph, brandishing a tankard of ale in the great hall of this very same manor house, as he complained to his men that he preferred the clamor of battle to the tedious diplomatic negotiations with Lord Hubert. But William also knew that the peace of the past several years had brought the townspeople a prosperity and happiness that no war booty could match.

"He did well for us, milord."

"Yes, yes, he did. But a melancholy seems to have come over him, as if a spell were cast. 'I have become a farmer, Gerhard,' he would sometimes say to me."

William looked up at the bailiff's face. In the pale blue eyes, the smith glimpsed a fear and a sadness he did not understand.

"William, he must recover. A knight who cannot ride . . ." he left the rest unsaid. A few yards farther on, they came to a low, stone bench. "Here is where he sat, where it happened."

William and Robin could see the disturbance of the ground. Goblin grew still but for his tail, which switched angrily, slapping from side to side. The cat picked his way slowly, almost stealthily, through the grass, pausing now and again to sniff first the grass and then the air. From time to time, he would lift his head and look around, once widening his eyes at Robin and William.

"Her ladyship was right. He does seem to know this place," said the bailiff. "Let me know—at my house—if you learn anything." He turned and walked back toward the manor house, leaving the three to their investigation.

Four.

GOBLIN CAME TO the place where the knight's boots had scraped the ground bare of grass. The ground had dried since the knight's fall, but two dusty scrapings remained, each about the length, the cat estimated, of three human feet. Goblin sniffed the earth and looked up again at the two humans. Then the cat put his head down and began to sniff the dirt at the end of one rut, running his nose over, and thoroughly inspecting every grain of soil. His cat eyes could not focus sharply on the imprint so close below his nose, but he gathered a world of information from the scent he was picking up.

William walked up to him slowly so as not to startle the big cat. "What is it, Goblin? What is so special about this little spot? Oh, I see. Come look at this, Robin."

The boy approached. "See this?" The father traced his finger over the indentation that Goblin had discovered. Being careful not to touch or change it, he moved his finger first in semicircle, then up and back five times.

"A handprint!" exclaimed the boy, "The knight's, I suppose."

Having finished his inspection, knowing now that he had the scent of a second person, the grey-striped knight trotted over to where a young apple tree had sprouted up from seed, pushing its way through the soil and rocks. It was under these rocks, in a hole dug out by another four-legged resident, that Goblin had found his rabbits. There were none there now. After losing one youngster, the mother rabbit had no doubt moved her nest—or perhaps Brutus had come back and emptied the nest for her, devouring all the little creatures. There was a heavy scent of dog on the grass. Goblin's nose turned over a few fluffy bits of fur and a tiny bone.

Goblin lifted his head and was studying the air again, disappointed that the rabbits were no longer around, when Robin ran up and squatted by the little hole. "What's here, Goblin?" He jabbed his finger at the bit of fluff. It blew against his hand. The boy spotted the little piece of bone. Brushing the fur from his hand and watching it float away over the valley, he called to his father, "Lady Alfreda was right. There was a rabbit."

Father and son stood looking around, wondering if there was anything more to see. Goblin bounced here and there in the grass, swatting at a moth and then diving for a beetle. The cat had no idea that he was part of an investigation. He was aware only that he had now both the scent and a visual image of another person having been present.

He had also a vague feline feeling that some violent deed had been done that night. He, a predator, was very knowledgeable about violence. Its uses were three: to provide food, to sharpen hunting skills, and to amuse. Batting down moths, as he was doing now, was most amusing, great fun. Even this amusement was related to the other two uses. It sharpened his hunting skills and provided snacks. It was like the knight, Sir Rudolph's, jousts and tournaments—basically entertainment, but with a purpose. But unlike human knights, Sir Goblin thought with a certain pride, he and the other tomcats never did deadly battle. Although he had to admit he had seen some tomcats come scar-faced and tatter-eared from fights for the right to hold a lady cat's paw. Still they did not have wars like the humans, making felines the better creature in the big cat's opinion.

Goblin was bouncing and pouncing merrily in the orchard when a butterfly led him over a little ridge. Had not Robin turned to look at the deep woods behind the orchard, they would have lost sight of their cat.

William was getting very hungry. His stomach growled, and he felt such emptiness in his belly that he thought if he could look down his throat, he would see his toes. "Let's go back. Where's Goblin?"

"Down there," answered his son, pointing to where Goblin had dropped over the edge of the hill. They hurried up to the cat and saw him strike at a beetle. His forelegs slid, scraping up the thin layer of soil and grass, and laying bare the smooth edge of a stone step. He was at the top of a series of steps that once led to an old building, long torn down. Goblin scratched after the beetle, skittering his claws on the stone. Blades of grass flew, and under the cat's paws, Robin saw a large circle of gold. "What is this? A coin? Father, come see this," said the boy.

William came over and, taking the coin, for that was indeed what it was, he rubbed its surface free of dirt with his thumb. "I have never seen a coin quite like this. Must be an old one."

"Meow."

"Look, Father. Goblin wants to go into the woods. See, the path continues," said the boy.

"No, I'm starving," answered the smith. "Get Goblin. We'll show this to Gerhard. The knight's people can follow the path, if they wish."

As they came up to the bailiff's big noisy house, young Gerhard was just staggering up to its door. He had a colorful bundle tucked under his arm. As he pulled the door open he staggered backward.

"Drunk as usual," whispered William. "Don't say anything about it," he warned his son.

A slow grin spread across Younger's face as he leaned against the doorjamb and gestured for the smith to enter. "Good day to you, Pushycat." He reached a finger to Goblin's chin.

Just then the bailiff filled the doorway. "What have you been up to?" he growled at his son. Then he saw William and Robin. After a quick glare at his son listing against the door, the bailiff asked William, "Have you learned something?"

Hurriedly, for he wanted to get back to town for some food and sensed a family row was about to break out at the bailiff's house, he explained about the hand print, rabbit fur, the coin, and the path leading further into the woods.

The bailiff held his hand out for the coin and polished it with his thumb, much as William had done. He flipped it over. "These have not been in circulation for a long time. Must go back to the last Elector." He folded his fingers around the coin. "I must show this to Sir Rudolph. You have done well, William."

Thus dismissed, the three—man, boy, and cat—walked down the hill to get some of the fair's fine food.

The bailiff shut the door to his house. If William had been expecting to hear angry words as he walked away, he was disappointed. Inside, he would have seen Younger drop down on a bench and pull the bundle from under his arm. Grinning, he looked from one little sister to the other, the same little girls who were usually pulling each other's hair and plaguing their half-brother constantly.

Slowly he unrolled the bundle and pulled out two beautiful dolls. Each was about a foot in height and dressed in exquisite material. One wore blue silk damask and a pointed headpiece in the French style, a cone from which a gauzy veil fluttered. The second wore burgundy and gold, not unlike what her ladyship had worn in the procession that morning. Younger jiggled the dolls in front of his little sisters, bobbing their heads with his index fingers. The two little imps squealed with delight.

"How about a little kiss for your penniless brother?"

The two girls jumped on his lap and threw their arms around his neck and kissed his cheeks until they were red. Handing over the dolls, he averted any arguments before they arose, saying, "Blue eyes gets blue dress. Yellow hair gets the gold. I should be so successful with all the ladies!"

Five.

WILLIAM AND ROBIN pulled stools up to one of the tables set outside the tavern. The smith plopped both elbows on the table and then waved for Joanna. "Two hungry beasts here, tavern mistress."

The big woman laughed, ducked into her establishment and returned with steaming bowls of stew, brimming with peas and large chunks of mutton. She pulled spoons from her apron pocket. "Be back with your drink."

Setting down two tankards of beer, a large for the father, and a smaller, weaker one for the boy, she nodded to the priest who had paused in front of their table. "Good day to you, Father Albert."

His grey eyes flicked toward her for a brief instant. He nodded, but his attention was on some activity at the fair.

Curious, because of his apparent rudeness, Joanna followed his gaze. People were moving all around, buying and selling, drinking, laughing. In the center of the fairground, a juggler was amazing the crowd by keeping five balls in the air and occasionally bouncing one off the top of his head. Among those gathered to watch were Stefan and Lotte, whose mother was, no doubt, taking her place at their doll booth. The priest's eyes were fixed on them. After watching for a minute, Joanna thought she knew why. From time to time Stefan's hand shyly reached for Lotte's. Their arms remained still, motionless at their sides. Only their fingers interlaced for a long moment and then broke away. *Oh, the poor dears*, thought the giantess, *we'll be hearing about unseemly demonstrations of affection in public places in Sunday's homily.* She wiped her hands on the towel that hung from her apron waistband and returned to her cooking inside, wondering why the priest focused on the innocent young couple when there were scores of beery louts nuzzling merry wenches all about the fair.

William and Robin scraped their bowls clean. Then, jingling a coin across the table for the serving girl, the smith took Robin to his mother's booth for more raspberry tarts. It would be Robin's third of the day, and William wanted to have at least one of his wife's specialties before the tarts were gone. They chatted while they ate. Rosemarie thought she would sell out of tarts before the dinner hour. Also, Anna had taken Maddie to her house for a nap, Rosemarie told her husband. A nap sounded like a good idea to William. He gave Robin some spending money and sent him off to have some well-deserved fun at the fair. The boy disappeared in an instant.

Wishing he had such energy after a heavy meal, William headed for home. On his way, he passed Stefan and Father Albert. Their heads were bent together; they spoke in whispers. "I can get you what you want," was all William heard the priest say as he strode by.

For the next several days, William heard nothing more of investigations or anything about the knight's health. On the second day of the festival, he and Rosemarie took the two children to see the joiners' guild play in front of the church. Rosemarie, indeed, had sold all her tarts the first day. She always did. After a day of rest she collected more berries and had a second batch ready on the fourth day of the fair. She sold all of those, too.

The weather had remained dry for the week. By now dust was kicking up under the horses' hooves and the air was hazy with swirls of brown dirt. The sun burned on relentlessly. The air grew very hot. Tempers flared and rumors flew. Rosemarie came home the fourth day with her ears full of horrible stories.

A brawl had broken out in the tavern with much smashing of crockery and flinging of stools. Younger now exhibited a bump on his head the size of a small hen's egg from being in the path of a flying three-legged stool. Surprisingly, he was not one of the instigators. The ruckus seemed to begin, as nearly as anyone could remember, by name calling from, of all people, the little crippled Stefan, who, feeling powerful—aided apparently by ale—accused a potter of inappropriate attentions to his sister. Other drinkers joined him, either to settle simmering grudges or just for the entertainment and exercise. Stefan now carried his right arm in a sling, in addition to dragging around his feeble leg. The regular denizens of the tavern were left shaking their heads and wagging their tongues about his odd words, something like, "You had your drink of power last night."

Then, overnight, a rash of robberies had left vendors and merchants howling for justice. The future of the fair was at stake, they claimed. Who would come if their merchandise and cash boxes were stolen while they slept? Most vendors now slept in their booths, pitching a cot or simply spreading some blankets across the dirt floor. Even the wealthier merchants, the sellers of cloth, rugs, pottery, porcelain and brass items, left their servants to guard their large booths while they accommodated themselves at the inn, enjoying good food but often elbowing in three to a bed.

Throughout the week of the fair, the knight's men patrolled the roads to the town. They escorted merchants—some laden with wares, coming to the fair, and some burdened with profits, leaving for their next market— safely along the roads as far as the knight's authority extended. This was a profitable time for bandits and a woeful time for any merchant fat with cash to venture forth without some kind of escort. Many brought their own stout men. But it was Sir Rudolph's responsibility, being the law, to guard the roads. This responsibility did not go unrewarded. In fact, it represented a sizable portion of the knight's cash income from the fees he collected for this protection.

As for the town, it had grown so fast from a hamlet to a fair-sized town that no organized system yet existed for its management. Guild members attempted to solve their problems within the walls of their guild houses. Other disputes and petty crimes were brought before the knight's court. Major difficulties had arisen in recent years over where to put new streets and houses, and even where the town began and ended, but no disturbances as major as this week's trouble.

The morning of the fifth day of the fair, the bailiff Gerhard and six of the knight's men-at-arms stopped in front of the smithy. William pulled a hinge strap, not yet red, from the forge fire and set it aside. He rushed outside quickly, hammer in hand, to see what all these men wanted. The bailiff asked him to check one of his horse's shoes. Gerhard dismounted and flung the reins over the hitching rail. Gently, William lifted the animal's front hoof. "A minor matter. Will take but a minute." He went inside for his tools. The bailiff followed him in.

"A word with you," he said, taking the smith by the sleeve.

William looked at him with some trepidation. Second only to the knight in authority, the bailiff now sounded very gruff.

"That coin, it hasn't been minted for fifty years. Where did you find it?"

"I told you. The cat found it on that square-shaped stone."

"The step. There are three of them. Apparently there was once a building of some sort there, but nothing now remains. But that path seems fresh trodden and continues for some way into the wood. I followed it a short way. I am here because my son says late in the night, the night before last, he heard voices."

William dropped his hammer and bent to pick it up. All the time his mouth worked hard, twitching on either side. Then his lips pressed firmly together. The smith covered his mouth with his fist and made a polite cough. It was all he could do not to laugh out loud at the thought of a drunken Younger hearing voices.

The bailiff's eyes squinted and blazed. He had not been fooled by William's polite fake cough, but the matter was urgent and he continued, "Voices from the woods after the curfew."

William did not ask how young Gerhard had managed to be out after the curfew. No doubt he was rolling home after a long night at the tavern.

"Doubtless you have heard of the troubles in town. The town fathers are most agitated. They would meet with his lordship, but . . ." here the bailiff stopped speaking, as if afraid he might say too much. When he resumed he admitted quietly, "I cannot say that I blame them for being angry, but my hands are tied until I escort all the visitors from town and collect the road taxes, and there is still the farm to manage. And," he paused, "yes, there is more, but that is enough for you to know, for now. I want you and your animal to take another look."

In the end, William had been granted permission to tramp through Sir Rudolph's demesne, taking whomever he wanted for assistance, even a horse from the knight's stable if he desired, all toward discovering the knight's attacker.

Six.

ROSEMARIE BEGAN CHATTERING like an angry squirrel as soon as William stepped into their house for supper. Her cheeks were as red as little balls of flame; her bodice was soaked through with sweat from cooking before the open fire. Little wisps of hair broke away from the long braid she had arranged down her back, and she kept swiping them back from her face. But it was not the heat from the sun or the hearth that was the source of her agitation. As William slid into his place at the table next to Robin, she ran her hands down her apron, smoothing it, and took a deep breath.

"William, I heard the most awful thing today. I went to the well an hour ago for more water and I met Anna there. She said to me, 'Rosemarie, I saw the most horrible thing. The poor little thing, so thin, so poorly she looked at the end. Last night, it was. I was coming home very late from attending a birth. The poor girl had such long labor for a first one. She was exhausted and so was I. No, I can't tell you whom I was attending. She doesn't want it known. These girls today. I don't know what the world's coming to. Well, it'll come out, but not from me.'

"Anna eventually got to the point. 'I was just walking past the church, when I hear someone cry out, "Get away! Get out of here!" Then a little squeal-like sound and a thump. I look up and I see Father Albert walking toward the church, as if coming from his house. Once again he was carrying a tall candlestick, like one from the altar; I swear it was one from the church. I didn't let him see me this time.'

"'This time?'" I ask.

"And she says, 'Yes, just like about a week ago. Another late baby delivery, you know, he saw me then and he asked *me* what I am doing out beyond the curfew. I stopped and said to him—I had my bag and my little stool, you know—so I say, "Father, it is I, Anna, the midwife. I have been attending to the arrival of a new soul."

"'And he says, "Humph! New soul? Children of the devil, as like as not, come at this hour. Old woman, mind what you do."

"'Rosie, I tell you, I have never felt so threatened in all my years! That voice! Then this morning when I came out for water, I saw the poor little thing. Just lying there up against the church wall behind some grass. Flies coming already. It's Magdalene. At least I think so.'"

Rosemarie stopped talking. She was wiping tears from her checks. Behind her, Goblin and Snow Beauty rose from their nap by the fireside and jumped up to the little window. They were out in an instant.

"Did you go look?" asked her husband.

"Oh, no! I couldn't."

"I'll go. The cats just left."

He got up and went out. Robin ran after him

"Me, too!" said Maddie.

"No! You sit right there and eat your food!" said her father.

Goblin, Snow, and their four nine-month-old sons Mrrt, Meouht, Meuht, and Meohie were standing before a small crumpled lump of matted fur when William got to the church. Silently, he and Robin looked upon the earthly remains of Magdalene, for it was indeed she. He thought of how the old priest had loved her, and he saw her once again in his mind's eye, curled up between St. Joseph and the Infant in the Christmas crèche. For years she had made herself part of the Christmas story in this way. Most children growing up in Johannesmarkt probably thought there really was a cat in the Christmas story. Magdalene had been special cat; of that there was no doubt. Now she looked very small. Her dull fur had been much matted in recent days, as she became too weak to groom herself. Her ribs were visible under her thin skin. A grey spot, round, and about the size of the toe of a man's boot, marked where her ribs had been crushed in. The cats stood with their tails hung down, drooped into despairing arches. Their heads dropped low. Very slowly, after standing quiet for several minutes, Goblin inched forward, one foot at a time, as if stalking a bird.

"Perhaps you shouldn't look, Goblin," said Robin. Tears ran shamelessly down the boy's cheeks. He had never known a world without Magdalene. He reached over to pick up Goblin, but his father stopped him.

"Let him. Let him say goodbye."

Goblin sat down close to the dead cat. Flies were already working over her eyes and mouth. The feline knight stretched out his neck and sniffed at the grey spot, once deeply and then again briefly. He got up and walked away; going over to Snow Beauty he rubbed against her cheek once. Magdalene had been the daughter from their first litter so many years ago. Then he crouched staring away toward the priest's house. He opened his mouth. Too quietly for human ears, he let out a long hiss.

"He understands everything." The speaker was Anna, who had seen the mourners from her window and come to join them. Joanna and Paul came over from the tavern and stood silently. Then Paul said, "He never fed her like the old one did. I gave him food for her but I wonder if she got it." Just the idea of one of the town's revered cats possibly going hungry appalled the round little innkeeper.

William sent Robin back to his house for a spade. Only then, while he waited for the boy to return, did he think of what the priest might say and what, if anything, was the church's teaching on animals buried in the churchyard. This, though, was not the side where the cemetery was, but merely the yard between the priest's house and the sanctuary. Frowning and chewing on his lower lip, the farrier glanced quickly toward the priest's house.

"Do not worry about him," Joanna assured him. "He is not here. I saw the cooper come for him. I think his mother, old Wanda, is going to her reward, at last."

Puffing for breath, and with sweat and tears both trickling down his face, for it was still a warm evening, the boy returned, rushing up with the metal-tipped wooden spade jouncing on his shoulder. William seized the spade and dug quickly and deeply, flinging dirt first left, then right. He did not stop for breath until he had made a hole three feet deep. After a few deep breaths, he scraped the loose soil from the bottom of the hole as if making it clean for Magdalene. Then taking the cat's stiff body by a hind leg, he pulled her over and dropped her into the hole. He shoveled dirt over her, not looking at where her body lay until all the fur was covered. When the hole was once again filled, he tapped the earth down firmly with the back of the shovel. Then he scraped a little grass and gravel over the spot to make it less obvious. Straightening up, he wiped his face dry with the heel of one hand and batted back an incipient tear. They stood a minute, each thinking their own thoughts, or perhaps prayers, for the little cat.

When they heard a door open across the square, the human mourners all left quickly for their houses, not wanting to encounter the priest. But the cats stayed a moment longer. Others of their kind joined them. They crouched and purred and clawed at the ground kneading it thoroughly. When they heard a door slam shut they ran off. A moment later the priest returned to his house, never noticing the dead cat was no longer lying there.

When William and Robin reached their house, Robin's father leaned the spade against the shed and dusted off his hands. Inside, he and Robin picked at their supper, now cold. It was a long silent evening broken only by occasional sniffing as Rosemarie or Robin wiped at tears. No one wanted to talk, and they filled the time until dark inventing little household tasks to keep themselves occupied. Just before they all got into bed there came a scraping at the door.

William let in Snow Beauty, Goblin and the four young toms. Snow Beauty lay down before the banked fire resting on her side and sighed. She gave her paw a listless lick or two. Then dropped her chin onto her front leg. She shut her eyes for a moment then opened them again and stared ahead without seeing. Goblin threw himself down and lay in dreary abandon with his legs and tail lying splayed as dropped, not neatly collected, as was the usual habit of cats. He groaned and turned his head to the side. His chest expanded and he blew out a great rush of air, a profound sigh, and groaned again. He was an old cat, some fourteen or fifteen years old. Never had he expected to outlive his favorite daughter. Now he felt like a very old cat.

Seven.

THE MORNING THAT the bailiff had stopped at the smithy, Stefan woke up feeling happy, strong, and in control. His injured arm was all but healed. Only a small bruise colored the tip of his elbow. True, his leg was still weak, but he had good hope for that. At noon today he would see Lotte and ask her to marry him. He smiled, as he pictured their life together. His smile was not entirely sweet or innocent. He would not hear of her saying no again. He was confident she would agree to be his, now, even before a house was ready. They would begin a new and different life together "in the Power." He would rise eventually close to the top of the House of the Power. They would have a wonderful life together, do things and feel things she had never imagined. He had paid his dues. He was in. For the first time he had tasted the Blood of the Black Spirit, and it had made him strong, exactly as the Prophet said it would. Strong and wild in excitement. And last night he had taken the test. How wild with eagerness he was! He had drunk deep of the Blood, and his heart pounded; he heard his blood rushing, beating in his ears. He danced with joy, leaping and turning in great circles when the Prophet gave him his assignment. He remembered again the screams. The Prophet said they were the music of the Power.

This morning he limped over to his toolbox. Throwing it open, his fingers played over the tools, caressing the chisels as if as if they were holy. A little frown momentarily marred his brow. "Oh, there it is," he said. He bent to the floor, holding on to the table's edge so his bad leg would not crumple under him and bring him to the floor. He picked up a chisel from where he had dropped it in his ecstasy the night before. It was finely made with a rosewood handle—one of his best. Lovingly he stroked it. He held it in both hands and brought it to his lips. He kissed it, whispering, "I do devote thee to the Power, the Black Spirit and the Blood." He ran his finger along where the blade joined the handle and scraped off a speck of something dark red. He laid it among the others in the box. He shut and locked the box. Hefting the toolbox to his shoulder by its leather strap, he left his house for his workshop.

As Stefan walked to work, he gnawed on a hunk of cheese that his mother had pushed into his hand as he went out the door. She believed he should always break his fast in the early morning.

He smiled as he walked. People smiled back, glad to see him not complaining sourly of his leg. Once he almost laughed out loud. "Am I a rat, nibbling on cheese?" He chuckled to himself at the image. "Lotte might think so, but I'll get around her. She'll understand. It was the rule. I had to do it to join. It was so simple really. Just to put that cash box below the counter when sneaking a kiss from Lotte. Then come back and 'find it'—looking the hero—while slipping the coins into my sleeve. And the old crone blamed Younger!" Stefan laughed out loud.

That evening, he whistled all the way home from work. He had his answer from Lotte.

All the next day it rained hard, and the day after that also. The farmers needed rain. But William, too, thanked God for the cooling downpour. His spirits had sunk very low and he believed his cats were, somehow, in mourning also. The rain made it impossible to start on the bailiff's mission. He indulged his melancholy by puttering around the smithy, picking up and pounding straight the occasional horseshoe nail. Fittingly for the mood of the village, the death bell rang on the second rainy day. He stepped away from his anvil and out into the rain to hear it better. Old Wanda had gone to her Maker at last.

The following morning, the morning of the funeral, the sky was a happy, brilliant blue, sunlight sparkled off wet leaves and dew glistened on the grass. The square before the smithy was busier than usual as people bustled about their morning chores. Wives were taking bread to be baked and older children were going for water, with yokes balanced across their young shoulders and the empty buckets dangling and swinging merrily. Children on their return trips walked straight, as stiff as bishops, so as not to spill the heavy buckets. Many of the men were making their way to the funeral out of respect for their associate, the cooper, rather than any true sense of loss for the ancient Wanda.

As she carried her dough to the baker, Rosemarie thought of Wanda, of how much trouble she had been for the cooper's family. The old woman sometimes did not know her own son, people said. Winifred, the cooper's wife, had once told Rosemarie that she often wet herself like a baby and that it took three people to clean her up every morning, two to hold her and one to wash her. *Very sad*, Rosemarie thought. How tired Winifred, ever the very particular housekeeper, had looked in recent days. Rosemarie wondered why God allowed it. *Must be a testing for sainthood*, she finally concluded after some thought.

At the baker's ovens, she remembered the priest's most recent homily and how he spoke at length of Purgatory and the Doom that awaited the unrepentant. Winifred, Rosemarie felt sure, had done nothing but good for her mother-in-law. She'd certainly spend little time in that mysterious in-between place. *She deserves to go straight to the angels*, thought the farrier's wife. *Yes, perhaps she is a saint in the making. Saint Winifred.* It sounded good.

Her husband's thoughts were of a more earthbound nature. Now that the weather was good, it was time for William to search the knight's demesne as the bailiff had ordered. The blacksmith lingered a minute in the square, speaking to one or two people, distracting them while Robin slipped away up the manor road. The blacksmith did not want his neighbors noticing that he and the crime-solving Sir Goblin had business up at the knight's house. *The knight's assailant might very well be standing in the square at this moment. Let them think I am going to the funeral*, he thought. He walked a few yards toward the church, chatting with people, and then made the excuse that he thought he had left a hinge strap in the fire and returned to the smithy. A moment later William slipped out the back door of the blacksmith shop and into his house. Here he slung a hempen bag over his head so the strap ran from one shoulder across his chest, and the bag rested under his arm against his side. It was a convenient carryall. Today Goblin would ride up to the manor in this sack. The smith believed his old cat was still too mournful to take much interest in his knightly duties. He scooped a sleeping Goblin into the sack and, holding it closed with his arm, he waited until most people were in the church for the funeral and then started for the manor road. He met Robin where the boy waited for him under a shade tree.

Eight.

U PON PASSING THE bailiff's house, Robin and William heard angry voices rising to a furious pitch.

"You would throw everything, your future, away! You drunken lazy wastrel! That cheese is soured! The cows are groaning to be milked! And you, you lie abed!" screamed the bailiff's wife.

"Father would make a milkmaid of me, a stable boy!"

"You have a living here always. Do not throw it away. Now go. Go on, git!"

The door banged open and Younger shot out, swinging a wooden bucket. William walked by Younger without breaking his stride. He clapped Robin on the shoulder and whispered between his teeth, "Keep walking. Don't look back."

They skirted the manor house. A stable boy waved. William nodded. Otherwise, there seemed to be few people outside. *Too warm*, thought the smith. *They should stand by my forge!* They had reached the first young apple trees. The breeze rustled in the delicate leaves like a whispered melody. For the first time, Goblin stirred in the sack. His head poked out and he yawned, displaying his long white fangs. The big cat looked around. *Good*, thought William, *he's taking an interest*. The two humans walked on. They came to the knight's bench, passed the old rabbit nest, and came to the older trees. Here the two stopped to survey the situation, looking for anything that might lead to the identity of the knight's assailant. A butterfly fluttered by, and Goblin reached out a paw to it. It was a pleasant grove. Bright and breezy. Nubbins of green baby apples bounced on all the swaying branches. It was a pleasant place, very pleasant, indeed, and perfectly normal, not a sign of anything out of the ordinary, of anything not right.

"The path is here, Papa. Shall we follow it?" said Robin, pointing to where the stretch of trampled grass, still visible, led deep into the woods. Suddenly Goblin squirmed. The sack was a jiggling, writhing bundle, and William could not keep it closed. Goblin jumped out and started walking down the grassy path. After a few feet he stopped and sniffed. The cat nuzzled aside some grass and pushed his nose to the ground. Here he seemed to smell something of interest. He looked up at William and then smelled the ground again. He laid his ears back and switched the tip of his tail, as if contemplating what to do next—or perhaps just waiting for the two humans to look at what he had found.

"What is it, Goblin?" William asked. After more than a decade of working together, he could tell fairly well when Goblin was sending a message. Here a wide patch of grass had been trampled flat. Goblin pawed the ground where he had sniffed. There might have been some trace of a dark stain there, but the two days of rain had made any evidence uncertain. And there were no prints of either shoes or hooves; Robin thought some deer might have bedded there for the night. William had to agree it was possible, having no better ideas. Goblin made a short derisive spurt of a hiss and started walking down the path. Robin and William stayed close behind him.

They were completely surrounded by forest now. Tall trees arched over them. All was silent in this dark, green world. Not a bird sang. The pleasant breeze did not seem to penetrate the woods and the air hung heavy and still. Once, Robin had to climb over a fallen tree trunk covered with wet moss—his hose were now soaked through and little pieces of moss clung to his legs. The boy wiped his hands together, brushing off dirt and moss, but he made no complaint. This was the biggest adventure he had been on, and he wanted his father and the knighted cat to have no doubts that he, Robin, was man enough for the task.

A green branch brushed William's chest. He pushed it aside, holding onto it until Robin could take it, so it would not snap into the boy's face. "This is an animal's trail," said Robin.

"Quite possibly, but let's follow it a little farther. If anything, it's getting wider," answered his father. A few yards farther on, they halted and looked about, surprised. The trail was indeed wider here, much wider. It continued ahead, but at this point a wide path joined it. The wide path came in from the right, the direction of the town.

"By the saints and all that's holy!" swore William. "This trail is fresh and much used. We must see where it leads."

Goblin was of a different opinion. He meowed repeatedly and

switched his tail mightily, whipping it back and forth in a half-circle arc. Laying his ears flat, he started to march straight ahead.

"Oh, no, you don't, boy, you are coming with us. We'll come back and do that path afterwards, I promise." William grabbed up the feline knight unceremoniously and went to put him back in the sack. "Here, Robin. Help me with this wriggly beast. Hold open the bag."

Once they had Goblin settled reluctantly in the bag, they started walking down the new path. It was an easy walk. They encountered no fallen trees to climb over and found themselves walking steadily but gently down hill. They walked a considerable distance—Robin thought they went half a mile—without seeing anything of note. Then, the path lurched to the right and again to the left around some huge boulders. As they stepped around the tall rocks, they found themselves looking at sky. The path dropped down precipitously by a series of terraces that, from the top, where they were standing, seemed like a cliff. Below them stretched the town and the brickyard. Robin let out a long, low whistle of amazement at the view.

"Quiet," said his father, who then apologized for surely no one could hear them.

"Papa, you are scared," Robin stated.

Then, proving the boy right, the smith jumped behind a tree and pulled the boy with him. Immediately he realized that it was not likely anyone would notice them standing on top of the hill. Still, there was something disturbing about the figure he had glimpsed going across the brickyard. What was it? He stepped out from behind the tree to take a better look. Yes, now he knew. The man walked with a halting gait—it had to be Stefan. *What was he doing at the brickyard? He could have no business there*, thought the farrier.

Then he saw a second man approach, a tall man. He stared and squinted, but could not make out who it might be. The two figures were engaged in animated conversation, it seemed.

"Who is that tall man, Robin? Can you make him out? What is he wearing?"

"A monk's robe," said the boy, "I think it's Father Albert."

"No, he's the one who says he doesn't have to dress like a mendicant. Why would he wear a monk's humble dress?"

"But he does sometimes, I've seen him! When he visits the poorer parts of town."

They watched the two small figures far below them for several minutes, until the two men parted. Then William, Robin, and Goblin—

who growled occasionally to let them know he was still there—started back up the path. They had not gone many yards when, this time, Robin noticed some cloth hanging on a low bush.

"Look at this," he said, gently lifting the scrap free. It was soaking wet.

"Well, it's been here through the rain, no doubt," said the father, "a piece torn from some man's hose, from the looks of it." He put the green scrap in the purse that hung from his waist.

"I do not know that it proves anything, but I'll show it to Gerhard." William was thinking that at least it proved that they had made the effort.

"Oh, but it does, Father! The man who tore his hose is probably the man who hit Sir Rudolph."

"Half the men in the town wear hose that color, and nobody would still have on a torn pair, or a patched pair, if he were the guilty one. We are going his way now," referring to Goblin. "Why carry twenty pounds of fur, when it can walk?"

William set down the wriggling bag and Goblin stepped forth, very regally, stopping to glare at the smith and his son before giving his fur coat a tidying shake and starting down the path. When they reached the place where the wide path joined the narrow, Goblin laid his ears back and switched his tail, slapping it into Robin's shin with a rhythmic thump.

"Yes, yes, we are going down that path this time," said William, swatting a gnat from his forehead as he spoke. The morning was growing warm and William's shirt was soaked through with perspiration. Half a dozen black specks on Robin's neck marked the final resting places of insects in search of a blood lunch, and the boy kept flicking more of the vicious devils from his brow.

"You're sweet, Robin. They really love you," joked William.

Goblin began to run and Robin trotted after him. They both stopped suddenly a few yards ahead. The cat began smelling and working over the ground like a hound.

"Would you look at this, Father!" Robin had stepped into an open area where no trees grew. This was the destination of the path; it went no further. The few trees that had appeared in recent years had been chopped down, their slim trunks pulled and stacked to the side. In all, the open place, roughly circular, was somewhat larger in area than the average house in Johannesmarkt.

They stood amazed. To their left were the most incredible trees they had ever seen. Around a large, brassbound chest stood four beech trees, one at each corner of the big box. They had been planted long ago, and, when still saplings, someone had bent their tender trunks together and bound them at a point some three times higher than the height of a man. Bound, their branches had intermingled and rose to the sky as if one tree. Whatever had been used to bind the young trees, whether cord or metal band, had disappeared, being incorporated into the flesh of the growing trees. The four corners of the chest had been overlapped by and fixed into the ever-expanding tree trunks.

While the humans stood staring at the box and wondering what it might mean, Goblin was scraping at the ground, growling and hissing. He moved to another place, and yet a third, always performing the same little ritual.

"He's finding much that interests him," noted William.

"That makes him mad," said Robin.

Acting on the cat's implied suggestion, they also began to inspect the ground. They began at the far right side of the grove, as if by tacit agreement to leave the chest for last. The ground was much trampled. Only herbaceous plants, no brush, were underfoot, and almost without exception these plants had been crushed under someone's feet. In a number of places the ground had been rubbed bare of green growth, but no clear footprint presented itself.

"Robin," said the blacksmith, "I think a great number of people have been coming here, and fairly often. The way the ground is trampled so much."

William stared off. A faraway look crept into in his eye. Robin saw how the corners of his mouth dropped down and knew his father was disturbed. Sir Goblin was slowly working his way over dead branches on the ground, at the side of the clearing opposite the entrance. Then Goblin pounced, distracted from his work by a fly, onto some branches on the far side of the circle. William saw a mat of dried foliage fall and rise like a wave. He sprang into action, snatching Goblin off the wobbly twigs. Their leaves were turning brown and curling, and as William pulled at one dead branch, the other branches next to it all moved as one. "These have been woven together!" he exclaimed.

"And tied!" Robin's sharper eyes had picked out the weathered cords holding the branches together. "It's like a mat."

They grabbed hold of the branches and pulled the mat toward the center of the grove.

"Holy . . ." That was all William could say. Before them was a black

Bound, their branches had intermingled and rose to the sky as if one tree.

pit, circled by cut stones, the open entrance to a well. Robin turned to look at Goblin, who was sitting behind him, licking a paw.

"You could have fallen in, Gobcat," whispered the boy, reverting to his childhood name for his pet and stroking the furry knight's shoulders. Goblin set his paw down and flicked his tongue around his lips a time or two. Then he looked into Robin's eyes.

"Looks quite proud of himself," said William. He was kneeling and looking into the well. "Let's find something and see how deep it is."

Father and son shifted the felled saplings and pulled at branches, but without an ax or adz, they could break nothing free that would be long enough to gauge the well's depth. Hot, dripping with sweat, and becoming the favorite feast of all the gnats and mosquitoes in the woods, they gave up. The well's depth would remain unknown. Robin threw in a stone. He heard the splash and thought he could make out the concentric rings spreading out. "There's water in it, and not too far down I'd guess."

"Let's move the cover back." They tugged the mat back over the well. Then, William and Robin began sweeping their feet across the ground to wipe out any tracks the brushy mat had made on the ground. When they finished, it did not seem as if the well had ever been uncovered.

"I don't want the people who come here to know the place has been discovered."

"Who comes here, Father?"

"I have no idea, but I have a feeling it's for no good."

Having returned the forest floor to its former well-trampled state, they went to look at the large coffer. It was securely bound, with many brass straps dulled with age to a tawny brown. William knocked on the wood in several places with his knuckles. It was very solid, not rotten at all.

"I don't know what kind of wood it could be made of," he said.

Robin stood on the other side brushing debris from a spot on the very top of the chest. He began moving his finger around on the wooden surface as if polishing it. "Father, Look at this— "

Just then Goblin let out a long howling meow. He had a piece of something long and stringy stuck in his mouth, and was snapping his mouth open and shut and tossing his head from side to side. "Wrahck, Ahrggh!" The cat made a horrible noise.

"Goblin, what is it? Don't choke!" The boy seized the cat and his father pulled the cord from the animal's jaws. It was a tie about six or seven inches long and apparently torn from a man's cap. It had come from a rather fine garment, for it was seamed, turned so the raw edge was on the inside, and filled with some sort of light batting. And it was embroidered. These particulars the smith would learn to appreciate after showing the tie to his wife that night. At the moment, it was just a cord made soggy by a cat's mouth.

"I wonder where he found it," said William.

"He was digging right here next to me," said the boy. "Ow!" He swatted at another devilish gnat, slapping his forehead rather hard. "How that thing bites!" Wiping his brow, and looking down as he did so, he saw Goblin paw a coin free of the dirt. The cat was very agitated still. Growling and occasionally hissing. His ears were flattened against his head and his tail switched violently. There were three coins altogether. William polished one with his thumb. It was just like the first one they had found before. Robin was working at something on the back of the chest.

"What is it, son?"

"Something here, stuck in the crack under the lid, just by the hinge. It appears to be—it is! Another coin. I can't get it out, though."

"Leave it," ordered his father. He spoke more sternly than he had meant to, and the boy jumped. *What if the chest was filled with money?* they each thought to themselves.

The smith's mind was awash with frightening possibilities, and he wanted to get away from the mysterious grove and its strange, immortal coffer. He wanted to hand everything over to Sir Rudolph or Gerhard. Gold coins suggested wealth and power, both more fitting to highborn men than to the humble. He wanted no connection with ill-gotten gains, or the power and danger that a chest of gold hinted at. This was not a farrier's business. He was just an ordinary man, and he wanted only to spend his days pounding nails into horses' hooves, as he understood this was God's will for him. Goblin had taken a seat on the treasure chest. William shoved the coins and the tie for the coif in his purse, snatched up Sir Goblin, and hurried them all out of the cleared circle.

The boy was bubbling with questions. His father kept saying only that they would discuss it with Gerhard. Where the wide path met the narrow one, the smith set Goblin down and the three made their way back through the woods to the orchard. When they came to the three stone steps, they sat down for a minute to rest. Here a warm and sultry breeze wafted over their faces. It was just strong enough to keep the flies and their stinging relatives from launching a major assault. Goblin found the only shade at the bottom of the three steps and crouched there, panting.

"Gobcat is tired and hot, too."

"We forget he is an old cat."

After another few minutes rest they continued on, passing through the orchard and by the knight's bench without pausing. Robin picked up Goblin from time to time and carried him a few yards. He had the cat against his shoulder when they dragged wearily into the manor yard.

They stood in the yard behind the main house surrounded by outbuildings: the stables, the kitchen, the springhouse, various sheds, and—farther off—the great barn and the animal houses. William was looking around for someone who could tell him where the bailiff was. He had about decided to look into the stable, the part of the demesne that he was most familiar with—someone there would, at the least, know if Gerhard senior had ridden out—when Younger came around the corner of the springhouse. "Gerhard," called the farrier, "do you know where your father is?"

"Oh, it's you, William," said the bailiff's son. "Don't the two of you look like a couple of badgers fresh crawled from their burrows," he added, as he saw their sweat-soaked shirts and the moss and twigs and leaves that clung to their clothing. Seeing Goblin was again panting, he said, "I have just the thing for you, kitty, and you two as well. Bring him here."

They followed Younger into the springhouse. They went down a couple of steps into the cool darkness of the little stone building. A slit of a window let in light enough for the work that was done there. It took a few seconds for their eyes to adjust to the dim interior. Then they saw a milkmaid ladling cream from a milk pan into a large crock for it to sit and sour before being churned into butter.

"Angie, bring us some cups, please."

The girl laid down her ladle and gave Younger a huge smile. Her eyes sparkled.

"Hurry about it. We have a manly thirst." He made as to swat her behind.

She skipped away, blushing a hot scarlet. When she was gone, Younger took her ladle and dipped it into the milk pan and then reached down and offered the fresh milk to Goblin. The cat did not stand on ceremony but lapped and lapped. He had paused for breath and would have gone back for a little more when Younger heard the girl's step and dropped the ladle back in the pan. The girl came in, radiant, with three large tin cups. The bailiff's son took them without so much as a glance at her and told her to be off.

"I think she likes you," said Robin softly.

"She can like till Doomsday," growled Younger.

Then he and William both said "What news?" at the same time and laughed.

"My father? Yes, well, as far as I know he is still with Sir Rudolph. I was playing midwife to a cow most of this morning." Younger filled the tin cups with water from the spring. "Now wrap your hands around that, Robin." The cup was icy cold and it felt so good. Robin drank heartily and then slowed. The water was so cold it hurt his stomach.

William sipped his more slowly. "Thanks much, Younger," he said. Young Gerhard leaned against the dairy table and gestured to William to take the one stool in the springhouse. Robin squatted on the floor, petting Goblin, who soon fell asleep lying on his side with his head upside down. They were silent for a minute, sipping their water. Then Younger began to speak.

"The townsmen have been making big trouble, wanting their own council and the complete government of the city for themselves. They want his lordship to continue ensuring the safety of the roads, all right. They know they can't do that themselves. But they want to police the town themselves—and I don't know what all—and, after this disastrous fair, they have something of a cause." He paused and finished his water and filled the three cups again.

After a long silence he started talking again. "And me. I am in big trouble, very big."

William thought he knew Younger's trouble—simply too much strong drink and hours wasted at cards, poch, and such games—but he was surprised and horrified by what followed.

"We just meant it to be a bit of fun, me and the boys," he began, picking his words carefully. Then followed a tale of how they had lured the squire Yodel into their drinking spot in town—not the tavern, Paul would never permit them to carouse there. They bought their drink and went to one of the boys' houses. Yodel was lured in with promises of a knucklebone tournament—a game the squire was very good at and thought he was sure to win—and they got the dimwitted young man sick drunk. He lost the tournament and what little money he had. He became so distraught and confused that he ran out of the house and into the woods, intending no doubt to find his way home. That was the last Younger's rowdy crowd saw of him.

"You are in trouble," said William.

"That is not what it is," answered the younger man, looking to the floor. He took a deep breath and let it out. The youth wiped his glistening eyes with the heel of his hand. After a minute he started talking again. Once started he might as well finish, he seemed to think, and the words tumbled out. "The next morning one of the farm hands heard the knight's dog, you know, Brutus, barking, and went to see what it was. He found Yodel lying on the ground. He was lying in the same place where the knight had been attacked! There were stab wounds all over his arms and legs and even one in his side, like Christ. He had lost a lot of blood. It is still doubtful he'll live. You did not hear of this?"

"I think that must have been what your father meant when he said there was more, but that I knew enough for the time being."

"Do I need to tell you, we had nothing to do with the attack on Yodel? Poor Yodel, poor dumb fool." His eyes glistened.

"No."

The two men were silent for a while. William looked down at Robin, who was sitting on the ground, wide-eyed and open-mouthed, entranced and frightened by Younger's words. Robin had heard many tales of brave knights and bloody battles, told and retold around the fireside, but never had he heard of anything so bloody and ugly really happening here in Johannesmarkt. His stomach rolled and cramped.

William reached down to his young son and said, "Robin, you have heard more than enough for your young ears. Best you go home. I want you to promise me you will not say anything to anyone about what you heard just now, not even to your mother. I will speak to your mother. It's just that the wrong ears, someone coming to the smithy, might overhear you."

Reassured that he was not being babied, the boy promised. The farrier pulled off the sack he had carried the cat in and gave it to Robin. "Here. Go home now and take Goblin with you. Carry him if he wants it. You can see he is tired." Then he added, "Be careful."

Not knowing if he would be able to see the bailiff today, William decided to tell what they had found to Younger. He left out only the part about the coin wedged in the chest, with its implication of a chest full of gold. Younger, perhaps to his credit, told William to keep his pieces of evidence to show to his father himself.

When he finally got back to his house, William ate a meal of cold beans and fresh bread. The air was heavy with moisture, and a thunderstorm threatened. The atmosphere fitted the turbulence of his mood. He looked at his bed where the entire cat family, all six of them, lay curled up in a mound, each with his head turned chin up. He thought they looked so peaceful and he wished he could feel so calm and join them for a nap. He was tired after his long hike in the woods, and his late lunch had made him even sleepier. But rest would not come to him. He could not get the picture of a bloodied Yodel lying on the ground out of his head. Something very evil was happening in Johannesmarkt.

Then he heard the clanging of the anvil next door. He knew Robin was there, trying his best "to do a man's work and appease an impatient customer," so his good wife informed him, as if he couldn't hear the pounding.

True, his failing hearing was a topic of many domestic debates—Rosemarie had even taken to sending their little daughter Maddie to the smithy to yank on his sleeve, rather than she, his wife, calling him to his meals. But this clamor was, as William put it, "enough to rattle open the gates of Purgatory itself." Of course he could hear Robin!

Rosemarie enlightened him further. "Everyone in the town wanted their horses shoed today, and I couldn't even tell them where you were." She stood with hands on hips. A little fluff of wool clung to the V of sweat on the front of her bodice. She had been spinning. He plucked off the wool fuzz. He patted his wife's warm pink cheek and went out to the smithy to relieve Robin. He longed to work his muscles and relax his mind.

Nine.

STEFAN HAD A task to accomplish and he, like William, had had to wait for the rain to stop. And, also like William, he ate a cold midday meal very late in the day. He was excited and eager to please the Prophet and waited most impatiently for the sun to come out and dry the ground. The other joiners thought his bouncy enthusiasm was because of his upcoming wedding and teased him, telling him he'd soon be working long hours to feed little mouths. But Stefan just whistled, as his plane slid over cabinet wood and told them nothing of his great hope. After his joyous dance and testing, the Prophet had deemed him fit for a certain important duty. *Surely, I have passed the initiation review, or I would not have been given such an important task,* thought Stefan.

And so it was not until late morning that he made an excuse—an outright lie actually, saying he had to carry water for his mother who was doing laundry—and left his workplace. He closed his toolbox, for he did not trust his coworkers with his fine tools. He slipped stealthily through the back alleys and came eventually to the cultivated fields on the far side of the town. He did not want anyone to say they had seen him going the wrong way from any of the public wells. It was not a crime to pick "pigkill," no more than it was to pick dandelions, but the Prophet had emphasized in very straightforward words that, for the time being, the work of the chosen must be kept secret. The time of fulfillment was coming soon, very soon.

It was, then, with a high heart and expectant spirit that Stefan worked his way through the wheat and bean fields. He was careful to walk along the edges of the planted strips, so as not to destroy the crops that would feed him as well as the rest of the town through the next winter. Coming at last to a fallow field, he set down his bag and pulled a knife from his belt. He began cutting the stout weeds, being careful to take only the ripest berries.

The ruby berries were squeezed somehow into the Blood of the Black Spirit, which the Prophet used. Stefan did not know how the rich invigorating drink was made; he just knew that he was to pick the fruit and bring it to a secret spot. "Let no one see you," the Prophet had warned.

It was the white liquid that oozed from the stems as he cut them that attracted swine. If a hog got a whiff of the lemony, sour, salty smell, it would come running, like a cat to catnip, and chew on the plant until it was drunk with it. Then, it would race around and around in a circle in the sun, until its nearly bare bristly body was a deep pink from sunburn. Still it would circle, until finally it would fall and roll onto its back, its bloated belly and four feet pointing to the sky.

Stefan had chosen this far fallow field because it was beyond the barnyards and there was little chance of swine smelling the cut canes. Otherwise, it would be seen as a deliberate malicious attempt to kill pigs. But it did not occur to Stefan, excited as he was to be a member of this blessed chosen circle, that pigkill might also affect people adversely.

Soon enough, his sack was full and wet with pigkill juice. Now, he had to get to the secret spot without being noticed by any of the foolish field workers hoeing around the bean plants. He could not let them see him if he was to maintain his alibi that he had been hauling water for his mother's laundering. He scurried along the far edge of the wheat field, running crouched and clutching the sack close to his side. Cutting through the woods at the northern perimeter of the town, he crossed the north road leading out of town.

Slowly he made his way through dense trees and brush behind the rotting wood of a palisade and earthworks that had once been the beginning of a town wall. Built by the townsmen many years ago, the wall had been pulled down by Johann de Forrest, so that Johannesmarkt would be defenseless and completely at the mercy of the cruel strongman. Stefan crossed the road to the manor. Running and still bent over, he ducked behind berry brambles and the young pine trees planted to grace the knight's demesne. When Stefan ran, his withered leg caused him to totter and wobble in such a way that if anyone saw him, they would know exactly who he was. This was the most risky part of his route. He did not want to be seen here because townsmen were not allowed to trespass Sir Rudolph's demesne land. If caught here, he would probably be whipped and certainly fined for more than he could pay in a year. But the Black

Spirit's power was with him, as the Prophet had predicted. He made his delivery.

He washed his hands at the brickyard well, and gave the side of his tunic a good soaking to get the smell of any pigkill off of it. He would say, if questioned, that he had been sloppy after washing his hands and tipped the bucket too far. In this heat his clothes would dry in half an hour.

It was after these brisk ablutions that Stefan met up with Father Albert in the brickyard. After a few cursory greetings, the priest said, "I have seen Lotte and her mother today. She is a lovely girl and will make a fine wife."

"That's wonderful to hear you think so, Father," answered the young joiner.

The Priest clapped him on the shoulder, and they parted. Stefan next got two buckets of water to bring to his mother's house, making sure he greeted and spoke to people as he carried the water.

Returning to his workshop, he pounded in a few pegs and planed some slats. When the apprentice working near him went out for a drink of water, Stefan pushed one of his chisels through the seam of his sleeve, ripping it open four or five inches. He now had a good reason to visit the seamstresses, Lotte and her mother. He rubbed a little sawdust into his sleeve to give the tear a more authentic look.

When he arrived at the house of the seamstresses, he could not help but let out a sigh of disappointment. On the bench outside his beloved's house, where she always sat to sew in the bright afternoon light, sat Lotte's plump mother, not the young maiden. Craning his neck, he looked hopefully over her shoulder into the doorway beyond.

"Looking for someone?" the mother asked sweetly, knowing full well whom he was hoping to see.

"I have torn my sleeve, Mistress seamstress."

"Let me have a look. Hmmm. Just an open seam. Take it off. It will be only a few minutes." With that, she jammed her needle into the bodice she had been sewing and got up. "You may sit inside."

She showed him inside and returned to the bench outside with his shirt. Plopping down on the bench, the seamstress turned so she would not cast a shadow on her work. She flipped the sleeve inside out, pinned the tear together, and began sewing, humming as she worked.

Stefan felt embarrassingly naked, sitting there wearing his undertunic, breeches, and hose, although in fact not one more inch of skin was exposed than before. Lotte's home was even more beautiful than he had imagined. There were tablecloths on all the tables, except their worktable, curtains fluffed at the sides of their little windows, even the fireplace had a strip of embroidered cloth draped along its mantel and hanging down over the ends. *They certainly do know how to exhibit their talents,* thought the young man. In one corner, a series of shelves were built into the wall. Here, rows of Lotte's brightly dressed dolls smiled down on Stefan. Most were beautifully garbed, like the most elegant ladies of the court. A few were naked; their chubby stuffed linen bodies awaited both garments and faces. Since he was looking at the dolls in the back of the room and thinking of how he could build Lotte a beautiful cabinet for them, he didn't at first see the arm jutting through the doorway and flapping his mended shirt.

"Don't you want your clothes?" sang out a honey-sweet, melodious voice.

Lotte! He snatched the tunic and pulled it on over his head, belting it with the girdle from which he hung his sheathed knife and purse. As he stepped through the doorway, Lotte whipped out her hand, jabbing him lightly with her palm open.

"Pay up."

He pulled open his purse and slapped a fairly large coin into her palm. "Keep it all."

"Mother has just stepped over to the neighbors. We have only a minute."

They smiled into each other's eyes. Then Lotte blurted out, "Father Albert came by today. I don't like the way he stared at me. A priest shouldn't . . ."

"Don't worry about him," Stefan interrupted her. "I will take care of you," he added, puffing out his chest and pulling in his lame leg, so as to stand as straight and tall as he possibly could. He clasped Lotte's arms just below her shoulders and drew her close. How sweet and luscious her lips looked! He wanted so much to kiss them. But he did not dare to, here where everyone could see them. He had to content himself with whispering. "Tonight then. You can get out?"

"Of course. I will simply tell mother I have a touch of something and must use the necessary house. I'll bring a light. Here she comes. Until then."

He squeezed her fingertips and in a louder, businesslike tone he said, "Be sure to thank your mother for her fine work," and then strode purposefully away in the opposite direction from the approaching seamstress.

Ten.

THE SIX CATS SLEPT soundly for a couple of hours. When the young ones stirred, still lying on their sides but stretching their legs and groaning in pleasure, Snow Beauty stood up, and patted each son with a gentle front paw, instructing them to be still because their father still slept.

The spinning wheel stopped its humming. Rosemarie put her waxy new wool yarn into a basket and carried the basket into the back room where the cats slept. She opened the back door and stepped out into the yard for a breath of air. A half-dozen speckled hens ran up to her looking for treats. The woman stepped back through the doorway, lifted the lid of a firkin, and removed half a round loaf of dried-up bread. Then, sitting outside on a bench by the door, she tore off little pieces of the crust and tossed them to the merrily squawking birds.

Whether it was the beam of light let in through the back doorway or the noisy hens, something woke Goblin and his entire family. It was conference time. If Rosemarie had been in the room, she would have seen her cats standing, stretching, turning around and settling down again. They sat with their tails carefully arranged across their front feet. There was much chortling and whispering of news. Then Sir Goblin began treading the bedspread and purring. They all kneaded the bedspread for a moment. Then all together they cried out, "Meow." And breaking from their huddled circle, they ran for the front door. Snow Beauty went only as far as the dooryard. That was her post. The others dashed out as a group, running across the square, four white cats with their grey-striped tails waving high behind their knighted tiger-striped leader.

Snow Beauty lay down, tucked against the house and the rain barrel,

The six cats slept soundly for a couple of hours.

a circle of white, lit like dazzling crystal by the dropping sun. She did not have long to wait to complete her assignment.

Young Gerhard trudged down the manor roadway to the village. He was going to the tavern for his supper but was later than usual. He walked awkwardly with his head bowed and his arms hanging stiffly at his sides, not moving in time with his stride. His heavy farm boots kicked up dust and rattled little pebbles as his feet dragged past where Snow Beauty lay. A dry shower of dust sprinkled her nose as Younger passed by, and she got up and followed him.

But despite the plodding walk, Younger was for once not drunk—quite the opposite. He trudged with gloomy soberness. Snow Beauty stood, arched, and followed the young man to the smithy, where Gerhard stopped in the doorway. He stood stock still, until William, Robin having nudged his arm, put down his hammer and looked up. Younger beckoned, and William stepped out into the sun, away from Robin and the customer's ears. Robin took up the hammer.

"Yodel is dead."

"Gerhard, I am very sorry," said William.

"Yes. He—my father—wants you to come up to the stable with the cat. He is taking some men into the woods to search. Come when the sun glints on those roofs." Younger pointed to where the sun was setting over the shops and nearby houses.

That said, Younger reached down and patted Snow Beauty. He turned on his heel and headed for the tavern where he was accustomed to take his supper—away from the shrieks and yelps of his little half-siblings and the demands of his stepmother. Snow Beauty trotted after him, meowing loudly.

Before Younger had plodded as far as the tavern, Goblin emerged from somewhere and circled around the youth's boots, polishing them with his flanks and meowing loudly.

"What's with you, cat?" said Younger, stepping trickily, as if performing some dance step, to avoid tripping over the cat.

Goblin persisted, running off a few steps but then coming back to rub around Younger's boots. Little by little, Goblin diverted Younger from his chosen direction. The youth noticed three of Goblin's sons, as he supposed they were, since they all three seemed to be working in concert, running back and forth on the rooftops. Now he heard the squalling of a cat howling in full caterwaul.

Something about the urgency of Sir Goblin's behavior made Younger decide to put off his supper and the gloomy thoughts that surely would have accompanied his meal. He followed Goblin down a narrow street of closely built houses, whose upper stories jutted out overhead on either side, blocking out the red light of the setting sun. Passing a narrow alley, still following the lead of the rooftop-prancing Meoht, Younger saw movement from the corner of his eye—a scuffle. Looking into the alley he saw a woman fall to the ground and a man working at something at her waist. The woman stirred. The man stepped back and slipped something into the neck of his doublet. The woman struggled to her knees; only then did she realize her purse was gone.

"Thief! Stop! My Purse! Thief! Help!" Standing up now, she reached for the fleeing figure, flailing her arms at him. The thief ran, but when he looked back at his victim, he ran straight into Younger.

Younger grasped the thief by his arms and shook him.

"Return what you have taken!"

The thief spread his hands. "I have nothing."

The old woman was now standing behind Younger, rubbing her knees. She pulled at the cut strings still at her waist. "See what that thief has done!" The woman waggled the sheared cords for them to see.

Younger shoved the criminal up against the wall of the nearest building in the narrow street. It was the stone wall of a stable, and the thief's head rang with a resounding crack. Holding the man against the wall with one hand well placed against his neck, Younger reached into the man's garments and pulled out a small purse trimmed by an elaborate white fringe across its bottom edge. His fingers told him there were not more than a few small coins in it.

"My name is on it."

Younger turned the small bag over. In the dusk he could just make out some ornate lettering. "Your name?"

"Frieda."

He handed her the bag.

Mumbling her thanks over and over, she dipped a curtsey and ran off.

"And your name, you cutpurse?" He gave the thief another shove against the wall. Younger stared at his catch, noting the two warts on the man's cheek, the pale eyes—it was too dark to tell if they were blue or grey—and the wispy yellow fuzz on his cheeks and chin. A short scar extended from his right nostril an inch or so across his cheek. It was an easy face to remember.

"Hans By-Well."

"You appear at the Knight's Court Thursday morning, or you'll wish you were never born. My father's the bailiff, you know."

He yanked the thief by the shoulder as if to throw him to the ground. The thief stumbled, regained his balance, and ran down the alley for home.

Younger dusted off his hands. Two cats were sitting a few feet away, watching. "Well, is this what you wanted me for? Now, how about some supper?" he asked, but the caterwauling continued.

Again, Goblin purred against young Gerhard's boots. Then the feline knight raised his chin and surveyed the rooftops, looking toward the squalling cat racket. He saw Meouht and Mrrt leap onto the roof of a nearby house. In this part of town, the newly built houses—usually those of merchants with little need of large gardens—were so close together that the cats could leap from one housetop to the next. In effect, they had an aerial highway system that allowed them to observe and track all the activities in town, both human and animal.

Now Sir Goblin sat up on his haunches and swatted with both paws as if batting invisible flies. It was the cats' agreed-upon signal. He walked a few steps away from the bailiff's son and then back again and then repeated this little dance twice more until the human caught on that once more he was to follow. Mrrt and Meouht trotted along, leaping from roof to roof, and their father and Younger followed at ground level, turning down one street and then an alley. They found themselves in a more humble section of town where quickly erected, old-style houses of wattle and daub lined the way.

Here, the four sons of Sir Goblin converged on one rooftop. They were quiet now. The front door of a neatly kept house stood open. The little house faced south on the sunny side of the alley. Its doorstep was swept clean, and bricks formed a path extending a few feet to reach the alleyway, obviously an attempt to catch dirt before it was tracked into the house. A boot scraper, probably one of those William frequently made, was bolted to the side of the stoop. At each side of the door, herbs almost burst from their boxes, spilling the scent of thyme, rosemary, lavender, and chives into the night air. Everything spoke of the pride of the householder.

But from within came a thumping sound as of a broom being swatted against a wall. "You lazy wench! I'll teach you!" a gravelly voice cried between thumps.

Then came a high-pitched cry of "No! Please! No!" It was a woman screaming. Something crashed to the floor just as Younger stepped inside.

A man of some thirty years, with a triangle of curly, chestnut hair

The four sons of Sir Goblin converged on one rooftop.

that came to a point between the balding upper reaches of his forehead, stood staring at what he had done, with a stout rod still quivering in his hand. His face was an angry blood red. But as Younger entered the room, the man's eyes grew round and his face began to whiten. He turned to Younger, and his chin quivered as he said, "But I had to punish her, to correct her. It is my right."

"Yes," answered the bailiff's son. "The law allows you to correct your wife, even to chastise her in this manner."

He took the rod from the husband's hand and slapped it against his own hand, testing its strength. It was a stout stick, totally inflexible and deadly.

"But remember," Younger continued, "she is the weaker vessel." Immediately, the youth hated his choice of words for it seemed he had heard them recently in one of Father Albert's gloomy homilies. He wasted little love on the dour, young priest; he was not Younger's kind of man at all.

The woman whimpered as she regained consciousness and lifted her head. Seeing her husband, her eyes filled with tears and she began to shake.

"Here," Younger turned to the man, "let us get her up." Together they gently lifted her to her feet. Already, the man was mumbling apologies to his wife. The back of the woman's dress was in tatters. Ugly red welts crisscrossed her back, and blood trickled from several cuts, making wine-colored stains on her shredded garment and matting it to her back.

"Let us take her to Anna the midwife. She has the salves for this," suggested Younger. Her husband found her mantle and gently draped it over her shoulders shielding her and, moreover, his pride from any further public embarrassment. As they stepped out of the neat little house, young Gerhard thought, *It was certainly not a lack of good housekeeping that had been her crime.*

There was not a cat in sight.

It was a long walk to Anna's house, and it was starting to get quite dark. They spoke little so as not to attract the attention of passersby. Younger walked a few paces behind the couple. He stepped up to take her elbow only when her steps faltered and it seemed she might fall.

Two women went by as they approached Anna's door. Their knowing nods and smirks told Younger that quite a different sort of rumor would be going around town regarding this couple—one of imminent parenthood. *Well, let it be,* thought Younger. *That is much better than wife-beating gossip and it may yet prove true.*

The bailiff's son remained outside the midwife's house, standing with his arms folded across his chest, glaring at anyone who dared stare at him to wonder what business he had there. His empty stomach growled.

After some time a very humbled husband came out. He seemed to want to talk, and so the two began walking back the way they had come.

"She is staying with Anna overnight," the husband explained. "The midwife was rather firm about that. She will come back when she wants to." There then followed a flood of words, recriminations, complaints, and apologies.

When at last the husband tired of talking, Younger remarked, "She is very much like my stepmother." A few steps further on he said, referring to his father, "But he says she'd be difficult to replace and he needs her. She says he 'corrects' her by his silences. She dreads his sulky silence more than any rod or lecture." Younger smiled to himself as they walked down the darkening street, thinking of the tense atmosphere that so often prevailed in his house. "He takes walks often, my father does."

The husband seemed to ponder this. "There is something to what you say. You speak wiser than your years, young man."

Shrugging his shoulders, Younger laughed and said, "Right now my stomach says it would be wise for me to turn off here and head for the tavern and my supper."

Later, when the bailiff's son left the tavern, he was well fortified with lamb stew and an extra serving of apple pudding that Joanna had insisted on setting before him. "For one of my boys," she said, rubbing her hands on her apron and confident that her grandmotherly attentions were well received. Younger strode home with only enough beer in him to wash down his food.

An observer might detect something of a spring in his step as the young man walked homeward, thinking over the evening happenings. *I wonder where the cats have gone. For a while we were quite a team—yes, actually, I think they planned it that way,* thought the youth. He walked on thinking over the ramifications and possibilities of these events. It was not until his house was in sight that he thought of Yodel.

Younger encountered William at the beginning of the manor road. William was returning home.

"We went to the stable and then searched the woods. No one came," the smith informed him. "I have given your father all the information I have." William then told Younger about the chest in the trees. "The knight's men are most eager to go there and chop it out in the morning," he said.

William then expressed concern over the whereabouts of his cat. Younger responded by relating his own strange adventures. They said goodnight, and returned each to his own house.

The bailiff met his son on the road outside their house. Gerhard was on his way to take the first shift sitting with Yodel's body in the little manor chapel. Younger was to take the next watch, four hours later.

Younger walked with his father as far as the manor chapel, telling him how the cats had pranced around him, urging him away from an early meal and into unexpected adventures. He said he thought they had sort of planned it, in a way.

His father laughed in disbelief but then shrugged his shoulders, saying only, "That Sir Goblin has done stranger things in the past. Who knows? Don't fall asleep and forget to relieve me."

William did not find Sir Goblin at home. And Snow Beauty seemed content to sit outside by the rain barrel. Sir Goblin and his sons dined exquisitely that evening outside the back door of the tavern, taking advantage of Paul's tendency to bake too much fish. Paul had a soft spot for "furry people," as he called them, and when teased he said it was, after all, nothing but his Christian duty to give alms. The neighborhood cats took full advantage of his generosity. After eating until their sides bulged, the four-footed knight and his entourage crawled between loose boards in the wall of the tavern's livery stable and curled up in the hay for a long digestive snooze.

When they awoke, it was well after the humans' curfew and fully dark. It was time to undertake the second part of their plan. They stole through a few of the town's darkened streets, and, seeing people moving about, they knew for certain that it was time to take action. Swift as deer, they flew through the streets toward the smithy, giving a hurried chirrup of acknowledgment to Snow Beauty as they passed by. They ran up the manor road, past Sir Rudolph's house, where dim flickering candlelight in the little private chapel shone through the stained glass windows, casting blue and yellow patches of light on the ground. They ran past the knight's orchard, into the woods.

Brutus, Sir Rudolph's mastiff, lifted his head sleepily and growled once as the little band flew past his master's porch. He was not chained but could not be bothered with such small intruders.

Eleven.

A S SOON AS she heard the first peal of the curfew bell, Lotte
stabbed her needle into the cuff of the linen sleeve she was
hemming. She ran it into the fabric once and then tipped up its point to
push it back through the cloth. This was how she marked her stopping
place and kept the precious little sliver of steel from falling out and
being lost. While the room was cheerfully decorated, Lotte's home—like
all those in the town—had small windows that did not let in brilliant
swathes of light. Even by morning's bright light, she would need a lamp
to find the needle if it dropped to the floor.

The young woman went directly to the fire and began stirring the
coals with the iron poker. Disturbed, the angry flames flared up for one
brief moment before settling down, hissing and muttering like old gossips
ignored. Lotte scraped the larger glowing chunks of wood together so
that the flames would rise, phoenix-like, from under a thick cover of
ashes when refueled in the morning.

She dipped her hands in the bucket of water that stood on a table in
the corner of the room where she both lived and worked. After rinsing
her hands, Lotte splashed her face with the water and then dried her
face and hands on an embroidered towel. When finished she carefully
folded the cloth and spread the towel on a bar so the embroidered edge
was displayed neatly, one more example of their needlework. Next, the
girl worked a salve that she had bought from Anna into her hands and
fingers. It promised soft and beautiful hands for eternity. She dabbed
a little on her neck too. Now Lotte removed her cap and let down her
hair. She brushed out her long tresses and braided them into one long
fat plait.

Noticing her mother, who was staring at her with a raised, questioning eyebrow, Lotte let out a delicate little cough—sure to put off any questions about why she was grooming so much right before bed. Immediately, the older woman inquired, "Are you feeling all right, my dear?"

"Oh, yes. I think so. Just tired. And a little cold."

Lotte knew her mother worried constantly about her health. The seamstress often wondered aloud about what would become of her in her old age if the angels took her daughter away first. Lotte had the same slender build as her dead father. While it lent a swanlike grace and beauty to the maid, the girl's slender neck was, to her stocky mother, a reminder always of how her thin-chested husband had died. Catching a chill, the tailor's narrow lungs had filled so quickly with fluid that he might as well have drowned in a river.

The older woman worried all the more because they had only each other. There were no relatives to lend a hand should things go wrong. Her husband had visited Johannesmarkt years ago to help his friend, a tinsmith, carry his pots and pans and kitchen gadgets to one of the town's summer fairs. He had liked the town and later settled his wife and daughter there, a distance of some twenty miles from their families.

In truth they were both sturdy and rarely suffered anything more serious than a queasy stomach. Regardless, her mother immediately suggested that Lotte wear her chemise to bed, so the night air would not get at her throat.

"Yes, mother." The maid rolled her eyes. Then she realized that going to bed in her chemise—rather than without clothes, as people usually did—would make her escape easier.

As she pulled the sheet up to her chin and sank into the feather-stuffed mattress, Lotte wondered why there was so much deception involved with young men. Several maids of her acquaintance constantly told their parents fibs and played sneaky tricks just to spend a few minutes with the youths they loved. Lotte hoped this would be the only time she deceived her mother, for she dearly loved the older woman. She recalled how her mother had wept when her father died. How hard the two had worked to make a go of their business!

As she heard her mother toss Pansy, their cat, out for the night, the girl remembered something—when Lotte was a child, she had once overheard her mother say to a man who had come to the house often, "I will not have my daughter made a stepchild. I will make my own living."

She really is a sweet old thing, thought the daughter, as her mother slid into the bed they shared.

Soon, Lotte heard the sound very like the soft, purring scratch made by Stefan planing wood—almost everything reminded her of Stefan. Slowly she turned onto her side. *Like a donkey braying in a whisper,* she thought, as her mother snored noisily but peacefully. Lotte closed hear eyes and dreamt of her wedding day.

Just as she dreamt of Stefan coming to the church door accompanied by a half-dozen groomsmen, her eyes flew open. Had she heard something? Was that the call of an owl? Her ears strained for any sound. Yes, there it was again, Stefan's signal. A "hoot-hoot" repeated four times, as no owl ever did. She turned back the sheet and slid quietly from the bed.

Lotte felt her way into the main room. She found her shoes where she had left them under her stool. With only a faint red glow from the slumbering fire to see by, Lotte sat down and tied on her shoes, pulling the strings tight around her ankles. She had not laid out hose for fear her mother would notice and say something. She lifted her cloak from the hook by the door and went out. Her mother had never stirred. Lotte did not need to tell her any lies.

Stepping out into the blackness, she stood a moment listening to the night sounds. A million spangling stars pierced the ebony sky. There was starlight and moonlight enough to see her way through the street, but Lotte turned into the little passage between her house and her neighbor's home and had to feel her way along the wall to the back of her house. Behind the house was a small garden where a viny patch of beans and bulging cabbages filled most of the space. The handful of speckled hens, perched in a shed built off the side of the outhouse, chortled in their sleep. The girl looked around. She saw no one. But once again, she heard the quadruple owl hoot.

Lotte walked up to the chicken coop. Its roof came to her chin and on it sat an overturned bushel basket. Lotte lifted it and pulled out a carefully rolled-up bundle of cloth. Tucking the bundle under her arm, she stepped up and into the privy.

It had a rough bench seat with a round hole in the center and a foot or so of space on either side. The summer weather had hurried the rotting of the human excrement under the seat to the peak of its fly-breeding potential. *We really must get someone to cover this and move the necessary house,* thought Lotte, gagging at the smell. She folded her cloak and placed it on the bench, as close to the wall and as far from the hole as possible. She didn't want even an edge to fall in. Then she set to opening her bundle. She drew from it a beautiful ivory gown of fine linen and wool. Its cut was simple. Its beauty was in the dip of the neckline, and the white embroidered roses at the neck and down the front of the bodice.

A circle of rosebuds and leaves ringed each cuff. If she had had more time, embroidery would also have encircled the skirt at the hem. It was her wedding dress.

She gathered up its skirt and, with considerable struggle in the narrow confines of the privy, dropped the gown over her head. She had to brace open the outhouse door with her foot to let in more moonlight before her arms could find their way into the narrow sleeves.

She jumped down out of the little building. It would not matter now if Stefan came. She had a proper dress on. She pulled at the lacing at the sides to snug the gown into a proper fit. She heard Stefan's call once more. This time, she answered with a single high-pitched, ladylike hoot.

She had just retrieved her cloak and set it over her shoulders when she heard Stefan's distinctive, halting footstep. Lotte pulled off her nightcap and tugged her fingers through the braid to let her hair fall loose around her shoulders. Two young hands gathered up her pale tresses and pulled her lips to his.

"Tonight we shall be handfast," he murmured.

The girl was stunned, and all she could manage to say was, "Shall it really be tonight?"

He laced the stem of one red rose between her fingers. Lotte drew the fragrance of the flower deep into her lungs and heart. Looking up at the brilliant stars, she felt her thumping heartbeat hammer in her ears. He had asked her to wear as much white as she owned for the meeting with the Prophet. Stefan could not have known that she'd wear a dress—the dress that she had been making for her wedding—that was whiter than any garment he'd ever seen. She appealed to the stars; they seemed to dance and sing with their twinkling.

"It is meant to be," the maid whispered, more to herself than her lover.

Taking her by the hand, Stefan led her to the road. He picked up the lantern he had left by her door. It cast but a feeble bobbing light as they made their way together through the narrow streets. They spoke only in whispers and then but rarely, because it was many hours after the curfew. No honest person should have been out of his house, except to bring aid to a woman in childbirth or to give last rites to the dying. The sweet-looking young couple would never be mistaken for a priest and midwife.

From time to time Lotte whispered into Stefan's ear for reassurance. She still had her doubts about the night's adventure. "What is it about the

Prophet that you like so much?" and then, "Are you sure he can properly marry us? I always dreamed of a wedding at the church door."

"Sweetest, after tonight you will always be happy."

She was still apprehensive. "But can he . . . I just don't think—"

Stefan cut her off. "See, the others are coming."

As they came near the brickyard, Lotte saw other people on the street. Most were men, but there were some couples also. From time to time they all seemed to stop in doorways and look around furtively. Seeing no one but their own group, the shadows flitted down the road, frequently pausing again to make certain there was no one around to report them. They were all headed for the brickyard.

They had come to the street of the tile makers, potters, and brick makers. The hastily tacked-together hovels huddled together around Johannesmarkt's new industries, next to the clay pits at the swale behind the church. Here, many doors stood open, and couples emerged smiling and laughing openly. Some of the younger women slowly spun and wobbled with their arms outstretched like tops coming to the end of a spin as they walked to the brickyard. They sang brightly, in spite of the night hour, "Looya, Looya, Ley, Ley," words that were meaningless to Lotte, but that cheered her, nonetheless. These people certainly did seem merry.

Broken chunks of discarded brick lay scattered around the brickyard. Lotte could not avoid all of them, and their sharp edges pressed painfully into her thin, leather shoes. Once she jumped aside, crying out, as one of the broken pieces nearly pierced her foot. "My rose! I dropped my rose!"

"Come on," said Stefan, taking her firmly by the arm, "there will be more up there."

"But you gave me it."

"Hurry, Lotte. We'll find it in the morning if you insist. We are nearly there."

Lotte looked up. They were facing a steep hillside. It rose, cliff-like, from the back of the brickyard. Directly before her face, she could pick out the stiff stems of burdock and clusters of button-like tansy flowers growing in silvery moonlit profusion against the hillside. As she raised her eyes, the tall trees seemed like a mass of impenetrable branches. She had to crane her neck far back to see the sky.

But the jubilant Seekers of the Power marched off to her right, and then she saw the little glints of their lanterns flickering between the trees as they walked up the hill, moving to her left at first, and then, higher,

She had not expected it to be like this.

moving to the right again. Apparently, she realized, there was a series of terraces, and a trail switched back and forth like a mountain road—for that was what it was, in miniature: a footpath of switchback curves.

She and Stefan started up the hill. She was glad now for the little lantern he carried. The trees canopied the path, blocking out most of heaven's light. Once or twice her cloak caught on twigs. She clutched her skirts close about her, afraid of tearing her lovely gown. She felt her feet growing cold. An early dew soaked through her leather shoes, and her feet were now quite wet. She had not taken time to put on hose for fear of waking her mother. Stockings would not have kept her feet warm, but at least her toes would not be rubbing against soggy leather. Determined not to think of her feet, she concentrated on the Seekers' singing. "They must serve sugared dates up there. They are all so joyful," she whispered to Stefan, trying to catch the lighthearted mood of her companions, because the Seekers still sang even as they tramped through the wet grass. Stefan made no answer.

At the top, the path curved to the right around a great boulder and became broad and easy. She now saw nothing of the town below, and very little moonlight above.

Were it not for Stephen's lantern, they would be encircled by absolute blackness. *Could even a cat see in this?* the young woman wondered. She clung tightly to Stefan's arm. There could be no thought now of not going to this ceremony, service, or festival—she still was not sure exactly what it was. In the darkness, she was completely dependent on Stefan's care. That is what she had always wanted, she told herself—a man to look after her. It was all so strange, so confusing, this, her first step into a life of her own. She had not expected it to be like this. She looked up longingly into his face and saw not tenderness, but a wild gleam in his eyes. She shuddered.

The path turned once more, and ahead she could see torchlight. Many torches. A few steps further and they were at edge of a cleared circle among tall trees. Lotte thought she saw something white flick behind a tree. She squinted and looked again, but saw nothing move. Stefan paused a minute, as if making a reverence, and then grasped her wrist and led her into the clearing.

Eight or ten torches racked in tall stanchions bathed the whole clearing in a red glow. The Seekers, still swaying gently but quiet now, stood in a ring around the edge of this opening in the forest, men on one side, women on the other. The hair on all the Seekers gleamed bright red in the torchlight. The women, Lotte noticed, all wore plain white robes not unlike her chemise.

The girl took in this scene all in a few seconds. But what seized her attention was the tall, black-robed figure at the opposite side of the ring. It stood motionless behind what seemed to be a brassbound altar. The hood of his robe hung low over his face—if the figure had a face, for she could see none. In one hand the motionless specter held what looked like a shepherd's crook, or perhaps it was a bishop's crosier. The curved head at the top of the long staff was golden and ornately carved. The brass straps on the chest—or altar, for the girl did not know really what it was—gleamed in the firelight.

Kneeling in front of it were two boys, each about twelve years old, she supposed. Their tunics, hose, and boots were all leather. They wore tunics belted low on their hips and cut very short in the most modern and elegant style of men's dress. The boys each knelt on one knee facing each other. Each held a large steaming ewer, apparently filled with a hot liquid. Slow curls of red mist wafted heavenward from the two vessels. The boys were as motionless as the silent figure behind them.

Lotte could not take her eyes from this tableau. It was hypnotic. She found herself holding her breath.

After all the Seekers had gathered and stood silently for several minutes, the apparition began to raise his arms, lifting them with snail-like slowness, first out to the side and then above his head. It must be a man, Lotte decided, for no woman could be that tall—with the exception of Joanna, but she could never disguise her womanly shape. The sleeves of his robe were deep so that with outstretched arms he resembled some great bird, heraldic perhaps, or maybe a monstrous bat. In the flickering flames of the torches, shadows played on these sleeves making them appear to move, to ripple. For one short instant Lotte thought he would fly.

Then he called out, his voice deep as rumbling thunder, coming from some dark cavernous place.

"Praise. Praise the Spirit of the Black Power. All praise," it commanded.

A growl rumbled from deep in his throat, a dark hum that repeated and repeated, eventually lifting to a higher pitch and becoming, "Looya, Looya."

The Seekers took up the call. Everyone whispering softly, as if shy, at first, and then with slightly more volume sang, "Looya, Looya, Looya, Ley."

Then the Prophet's arms dropped so suddenly that his garments flopped and snapped like a flag in the wind. The chanting ceased and, but for the flicker of the flames overhead, the woods were silent. But not peaceful. All the Seekers looked toward their leader. Stefan squeezed Lotte's wrist. She could feel that her lover's whole body was tense and squirming with anticipation. The young seamstress, too, stood very still, tense with anxious excitement, tinged with not a little fear.

Again slowly, so slowly, the Prophet moved, this time raising just one hand, lifting it palm turned down, and pointing to one of the boys. "A taste. Pass."

The boys stood up and walked to the nearest of the Seekers, one going to the women and the other to the men.

"Oh. Yes! Yes!" whispered Stefan, rising to the tips of his toes and stretching his neck forward like a thirsty dog pulling at his chain. He gave Lotte a wide-eyed, glowing glance, squeezing and jiggling her hand in excitement. He brought her hand to his lips and stole a momentary brush of a kiss. His eyes, she saw, caught the light of the torches and blazed with a glory all their own.

The boy acolytes moved in opposite directions, each serving half of the circle, offering each Seeker a small sip from a chalice and refilling the smaller vessel once or twice from the ewers. They both arrived together at Stefan. Having been given their instructions before the ceremony, the two youths turned on their heels and walked back to the brassbound chest, leaving Stefan thirsting.

Stefan sucked in his breath, startled and even a little frightened at being turned down. He had been so sure of his place in the group. Lotte felt his hand grow damp and begin to quake.

"Stefan," boomed the black-robed Prophet. The sudden, loud voice made Lotte jump. Her foot toppled the lantern Stefan had set on the ground before them. Little licks of flame grabbed at the grass at her feet. She jumped back again, whimpering, "Dear Jesus!"

"We don't say that here," whispered Stefan as he stamped and rubbed out the little fire. Water buckets stood at the base of each torch stanchion for dousing the light at the end of the evening. One of the Seekers carried over a bucket and deftly tipped a little water over the flames, drowning the fire.

Lotte looked down at her feet and held her hands against her face, a picture of embarrassment and consternation. Then she heard a rustle, the crackle of twigs underfoot. She looked up. To her horror, the Prophet was coming slowly toward her and Stefan. He was holding out both his arms toward her, still carrying the crook in one hand. When he stood in the middle of the circle, his voice boomed out again. "Stefan, you have done well. You have passed the great test. You have ended the old life assigned to you."

Stefan beamed. Lotte shuddered at what that might mean.

The Prophet lowered his voice. "Their runny-nosed cleric gave him last rites, and the half brained fool left this world assured of a vision of angels." The Prophet's voice cackled with amusement.

I know that voice from somewhere, Lotte realized.

Raising his voice to its ceremonial volume, the Prophet intoned, "Tonight you will drink deeply. Never again will your leg trouble you, and you will dance the immortal dance. Do you wish to take this vow and receive this cure?"

"Oh, yes, my Prophet. I do," answered Stefan, kneeling on the ground before the black-cloaked form.

"Rise and drink."

One of the leather-garbed acolytes brought him a ewer and chalice, poured out the potent drink until it overflowed the cup, and handed it to Stefan.

The other Seekers, feeling the effects of their drink, began chanting again, still softly but with slowly increasing volume, "Looya, Looya, Ley."

With the lightning swiftness of a striking snake, the Prophet stepped up to Lotte and cupped his free hand hard about her chin. The girl still could not make out his face well. It was swathed in black cloth, but for his hard eyes, eyes that glinted in the firelight like clear glass. Grey, colorless, dead eyes.

"The bride. Yes, perfect." He seemed to consider her face, twisting it from one side to the other. His low voice went husky, becoming almost a purr. "You, dear girl, will rule!" He made a sweeping gesture with the crook. "All Johannesmarkt and the knight's demesne. From my side, as my beloved!"

Lotte gulped and blurted "No!" Then with dawning recognition, "Father . . ."

Everything began happening very quickly.

Stefan lowered his cup. In his last sane moment he cried out, "No! She is to be my wife!"

Still clamping his fingers hard into Lotte's jaw, the Prophet whirled around. "No, Stefan, the immortals cannot marry. You have what you said was your deepest wish. Look, your leg already grows thick and strong. Dance!"

Stefan looked down at his legs. Indeed, his hose was stretched taught over the once-withered leg. Both legs looked whole and well formed. At that very moment, the pigkill juice soaked into his brain and he began to dance.

"Stefan! No, No! Come away! Come home!" screamed the girl.

"You will be my bride."

"No. Never." Lotte twisted loose from his hand, only to be seized by two bulky Seeker men.

"If that be her answer, then she must be corrected. She will partake of the Cooling Sacrament until she will be my bride," intoned the Prophet, his voice booming across the clearing. Stefan was leaping and twirling in the center of the ring, oblivious to Lotte and the world, answering only to the Spirit of the Black Power.

The Prophet turned to face Stefan, held out his arm, and snapped his fingers. Immediately Stefan's gyrations jerked to a stop and he stood still as one turned to stone.

One of the burly Seekers drew a cloth across Lotte's mouth, pulling it tight between her teeth and gagging her. Another tied her hands behind her. Two other white-robed Seekers dragged the mat of branches across the ground. Lotte's captors pushed the girl along a few yards, and then lifted her and dropped her, feet first, into the well. The Seekers' Looyas rose to a frenzied pitch. Her cloak and lovely white gown floated out around her like a great round tent and then, becoming water-soaked, sank. The girl gurgled a long sobbing cry as the icy water rose up her thighs, but her muffled voice, if heard at all above the singing, only roused the Seekers to more furious dancing and shouting.

A screaming war cry rent the forest. When the man who had dropped Lotte into the well straightened up to see what the noise was, he was hit in the face by ten pounds of white furry beast. Meuht yowled a meowing battle cry, and dragged claws down the man's forehead and cheeks. All around him, the sons of Goblin hurled their assaults at the Seekers, jumping from trees and leaping up again from the ground. Sir Goblin chose the Prophet.

Springing from his hiding place, the great cat plunged onto the Prophet's shoulder as the man turned toward the skirmish at the well. Then, biting the black hood with his teeth and ripping it back, Goblin twisted around to dig his claws into the evil man's face. Ten claws sank into the angry brow and began their rapid descent down through the eyebrows and lids, carving red tracks down the broad cheeks. All this happened in an instant. The priest swirled around, his robes flying out, bat-like. He grabbed onto the cat's fur with a tight fist. Flinging Goblin into the air, the priest then struck out with his crosier, jabbing the cat hard in the abdomen and cracking his ribs with the twisted head of the staff. Screaming with pain the feline knight fell backwards. The priest swung the staff again. The vicious hook caught and snapped the cat's hind leg. Goblin dropped to lie motionless in a thicket of beech saplings.

Twelve.

U NAWARE THAT THEIR father had fallen, Meouht, Mrrt, Meuht, and Meohie kept up their attack, jumping, clawing, tearing at clothes, and spitting in the faces of the intoxicated Seekers. The assault continued for only a few minutes, but it seemed an eternity to the besieged. Nearly all of the Prophet's chosen were bleeding by the time some of the larger men, being less affected by pigkill juice, took courage, shook off the cats and began to douse the torches. They fled down the hillside. Seeing the circle darkening, and wanting to appear to retain control of his people, the Prophet called out his formal benediction, "Next moon! Next moon! Return in joy next moon to praise!"

The men doused the last of the torches. The disappointed but now less ardent Seekers retrieved their lanterns and made their way through the woods to the terraced path and back to the town.

Just as he was leaving the clearing, the Prophet spun back to stare into the pitch-black, sacred grove. He thumped his staff against the ground and snapped his fingers. "Home, Stefan. Next moon."

The obelisk in the center of the clearing jumped to life. Drunkenly Stefan staggered after his master and ran down the hill.

Meouht, Mrrt, Meuht, and Meohie sought their father's scent and found him lying on his side, motionless. They stretched out their necks, sniffed, and twitched their whiskers, feeling for vibrations, seeking any sign of a breath of life. Mrrt, nearest Goblin's head, licked his cheek gently, stroking back the old cat's fur and whiskers. Meohie, less cautious and always more impetuous than his brothers, poked his nose into Goblin's side and unwittingly jabbed the center of his injuries. "Merrrour!" screamed the knight. His whole body flinched and flipped over so that he was now resting on his stomach with his feet under him. Again he lay apparently lifeless. The cat brothers began licking his fur, caressing his shoulders, and purring a gentle song of hope.

As Meouht's rough tongue stroked his father's throat, separating the hairs and smoothing them down, he felt a feeble vibration begin. The vibration became a faint but regular rumble. Goblin was purring. It was not the happy purr of a contented cat, but a desperate plea for consolation and comfort that comes only from the injured and dying.

Minutes passed by. Goblin's eyes opened, his third eyelids sliding back into their corners to reveal shiny black dilated pupils. The knight shakily pulled himself up to his feet. *William*, he meowed, *must get to William.*

He took a step forward. He tried to take another, and screamed out in pain. But the noble cat remained on his feet. He pushed out of the thicket slowly, one footstep at a time, and began to hobble toward the orchard. Every time he moved his left back leg, he yowled.

He rested, saying nothing more to his sons. His sides rose and fell heavily. Again he got up and tried to walk on. His sons fell in at his shoulders and hips and, after several tries, synchronized a system of nudging with their noses that lent support to the cat's attempts to walk.

It was the second hour of the morning when the cats came close to Sir Rudolph's bench. Goblin fell to the ground at just about place where he had found the nest of baby rabbits.

I can go no farther—must rest—get William, he mewed into Meuht's ear. Goblin's sides fluttered fast but shallowly as he fought for air. His voice sounded little stronger than the whisper of a blade of grass in the breeze. A death rattle of a purr rumbled in his throat. He dropped his head to the ground.

Get William. He closed his eyes.

A dog barked in the distance, but he was fast coming closer. It was a thunderous bark.

Run. Get William. Save yourselves.

Whether in answer to Goblin's orders or to some survival instinct, when they felt the dog's feet pounding the ground, the four cats ran. Meohie circled out into the orchard in a diversionary maneuver attempting to distract the dog before he made his dash for home.

Goblin could hear the pounding feet, feel the panting, slavering breath. He opened his eyes for one terrified moment and saw the great saber-like teeth snapping toward him.

Oh, Creator Cat, he prayed, *Lord of Lions, don't let me die by dog!*

He saw a fire. A human was approaching with a torch.

"Quiet, Brutus. What is all the fuss?"

A dog barked in the distance, but he was
fast coming closer.

The dog turned toward the human and whined. Goblin opened his eyes. Younger saw the two orange discs reflecting the firelight.

"It's a cat." The youth knelt. "Goblin! And you're hurt." Younger stood up and, pointing toward the manor house, shouted at Brutus. "Hans! Get Hans!" The huge dog galloped off to find the pageboy.

In the black of night, what seemed an army of cats had come teeming through the little front window and now pawed at William's blanket and pulled his hair. He dreamt he was on a ship being tossed in a stormy sea. William had never seen a real ship, or even the sea—only the props used in the midsummer morality play of Jonah. But this dream-sea grew violent. He could hear his wife Rosemarie screaming his name. He must save her! Now Rosemarie was shaking his shoulder and calling to him, "William, William, wake up! All these cats!"

A few minutes later he staggered, sleep-sodden and cat-led, out of the house. On the manor road, he met a procession of dog, a torchbearer, two other humans, and Goblin carried gently on Sir Rudolph's best silver salver. They brought the old cat into the house and laid him before the fireplace. William stirred the coals to cast a little light. He doubted his old friend was alive.

William did not like to wake Anna in the middle of the night, although it happened often enough when she was called to deliver babies. But Sir Goblin lay so still, the rise and fall of his breathing barely perceptible, that William, watching his family wringing their hands, crying and praying, had gone for Anna at the first sliver of light.

Now the room was filled with hushed activity. Little Maddie squatted before the fire stroking Goblin's forehead between his ears, with her tiny middle finger. Rosemarie tiptoed about, trying to make poultices and tisanes, according to Anna's order, and also fixing something to break her family's fast. Over and over she brought her apron to her face to stifle wracking sobs and wipe her tears.

It was Robin who kept his head in emergencies. With stoic calm, he pulled out the trestles and set up the table for the morning meal. He gave up trying to place the stools around the table, because the room was so small that the broad midwife nearly knocked them over whenever she stood up. If they ate, they would eat standing.

Anna scuttled back and forth, applying this and that, and then running deft fingers over his legs and tail. She followed this with a series of incantations, often invoking the Blessed Virgin and making signs of the cross over the poor cat's body. Then she'd begin again with the poultices, wrapping boiled herbs in linen cloths and applying them to the cat's side and chest. The strong sour odor of sage, that hoary herb thought to grant long life, filled every corner of the little room, making the humans cough and clear their throats and step outside from time to time for a fresh breath of air.

Rosemarie took a place at the end of the table nearest the back room and cut day-old bread into round trenchers. Maddie, dressed only in her chemise, would not leave the cat's side for the smallest breath of fresh air, and stayed squatted barefoot next to the feline knight, stroking Goblin between the ears. The little girl had kept up this comforting massage for hours, only switching fingers as one tired. William was surprised that Anna let her continue, even encouraging her, whispering, "You have the gift, girl."

Snow Beauty lay, very hot, between Goblin and the fire. She too kept up a steady kneading motion, opening and closing her front paws, touching her best mate's shoulder with but one toe.

Goblin's four sons all sat in one corner, quietly watching. After waking William and getting him to open the house for their injured father, there was nothing else they could do.

William tried to oblige Rosemarie by taking a sip of his morning beer and a bite of cheese, but he had no appetite. The cheese scraped like a sharp-edged piece of wood against his throat and, once swallowed, rolled in his stomach like stone tossed about in a spring freshet.

Anna stood up. "There is nothing more I can do. We can only wait."

That sounded ominous. William's heart sank, and he had to get out of the house with its sickroom odors. The muscles of his chest pulled tense against his heart, taut as bowstrings. His stomach rolled violently and he grasped at his abdomen and stepped out into the cool morning air.

He waved Robin out of the house and sent him to the blacksmith shop, saying, "You can get the fire going. I'll be with you in a few minutes. There is something I have to do."

William looked down at his feet as he walked, too sad to look at the sparkling new day or listen to the birds twittering in the trees. The morning dew dampened his work boots, spotting the brown leather black where the droplets landed on his toes. The little black spots brought to mind thoughts of earlier walks with Goblin, of Goblin leading them past the mill to find Robin, of Goblin trotting ahead of them over the icy road on the dragon hunt. But most of all, he remembered Goblin traveling with them through unknown forests, week after week, thin with hunger, on the journey that brought them to Johannesmarkt where he rescued the Baron. He had always been with them, it seemed. It was because of him that they had this good life. And now. Now! He did not want to think of it.

He hastened to the church. Stopping only to dry the tears that threatened to run down his face, the smith climbed the steps and pulled open the church door. Inside, a few flickering candles warmed the dark interior with a rosy light. The sun had not yet come around to throw in its multitude of colors through the stained glass. A figure knelt at the altar.

William knelt and drew his fingers across his chest and forehead in the sign of the cross. He rose. He went over to the statue of the virgin and knelt again. The blacksmith looked up into her gentle, kind face, and a tear ran down his cheek. He could not help it. He reached out as if to touch the white hem of her gown. Humbled before her comforting presence, he drew back his hand and began to pray.

"Ave Maria." The Latin words, so often recited, would not come. The smith shifted his knees on the stone floor and tried again. "Blessed Virgin, Goblin is a good cat." He drew in a deep breath. "He is such a good cat. Please, Holy Mother, if you will." Here William buried his face in his hands. "We need him. He is a good cat." He was crying as he said "good cat," and the words tumbled out louder than the others.

"My son," snarled a deep voice. William jerked his head up. It was the priest, Father Albert. "We do not pray for cats."

William looked into the face of the priest and his own face hardened. His lips pressed into a hard thin line. He made his face a mask to hide his emotion—especially his anger.

Father Albert had chosen that day to dress more austerely than usual, assuming his monk's garb. He had the cowl pulled low over his face. Still, from where William knelt on the floor, he could see a single embroidered tie dangling from the priest's coif. Father Albert had kept the little cap on under the hood. His sartorial vanity would not let him give it up. But the monk's hood was clearly an attempt to put in shadow the long scratches that marred his forehead and cheeks. William knew Goblin's work. He had seen it before. He understood.

Rage swelled in William's belly, rose, seized his heart and filled him with a powerful determination. Without showing the priest a flicker of emotion or recognition, William's face took on the mask of an actor about to play his greatest role. In his most sheep-like, innocent, and obedient voice he pleaded, "Forgive me, Father. Bless me, Father." Father Albert drew a cross in the air over William's head with a flat, vertical hand. The blacksmith rose, and, with bowed head and hands folded prayerfully before him, he walked penitently to the door. At the door, still the actor, he remembered to pause and fumble in the purse at his waist. He drew out a small coin and dropped it in the alms box. He pushed open the door. Once out in the sunlight, he looked back quickly over his shoulder to make sure the priest was not looking out the door and watching him. Then he ran. He sped past his shop, past his house, past the north road and did not slow to a walk—and then only for breath—until he was well up the manor road.

Thirteen.

N OT LONG AFTER William left their house, Rosemarie stepped outside her front door to catch a breath of fresh air. She needed to turn her eyes away from the sad group of cats and humans around her hearth. When Rosemarie saw William loping up to the house, he was breathless and dripping with new sweat. She held out her arms to him. William draped his arms around his wife and dropped his head against her neck.

Since the middle of the night, William had been running to one place and then another. He would have liked to sleep. But he could not bear to lie down in that house with Goblin dying on the hearth.

"Oh, I am so tired, Rosie. The bailiff rides for the fighting men. How is Goblin?"

"He still breathes."

"He did it again, you know. He found the monster who attacked the knight."

Rosemarie pushed him away and, holding her husband at arm's length, searched his face for an explanation. His face was grey with dark, puffy circles under his eyes.

He had to tell her. Soon the whole town would know. Part of him still didn't believe it was really true. But it was. He took her hand and patted it. This was going to be hard for her to accept, too, he knew. Then, still holding her hand, he drew her around behind the house to the garden where they could sit away from passersby and from the busyness and sadness inside. A few chickens cackled and scratched at their feet, but otherwise it was a quiet spot. Slowly he forced words out of his mouth, ugly but true words, and told Rosemarie every detail of what he had seen in the church and of how the priest's hat string matched the one Goblin had found earlier. He told of the scratch marks and then how he had alerted Gerhard the bailiff who even now was riding out to bring the knight's fighting men off their farms.

"But he's our priest!" wailed Rosemarie, shaking her head. She shifted on the bench, murmuring in disbelief. After a moment she stood up and sat back down, resetting her skirts and smoothing them out as if to rub away this awful knowledge. "A man of God."

"I know. I know." He squeezed her fingers, then stroked her arm. "He has listened to the Devil," was all William could offer by way of explanation.

"It must be true. Cats do not lie." Thinking of Goblin stretched in front of her hearth, Rosemarie burst into tears. "He really is," she said, sobbing, "a true knight: honest and good."

When her tears stopped, the two sat together in silence for a few minutes. Finally Rosemarie stood up, smoothed her apron, and, sighing, said, "I must see how Goblin is."

William went into the blacksmith shop to try to pass the time with mindless chores. Pounding on iron cured many ills. A nicely flattened chunk of hot metal, he often found, straightened out and made sense of the world.

Rosemarie did not often sit in the backyard to work, but now Anna and Maddie were taking up so much room in the house, doing all that could be done for Sir Goblin. So just to keep busy, she sat with her sewing on the bench. She was still working with her needle in the middle of afternoon when Anna stepped through the back door.

"Rosemarie."

Rosemarie's heart went cold. She searched the midwife's eyes, afraid of what she might read there.

"No. He still lives." Was that a flicker of a smile at the corner of her mouth?

"What then?" asked Rosemarie.

"Come see this." The midwife ushered Rosemarie through the back room and into the main living space where all the cats lay arrayed around their leader, who still lay stretched full length before the fire.

Little Maddie was on her knees offering Goblin a saucer of fish broth. With one hand she held up his head so he could lap up the nourishing drink and with the other she kept the saucer tucked tightly under his chin.

"She does have the healing gift. I'm sure."

The little girl smiled up at her mother. "I think he is a little stronger, Mama."

"But the broth?" asked Rosemarie, tipping her head toward her daughter and lifting an eyebrow, "Where did it come from?"

"Oh, Joanna stopped in a minute ago while you were in the garden. She brought it for him, and this for you and Papa." She gestured toward a steaming iron kettle, its metal bail wrapped with heavy cloth so it could be carried directly from the fire. It sat on the trestle table beside a smaller iron pot of fish broth. Only a giant of a woman could have carried two such cauldrons all the way across the square.

"I haven't thanked her."

"She had to hurry off to feed visitors from 'away,' is all she said."

They stopped talking when they heard the clop of horses' hooves in the dirt and the rattle of arms outside. The knight's men had arrived. They had ridden in from their farms and now were dismounting, adjusting their weapons and shields. An archer inserted a bolt into his crossbow and cranked.

Robin alerted his father and they went outside to watch, wondering how the men-at-arms would go about arresting a priest. Rosemarie and Anna were soon outside as well. Anna stood just outside the doorway, ready to slip back inside at any change in her patient's condition.

The fighting men were not yet watching the church; their attention was fixed on the manor road. People all around the square had stopped what they were doing. They watched expectantly, perplexed. They had no idea of what was about to happen. Anna's skirts stirred. A small white face poked out between the doorjamb and the hem of her garment. It was Meouht, the self-appointed representative for the feline family.

Everyone stood still, hushed, expectant, apprehensive; not a few were afraid.

A little cloud of dust rose on the manor road. They soon heard again the majestic clop of horses' hooves. A small band of men drew near. Sir Rudolph rode his warhorse and was resplendently garbed in a gold-edged burgundy doublet over a mail shirt. A short cape fluttered at his shoulders, and a feathered velvet hat of the same burgundy hue crowned his yellow hair. He wore a mail shirt but no armor—he had no squire to fasten it on him. But the splendor of his raiment, the mighty sword that hung from his waist, and the war hammer he carried like a scepter spoke as plainly of his authority as any plate of steel. Close at his side rode the young page, Hans, mounted on a palfrey and also wearing the knight's colors. Behind them rode the bailiff, Gerhard, and his firstborn son, Younger.

The knight joined his foot soldiers in the square, spoke briefly, and sent two men to search the priest's house. Then a woman shouted. Again and again, she cried out, each time louder, as she ran toward the square.

"Stop! You! What have you done with her?"

Stefan broke through the crowd of onlookers skipping, jumping, and spinning as he ran. Following just behind him came Lotte's mother. Her cap was awry; her hair streamed in sweaty ringlets down her face; her bosom heaved heavily from running. The old woman reached out and grazed Stefan's sleeve with her fingers. He twisted, and she stumbled. She cried out, but got immediately to her feet. The woman called out again to Stefan as he danced and twirled. "Where is my daughter? I saw you two walk off together last night with a lantern!"

She saw the men-at-arms standing before the church. She immediately recognized the burgundy and gold colors as the knight's. Taking a deep breath, she hitched up her skirts to her ankles and ran up to the nobleman. The distraught woman fell on her knees before Sir Rudolph and, clasping her hands over her heart, pleaded.

"My lord. Sir Knight! I implore you. I beg you. Last night, that man took my daughter Lotte away with him." She pointed at the twirling Stefan. "They were lovers, I know." Here she choked back tears and swallowed, pursing her lips until she regained control of her weeping. She continued, "She has not returned. I have looked everywhere and asked everyone. Help me. Oh, please, help me find Lotte."

"Rise, woman," said Sir Rudolph. Then, pointing with the war hammer to the gyrating Stefan, he ordered, "Hold him." Two of the knight's men seized Stefan by the arms and held him, but it was a struggle to keep him still. Stefan's feet kept moving, dancing in place.

"What have you to say?"

Stefan only smiled and kicked and hopped a sort of jigging dance. The knight, impatient to have the matter with the woman cleared up—he was, after all, in the middle of pursuing his attempted assassin—commanded, "Make him speak."

One of the men holding on to Stefan pricked the joiner's throat with a dagger. Stefan sang, "Well, well, well. She's cooling in the well." Then he threw his head back and laughed a great roaring laugh, ending with burbles and a hiccup.

"He's mad!" said an onlooker.

Younger leaned over and whispered to his father, who then spoke to the knight. Quietly the bailiff's son turned his horse toward the tavern.

"Thirsty?" jeered a bystander, upon seeing the youth head for his favorite drinking place.

Younger waved William over to him, shouting, "Come here." Within minutes, they had freed the rope that was affixed to the tavern well's bucket.

Younger started for the manor road but William stopped him with, "No, I know a shorter way." Then, with the rope coiled over his saddle horn and William walking beside Younger's horse, the two set off toward the brick makers' yard and the switchback trail.

Only a few people in the crowd noticed them go, for at this moment two things happened.

First, Stefan broke free of his captors and ran into the church, thumping the heavy door shut as he disappeared inside.

Just as the church door slammed behind Stefan, the men sent to find Father Albert came out of the priest's house. They had with them a black robe and a medallion on a neck chain. They held up the medallion. It was shaped like a shaft with two upward pointing pieces like a V at the base.

"The downward arrow!" exclaimed Gerhard. Addressing Sir Rudolph, he said, "You were ill that night, my lord, but as Yodel lay dying, he spoke of a man wearing a downward arrow who ordered another to pierce his flesh with a chisel. You know how simple his mind was, and we just thought him delirious, besides. But the wounds could have been made by a joiner's chisel, I suppose."

The knight's face blanched, and he passed a gloved hand over his eyes.

"Proof then—," he started to say, but the church bell rang out over the town. Two peals, then one. This signal, for a signal it was, rang out four times. People from the edges of the town—brick makers, tile makers, and carpenters, all free men, but mostly poor laborers—came running to the square. Some held sickles tucked under their arms. Others carried cudgels at their sides or behind their backs. There was much murmuring among the people already gathered as to what this might mean. The answer came immediately.

The church doors flung open. Father Albert, with Stefan just behind him, stood on the step. His voice boomed out for all to hear. "Seekers, the time has come. Arise! I am Albert de Forrest! Son of Johann de Forrest! I claim this town, this manor, and all lands attached as my own true and justly inherited demesne!"

Sir Rudolph urged his horse forward a few steps. Although very pale, he sat straight and tall and seemed calm when he spoke. "Father Albert, I know nothing of your claim. I will not contend with you. What I do know is that I hold this fief at the pleasure of my liege lord, Baron von

Schwartzfeld. It is to him that you must put your claim. But I come today—"

The priests' arms immediately flew up as if in benediction to the gathered crowd and he called out, "Seekers! Arise! The time has come to receive the Great Power." Shouting now, he continued. "Arise! The Black Power has delivered the enemy into our hands."

At this call, the sickle holders and cudgel bearers rushed forward. The knight's men charged the mob. The homemade weapons proved no match against sword, mace and lance, despite the extra strength the pigkill juice imparted to the Seekers. Most of the would-be conquerors slunk off to their houses after an eager crossbow bolt found a home in a tile maker's shoulder. He, a poor man who never before had harmed a soul, fell as blood gushed from his wound and spewed from his mouth.

The page's pony and Gerhard's horse had made runs at the rebels but Sir Rudolph's war horse halted before coming within striking distance. The noble beast, though well trained, was confused and shied upon feeling his master's warm breath on his fuzzy neck. Sir Rudolph's world had blackened again, and he would have tumbled from the saddle had not the page Hans pushed him upright and fixed his fingers into the horse's mane. This time, color came quickly back to his face. In the moment that he sat straight again, the Seekers turned heel and ran, never coming close to capturing the knight.

"Let them go!" called Sir Rudolph to his men, pointing his war hammer towards Father Albert. "It's him we want."

Father Albert had not realized how close his chosen adversary had come to falling. As his Seekers ran for home, and the knight's men turned toward the priest, Father Albert grabbed hold of the church doors. "Sanctuary! Sanctuary! I claim sanctuary!" The heavy doors thundered shut and inside a bar rumbled across, locking them closed.

"After him!" demanded Gerhard, swinging his mace over his head and spurring on his horse. Such heavy weapons would have reduced the church door to splinters in no time.

"No!" commanded the knight, "I will not have the church's sanctuary violated. We will wait him out. There is little to eat in the church. He will not last more than a few days. We'll post guards at the doors." Then, raising his voice and addressing the townspeople, "No one is to go in. No one is to bring food or drink." Pausing for breath, he added enigmatically, "God will provide."

This last was said with a certain sarcasm and some of the townspeople snickered. But it was not beyond their belief that a miracle might happen if the priest should prove blessed by God. The nobleman posted his guards and rode home with his page and bailiff.

Anna and Rosemarie had ducked into the house when the fighting began, but Meouht stayed on the doorstep and watched it all. Now he saw a distant blur of movement across the square. As it drew closer, the cat could discern two figures coming toward him. One was William coming home. The other he could just make out as a man on horseback with a maid in the saddle before him, her head tucked against his chin. The young cat treaded his feet and switched his tail in excitement. Now they would hear the story!

But before William reached the door of his house, one church door opened and an arm plunged forth, pushing a prancing Stefan out before it. Some people later claimed to have heard a voice saying, "Go drink the juice of the Black Power, you fool!" Others said Stefan simply burst through the doorway singing, "Looya, Looya."

What everyone would agree upon later was that the joiner skipped and pranced down the steps, slurping some purple juice from a chalice. He danced in the square, turning in smaller and smaller circles. Then he tossed away his cup and twirled faster and faster until he dropped to the ground. He lay on his back. His body jerked once, then again. His arms shot skyward, stiffened and held. His toes too jerked up. He lay still, dead. One old farmer remarked that he looked like his old sow that had rooted up pigkill.

By the time Sir Rudolph's warhorse clopped into the knight's own stable yard, the nobleman was whistling. He had not felt so well in many a day. With his quarry trapped in the church, the man was, as far as Sir Rudolph was concerned, as good as tried, drawn and quartered. *An execution I would not mind observing,* he told himself. In his imagination, he saw the priest and heard his howls of agony as four oxen pulled his arms and legs in four directions. Sir Rudolph shook the thought from his head, deeming it unworthy of a knight. There remained only the satisfaction of getting a confession from the wicked priest that he—or perhaps that fool disciple of his, the cripple—had killed Yodel. *Poor Yodel had been a good soul,* he thought to himself, as he dismounted.

There was one other task that must be done before nightfall, the knight decided, but first he would rest a little.

Fourteen.

L ADY ALFREDA MET her husband in the stable yard. She had just come from the kitchens and was still fingering the keys that hung on a chain from her waist. She had been taking inventory of the spices, unlocking and inspecting the level of the precious condiments in each box; she had been preparing for an upcoming feast with her chefs and butler. The visitors from "away," as Joanna had described them, had changed everything. They had brought the news that the terms for Ruth-Anna's arranged marriage to young Prince Engelbert were accepted. Lady Alfreda's plans had all worked out. They would give a great feast to celebrate the occasion, and the lady of the manor was radiant with expectation. Ecstatic with anticipation of her only child's marriage, Lady Alfreda was also happy to be hosting a grand social event, the likes of which their country life seldom called for. She had the guest list already prepared, and riders were even now saddling their horses to deliver invitations. The lady's eyes sparkled in merriment as she spoke. "How went your battle, my lord husband?" She dipped a quick curtsey for the notice of the servants standing around.

"Never better." He took her by the shoulders and smacked a kiss on each of her cheeks. They exchanged a few quiet words together.

The manor would soon be packed with guests, wedged into every corner of the hall, and the knight wished to finish his remaining task while there were still few eyes to observe it. So, later that afternoon, Sir Rudolph led a small group of his men into the woods. Following the well-known path, they went supplied with axes and an ox-drawn sledge. In spite of his bailiff's description, Sir Rudolph was amazed at the peculiar binding of the beech trees and the size of the chest. "Verily, it is the size of an altar," he exclaimed to no one in particular. He set the men to chopping at the trees, and when they had freed the chest he had them drag it onto the sledge. Only then would he allow it opened. The lid creaked back on its hinges, and the sparkle of gold lit the clearing with a yellow radiance, as it reflected the low, afternoon sun.

"Gold! So much gold!" said one of the men, astonished. The trunk was filled to its top with gold and silver coins interspersed with necklaces, bracelets, earrings, brooches, and every sort of ornament, many studded with jewels.

"Johann de Forrest's treasure," declared the knight in an awestruck whisper. Even he was amazed at how much gold was in the chest. Then, as if on a sudden impulse, he jumped up onto the sledge. He drew his dagger, felt its keen edge and squinted at his men. The nobleman eyed each one of the men who had chopped down the trees and dragged the chest onto the sledge. They were all dripping with sweat, and their shirts were soaked through.

"Gold makes all men greedy and some men thieves. But the laborer is worthy of his hire." Then he thrust the knife toward the bailiff's stomach. His intention was to point, but Gerhard instinctively jumped back, sucking in his belly, and tottered off the sledge. "Get up here, Gerhard. Take what you can in your hands." The bailiff raised a questioning eyebrow. "Yes," said his master, "dig in!" The bailiff stepped up and scooped out as much as he could with his two hands. "Now you." He pointed to one of the woodsmen. "Your turn." He pointed to each of the men in turn. Younger was the last to reach in.

Younger's portion included a ring. It was a petite gold lady's ring, set with three rhinestones. He put the coins in his purse and pushed the gold band up on his little finger as far as it would go. *Someday this will go on a special lady's finger,* he thought to himself.

Sir Rudolph knew well what the mere sight of gold did to men's hearts. But now, none of the men could say he had not been generous to them—and still, the chest seemed to be as full as ever. Gerhard shut the lid. He touched the prod to the ox's haunch, and they began their slow return to the barn. At the manor yard, the workers were dismissed. After dark, Gerhard, Younger, and the knight himself emptied the chest and hid the gold.

That night, a melodic sound woke Rosemarie up in the middle of the night. She turned onto her side and lifted her ear away from her pillow so she could hear. Yes, it was a meow, followed by many more little mews. It sounded to her like a cat conversation. She slipped from bed and peeked into the next room. There, she saw the entire cat family gathered together and sitting around Sir Goblin by the fireside. He was resting upright on his belly, with his legs nicely tucked under him. His eyes were closed, but his ears flicked in turn toward each meow. Meouht was doing most of the meowing, but the other sons added anxious mews of their own. Then Goblin raised a front paw. They fell silent, expectant. His eyes slid open. The inner membranes retreated to their corners.

"Meow-ow-up," he said. If translated into human speech, Rosemarie would have heard, *Like a mouse he will come out of his hole.* Then the great cat went to sleep and the house was silent.

On the morning of Father Albert's second day of sanctuary, a pageboy, dressed formally in burgundy and gold, rode up to William's house. His orders were to invite the knight Sir Goblin to the celebration given by Sir Rudolph and his lady Alfreda at one hour after the noon bell rang, or in three turns of the glass. He had come prepared and held out an hourglass to William, because they could not now expect that the priest would ring the church bell at the noon hour. "William may escort Mistress Rosemarie to the feast," added the page, speaking most formally and looking at the woman standing just behind her husband. Rosemarie was delighted that the noblewoman had recognized their slight and long-ago acquaintance. But after a moment's thought she rather suspected that, for the highborn lady, the peasant woman and her cat would be more like entertainment for her other guests than guests themselves.

They begged forgiveness and turned down the invitation. Goblin, though somewhat better, still was certainly not able to travel. Goblin had, in fact, risen that morning, but took only a step or two before dropping back to the floor. One back leg dragged badly. Maddie was at that moment squatting in the back garden, sifting dirt into a basin to make the big old cat a portable commode.

Even without the cat present, Lady Alfreda's banquet was a great success. The servants had set up three long tables in the hall and covered them with fine linen tablecloths. Sunlight flooded the center table, behind which the knight and his lady sat in their throne-like chairs. Eight-armed candelabra graced the two side tables, adding a festive glow to the table setting. The noblewoman had given great attention to the location of the silver nefs, her fancy saltcellars, making sure that nobody of any importance would be insulted by having to sit below the salt.

Most of the guests were members of the nearby nobility. The monastery's abbot superior and a few very selectively chosen couples from among the most prosperous of the town's businessmen and merchants also attended.

Of the many courses served, she took particular pride in her chef's seethed chicken galingale, seasoned with grains of paradise. Pages kept the wine flowing. Everyone grew very merry and began to entertain each other with jokes and riddles. Lady Alfreda, Ruth-Anna, and Gerhard the bailiff attempted a song, a madrigal, but the bailiff could not find the right notes, gave up, and soon had everyone laughing. It was time for toasts.

"To the lovely bride!" they all shouted. "To His Highness and young Prince Engelbert," toasting both the young groom and His Highness, the young man's father. Ruth-Anna nodded and smiled, maintaining a serene expression and covering well any doubts she may have had about marrying a man she hardly knew.

Lady Alfreda would not admit it, but a good deal of her excitement stemmed from the wedding gift the bridegroom's father had bestowed on his son's future parents-in-law: a castle overlooking the River Wort. It was a considerably larger fief than their present holding, and she foresaw that they would no longer be spending much time in "boring" little Johannesmarkt.

After toasting everyone they could think of, including Sir Goblin, a trumpet fanfare blasted through the hall, and pages streamed in with pie after pie. Once all the pies were set down before the guests, they were cut open, and out flew dozens of twittering goldfinches. Festive in their gold, white, and red plumage, the little birds tweeted and circled in confusion about the laughing guests' heads. A few found their way out the windows. Most of the rest eventually settled on the rafters, where they kept up a lively chatter. Younger, sitting well below the salt, thought of how Goblin would have loved to be there for the birdy-ing.

Pages changed the tablecloths, cleaning up the gravy stains and bird droppings, and served the real dessert: a mouth-watering display of candied, dried, and fresh fruits.

Fifteen.

WHILE THE KNIGHT and his lady feasted, Father Albert was getting very hungry inside the church. He had always eaten the best of food and slept in a soft bed, never denying his soft body any luxury. But in the sanctuary of the church—where he was safe from capture as long as he stayed within its walls—he slept on a stone floor and ate communion wafers. No angel came down from Heaven with dinner or a soft blanket. Hunger gnawed at his belly, and thirst made his mouth feel as though it was coated with mouse fur. He paced the length of the church over and over again, twisting his hands together and rubbing each knuckle until they were all red. He did not pray. He never did. He thought about the opportunities he had missed. How close he had come to ruling the town! He cried, cursed, and cried again. "There is no way out," he muttered, "I shall be tortured to death." He had seen executions. It was not a quick death.

On the eve of the third day, the priest stood in his sacristy staring at two jars. One was filled with communion wine and the other with his supply of pigkill juice, enough to kill ten men. He stood for an hour. Then he reached for one of the jars. He took a drink, then threw his head forward and spit the juice out in a violent spray that left the table, the wall, and the floor streaming with little rivulets of purple. "No! I cannot do it. I am a coward. A weak fool coward!" Then he lifted the jar of wine and drank deeply. The wicked priest snored loudly all night, lying in a drunken sleep on the sacristy floor. He dreamt wild golden dreams of the money in the chest up on the hill.

In exactly the three days, as Goblin predicted, the mouse came out of his hole. Father Albert woke after his drunken sleep, still thinking about the chest of gold. He was weak and shaky and so hungry that his stomach growled and hurt. The alcohol in the wine had made him thirstier than ever. But he had a wonderful idea. If he could only get away from the church, he would go up the hill and get himself enough money to start over. He staggered into the sanctuary and grabbed one of the huge candlesticks from the altar. He would use it to pry open the chest and, if need be, to smash the heads of any guards outside. It had nearly killed the knight, after all. Laughing out loud, he peered out the tiny window of the side door. He saw no one. A wide grin spread across his face as another idea came into his evil head.

I might even get across to my house to pack some stuff, said his dry, drunken brain. He tore open the door and dashed out, right into the arms of two of the knight's guards. They had been standing on either side of the door, just a few feet out of the priest's line of sight. Quickly, they tied his hands behind him. Relieved to have their boring guard duty over, four guards walked him, hungry, thirsty, and wobbly, up the long road to the manor. From the corner of his eye, the priest saw a white cat with a grey-striped tail that scooted off toward the farrier's house, kicking up dirt with his back feet as he streaked by the military men and their prisoner. The prisoner cursed the little animal, calling it, among other things, a filthy brat of the Devil.

Meouht burst through the little open window at the front of William's house like a cannonball, and landed with a thump in front of the cats gathered at the fireside. *Magdalene is avenged!* he yowled. Then he explained about the capture of the priest. Goblin sat up. His sons all rubbed their whiskers against his cheek. Then all the sons wove around one another, brushing against each other's long sides in a feline victory dance of joy and loud purrs. Their job was done. They had accomplished what they had set out to do: make that evil man pay for killing their sister and daughter.

That the priest was also the knight's assailant was not nearly so important to Goblin and his sons. First, it was Magdalene's mistreatment by the new priest that had saddened Sir Goblin. Then, the boot print on her side as she lay dead by the church made the cat determined to seek justice for his daughter. The scent of the priest was on it, as it was on the embroidered tie, and several places in the orchard, woods, and even on the chest. The difficulty for the cats was in bringing this to the attention of the humans.

Sir Rudolph had the priest clamped in irons in the old dungeon where Albert's father, Johann de Forrest, had once kept the Baron von Schwartzfeld so many years ago. He lay in utter darkness that was lighted only when Gerhard came with a torch to give him his morning or evening cup of water. When Gerhard came, his torch lit up the thousands of golden coins and jewels that were lying in piles on the floor, and, for a few minutes each day, made the prisoner's hole gleam like the sun. Sir Rudolph had stored the great treasure in the dungeon, the safest place for it. Albert sat on the damp ground with his wrists chained to the wall and enough gold to have fulfilled all his wicked dreams of empire lying just beyond his fingertips.

After two more days, Sir Rudolph and Gerhard entered the dungeon. They offered him bread in exchange for his confession. The starving man confessed to all. He babbled on and on, as Gerhard waved a crust of bread in front of his mouth, about his dreams of ruling Johannesmarkt, about how he controlled his followers with pigkill juice, and about Stefan's ambition to be his chief assistant. How clever he was, the self-proclaimed Prophet bragged. He had convinced the lame joiner that his leg was restored, when it was actually bloated with pigkill poison. And the ambitious fool had ritually pierced the arms, legs, and chest of Yodel with his finest chisel as part of his initiation into the sect. They had then dragged the dying squire into the orchard. The priest actually smiled and his eyes glowed in the torchlight when he thought again of the joy and sense of power he had when he watched the joiner kill. "I told him he had to give everything to the Black Power, his best tools, even his intended bride!" Here, in spite of his great hunger, the priest threw his head back and laughed uproariously. "He believed me. He was such a fool!"

The knight stuffed the chunk of bread into the priest's mouth, saying, "Who was really the fool, I wonder?"

Ruth-Anna's marriage to Prince Engelbert took place at the end of the summer, just before Michaelmas. The young man was totally enchanted by his bride, and the arranged marriage seemed off to a happy start. As Lady Alfreda had planned, she and her husband were caught up in whirlwind of social activities, jousts, tournaments and feasts. Sir Rudolph now looked out from a high castle tower at the River Wort rather than at his old orchard. He rarely returned to Johannesmarkt. He was more than happy, then, to intercede with the aged Baron von Schwartzfeld on behalf of Johannesmarkt, when town fathers petitioned for free city status. They had their charter by the following fall.

Gerhard the bailiff still managed the demesne lands for Sir Rudolph and saw that the farm returned a profit to the absent knight every year. The senior Gerhard liked this peaceful work, but Younger loathed cows and pigs. He spent achingly boring days at his father's side on the farm. Were it not for Yodel's horrible end and his dream of someday winning Lotte's heart, Younger would have gone back to his drinking and card playing.

At first, the new town council wanted to elect Sir Goblin honorary mayor, because he was a knight, and had helped them so much in the past. But William did not want his beloved old cat, now crippled, carried to and from the Town Hall for ceremonies and pressings of his inked paw as his seal of approval on documents. No town hall would have enough mice to satisfy Goblin, William claimed.

Goblin's back leg never healed properly. He walked on three legs and sort of dragged the fourth. In wet weather he ached. For these reasons he preferred to stay close to home, sitting by the fire or in a sunny doorway. He did, however, make occasional trips across the square, in the company of his four sons and Snow Beauty, to the tavern. Here, he feasted on innkeeper Paul's "Fish Feast for Cats," and kept informed of events in town.

With Sir Rudolph living in a castle on the River Wort, the newly independent town had no one to enforce the laws. The cooper was elected to be mayor, because his prosperous, well-managed business suggested that he would do a good job. Also, since Winifred was a meticulous housekeeper, the town council enjoyed meeting at her comfortable home. But Winifred was not going to have twenty councilmen tramping into her house with their muddy boots. Nor did she see herself providing refreshment every week to a sometimes-cantankerous group of men. They could go to the inn for their meetings, she suggested. But Paul the innkeeper was also on the council. He immediately said the inn had no meeting room large enough, and he did not want his regular customers inconvenienced. They considered the various guildhalls and even the church, but there seemed to be objections to every place. It was at this point, when the hour was growing late, that Gerhard suggested the usually vacant manor house. The manor house became the new Town Hall.

Next they voted on how to use Johann de Forrest's treasure, still hidden from everyone but Gerhard. Sir Rudolph had commanded that the town use it to good purpose. He did not need it, nor did he believe that it was rightfully his. This discussion took much less debate than choosing a site for the town hall. They would rebuild the town wall for protection against attackers, and they would establish a town watch to police the streets.

At the council's first meeting in the manor house the following week, when they began to discuss how to set up the town watch, three women arrived and asked to speak. One was a seamstress; one an old woman whose purse had been stolen, but returned; and one had had troubles at home—now no longer occurring, she happily reported. The councilmen listened intently to their recommendation. Next, the mayor made a proposal, and then reworded it several times. By the time the council voted, they all believed they were voting on the mayor's suggestion and had forgotten that the original idea came from three non-voting citizens—and mere females, at that.

The next evening, as Younger was spooning down one of Joanna's hearty soups in the tavern, ten prosperous-looking men, including the cooper, approached him with a document. A wax seal and ribbon dangled from its lower corner.

"Put your mark here, young man," said the barrel maker, recently elected mayor, pointing to a clear spot on the parchment. "We have elected you Chief Constable, head of the town watch." He set down an inkwell and a quill pen.

The appointment came with a sizable salary and a stipend for four feline assistants. Younger thought it over for about one minute. He had already apprehended several criminals, aided an abused wife, and rescued Lotte from the well. He knew he had the necessary experience. Suddenly, his days of milking cows and picking apples were behind him, and an opportunity for a life of adventure lay on the table before him, in the form of a piece of parchment. He marked the spot where the mayor pointed.

The next day was Friday. Younger would pay a visit to the seamstresses. He had last been there on Tuesday, with a fine clutch of extra-large eggs. He would often ask his stepmother if she needed any sewing picked up or delivered. He suspected his stepmother knew he had no objection whatever to paying a call at Lotte's house—none whatsoever. As he began frequently running these errands, Younger was shocked to realize how much effort it took to keep these women, his stepmother and sisters, dressed.

On the day she was pulled from the well, so many months ago, by William and Younger, Lotte was exhausted and shivering from cold and shock. She had tried all night to struggle up the side of the well, to get above the icy water, to maybe reach the top of the well. Her hands had been tied behind her, and her palms and elbows were raw and bleeding from her efforts. When William pulled the gag from her mouth, the only intelligible thing she said was "Oh, thank God," and then she babbled on about snakes and monsters slithering around her in the well, about yellow eyes peering down at her from the top, strange beasts laughing and screaming down at her, black powers, evil spirits. It would be weeks before she was calm enough to talk so people could understand her. Her mother immediately took her home and tucked her into bed, with hot water jars snugged against her sides. Anna came, straight from nursing Sir Goblin, with hot teas and incantations.

After almost a year, the terrifying memories still came, but only in her dreams. For a long time, she spoke to no one except her mother, and then only rarely. Yet every week, Younger came to the house. First he brought delicious foods fresh from the knight's farm, saying they would restore the girl to health. Apples, bacon, butter, eggs.

When he came, the girl darted into the back room at the sound of his footsteps. He had to conduct all his business with her mother. But day by day and week by week, Lotte began to trust life again. She returned to her sewing and now occasionally sat outside in the light to work.

In recent weeks, she had given Younger long glances before fleeing to her back room. And last week, he made so bold as to call her "old and ugly." She had looked straight into his eyes as if to see that he was joking. He thought he saw her mouth twitch ever so slightly, as if it wanted to smile.

Then she dropped her eyes and said, "I'll find out what you owe," and walked slowly into the house. Her mother came out, and he paid the money for his stepmother's bill. Lotte's mother winked.

The previous Tuesday, once Lotte had taken the eggs from him, she said, "Thank you. They are lovely." Had her fingers lingered against his hands?

He said, "Beautiful day."

She said, "Yes, yes, it is." Then, a hesitant smile broke across her face. Her cheeks turned pink and she ran into the house.

Younger had given much thought to today's visit. For once, he wanted to see the mother first, so he could tell her of his new circumstances. But Lotte sat outside the door. His carefully planned speech died in his throat. All he could say was, "Lotte, Lotte, some day . . ."

Her blue eyes met his. Her fingertips, fluttering for a moment like a falling leaf, grazed his wrist and then drew back. "Some day . . ." she started to say.

Her mother bustled through the door. Younger suddenly heard these words tumbling from his mouth. "I have to stop by the farrier's house on business—very important. Perhaps you have some business in that part of town. It is a lovely day. We could," his glance took both women pointedly, "walk together."

The mother pinched her daughter's elbow. "Fetch my basket, Lotte."

They walked. The women had not heard of his appointment. This made Younger happy. He knew the girl was walking with him because she liked him, and not his new important position in the town. *It is me she wants, praise the Lord,* thought the new-made constable.

Sun bathed the doorway of the farrier's shop.

Sir Goblin sat in the pool of golden light. Spread in front of him was a half circle of white cats, all wearing the usual grey-striped tails. A veritable chatter arose from the little group. The babble of mewing was interspersed intermittently with sharp corrective meows. They paid no attention to the approaching humans.

Robin yanked on his father's sleeve as the older man, not hearing anything but his own hammering, pounded on a horseshoe. The boy pointed toward their visitors. William went outside. Younger explained about his new work, and how the cats were on the payroll. As he talked, he pointed down to Sir Goblin. "They get orders from him. I'm certain."

The great cat's ears rotated back as if to take in what Younger was saying. Then they spun forward. His whiskers flicked toward his nose and then back. He lifted a forepaw in gesture and continued with his mewing lecture to his disciples.

"Some people say he's running a school for cats," said William. Then, laughing, he added, "Those mousers really had a long and loud conversation a couple of days ago. Even I had no trouble hearing them."

"Yes, they led me on a merry walk, and I bumped into some youths about to steal nail kegs from a wagon after beating up the driver. I put a quick stop to their little party," Younger told him.

"Perhaps you are right, and it is a school for the night watch," said William.

They talked a while longer, mostly about how the four cats' stipend would be paid.

Snow Beauty came out of the shop and rubbed around Lotte's ankles. Then she slid a smooth figure eight around Younger's boots and pressed again around the girl's skirts, twisting, and then, as Goblin pointed a paw, she looped back around the man's boots.

"This cat is pushing me over," Lotte laughed. She took hold of Younger's arm to keep her balance. Laughing again, she suddenly whispered none too softly into his ear, "Two dolls for a kiss." Younger took the girl into his arms. Her mother fumbled around in her basket and drew out a small cloth. She blew her nose and went to have a word with Rosemarie. William and Robin both blushed as red as their forge fire. They hurried into the blacksmith shop, leaving the two young people alone. A rhinestone ring changed fingers.

The End.

Afterword.

SIR GOBLIN DID many other things that are not written in this book, but these are written so that you may believe that Goblin was a good cat and a true knight.

Glossary

acolyte. An attendant to a priest, assists in religious services.

adz. An ax-like tool with its arching blade at right angles to the handle, used for dressing wood; also spelled adze.

almoner. A servant who distributes alms or charity for a nobleman.

alms. Money, food or clothing or anything given away free to help the poor.

armoire. A large cupboard or cabinet to keep clothes in.

bank. To arrange a fire by covering with ashes or adding fuel, so that it will burn slowly and keep for a long time such as overnight.

banns. A proclamation of a proposed marriage read by a priest in church.

bier. Frame of wood on which a coffin is placed; sometimes also the coffin itself.

bolster. A long narrow pillow used to support the head of a person lying in bed. Often pillows were placed on top of it. For many centuries people slept in a semi-sitting position.

book of hours. A devotional book containing prayers and meditations appropriate to various seasons, months, days of the year, and hours of the day, usually beautifully illustrated.

brazier. A metal container used to hold burning coals or charcoal for heat.

caparison. To cover with a cloth, especially covering the saddle of a horse for a special occasion.

carding combs. Combs used for disentangling and smoothing wool and cotton fibers in preparation for spinning.

childbed. The state of a woman giving birth to a child.

coif. A brimless cap that fitted closely on the head like a baby's bonnet and tied under the chin; kept a workman's hair clean and protected knights' heads when wearing helmets and mail.

coppice. A thicket of small trees, where firewood is cut at certain times.

cowl. A hood, especially one worn by a monk.

crone. An old woman.

crosier. The staff with a curved end carried by a bishop, symbolic of his role as a pastor, patterned after a shepherd's crook.

cuirass. A piece of close-fitting armor for protecting the chest and back.

cuisse. A piece of armor to protect the thigh.

demesne. Manorial land retained for the private use of a feudal lord. Here, the knight's farm, orchards, and yard.

doublet. A man's close-fitting garment covering the body from the neck to just below the waist. It may have sleeves or be sleeveless.

duchy. The land ruled by a duke.

ewer. A pitcher with a wide spout.

faggot, fagot. A bundle of sticks, twigs, or small branches used for fuel.

farrier. A blacksmith who specializes in shoeing horses.

feudal lord. A nobleman who held land in return for service, usually military, to the higher-ranking lord who assigned him the land.

fief. In the feudal system, heritable land held from a lord in return for service.

filigree. Delicate, lacelike ornamental work of intertwined gold or silver wire; any work like this.

firkin. A wooden bucket or small container usually with a handle; also a dry measure equal to one fourth of a barrel.

flagon. A container for liquids, usually has a handle and sometimes a lid.

galingale. The spice ginger.

girdle. A belt.

grains of paradise. The spice cardamom.

greaves. Armor for the shins.

handfast. To become engaged or married.

hempen sack. A bag made of hemp; the fiber was used to make rope and sailcloth. Hemp is the common name for plants of the entire family of *Cannabis*.

heraldic. Pertaining to heraldry, which is the study of coats of arms, tracing genealogies, and devising designs on shields for the identification of knights, who were covered completely in armor when in tournaments.

horn spoon. A spoon made of cow's horn. Horn becomes bendable and workable when heated and served more or less as the plastic of the Middle Ages.

houppelande. A woman's or man's gown with a high neck and wide sleeves, sometimes lined with fur. Women's houppelandes were always floor length and belted under the bust, which gave the appearance that the wearer had a rounded stomach, which was a desirable look in Rosemarie's time; the men's houppelandes were either ankle or mid-calf length and belted at the waist. The men's garments may have been padded in the upper body.

iron crane. A horizontal iron rod that swung across the fire in a fireplace on a vertical hinge, from which pots and kettles could be held over the flames.

itinerant. A person who travels from place to place, especially a preacher, tradesman, or other type of worker.

joiner. A carpenter, especially one doing interior work.

lay brothers. Men received under vows into a monastery but not into holy orders and therefore not monks; generally they did manual labor.

litter. A frame with two long shafts enclosing a chair or couch on which someone—often the sick, wounded, or aged—is carried by two bearers.

lout. A stupid, awkward person, a boor.

mace. A heavy armor-piercing club with a spiked head; also, a spice made from the outer covering of nutmeg.

manor lord. The ruler of a manor, which was land granted to him by his overlord in the feudal system; the manor consisted of land for his own use and could also include land farmed by peasants who paid rent. Residents were subject to the jurisdiction of his court.

mendicants. Beggars.

Michaelmas. The feast of St. Michael, the archangel, September 29th.

millrace. The channel that water flows through to turn a millwheel.

name day. The feast day of the saint a person is named after and often celebrated instead of one's birthday.

narthex. A lobby at the entrance of a church, leading to the nave.

nave. The main, central space of a church where the congregation worship.

necessary house. A pit privy, often located in a little building separated from the house.

nefs. Elaborate saltcellars (containers). The higher one's social importance the closer one sat to a nef at a banquet.

obeisance. A bow or curtsy, also called a reverence.

page boy. Young serving boy, attending a person of high rank and sometimes in training to become a knight.

palfrey. A small, gentle horse.

palisade. A fortification made of stakes set in the ground vertically and sharpened at the top.

pattens. A wooden over-sandal strapped to the shoes and keeping the feet an inch or two off the ground. It was used to protect leather shoes from mud, water, dung and dirt.

pauldron. The shoulder piece of armor.

peel. A long, flat, wooden shovel used by bakers to move bread in and out of an oven.

poch. A medieval card game somewhat similar to poker.

poleyn. Armor over the knee.

pottage. Boiled grain, served as a main or side dish.

poultice. A hot, soft mass of flour, bran, or similar substance mixed with mustard or other ingredients and applied to sores and inflamed parts of the body. A hot mustard plaster.

prie-dieu. A small reading desk with a ledge for kneeling at prayer.

pullets. Young hens.

rain barrel. A barrel used to catch rainwater, which water could then be used for washing, watering gardens, and so forth.

relic. An object, or body part of a saint, such as hair, bone, or finger, kept and reverenced in memory of the saint.

reliquary. A box, chest, or any type of container in which relics of saints are kept.

sabeton. Armor for the foot.

sacristy. The part of the church used to store sacred utensils and vestments (priestly robes).

salver. A tray.

scullery. The part of a kitchen where pots and dishes are washed.

scullions. People who work in the scullery.

serf. In the feudal system, a lowly person bound to serve on his master's land. He was not a slave because he could not be sold, but he went with the land if the land got a new owner.

settle. A long bench with a backrest and arms.

shift. A woman's undergarment.

sirrah. Mister, fellow, a derogatory form of address to a man.

smithy. The shop of a smith, especially a blacksmith.

snood. A netlike bag worn at the back of the head to hold the hair.

solar. An upper room, the private chambers of the lord and lady.

stanchion. An upright prop or post for support.

stoppered vial. A small container with a cork or other type of plug to keep the contents inside.

stoup. A basin for holy water in a church.

swale. A hollow in wet, marshy ground.

travail. To suffer the pangs of childbirth; the labor of childbirth.

trencher. A slice of bread used as a plate or platter, a platter of any sort, especially wooden.

trestle table. The trestle—most frequently seen today as a sawhorse—

was a frame consisting of a horizontal beam fastened to two pairs of spreading legs; planks set across two trestles would make a temporary table.

troth. Faith, belief, loyalty; betrothal.

tureen. A large, deep dish with a lid, for serving soup.

vassalage. The state of being a vassal and owing homage, loyalty, and service to one's overlord.

wattle and daub. A network of twigs daubed over with mud and clay to build a primitive house.

wench. A girl or young woman, often a derogatory term.

wimple. A cloth covering worn around head and over the chin and neck, leaving only the face exposed, still worn by nuns in some orders.

Barbara Edinger Moss has had a life-long love of cats. As a baby she pointed to the family cat and said her first word: mao-wow. Her parents thought that was the infant girl's attempt to say meow and communicate with her kitty in its own language. Languages always intrigued her, and as a student she studied Spanish, German, and when Sputnik was sent heavenward, she began the study of Russian. She translated professionally until the mid 1990s, usually rendering Russian scientific journals into English for the  benefit of American scientists. She holds a degree in zoology from St. Lawrence University and attended graduate school at Cornell. She worked as a research assistant at the Bingham Oceanographic Laboratory at Yale University before moving to Massachusetts and raising three children.

Mrs. Moss began writing in the 1970s and is the author of two books, *Mo, Cat of My Heart* and *Working Cats of Southern New England* and many magazine and newspaper articles. In 2006 she was a prizewinner in the Amazing Cat Tales contest, and her work appears in the anthology by that name published by Linden Hill Press.

The author lives in Westport, MA, with her husband and their cat Dexter.

Emily Marie Dueñas Cornell du Houx studied fine art and English at Amherst College in Massachusetts. She has illustrated several books for Polar Bear & Company, including a Biblio Bestseller. She illustrated *The Adventures of Sir Goblin* in 2008,  while working freelance in Brooklyn, NY, with her four cats, Puma, Nikki, Guapo, and Leonard. She is a professor at the Rhode Island School of Design, where she received her master's degree. She is also a graduate and director of The Apprenticeshop in Rockland, Maine, a nonprofit inspiring personal growth through craftsmanship, community, and traditions of the sea.